SECRETS

TYPED

IN BLOOD

Also by Stephen Spotswood

Murder Under Her Skin

Fortune Favors the Dead

SECRETS
TYPED
IN BLOOD

A PENTECOST AND PARKER MYSTERY

STEPHEN
SPOTSWOOD

DOUBLEDAY   *New York*

Copyright © 2022 by Stephen Spotswood LLC

All rights reserved. Published in the United States by Doubleday,
a division of Penguin Random House LLC, New York, and distributed in
Canada by Penguin Random House Canada Limited, Toronto.

www.doubleday.com

DOUBLEDAY and the portrayal of an anchor with a dolphin are
registered trademarks of Penguin Random House LLC.

Jacket design and illustration by Michael J. Windsor

Library of Congress Cataloging-in-Publication Data
Names: Spotswood, Stephen, author.
Title: Secrets typed in blood : a Pentecost and Parker mystery / by
Stephen Spotswood. Description: First edition. | New York :
Doubleday, [2022] | Series: Pentecost and Parker; vol. 3
Identifiers: LCCN 2022013531 | ISBN 9780385549264 (hardcover) |
ISBN 9780385549271 (ebook)
Subjects: LCGFT: Detective and mystery fiction. | Novels.
Classification: LCC PS3619.P68 S43 2022 | DDC 813/.6—dc23/eng/20220321
LC record available at https://lccn.loc.gov/2022013531

MANUFACTURED IN THE UNITED STATES OF AMERICA

10 9 8 7 6 5 4 3 2 1

First Edition

To Jessica,
the best co-conspirator I could ever ask for

I think everyone enjoys a nice murder . . .
provided he is not the victim.

—ALFRED HITCHCOCK

CAST OF CHARACTERS

WILLOWJEAN "WILL" PARKER: Partner in crime-solving to Lillian Pentecost. She loves her job, but it doesn't always love her back.

LILLIAN PENTECOST: Arguably the greatest detective in the five boroughs and beyond. On a two-woman crusade to make the world a better place, one captured criminal at a time.

HOLLY QUICK: Prolific crime-magazine writer. She's killed a thousand people under a dozen pseudonyms. Now someone's ripping her murders from the pulp pages and trying them out for real.

MICHAEL PERKINS: City health inspector and boozehound. Someone thought hanging wasn't good enough for him, so they shot him for good measure.

CONNOR "CONNY" HAGGARD: Army veteran and unemployed machinist. He got caught napping and ended up with a blade in his belly.

FLAVIO CHECCHETTO: Art and antiques dealer. Was his sideline selling murder memorabilia the reason he was left gutted?

DARRYL KLINGHORN: Private investigator with a nose for philandering. He can sense when someone's lying and he's sure Pentecost and Parker aren't playing him straight.

BRENT AND MARLO CHASE: Owners and co-editors of *Strange Crime*. Has their love of crime bled into the real world?

JESSUP QUINCANNON: Wealthy philanthropist and student of history's bloodiest murderers. Does his patronage extend to killers who are still building their résumés?

DETECTIVE DONALD STAPLES: Up-and-comer in the NYPD. Smart, ambitious, and more than willing to toss a private detective or two behind bars if it gets him a collar.

LIEUTENANT NATHAN LAZENBY: The top homicide cop in the city, at least for now. He'll let Pentecost and Parker bend the law, but won't sit by while they break it.

ELEANOR CAMPBELL: Scottish émigrée and faithful housekeeper. Worth her weight in scones.

SAM LEE BUTCHER: Circus roustabout turned morgue orderly. Learning how to speak for the dead but willing to put his life on the line to help the living.

KEN SHIRLEY: Senior partner at Shirley & Wise. What does a middling tax lawyer have that Olivia Waterhouse wants?

OLIVIA WATERHOUSE: Shadowy mastermind with a grudge against the rich and powerful. Good intentions don't give her a pass from Pentecost and Parker.

SECRETS

TYPED

IN BLOOD

CHAPTER **1**

The kidnapper was good, I'll give him that.

He parked himself right next to the trash can, then pulled out a cigarette and a book of matches. He flubbed the first match and tossed it in the bin. That gave him the chance to eye the paper bag sitting on top of the lunchtime leftovers and discarded morning papers.

He flubbed the second match—not a hard thing to fake on a blustery January day. He tossed that second match in the bin, which gave him the opportunity to glance around and check out the people in his immediate vicinity.

There were plenty.

There might have been busier intersections in New York City than the corner of Forty-second Street and Madison Avenue, but you'd have to go hunting. Two dozen restaurants, bars, and greasy spoons were throwing their lunchtime crowds onto the sidewalk. Everyone was hustling to get out of the cold and back to work, warmed by overcoats, hats, and three-martini lunches.

It was a smart place and a smart play. It gave the kidnapper cover, and it made anyone standing still look mighty conspicuous.

People standing still included:

The newsstand owner hawking the latest copies of *Life* and *Vogue* and the Monday, January 20, 1947, edition of the

Times and its competitors. The kidnapper had probably scoped this spot out several days running, so he'd recognize the owner for genuine.

The drunk panhandling at the mouth of the alley twenty yards down. Too old to have served in the Pacific, but that's what his cardboard sign proclaimed. The line seemed to be working for him if the pile of coins in his hat was any indication. He was a regular, too.

The girl in the phone booth, the one in the private-school uniform arguing with her mother in that kind of why-me whine fifteen-year-old girls hold a patent on.

"I want to see the matinee and it's closing this week and Billy invited me! . . . He is not. . . . He would never. He's a gentleman. His dad is vice president at Mavis and Mulgrave."

No one to set off the fine-tuned alarm bells wired into the kidnapper's nerves.

The man in question was dressed in assorted grays—light-gray suit, charcoal overcoat, gunmetal-gray porkpie. He had the kind of easy-smiling face you'd hire to play second-fiddle in a Seagram's ad.

Pleasant and forgettable.

That forgettable mug and careful planning were the reasons he hadn't gotten caught. And we were pretty sure he hadn't gotten caught a lot.

This was a sample of what was going through my head as I defended fictional Billy to a dead telephone line: "I'll come home after the show, I promise. . . . But, Mom, we've already got our tickets."

I was thinking he didn't look much like a kidnapper. Then again, they never do.

To be fair, I didn't look much like a fifteen-year-old girl playing hooky. Even with the wool skirt and the school jacket and my frizzy red curls pulled into place with plastic barrettes.

Up close, I looked every bit my twenty-four years. Maybe

a couple more, once you factored in mileage. But through the smeared, breath-fogged glass of the telephone booth, I could pass.

Also, I had the whine down pat.

"No, Mom, I love Billy. I loooove him."

The easy-smiling man tore off a third match, struck it, and lit his smoke. He shook the match out. Then he carefully placed it in the garbage can, dipping ever so slightly to scoop up the paper bag at the top.

He took a moment to feel what was inside—three stacks of tightly bound bills. Then he was off, moving as fast down Madison Avenue as the post-lunchtime crowd would let him. I was out of the phone booth a moment later, hurrying to keep up, slipping in between the cracks in the masses with ease. I top out at five-two in flats, with a narrow frame that makes dress-fitting a pain but helps when I need to tail a crook.

Twenty seconds in and I was only three people back. The hope was that I could ride the kidnapper's slipstream all the way to Wyatt Miller.

Wyatt had been snatched from his pram in Central Park three days earlier. His mother had been distracted giving directions to a German tourist, and when she turned back she found her fourteen-month-old darling gone. In his place was a typewritten note.

WE HAVE WYATT.

DO NOT CALL THE POLICE.

WE HAVE PEOPLE ON THE FORCE.

WE WILL KNOW.

GO HOME AND AWAIT FURTHER INSTRUCTIONS.

Gloria Miller ran back to her Upper West Side apartment and showed the note to her husband, who did the reasonable thing. He picked up the phone and asked the operator to connect him with the cops.

An overly gruff voice answered.

"Twentieth Precinct."

"This is Simon Miller. My son's been kidnapped. My wife was in Central Park and—"

The voice cut him off.

"What did we tell you, Mr. Miller? We told you not to call the police. We have people everywhere. This is your only warning if you want to see your son again."

Then the voice instructed the Millers to gather ten thousand dollars in ransom money. The voice went so far as to instruct them on the best way to do it, naming bank accounts and telling them to cash in this or that stock.

The kidnapper really did seem to know everything.

What he didn't know was that Mrs. Miller played a weekly bridge game with a group of wives, one of whose sister's best friend had had something similar happen to her daughter a year before.

Back when it happened, it had made for juicy conversation between bids or rubbers or whatever the lingo is. I'm a poker girl, myself.

Naturally, the chatter had expanded to include what each card player would have done if such a thing happened to them. Someone had suggested that a private operator would be the best choice—someone who could work to bring the child back without the flash and show of the NYPD.

Gloria Miller raised the idea with her husband, who quickly nixed it. Private detectives were nothing but glorified grifters, he told her. While Mrs. Miller loved and cherished, she didn't always obey. Which is why, with her husband tying up the house phone making calls to his bank, she walked down the street and made a call of her own. This one to the offices of Pentecost Investigations, Lillian Pentecost being known far and wide as the greatest private detective working in New York City in that year of our Lord 1947.

That reputation was kept fresh through the efforts of her

erstwhile assistant, Willowjean "Will" Parker, who made sure her boss's name appeared in the paper as often as legitimately possible, sometimes going so far as to flirt shamelessly with the editors. Which, if you'd met the editors in question, you'd know took a lot more acting chops than playing a whiny schoolgirl.

We took the case.

What followed was a whirlwind seventy-two hours. While the Millers got the ten grand together, Ms. Pentecost and I tracked down the friend of the sister of the bridge player—a Mrs. Diane Neary.

We couldn't pick apart the Millers' lives. There was a chance the kidnappers had them under surveillance, and we didn't want to trip any alarm bells. So we dissected the Nearys'.

We talked to grocers and bankers and lawyers and landlords and housepainters and hairdressers and everyone listed in their address book. If we'd ever worked faster, I couldn't remember it.

By the time the Millers got a call from Mr. Gruff giving them the details of the ransom drop, we had a theory and a plan and I was the first person on Mrs. Miller's phone tree.

When the call came, I was camped out at a hotel two blocks from the Millers' apartment. I'd spent the morning lounging in a robe, waiting as patiently as humanly possible. Laid out on the bed were a dozen choices. There was housewife, cabdriver, delivery girl, socialite, and barfly, among others.

As soon as Mrs. Miller told me the drop location, I hung up and placed a call of my own, relaying the information and confirming my own quick calculus that schoolgirl was the way to go.

I set a land-speed record for dressing, then ran downstairs and took a cab in the direction of the ransom drop. I got out five blocks short and walked the rest of the way in character, just in case the kidnappers had a lookout.

I got there about ten minutes before Simon Miller arrived, clutching the paper bag in both hands and looking terrified. I had already grabbed the phone booth, dropped in a nickel for show, and was deep into my one-sided conversation.

Ten minutes later, Mr. Pleasant-Face showed up.

Two minutes after that, I was riding his wake down Madison Avenue.

Now you're all caught up.

I was two arm's lengths away when Mr. Pleasant-Face made his move.

He put on a big show of looking at his watch, then took off running. I'd expected it. The fastest way of checking for a tail is to start sprinting and see who keeps pace.

Forewarned or not, he gained half a block on me before I got up to speed.

Luckily I'd added a pair of ten-inch military-style boots to my schoolgirl uniform. Not easy on the feet, but great for getting traction on the slush-slick sidewalk.

Early in the chase he glanced back and saw I was following. He picked up speed, then without warning dove into traffic. He slipped through unharmed, but I had to juke and dodge. A delivery truck screeched to a halt, its grille coming so close to my face I could feel the heat of its engine blast against my cheek.

At the end of the block he turned right on Thirty-ninth Street, sprinted the long block, turned left, sprinted another two blocks, then turned right again.

It seemed random, but I knew it wasn't. This guy was a planner. He would have an escape route.

The best-case scenario had been trailing him unawares to wherever he was keeping Wyatt Miller. That was out.

The worst-case scenario was that he disappeared into

one of the many office buildings we were passing. Then it'd become a snake hunt, and we didn't know how much time Wyatt had.

I saw the move before he made it.

There was an alley halfway down the block. He sped up, glanced at the alley, then quickly looked away. I waved my arm in a circle over my head, sending a signal I hoped would be understood.

He darted into the mouth of the alley and I followed a second later.

Halfway down, he leapt over a broken crate. I opted for around rather than over, seeing too late the chain that had been stretched knee-length across the width of the alley.

I hit it full speed and went ass over teakettle, landing hard on concrete and filthy snow.

I wasted half a second making sure nothing was broken, then stumbled to my feet and started running again. By then he was nearly at the end of the alley. There was no hope of catching up.

A squeal of brakes and a chorus of car horns, and suddenly the mouth of the alley filled with the broadside of a yellow cab.

Pleasant-Face slammed against it and rebounded. He managed to stay on his feet and began a stumbling run back toward me. By that time I was up to full speed.

I brought my right leg up, kicking straight out and sending my size-seven boot deep into his gut.

He collapsed like someone had cut his strings.

I took the paper bag out of his limp hand and tucked it in my coat pocket. He groaned, and I saw him shoot a look past me and back to the end of the alley where we'd come in.

"Please don't," I said, unzipping my school jacket and giving him a peek at the holstered Browning Hi-Power. "My boss would like a word."

The door of the taxi creaked open. I helped Pleasant-Face to his feet and led him over. He slid into the backseat of the cab and I followed.

Inside, he found himself sandwiched between me and a woman of about fifty, wearing a black overcoat and a three-piece suit tailored in heavy black wool. Her elaborate braids were hidden by a matching watch cap, her long-fingered hands kept warm inside tight leather gloves. Both were clasped on the silver-headed cane propped between her legs.

Lillian Pentecost was not a fan of the cold, thus the bundling and having the cab's heater cranked up to sauna. The cold burrowed its way into her bones, she said, and turned the periodic ache from her multiple sclerosis into a consistent throb that lasted from Christmas through April.

All that is to say that she wasn't in the best mood for a number of reasons, and you could see it on her face: lips pressed in a line so straight you could use it as a level, almost-hook of a nose looking sharp enough to cut. Her eyes—glass and good alike—might as well have been windows into the cold, blue-gray January sky.

I slammed the door and nodded to the driver to start moving. Then I tossed the paper bag into my boss's lap.

"One kidnapper, complete with ransom, delivered as promised," I said. "I'd have gift-wrapped him, but I forgot to bring a bow."

"Look, I don't know what's going on here," Pleasant-Face said. "This dame started chasing me and I was just trying to—"

My boss held up a hand.

"Please, Mr. Kelly. We don't have the time for excuses or equivocations."

If her tone didn't put him on his heels, her use of his name certainly did. She pressed the advantage.

"You are Thomas Kelly, currently employed as a technician with the Bell Telephone Company. You have been arrested three times, twice for mail fraud and once for assault, though that was under the name Thomas Koon in Newark, New Jersey—a charge for which there is still an active warrant for your capture."

She gave him time to process.

"Fine, my name's Kelly and I did my time," he said. "But I don't know who this Koon guy is. That's not me. You got it all wrong."

"Would you like to see the mug shot?" Ms. Pentecost asked. "While you've dyed your hair and shaved your mustache, the resemblance is still unmistakable."

Another pause.

"You wanna run me in, go ahead," Kelly muttered. "But I ain't talking."

She shook her head.

"I am not the police, Mr. Kelly. This charge in New Jersey is not my concern. What is my concern is the health and well-being of Wyatt Miller."

"I don't know what you're talking about," he said. "I don't know who that is."

He cast a quick glance at the doors of the cab, doing the math on how fast he could leap across one of us, open the door, and dive. The cab was at that moment making its way along Eighth Avenue, managing to miss the lights and staying at a decent clip. If he dove, he'd be rolling the dice.

Maybe he was willing to chance snake eyes.

I slipped the nine-millimeter out of its holster and held it in my lap, barrel pointed casually at his gut.

"Get those thoughts out of your head," I told him. "A bullet will hurt a lot worse than my boot."

He eased back into the seat, unhappy but resigned.

My boss continued.

"Your methods were really quite ingenious," she said. "By tapping the Millers' phone lines you were able to glean information about their habits and their finances. You were also able to intercept their call to the police, pretending to be a corrupt officer and ensuring they would not go to the authorities until after the ransom was paid."

I kept an eye on Kelly's face, but I didn't really need to. I'd helped with the homework and was confident we had him nailed.

"I am assuming that Wyatt Miller is currently in the care of Beatrice Little, your common-law wife and past collaborator. I'm also assuming she was the one who physically took him from his pram while you distracted Mrs. Miller by acting the part of a tourist and asking for directions during her walk in the park three days ago. Both of you deserve to be locked away for the rest of your natural lives."

With each word I saw the hope in Kelly's eyes die just a little more.

"But your imprisonment is not my goal," she told him. "I was hired to deliver Wyatt Miller safely back into the hands of his parents. If I were to take you to the police now, you would be arrested, arraigned, interrogated—all of which takes time. Time during which Miss Little might panic. She might try to dispose of the evidence."

The implication being that "the evidence" included a fourteen-month-old boy. I'll leave "dispose" to your imagination.

"I would like to propose a deal, Mr. Kelly. One that will give us both what we want."

The light reignited in Kelly's eyes.

"You will lead us to where Miss Little has Wyatt Miller. Once he is recovered, I will release you. You and Miss Little will leave this city and never return. I will even let you keep the contents of this bag. You may use it to start a life somewhere far away from here. One that does not include the abduction of small children."

I waited as Kelly worked through his options. His face didn't seem all that pleasant anymore. It was the hard, ruthless mug I'd seen on a hundred wanted posters and one New Jersey mug shot.

"How do I know you're on the up-and-up?" he asked my boss.

"I'm afraid you will have to take it on faith, Mr. Kelly," she said. "And on whatever knowledge you have of my reputation for keeping my word."

Apparently he knew something about something, because after a thought or three, he nodded and told us the address. Ms. Pentecost repeated it to our driver, and a few minutes later we were pulling up to a run-down apartment building in Hell's Kitchen.

I hopped out and went inside. Keeping the Browning down at my hip, I made my way up to a third-floor apartment and used the key Kelly had given me to unlock the door.

Inside, I found a bleached blonde, who might have been a looker twenty years and a hundred hard miles ago. She was lounging on a mattress on the floor, applying a fresh coat of Revlon to her toenails.

"Hiya, Bea."

"Who the hell are you?" she sneered. "Get out of here!"

I showed her the gun and that put a quick end to her attitude. She shrank back, her bottle of polish tipping over and spilling crimson onto the floor.

"Where's Wyatt Miller?" I asked.

Her mouth said, "I don't know who you're talking about." Her eyes pointed to the bathroom.

I found Wyatt in the bathtub. A sheet of chicken wire had been laid on top and bent around the tub's edges to create a makeshift cage.

The toddler was curled in a ball, naked and covered in his own filth. As I tore the chicken wire away, his eyes fluttered open. I let out a breath I didn't know I'd been holding.

I grabbed a ratty towel that was lying on the floor, wrapped him as best I could while holding the gun, and walked back into the living room.

I'd half expected Bea to make a break for it, but she was still on the mattress, frozen and mute.

There were a lot of things I could have called her, but none of them seemed up to the task. I walked out and went back down to the cab. I opened the door and let Ms. P see the squirming bundle in my arms.

She nodded.

"See—the kid's fine," Kelly said. "Now give me the money and let me go."

My boss gave him a smile, and not a friendly one.

"This money, Mr. Kelly?" She turned over the paper bag and three bundles tumbled out—the Sunday *Times* cut to size. "Mr. Miller wanted to use real currency, but I convinced him that would be unnecessary."

"We had a deal," Kelly growled.

"Perhaps you'd like to complain to the police," she said. "Lieutenant, would you mind taking his statement?"

The cabdriver swiveled his bulk around. Granite eyes peered out over a salt-and-pepper beard.

"I'd love to have a chat with him," said Lieutenant Nathan Lazenby. He honked the cab's horn and half a dozen police cars came roaring from both ends of the block, discharging a battalion of blue.

Kelly made a move for my boss, but before he could get his hands on her, Lazenby grabbed him by the collar and yanked.

"You gave me your word!" Kelly sputtered.

Ms. Pentecost's smile winked out.

"Yes, I did," she said. "But I also gave my word to Diane

Neary. Do you remember her? She was the mother of two-year-old Clara Neary. She paid the ransom, just as you instructed. But her daughter was never returned. The remains of the child's body were discovered three months later in an abandoned lot not ten minutes walk from here."

She leaned toward him so that they were nearly nose to nose.

"My word is very important to me, Mr. Kelly. It's the currency I trade in. But I'd rather spend every cent of it than let the murderer of a child walk free."

A couple of sergeants reached in and grabbed hold of Kelly, pulling him out of the cab and into the cold.

"Enjoy the fresh air, Mr. Kelly," my boss said before he was marched off. "It will be the last you breathe for a very long time."

CHAPTER 2

The wren was waiting across the street when we got home. Home being the three-story brownstone in a tucked-away section of Brooklyn that served as both office and residence to myself, Ms. Pentecost, and our Scottish-émigrée housekeeper and loyal watchdog, Eleanor Campbell.

I call her a wren because she was shortish and plumpish and wearing half a dozen shades of brown—chocolate-brown coat, sandy-colored skirt, chestnut boots, and a russet tam hat, under which I assumed was tucked a head of brown hair.

The only thing not brown was the giant black handbag she was clutching in her lap.

The resemblance to a bird didn't stop with the color. She was cocking her head this way and that in tiny adjustments, her eyes darting around behind a pair of thick glasses with square black frames.

She was perched stiffly on a bench halfway down the block from our door when I eased the Caddy into a space in front of our office. She drew the last puff out of a cigarette, then dropped the butt on the pavement, where it joined a half dozen of its brothers. She looked at us, quickly looked away, cautiously looked back.

"I think that might be our five o'clock," I said as I helped Ms. P out of the backseat.

She checked her watch.

"It's only twenty minutes after four."

"Yeah, but she's got that look about her."

I threw a wave to the bird on the bench. She got busy brushing some loose ash off her skirt.

"Or maybe not," I muttered.

We went inside out of the cold.

We'd spent the last hours with an assistant district attorney unloading the lot we'd collected on the kidnapping scheme. Lazenby was there for the start, but then had to run.

"Home burglaries are up across the city, and the mayor wants something done," he told us. "So we're rousting the usuals and putting the fear of God into them."

"I thought they only called you in when there was a body on the ground," I said.

"The newspapers are making it a problem for the mayor. Some wordsmith at the *Times* called it 'a pernicious crime spree targeting the workingman.'"

"That's dramatic."

"Yeah, maybe. But the mayor made it the commissioner's problem, and the commissioner thinks the robbery boys dropped the ball, so he made it my problem."

He squared a cap onto his granite block of a head and reluctantly turned toward the door.

"I'm working a dozen homicides, but I've got to spend the rest of my day rousting fences."

I wished the lieutenant well and told him I hoped he'd shake out some squealers.

Meanwhile, we became the DA's favorite people. The evidence against Kelly and Little was enough to put the two away for three lifetimes. Want to see a prosecutor salivate? Hand him a slam-dunk case that'll generate good press for everyone who touches it.

To ensure that, I'd slipped out to use the facilities and, instead of powdering my nose, placed calls to the *Times,* the Associated Press, and the New York City office of Reuters. I decided to save *Time* magazine for the morning. They were a weekly, after all, and could wait.

I'd also had the pleasure of delivering a freshly scrubbed toddler into Gloria Miller's grateful arms. Her "Thank you" was barely understandable between the sobs. I pocketed the bright little moment away for safekeeping.

Back at the office, Mrs. Campbell swapped hot mugs— coffee for me; water, honey, and lemon for my boss—in exchange for news of how things had gone. When we finished with the tale, she gave a single brusque nod.

"Good," she said. "Too bad you weren't able to shoot the bastard."

She may look like the graying matron of an all-girls' school, but Mrs. Campbell is one part midwife to two parts mastiff. When it comes to crimes against children, she shared my boss's philosophy: Let 'em rot.

Three coffees later, the Swiss clock on the wall began to announce the hour. It was on its third of five chimes when the doorbell rang. I found the wren standing on the stoop.

"Hello, I'm Holly Quick. I have a five o'clock appointment with Lillian Pentecost for a consultation," she said in clipped words that suggested she'd spent her hour on the bench rehearsing.

"Come on in," I said.

I'd pegged our potential client as middle-aged when I'd glimpsed her outside. Once she was inside, her cheeks healthy and flushed, I re-evaluated to a few years over thirty. On her feet, she was an inch or two taller than me, depending on footwear.

I relieved her of coat and hat, though she kept hold of the giant handbag. I'd also been wrong about the hair. It was thick and black, parted left in a big Lauren Bacall wave that was about six months overdue for a trim.

Not that I could judge. My own hair hadn't seen shears in over a year, and my wiry red curls were starting to creep down my back. Every morning when I looked in the bathroom mirror I got a fraction of an inch closer to mistaking my reflection for my mother.

Her eyes matched the ensemble, though—chocolate brown and about twice as big as her face required, though that might have been the specs. The eyes, combined with her complexion—about three shades too dark for January—gave her a very Lupe Vélez look. If the smoldering Mexican actress had ever decided to play a nervous schoolteacher.

"You could have knocked earlier," I told her as I led her into the office. "You didn't have to sit out in the cold."

"No, no, that's all right. I don't mind the cold." The shiver in her voice said she minded it at least a little.

In the office, I maneuvered her in front of the choicest of the armchairs facing Ms. P's half-ton oak monstrosity before moving to my own, much more modest, desk. My boss rose long enough to extend a hand.

Our guest took to the handshake like she was diving out of a foxhole.

I offered refreshments, she declined, then we all sat on cue. I grabbed a notebook and prepped my Pitman.

"A pleasure to meet you," my boss said. "Do you go by 'Miss,' 'Mrs.,' or something other?"

Our client treated the question like it was an episode of *Quiz Kids* and a new Zenith was on the line.

"Well, I'm not married, so— Wait. What do you mean by 'other'? Oh, that's right—you go by 'Ms.,' don't you? I've heard of it—seen it written out somewhere, I suppose—but I've never known anyone to actually use it. Until now. By you, I mean. It's very interesting. No, that's not the right word. I mean, it is interesting. But also off-putting. It calls attention, doesn't it? Anyway, I think if I tried to use it, people would think it was a typo. So 'Miss.' I think I'll stick with 'Miss.'"

However this meeting was going to go, I didn't think it would be brief.

My boss and her off-putting title took it in stride.

"How can I be of assistance, Miss Quick?"

No answer. Instead Holly Quick did the bird impression again, hands twitching, head darting this way and that to take in the bookshelves and their rows of well-thumbed tomes, the modest drinks trolley, the clock ticking away, me at my desk, the massive oil painting hanging on the wall above Ms. P's head. The tree, wide and yellow and gnarled, standing alone in the middle of some parched prairie. The woman nearly lost in its shadow.

She lingered there a moment, possibly wondering the same things I did every time I looked at it.

"Miss Quick?"

Our guest snapped back into focus.

"Yes, I'm sorry. This is difficult," she said. "I knew it would be. I prepared for it to be difficult. But—"

"I assure you, Miss Parker and I are experienced dealing with problems of the most personal nature."

"Oh, it's not personal. Not really," she declared. "No, I take that back. It *is* personal. Very personal. Do you mind if I smoke? No, no, never mind. There's no ashtrays. Context clues. Have to remember context clues. Anyway, where was I? Right. Personal. Yes, very personal. Somebody is stealing my murders."

I paused my shorthand.

"Stealing your murders?" I assumed I'd misheard.

"Yes," she said, looking my way but not quite meeting my eyes. "It's really . . . I don't know the proper word. Infuriat-

ing. Insulting. Violating. Yes—a violation! It's a violation of
the most profound sort."

"That someone is stealing your murders."

"Exactly!"

I shrugged an apology at Ms. Pentecost. Usually I did a
quick background on a potential client. But Holly Quick had
made the appointment about ten minutes before we got the
call from Gloria Miller. I'd been too busy running hell for
leather to even look her up in the phone book.

No harm, I figured. In every life a few nuts must fall.
Though I shot a nervous glance at the giant handbag she'd
stashed beside her chair. It was big enough to conceal a sawed-
off. I tried to remember how heavy it had seemed when she'd
carried it in, and came to the conclusion that a shotgun was
pretty unlikely, but a handgun wasn't out of the question.

I started calculating how I could eject Miss Quick with
the least fuss, preferably in time for an early dinner and without getting shot. Mrs. Campbell was making fresh bread and
tomato soup, and the smell was starting to waft in.

"Perhaps," my boss said, "you could clarify. What murders are you referring to? And who is stealing them?"

"I don't know who's stealing them. That's the problem. If I
knew, I wouldn't have come here. I didn't want to come here.
I was hoping it was a coincidence. The first two could have
been. Or maybe I was hoping they were. But the last one—he
used 'The Curse of the Red Claw.' That one was really impossible to miss."

Somewhere in my head a very faint bell rang.

"No, after that one I couldn't sit back and do nothing. But
I didn't want to go to the police, because . . . I didn't want
to, that's all. I knew about you from your work, of course.
I've followed it for some time. I've even used some of your
cases as inspiration for my stories. Just inspiration, mind you.

I would never directly reference real events. It would be a . . . well, I don't like using the same word twice in this way, but a violation."

Ms. Pentecost waited a breath to see if there was more to the monologue. Then: "You're a writer?"

Miss Quick fluttered.

"Yes, of course," she said. "I'm sorry. I should have led with that. My editors are always chiding me for not including enough exposition. I like to throw my readers into the middle of the action and let them put the pieces together as they go. But Marlo's always telling me, 'No, Holly, people don't like to be confused. They like to know what's happening.'"

"How about you spoon-feed us?" I suggested. "Just this once."

She did some more head-cocking and hand-wringing and then settled in.

"I'm a writer," she began. "Crime stories, mostly. Sometimes horror or science fiction. I've had a few pieces in *Weird Tales*. They only pay three-quarters of a cent per word, but those pieces have more words. It's all the exposition, you see? But most of my work has been through detective magazines, and my best work—I think it's my best, anyway—and the stories that are relevant in this instance, have been published in *Strange Crime*."

Ms. P tossed me a look.

"I know it," I said. "Mostly short stories and novellas, but with some true crime stuff thrown in. I've got a few issues under my bed. Don't remember seeing Holly Quick as a byline."

Miss Quick let out a bark that took me a second to realize was a laugh.

"Oh, I don't publish under my own name!" she exclaimed. "I use a pseudonym. Several, actually, depending on subject and style. And I frequently have multiple pieces in the same issue, and editors don't like repeating bylines. It makes the magazine look cheap. Also, I'm a woman."

"Is it difficult for women in your industry?" Ms. P asked.

Miss Quick froze, like a windup toy whose spring had locked. Abruptly she started up again.

"*Difficult* isn't quite the right word," she said. "But I don't know if I have a better one. At the very least, using a male pseudonym cuts out a lot of silliness. The stories in question were all published under the pseudonym Horace Bellow."

That was the bell I'd heard ringing. "The Curse of the Red Claw": It was a novella by Horace Bellow. I'd read it not too long ago. I'd actually read a lot of his work.

Her work.

"You're Horace Bellow?"

"Yes. More accurately, Horace Bellow is me."

I turned to my boss. "She wrote that story I tried to press on you last summer. The one about the widow who kept a poison garden on the roof."

Our maybe-client perked up. "'The Garden of Earthly Destruction'!"

"That's the one," I said. "I thought Ms. Pentecost would appreciate the horticultural details."

The detective in question shifted her weight from starboard to port and back again. A sign she was getting impatient.

"Let's return to this belief that someone is stealing your murders," she said. "If this is an issue of plagiarism, I recommend you consult an attorney."

"Oh, it's not plagiarism," the writer assured us. "Certainly not in the traditional sense."

She went spelunking in her handbag and pulled out an inch-thick folder. She passed it across the desk to my boss.

I got up and walked around Ms. P's desk so I could play backseat detective.

Inside the folder were issues of *Strange Crime*, each with

pages bookmarked, along with several newspaper clippings pasted to heavy bond typing paper.

There were clippings on three murders: a hanging in Stuyvesant Square in August, a stabbing in Sunnyside in November, and a third death at an antiques shop on the southernmost edge of the Upper East Side four days prior. In the latter, the cause of death was omitted but a quote from the police saying the death was "originally suspected to be a wild-animal attack" suggested it wasn't pretty.

All of the murders were familiar to me and my boss. We had identical clippings in the file boxes on the third floor. Every day I scanned the city's major rags for interesting crimes, as well as bits and bobs about notable figures. All three had qualified as interesting.

"How closely do these crimes adhere to the details of your stories?" Ms. P asked.

"Very closely," she said. "Or at least I think very closely. Reporters only provide so many details. It's quite frustrating. For example, the hanging—a Mr. Michael Perkins. The paper mentions that he was also shot, but they don't say where. On his body, I mean. I have my character shot in the head. And the stabbing incident mentions that the victim was found with a piece of horn projecting from his stomach, but they don't mention what kind of animal. In my story, it's a deer antler."

More head-cocking and hand-wringing. I had the sense that despite the volume of words tumbling out of her mouth, she wasn't used to talking so much.

"However, in 'The Curse of the Red Claw,' the murderer uses a glove to which he's attached a set of panther claws. The victims were partners of his in a jewel heist. The killer was the only one who was caught, and he went to prison. Now he's exacting revenge. His first victim operated a jewelry store."

Ms. P and I quickly scanned the clipped articles on the third murder. There had been several over the last few days, not just because of the sensational nature of the crime, but because of some of the characters the victim spent his off-hours with.

The body of Flavio Checchetto was discovered around noon on Friday in the office of his store, Checchetto Curios and Consignment, located in the shadow of the 59th Street Bridge on First Avenue. Police originally believed it had been some kind of wild-animal attack because of the "horrible wounds on his body."

Halfway down the article, Miss Quick had circled a sentence noting that the body had been found lying atop a desk.

"I assume this detail about Mr. Checchetto being discovered on his desk has an echo in your story?" Ms. P asked.

"Yes. In my story the victim—a Mr. McKray—struggles with the killer, falls back onto his desk, and then is . . . well . . . killed."

The articles that had come in the Sunday editions were skeptical about the animal attack theory, humans being easier to find in New York than wandering tigers. There were also the inevitable parallels to the Black Dahlia thing that was eating up the headlines in Los Angeles. However, they didn't spend too many column inches on it.

What they did spill a lot of ink on was the fact that Flavio Checchetto had been a member of the Black Museum Club, the famed murder salon run by noted philanthropist Jessup Quincannon.

The group's name came from the fact that Quincannon was rumored to have the largest collection of crime memorabilia outside of Scotland Yard's Black Museum.

His salon, which met monthly, was very exclusive. Its membership was a loose secret, but it was rumored to be made up of a number of respected scholars, socialites, politicians, and other wealthy so-and-sos who got their jollies chatting homicide.

It was also rumored that guest speakers included people with more firsthand experience on the topic—killers and crime fighters, alike.

Ms. Pentecost received an invitation from Quincannon at least twice a year, and at least twice a year I typed out her polite but firm refusal. After the third or fourth time, I'd dived into the third-floor files and found a thick folder on Quincannon and his salon and made a point of learning who I was wasting two stamps a year on.

I went back to my desk and took up my notebook again. If Miss Quick was on the up-and-up, and the other killings shared a similar number of details with her stories, then I had to agree with her assessment. The first two murders could be chalked up to coincidence. Enough people get offed in New York City, it would stand to reason that a few would resemble fiction.

But three murders in a six-month span? All echoing the same writer? That wasn't coincidence. Someone was making a point.

What the point was, I had no idea.

"Assuming the content of your work is as you say, then there is the possibility that someone is utilizing your stories in the most disturbing way," Ms. Pentecost said. "The best course for you would be to contact the police."

Our guest started shaking her head. My boss barreled on.

"These murders happened in different jurisdictions. There will be different officers investigating each one. If they are connected, the authorities need to know so they can—"

"No, no, no. No police," Holly said. "That's why I came to you. No police."

Ms. Pentecost took a breath, then rearranged her pitch.

"It is not merely about solving these crimes, but the prevention of future ones. If someone is copying your stories, then—"

"I know how the police work, Ms. Pentecost. Crime is as

much my vocation as yours. They peer into every crack and crevice of a person's life."

"Do you think Miss Parker and I will not do the same?" Ms. P countered.

"I think that you will do so discreetly," Holly said. "I do not think you will leak information like a sieve. I do not think you will sell details to the press."

She shifted in her seat. Actually, I'm not sure she ever quite stopped shifting.

"I'm a very private person. If I go to the police, then eventually I will be paraded out into the spotlight. That is something I adamantly do not want."

I jumped in.

"Look, we have relationships with a lot of cops. Some with bars on their shoulders. They can be discreet when they want to," I assured her. "They put out the word to their officers to keep mum about you, then—"

"Do you think I'm stupid?" she snarled, managing to hold her eyes on mine for the first time that evening. "I know what makes a good story. This is a good story. It will get out. A reporter will bribe a policeman—maybe not your friends, but others—and it will get out. My name will be splashed across the papers. I don't want that. I don't—"

She twisted her head away, snapping off the end of the sentence. Any resemblance to a fluffy bird had disappeared.

She turned back to my boss.

"Will you take my case or won't you?"

Ms. Pentecost leaned forward half an inch. "You wish us to discover whether these murders are linked, whether they are indeed inspired by your work, and I assume catch the person responsible. But without involving the authorities in the attempt."

Miss Quick nodded.

"And if we succeed? What then?" my boss asked. "If we

catch this murderer and bring him or her to justice. There will be a trial. Evidence will be presented. It's very possible that your connection to these crimes will become part of the public record. Have you . . ."

My boss trailed off, her good eye going unfocused. One second. Two seconds. Three. Holly's fidgeting increased. I started to get concerned.

We got to seven seconds before the needle dropped and my boss came back to herself.

"Have you considered that?" she continued, as if no time had elapsed. "The inevitability of your involvement if we are successful?"

No answer from our guest. She just sat there, eyes on her lap, fingers plucking at her skirt, the pulse in her throat thrumming to beat the band.

"Miss Quick?"

"Yes," she said, her voice small and fragile. "I've thought of it."

"And?"

She looked up.

"If it comes to that—and I don't believe it is inevitable— I will deal with the consequences," she said. "In the meantime, if you take the case, I insist on anonymity. For that to be achieved, I believe you cannot contact the police."

The three of us sat in silence for a moment. Outside, the wind was picking up, rattling the windows in their frames. The last of the January sunlight had vanished, and the office was lit in the warm glow of the room's lamps.

Eventually, Holly Quick asked her question again.

"Will you take my case?"

"I will need to consider it," Ms. P told her. "And to confer with Miss Parker."

Our maybe-client opened her mouth to object, but my boss stopped her.

"You ask a great deal, Miss Quick. It would be unfair of me to agree to take the case and then find I am unable to operate within your parameters."

Our guest thought about that for a moment, then nodded.

"How long?" she asked.

"Twenty-four hours. Miss Parker will call you with my decision."

Another thought and a nod. A couple of awkward handshakes later, I fetched her hat and coat and showed her out.

I watched the curious woman disappear into the night.

CHAPTER 3

Back in the office, Ms. Pentecost and I settled into the familiar argument: Do we or don't we? If we disagreed, the tie went to the boss. It was her name on the business cards, after all.

"What is your sense of Miss Quick?"

"I honestly don't know."

She gave me a dubious look.

"Really," I said. "I couldn't read her. I mean, if she is who she says she is, then she makes up stories for a living. Any or all of what she told us could be fiction. And if she's got a tell, I couldn't find it in that haystack of tics and twitches. I'll say this, though—she refused to meet my eyes. That screams someone with something to hide."

My boss shook her head.

"I don't think that was intentional," she said. "I believe she is merely someone who finds eye contact uncomfortable."

"Well, I find her lack of it uncomfortable."

"A reaction I'm sure she's familiar with."

My boss was being argumentative. That meant she was interested. Which was the first step to her taking the case.

"Surely her peculiarities are not the real reason you don't care for her," Ms. P said. "We have trucked with far more peculiar people."

She had a point. Our address book was chock-full of oddballs.

"You're right," I said. "It's not just her mannerisms. It's what she's asking. No police involvement? It's begging for trouble down the road."

"We've crossed such lines with the authorities before."

"Sure, but it's always been our call, not the client's," I reminded her. "Three murders, no cops, and I'm about to be out of pocket for three weeks in case you've forgotten."

"I have not."

I was about to push the issue, but was interrupted by a shout from the kitchen.

"Dinner's up!"

The scent of tomato and basil and hot bread was filling the entire house now, and my stomach rumbled. I'd skipped lunch, being too busy preparing for my starring role as Billy's devoted girlfriend. It was a nasty habit I'd picked up from my boss—skipping meals when we were hot on a case.

We'd been hot for the better part of six months, taking on one job after another, sometimes two or three at the same time, not to mention our pet projects. It wasn't that Ms. Pentecost was running herself ragged. I was the pressure valve that was meant to keep that from happening. It was more like she was testing her limits.

Following our adventure in Virginia the previous August—one that left her with a twisted ankle and me with a battered everything else—she paid a visit to her longtime doctor.

All she wanted was a cursory check on her hoof to make sure no lasting damage had been done. But while he had her on his table, the doc put her through the series of tests that she was supposed to have on a regular basis and that she'd been avoiding for the better part of a year.

The tests that tracked how her multiple sclerosis was progressing.

I didn't know how things went. Our relationship did not extend to having access to her medical records. Whatever the results, she came out wanting to take on every case that walked in the door.

Make of that what you will.

At that moment I was making what I would of Ms. P's seven-second silence during our interview with Holly Quick. Maybe she'd just been gathering her thoughts. She had a lot of them, after all.

On the other hand, I'd done more than my share of reading on multiple sclerosis and I knew that it could eventually start throwing a whole bucket of monkey wrenches into Ms. P's mental machinery.

I could have just asked her about that seven-second pause, but I was afraid. Afraid the answer would be "What pause?"

We had no hard-and-fast rule about working during meals, so we spread out the contents of Holly's folder between the plates of grilled cheese and bowls of soup.

For the thousandth time, we invited Mrs. Campbell to join us, and for the thousandth time, she opted to take her dinner in the renovated carriage house that she called home.

Already familiar with the news articles, we started with Holly's stories, reading them in the order of the murders they resembled. My boss was a slower reader than me, at least over the long run. Her disease let her have about fifteen minutes of good reading before she had to give her eyes a couple minutes' rest. To accommodate, I gave her a two-story head start before I started running.

"The Last Drop," published in the March 1942 issue of *Strange Crime,* was about a mutt named Chester, an alcoholic crippled by guilt. Driving home from a bar one night, he hits a mother and child crossing the street, then speeds off. The story opens with the boozehound in his fleabag apartment, tying his own noose.

As he's setting up his low-rent gallows, he reminisces about the cascade of bad decisions that got him to this point. Just as he's about to step off his stool and take that final drop, he has second thoughts. What if he could change? What if he devoted his life to helping people?

He's about to take the noose off when a voice speaks from the doorway.

"Looks like I got here just in time."

It's the man whose wife and child the boozehound left dead by the side of the road. He's come to shoot the old alkie dead. He gives him a choice—the gun or the noose.

Chester decides that he doesn't want his death on anyone's conscience but his own, so he takes the drop. But as coroners—and also, apparently, Holly Quick—know all too well, unless it's a long drop, you don't break your neck. You strangle to death. And strangling is a slow way to go.

The man is hanging there, dying by degrees. The grieving husband and father can't stand to watch it.

"You don't deserve mercy. But here it is."

He shoots him square between the eyes.

March 1942: Not too long before I crossed paths with Lillian Pentecost and she turned me from a circus Jill-of-all-trades to her—handler? Co-conspirator? I had a hazy memory of reading the story when it was first published, sitting at a chow-tent table, killing time between acts while the circus rumbled around me.

The second story was titled "Five-Minute Head Start" and had been published in May 1944. It followed a woman, a grifter who sets her sights on a millionaire. Her plan is to seduce him, get access to his bank accounts, then drain him dry.

He takes her on a weekend getaway to his hunting cabin, where he reveals that she's the prey, not the predator. His plan is to hunt her through the woods like an animal and kill her. He shoots her and leaves her for dead, but she ends up surviving, then comes back to the cabin and stabs him in the gut with a broken piece of deer antler.

It was a gruesome little take on "The Most Dangerous Game," which Holly made messier by making the prey a woman.

The cover of that issue depicted the lady grifter lying helpless on the forest floor, her paper-thin negligee torn in every spot the censors would allow. The hunter loomed over her, leveling his rifle.

It didn't take Freud.

The third story, "The Curse of the Red Claw," had been published only a month prior, in the December 1946 issue of *Strange Crime,* and went as Holly described, ending with the first victim sprawled across his desk, gutted from stem to stern. Though it had less to do with the revenge plot and more about how the drive for vengeance ate away at the protagonist over time.

Holly Quick might be annoying and demanding and an assortment of other adjectives, but she wasn't a bad writer.

She also wasn't wrong. The resemblance between her stories and the crimes in question was clear.

As she put it, someone was stealing her murders. Now all that was left was to decide if we were going to take the job of finding out who.

Ms. P was leaning back in her seat, plate and bowl empty, fingers twisting at the corners of the tomato-stained napkin in her lap. I didn't mistake the posture for a nap. That was her thinking pose. She was going through the same mental checklist I was.

The list contained three boxes that could be checked off, each one adding to the likelihood of us taking the case.

First question: Could we do a better job than the police?

I gave that half a check. Without knowing about Holly Quick and her stories, it was doubtful New York's finest would ever link the three murders. But their not knowing was on our client, not on their incompetence.

Second question: Was the case deserving of our time? In other words, was there some aspect of the case that plucked our heartstrings? No check in that box. At least not for me.

And finally, in the absence of a check in box two: Could the client pay enough to make it worth our while? My boss frequently skipped over this box. I did not.

In addition to being Ms. P's leg-woman, sounding board, note taker, occasional browbeater, and sometimes translator, I was also the office manager. Which meant I knew the cost of a loaf of bread.

I also knew the cost of running an office and a household that included two full-time staff and an owner who needed to sock away for a rainy day.

I didn't know what *Strange Crime* or *New Detective* paid, but I was betting it wasn't a mint.

Half a check out of three is not great. Also, I had the feeling that Holly Quick would be more trouble than she was worth. Not only should we take a pass, but we should send a polite, anonymous note to the NYPD letting them in on the connection between the killings.

I was drafting out this line of reasoning in my head when Ms. P opened her eyes and stood up from the table, brushing errant crumbs from her lap.

"Call Miss Quick," she said. "Tell her we'll take the case."

Checkboxes be damned.

Maybe it won't be so bad, I thought, as I began clearing

the table. Three murders, no tipping off the cops—at least it would be a challenge. It might even be fun.

Hindsight doesn't wear cheaters, so I feel awful typing that out.

Fun.

But I didn't know what I didn't know. That before we were done I'd be standing over two more bodies, and our professional reputations and our lives would be on the line.

CHAPTER 4

We moved back to the office, where I called Holly Quick and told her we'd take the job. Then I set up an appointment to interview her the following evening at her apartment.

She bucked at that, but I held firm. Sure, we could have had her come to us again, but then we wouldn't also be able to snoop.

With that settled, we moved on to a problem that we had been picking at for over a year and the reason that the next three weeks were going to be trying ones: the Waterhouse Project.

I referred to it as a "project" because there was no client to speak of and "case" was too small a noun to encompass Olivia Waterhouse.

She had crossed our path during the Collins Case, an adventure that ended rather bittersweetly for everyone involved. She was introduced to us as a passionate but unassuming university professor. While her subject of choice was anthropology, she also had a fascination with high-end hucksters and fraud spiritualists and had even written a book on the subject. All seemingly aboveboard.

Then we learned she was a fraud herself. That she'd orchestrated the blackmail and sometimes death of prominent men—mostly wealthy businessmen with blots on their ethical record.

These were the kind of men for whom human life was no more precious than pocket change, and Waterhouse believed they needed to be taught a lesson. One that sometimes ended in a very final exam.

She confessed as much right in our office, admitting to my boss that a long string of deaths and disappearances that Ms. P had been investigating could be chalked up to her.

The next day she vanished.

Her office was cleaned out and her apartment emptied of everything but the Frigidaire. The university had no way to contact her. Neither did her publisher.

Her résumé turned out to be a tissue of lies. When the school originally hired her, they had done due diligence. They made calls, asked questions about the esteemed Dr. Olivia Waterhouse, and were given suitable answers.

From someone.

Even her name was up for grabs. If you're lying about everything else, why stop at your moniker?

All we had to prove the woman even existed were a set of fingerprints lifted from a book, a single off-center photograph, and a collection of crimes, some of which we couldn't even prove were crimes and none of which could be linked to Waterhouse.

For the last year we'd been pursuing what avenues we could, including paying to have that one picture of Waterhouse printed in newspapers across the country.

It had been taken at a masquerade party and showed a petite woman, a head shorter than the men around her, caught in the act of looking warily at the camera. The top portion of her face was obscured by a black half-mask, but you could still see her wiry, somewhat windswept hair, the button of a nose, the squared-off chin, and the ever-serious mouth caught curling at the edges, as if contemplating, but not committing to, some private amusement.

If the photo allowed you to see into the holes of her mask, you'd have found eyes so dark they were almost black. Not knowing what we knew, you'd easily mistake her for an unkempt, awkwardly charming academic playing dress-up with high society.

Knowing what I knew, when I looked at the photo I saw a shark swimming in the shallows.

Along with the photo was a message promising a reward for reliable information about the woman in the picture and instructions on how to contact us.

Since Waterhouse had disappeared, we'd identified another half-dozen crimes that smelled like her—some taking place after she'd vanished and not all of them in New York City.

There was a paper baron in Maine who'd signed an order turning his ten thousand acres of old-growth forest into a national preserve before going for a walk in the Great North Woods, never to be seen again.

Then there was the high-priced D.C. lawyer who didn't show up for the defense's closing arguments in a massive anti-trust case. They found him gone and his office stripped of years' worth of files—many containing incriminating information on his clients. As for the lawyer, rumors put him on a South American beach, the bottom of the Potomac, or anywhere in between.

Again like a shark. Visible only by the blood left in her wake.

Whenever we weren't actively working a case, Ms. P would take up the Waterhouse file and pick at it. Or go through the third-floor files searching for unsolved crimes that she could pin on the not-so-good doctor.

We stopped going to lectures. Books languished on shelves. Ms. P's collection of esoteric magazines piled up. I made it a twice-weekly practice to suggest she relax. Stress, I pointed out, did her disease no favors.

"Wherever Dr. Waterhouse is, I doubt she is relaxing," Ms. Pentecost told me on one of these occasions. "We are the only ones who are looking for her, the only ones who can discover her intentions. If we fail, more will die."

A hard argument to budge.

Then, after months of fruitless fishing, we had a bite. A woman recently retired from a Financial District law office recognized the photo. She fingered Waterhouse as having worked for the office as a temp secretary for about two months in the summer of 1940.

I figured it for a mistake or a goof—someone taking a flyer on collecting the reward.

But when I called the retired clerk, she had enough details about Waterhouse—including those deep, dark eyes—that I had to admit she was on the level. Waterhouse had worked as the personal secretary to Ken Shirley, one of the two founding partners at Shirley & Wise.

The question was why?

The firm handled mostly tax law, and their clients were more in the range of corner dry cleaners than titans of industry. Nothing sinister had befallen Shirley. He was still alive and well and helping Mom and Pop wrestle with the IRS.

According to our source, Waterhouse had been employed under the name Emily Ginsburg and had done the job for eight weeks with neither distinction nor demerit.

At first, Ms. Pentecost had considered scouring the firm from top to bottom, interviewing every employee, nosing into every hidey-hole. We quickly realized that even if we were allowed access, it was possible that Waterhouse's goal was a more subtle one. Our questions would get us nowhere, and they might tip off Waterhouse that we had a line on her.

It was decided that I would do a little acting, this time with a role that went beyond some monologuing in a phone booth.

Mr. Shirley's current secretary had just received an all-expenses-paid three-week trip to the Florida Keys courtesy of a newspaper contest she didn't remember entering. Thanks to a few well-placed bribes, her replacement would be a loquacious redhead who could type seventy-two words a minute and asked a lot of silly questions.

I didn't think it would be that hard a chore. I'd taken all the right secretarial classes and could file as fast as the next woman.

I had been set to start that morning, but the kidnapping case had complicated things and I'd called out of my first day of work, blaming it on a bout of food poisoning. The folks at Shirley & Wise were annoyed but understanding, and I assured them I would be there bright and early Tuesday.

"Three weeks should give you adequate opportunity to deduce Dr. Waterhouse's purpose, if such a thing is possible," Ms. P said.

"Three weeks chained to a desk and trying to keep the swears to a minimum," I said in a half-feigned lament. "I can't tell you how thrilled I am."

"If you don't think you can play the role—"

"It's not that," I said. "I just hate pencil skirts. I can never fit a holster under the things."

She grabbed a bottle of wine and a glass from the drinks trolley and retrieved her cane from its place propped against her desk.

The cane had the same silver head as its predecessor, having been made by the same manufacturer. The last one was a sword cane that had spent several months in the custody of the Virginia state district attorney's office. When it was finally returned, it was covered in long-dried blood.

While the sword cane had been a gift from her most loyal, diligent, and attractive-in-the-right-light employee, she'd decided to chuck it. Her loyal employee didn't blame her.

She had this new one made to her specifications, housing more than a single trick in its black wooden shaft.

"I'll be in the archives," she said, making her way toward the stairs. "Don't forget you have an early day tomorrow."

"Don't you worry," I told her. "I'll get my eight hours and change."

I stayed at my desk, mentally preparing for the next day. Who knows? I thought. Pretending to be a working stiff might not be so bad.

Again, I thought, it might even be fun.

CHAPTER 5

You know what isn't fun?

Getting up early enough to straighten and pin your curls into something resembling a wave, finding your white Bloomingdale's blouse has burst into wrinkles overnight, realizing that you have to hold your breath to squeeze into your best black pencil skirt, then doing your makeup at a record pace only to have it scoured off by an Arctic blast on your walk to the subway. All before eight a.m.

This, I thought as I shouldered my way into a standing spot on the 2 train, was a good reminder of why I was a detective.

Shirley & Wise took up a decent chunk of the fourth floor of a high-rise on the fringes of Wall Street. I glanced at the directory on my way into the elevator. It listed half a dozen law firms and accounting offices, as well as a high-end portrait studio, a catalog company selling household appliances, and businesses I couldn't classify by name alone, like Sunshine Services and Choc-O-Love, Inc.

My first day was like every first day of work since the invention of the office. There was half an hour of paperwork with a dour-faced woman in payroll to ensure my checks were sent to the right address. In this case, a PO box registered to "Jean Palmer," my alias for the duration. I had ID to match the name, courtesy of our favorite forger.

We didn't go to the trouble of setting up fake references. It wasn't likely they'd dig deep for a three-week temp girl.

Shirley & Wise was laid out in the popular style: a big open space with about two dozen desks at even intervals, all facing the same direction. They were filled with a grab bag of men and women rubbing the sleep out of their eyes while sorting through papers, punching calculators, and composing a veritable Bach fugue on their typewriters. Along one side were doors leading to private offices. Along another was a bank of windows looking across the street at an identical bank of windows that framed an identical set of office workers. And along a third wall were three rows of filing cabinets containing what I assumed was client paperwork.

Knowing how much paper you can pack into a single file drawer, I did some quick back-of-the-envelope math. I estimated I was looking at around a quarter of a million individual sheets. If whatever Waterhouse had been looking for was in there, I would be collecting Social Security before I located it.

With my own paperwork sorted, I was escorted across the floor to meet Mr. Shirley.

The senior partner had a corner office with a bank of windows along one side and a desk that was nearly the size of Ms. Pentecost's but with none of the personality. Kenneth Shirley was one of those men whose faces had stubbornly held on to its baby fat well into middle age. He had a thick mop of sandy-brown hair that took me an impressive ten seconds to clock as a toupee, and a shape that was slowly drifting toward pear. He was about half a head taller than me, but that isn't saying much. All in all, not the most impressive physical specimen. But you didn't need a beach body to wrestle balance sheets.

"A pleasure to meet you, Miss Palmer."

His handshake was firm, his voice strong, his eyes sharp and focused.

"Mrs. Palmer," I corrected. "If you don't mind."

"Ah, sorry. I didn't see a ring."

Definitely sharp.

"Widowed," I explained. "Three years now. I keep the ring in a safe-deposit box. I'm absolutely terrified of losing it."

I said that line with a delicate warble and added a bit of midwestern drawl. Jean Palmer was originally from Ohio, or so said her résumé. I also had on a pair of horn-rimmed glasses with uncorrected lenses. Combined with the accent, the outfit, the shape I'd hammered my hair into, and some judicious use of Max Factor to conceal the freckles stubbornly clinging to my cheeks through the winter, anyone who had seen a picture or two of Will Parker in the papers would have a hard time making the connection.

I wasn't too worried. Generally people don't see what they don't expect to see.

"My apologies, Mrs. Palmer. Foolish of me for assuming," Shirley said, giving a little half-bow of contrition. "I'll let Peggy get you settled. After lunch I should have some letters to dictate."

Peggy was a fortyish office manager in a Chanel suit and lacquered bumper bangs who had probably dreamed of growing up to be called Margaret but had to settle. She pointed me toward my desk, which was parked just outside Shirley's office. Good for keeping an eye on him. Less so for being able to wander unnoticed.

The desk came complete with a well-oiled typewriter, a stack of notepads, pens, and assorted bric-a-brac. It also featured your standard model 302 Western Electric with complementary handset and rotary dial. Peggy spent a solid three minutes explaining the procedure.

"When you answer, just say, 'Kenneth Shirley's office, how may I help you?' If he's in, tell them he's in. Then go and tell Mr. Shirley who's on the line and he'll pick up. I keep telling him he should get a second line for an intercom, or maybe one of those ones with the speaker you talk into. I have a friend who works at a patent firm on nine and they've got those and she says they're great. Mr. Shirley says that would be silly since his desk is only six feet away through that door, but it would save a lot of getting up and down and knocking and anyway, where was I? Oh right. If he's out you can just take a message and tell them he'll get right back to them. Sometimes he's in but he doesn't want people to know he's in, so you tell them he's away from his desk at the moment and you take the message. He'll let you know when he wants you doing that. Usually the hour after lunch. Except on Thursdays. On Thursdays he always takes a long lunch and doesn't get back until three, but then he's raring to go. Now there are some people you disturb him for no matter what. His top clients. Their names are typed on this sheet right here by the phone. Do your best to memorize it so you don't make any mistakes. A quick girl like you shouldn't have any problems. If you need anything, don't hesitate to ask—I'm right over there."

Ears a little numb from the barrage, I nodded and smiled. Then I was left alone at my freshly waxed desk. I glanced at my watch: 9:07 a.m.

It was going to be a long day.

The report I eventually typed up for Ms. Pentecost presented that first day in excruciating detail. I wanted to impress on my boss the sheer weight of the tedium I was shouldering on her behalf.

It took the better part of three hours to type, even at seventy-two words per minute, and from where I stand now I can safely say that nearly every bit of it was worthless. Only one moment in that entire day held a nugget worth polishing.

It came flying a flag so bright, it was practically semaphore.

It was early afternoon and I was sitting at my desk jotting down notes of what I'd learned at lunch. This included that most of the staff ate lunch at the Automat down the block; a ham-and-cheese did not taste better when paid for with nickels; and that Wilson in personnel would hit on a department store mannequin if you put it in heels.

Not a whiff of what could have interested Waterhouse.

That is until, shortly after lunch, Shirley appeared at the door to his office.

"Mrs. Palmer, I'm ready to dictate those letters."

I followed him into his office and he directed me to a chair that had been pulled up to the side of his desk. I settled in with my notebook, conscious that my chair was only half an arm's length from his.

He very firmly closed the door.

Was a pass on its way? Was he that fast a mover?

Ms. P and I had settled on Jean Palmer being a widow to allow for just this sort of eventuality. It made me seem available and made men more likely to get flirty and chatty, but allowed me to play the "Oh, you're so sweet but I'm still grieving" card.

While I was perfectly willing to return the occasional serve, I wasn't letting the game go any further than that. To mix my sports metaphors, if it came down to it, Shirley was getting thrown out at first.

It did not come down to it.

Shirley had put me behind his desk because when he was dictating letters he didn't use it. He was a pacer.

Back and forth and back and forth, rolling out one client letter after another. When he saw how quick my shorthand was, he only went faster.

He barely got within spitting distance of me, much less groping.

So the red flag?

Halfway through one of the letters—this one to the owner of a chain of grocery stores—he paused.

"One moment. I need to check something."

He went to a painting on the wall—a passably pretty watercolor of a sailboat. He clicked a hidden switch on the side and the painting swung out to reveal a safe.

In a corner of my notebook I started jotting shorthand of my own.

Murphy safe. Hotel-style. 14" x 10" x 18." Bought used?

It was a three-digit combination. I thought the first number was in the thirties, but then his shoulder nudged the picture and all I could see was sailboat. There was a quiet clunk and he swung the safe open and pulled out a file folder. Craning my neck to peek, all I saw was paper. No stacks of bills, no hidden pistol.

"That's what I thought. Their Long Island branch opened in 1939. That changes things. Mrs. Palmer, please cross out the last two sentences. Replace with . . ."

The dictation continued. He put the file back, locked the safe, and swung the painting back into place.

Later on I cornered Peggy at the watercooler, pretending to be interested in where she got her shoes, and eventually working the conversation around to "Mr. Shirley's neat little office safe."

"Oh, yes, it's so fancy, isn't it?" Peggy exclaimed. "He had to get it, you know? After what happened."

I asked the obvious.

"It was about six, seven years ago now," Peggy said. "Right after Mrs. Baxter left. She was Mr. Shirley's secretary for the longest time. Anyway, it used to be that all the partners kept their most important clients' files in little personal filing cabinets in their office. So they could get to them right away. That just makes sense, doesn't it?"

I concurred.

"Anyway, one morning Mr. Shirley comes in and finds his filing cabinet had been broken into and a whole heap of files were missing. The police were called and everything."

That was a surprise. I'd done my due diligence, and looked for any police reports involving the firm. I'd come up dry.

"What did the co—the . . . um . . . police say?" I asked.

"Oh, I don't know," Peggy said. "I never talked to them. Mr. Shirley handled it all. Poor man. It took him forever to re-create those files. His reputation took a blow, I'll tell you. That's why Dan Wise can holiday in the Caribbean through March and Mr. Shirley has to stay here and hold down the fort."

"So all those files are in Mr. Shirley's neat little safe?" I asked.

"They sure are. Now the only person who's allowed to touch them is Mr. Shirley."

We'd see about that.

CHAPTER **6**

I joined the deluge of nine-to-fivers cascading out of Lower Manhattan into the outer boroughs and made it back to the office just as the clock struck six. We were due at Holly Quick's apartment at eight.

I discarded my office attire for something more . . . well, something more anything. I settled on a blouse in lavender rayon over a pair of checked purple slacks that had been pressed on me by the women's wear clerk at Bloomingdale's during a recent shopping spree.

"In the winter, redheads should embrace purple and blue wholeheartedly," she declared while silently calculating her commission. "Then start bringing green—oh, yes, dear, absolutely include the hat; it adds a certain daring frisson— bringing green back into your color palette in the spring. Just because the world is gray does not mean you need be."

I walked out with five bags and the realization that I might be turning into something of a clotheshorse.

Having made the transition from black and white to color, I went downstairs to the office, where I gave my boss the highlights of the day—or highlight, singular.

"I double-checked the timing, and all of this went down right after Waterhouse finished her eight-week stint as Emily Ginsburg," I told her. "It's a Murphy. Like the kind some older hotels have in their rooms. As safes go, it's pretty basic. Give me a couple of hours with Jules and I'm pretty sure I could get into it. Unless you want to bring him in to do it himself."

Jules was a semi-reformed safecracker. "Reformed," because after a stint in Sing Sing, he'd made a few lifestyle adjustments and now got the majority of his income as a security expert for the rich and famous.

"Semi," because he occasionally still liked to rob those same rich and famous.

Ms. P shook her head. "We should keep this endeavor to ourselves. And while I agree that it is necessary to know what's in Mr. Shirley's safe, we should wait. Perhaps until the end of your three-week contract."

"Why the delay? I can get hold of Jules now, set up some lessons for tomorrow. I could be inside that safe by Friday night."

Another head shake.

"The safe may not hold the answers we seek," she said. "If that's so, and you're caught or—"

"I won't get caught!"

"Or they suspect that the safe has been tampered with, even if they don't know by whom, it could prematurely end our investigation."

I knew she was right. I just didn't want to spend three more weeks chained to a desk watching everyone else watch the clock.

I'd have argued more, but it was time to go.

While Ms. P stitched herself into her Arctic-explorer gear, I shrugged into my overcoat and grabbed my hat from the rack by the door. A gray fedora with a medium brim and a low crown encircled by a ribbon in a shade of purple somewhere between my blouse and pants.

Though most of her face was obscured by wool cap and muffler, I caught my boss's look.

"What?" I said, slinging my purse over my shoulder. "I have it on very good authority this adds a certain frisson."

———

Holly Quick lived in an apartment building in Morrisania—a neighborhood in the southwestern section of the Bronx about a hundred blocks north of the skyscrapers you see on the postcards. Her building wasn't quite run-down but was leaning in that direction. It was four stories, and its flat-faced brick might have been red if you scraped off half an inch of soot.

Mind you, it was eight p.m. and streetlights are not the most forgiving. However, I would eventually see the building in the daylight, and sunshine did it no favors.

I'd also eventually learn that the place housed twenty-four apartments split evenly among youngish professionals, married couples with and without babies, and elderly tenants who had been there for years, most of them Russian or Central European. The building's owners had retired to Boca Raton and left the day-to-day in the hands of the super, an elderly Hungarian named Kolompar.

"But please call me Mr. Cosmo. Everybody calls me Mr. Cosmo."

When we arrived we found that there were working buzzers for every apartment except Holly's. She'd warned us ahead of time and instructed us to hit the one marked SUPER. Thus the introduction to Mr. Cosmo, who insisted on walking us up the three flights to Holly's place.

I made conversation while Ms. P concentrated on the stairs, the banister for which was attached with finishing nails and hope.

"She is very private," he said, explaining about the lack of a buzzer. "Very smart to be careful. A girl living alone."

I asked whether there had been any incidents in the building or neighborhood. Specifically of the untimely death variety.

He chuckled. "Miss Holly ask me very same question. She ask if there had ever been a murder in the building."

There hadn't, he said. The only untimely death that had occurred under his watch had happened four years previous, when a widower with a dodgy hip tried to change a light bulb, fell off the stool, and cracked his head open on the edge of the stove.

"Was very terrible. Very nice man. He should have rung. I would have changed the bulb for him. Easy as pie."

When we arrived at Holly's door, Mr. Cosmo did the honors of knocking. His fist hadn't hit it twice before she opened up.

"Thank you, Mr. Cosmo," she said.

"My pleasure. You need anything, you ring. Okay?"

"Okay, thank you."

He tottered off and we went inside.

The first thing I noticed were the books. The second were the locks. The third was Holly's outfit.

In reverse order. Our client had turned from wren to cardinal, courtesy of a dusty-rose wool cardigan, red blouse, and burgundy slacks. She was barefoot and her toenails were painted bright red to match her lipstick.

There were five locks on the door. Two heavy-duty sliding bolts, the key lock, a chain, and a floor bolt. None of them looked newly installed.

As for the books, there must have been thousands. She settled us in the living room, where bookshelves were fastened against every available wall, every shelf filled to capacity.

Books were stacked in towers on the room's two coffee tables and piled on the floor beside the room's two overstuffed armchairs. The only place where books didn't dominate the landscape was the tiny secretary's desk sandwiched between two of the bookshelves, but that was only because it was taken up by a battered typewriter and neatly arranged piles of typed pages and carbon paper.

The room had two windows facing an alley and the building beyond. Both were equipped with two bolts apiece that slid into the window frame. One window was painted shut; the other led to a fire escape. The scuff marks on the windowsill told me it was regularly used. The cigarette butts scattered across the fire escape's landing told me why.

Holly directed us to the armchairs while she took the swivel chair at the desk.

I looked at my boss to kick things off. We'd talked about it on the way over and had come up with a preface to the interview. Yes, we'd take her case. But we would make it clear that if we found any evidence that another murder was on the horizon we would have to tip off the cops.

I waited for my boss to lay down the law. Instead, she seemed more concerned with browsing the books. Five seconds passed while she tallied titles. Ten seconds. Twenty.

Holly started fidgeting. First her hands, then her head, then she started digging her toe into the carpet, swiveling her chair from side to side. I wondered if Ms. P was employing a new interview strategy: pummel them with silence until they spilled the beans.

Finally my boss moved her eyes from the shelves to the client.

"Thank you for hosting us, Miss Quick."

Holly twitched her lips into something I'd call a smile if the word *grimace* hadn't been available.

"I'm not used to . . . I don't have visitors often. Ever. I don't have visitors ever," she said. "I would have come to your office again. I wouldn't have minded. Really. Or we could have spoken over the telephone. I'm very good on the phone."

I had spoken to her on the phone twice, albeit briefly, and I could testify that she was as prickly over the wire as she was in real life.

"As I believe Miss Parker explained when she called,

whenever possible, I like to visit clients in their homes," my boss said. "It provides much-needed context."

In this case, I wasn't sure how needed that context really was. She liked books; she didn't like people. End of story.

Holly shifted uncomfortably, fiddled her fingers, swiveled her stool one way, then the other.

"Can we . . . can we start?" she asked. "I'm in the middle of a very tense scene. The hero—well, he's not so much a hero in the classical sense, but he is the protagonist—just found the remains of his partner and is trying to decide between seeking vengeance or fleeing the city because he knows he'll be next."

Having read a thousand of these stories, I was putting my money on vengeance. God forbid we leave the guy hanging.

CHAPTER 7

There was the ritual signing of the contract and writing of the check for our retainer. With those safely tucked away in my purse, we got to work.

The interview took the better part of two hours, with Ms. Pentecost peppering Holly with questions, sometimes backtracking, frequently performing loop-the-loops, going over the same ground again and again. If I hadn't been jotting shorthand the entire way, I'd have been wondering where we were in the narrative.

In short—the usual.

What made it unusual was our client.

Some questions sent her into a monologue that would have made Eugene O'Neill call for the bell. With others, it was like pulling teeth. All of it accompanied to a greater or lesser degree by her constant movement.

I tried to use Holly's twitching as a barometer for how she felt about a given question, but eventually gave up. If there was a pattern, I didn't see it.

To save you from wading through half a notebook, here's the abridged version.

To begin, Holly Quick was a New Yorker, born and bred. She kicked off life in 1913 as the daughter of John and Naomi Quick, a pair of Okies who came east instead of going west. For the first few years of Holly's life, the trio lived happily, if frugally, in one of those honeycomb tenements on the Lower East Side.

Trio got demoted to duo in 1918, when John, who had a job changing sheets and bedpans at the Willard Parker Hospital, came down with the Spanish flu and went from employee to patient to statistic over the course of two weeks. Left with a pittance of a pension, Holly's mother took a job as a librarian.

"Every day after school, I would go to the library and wander up and down the aisles and collect an armful of books," Holly explained. "Then sit at a table and read until closing."

Considering Holly's apartment, it was easy to imagine her growing up in the stacks. I wondered if she found solace in the library because of the way she was. Or if she became the way she was because she'd spent her formative years scanning pages instead of people.

"We had to move when I was eleven—the rent had gone up. That's when we moved here. Naomi—my mother—she got a job at the library a few blocks away. It's a nice building. Not as nice as where we were, but very affordable."

Cue another five years of librarian mother, bookworm daughter. It might have gone on like that for another fifty if Naomi Quick hadn't had a stroke the day before Holly's sixteenth birthday. She was found by the library's janitor, sprawled out in Poetry, a volume of Whitman clutched in her hand.

Naomi Quick recovered, but not entirely. She couldn't walk as well, or carry as much. She managed to keep her job at the library, but her duties were limited, and her hours were eventually halved.

With less money coming in, Holly quit school in favor of a job stocking shelves at Hayward and Sons, a bookstore in Jefferson Park. I thought I knew every bookstore in the five boroughs, but I'd never heard of this one, and told her so.

"Oh, of course you haven't," Holly chided. "You're probably too young."

I was about to point out that having nine years on me did not make her a tribal elder, but decided that wasn't a swamp worth wading.

"Mr. Hayward had to close the shop in 1934," she explained. "He said that people weren't spending money on books like they used to. His sons had left. It was just him and me, and it was too hard to keep it going."

She drifted away for a moment, and Ms. P and I waited patiently for her to come back.

"He owned the building and when he sold it he gave me five hundred dollars. I thought it was a fortune. The first thing I did was buy a typewriter. This one right here. I started writing stories on it that very night."

Finally, I thought, now we might get something useful. The childhood history portion of our program had been courtesy of Ms. Pentecost, who felt that when it came to understanding people, there wasn't a stone worth keeping flat.

"Was this your first foray into writing?" Ms. Pentecost asked.

"Oh, no, no," Holly said. "I've made up stories for as long as I can remember. At the library, my mother would give me paper and I would write and write."

"About murder?" I asked.

"Don't be ridiculous. I wrote what little girls write about. Fantasies. Silly little . . . childish things." She trailed off in a flurry of tics before coming back. "Later, I started writing other things. Detective stories. Crime stories. I found crime easy to write. There's a formula. Things happen in a certain order."

Having more than a passing familiarity with the subject, I wished that were true. In my and my boss's experience, order was a commodity that was hard to come by.

"I showed my mother my stories. She said they were good and . . ."

Again she trailed off.

"Miss Quick?" I don't think I let the impatience show in my voice, but I make no promises.

She snapped back into focus.

"I don't see how any of this is relevant," she said. "Whoever this person is has focused on Horace Bellow's stories, not mine. On him, not me."

My boss opened her mouth to answer the question but Holly got there first.

"Unless you think . . . that whoever is doing this knows who I am. Why would you think that?"

That was a good question. I wanted to know the answer, too.

"We must explore that possibility as one of many," Ms. P said. "And if, as you believe, this person is fixated on your pseudonym, Horace Bellow does not exist except as a product of you. So understanding your background will be useful regardless."

It was a little out there, even for my boss. But eventually Holly relented. After all, she'd approached us, not the other way around.

Lillian Pentecost: Were you able to make a living right from the start?

> **Holly Quick:** Oh, no. It was over a year before I sold my first story. To *New Detective* for twelve dollars.

LP: Under a pseudonym?

> **HQ:** Oh, yes. That first one was under Ronald Mitchell. I sold another to *New Detective* two months later under the same name. Then one to *Black Mask*—that was for twenty-five dollars. That was under the name John Gallagher. Then three in quick succession to *Detective Fiction Weekly* under Simon Doyle. It was another year before I was selling enough to support myself and my mother.

LP: Where is your mother now? Has she passed?

HQ: Passed? Oh, no, she's in Brooklyn. At a convalescent home. She had another stroke. A tiny one, the doctor said. But it meant she couldn't work. I tried to take care of her. I really did. But it was too hard. To see to her and have enough time to write. So I took her there. And now I'm all by myself and I have the time to write as much as I can and I can pay for her to have a nice place.

Which it is. It's a very nice place.

LP: I imagine the cost of such a facility must take a lot of writing.

HQ: Oh, yes! Every year it goes up a little. Sometimes I think they make up things so they can increase the fee. Last year they started including a nutrition tax. What the hell is that? Thirty dollars more a year is what that is.

Although Mr. Dobbin—this is the manager—he's good enough to let me know in advance when increases are expected.

To keep up with it and everything else, I have to write an average of four stories a week. Two if they're longish.

If I were smart I'd write Westerns. There seem to be twice as many of those sorts of magazines and they pay all right. But I've only ever thought of a couple. Murder stories, of course, involving a tin-star sheriff.

Most things I'm able to sell. These days, more than half of my work is published through *Strange Crime.*

LP: Why is that? Do they pay more?

HQ: Oh, no. Technically, they pay less. But that's because they buy in bulk. I write a full third of their content. Under various pseudonyms, of course.

LP: How did that arrangement come about?

HQ: I met Brent and Marlo Chase—they're the owners. This was just before the war. They'd published my—or Horace's— stories before. Including two novelettes.

They contacted me and said they wanted to meet. I'd never

met with the publishers or the editors before. It was all through the mail. And never under my real name. I have a post office box. Three post office boxes, actually. And I have them make my checks out to cash.

LP: None of these other magazines knew that you were the person writing all of these stories?

HQ: None of them. Some of them probably knew I was using multiple pseudonyms. I couldn't have a post office box for each one. That would have been ridiculous. But none ever mentioned it.

Certainly none of them knew I was a woman. Some of the editors got very, well, frank in their notes on my stories. It's fascinating how men will talk with other men. As a writer, it's very informative. Much of it unprintable, but excellent background.

LP: You were saying that with Strange Crime, *this was the first time you met your editors. Why did you relent to meet them?*

HQ: My mother urged me to. This was back when she could . . . when she could talk more. She was afraid I was becoming too . . . Well, anyway, I met with Brent and Marlo and they were so surprised I was a woman. Or maybe not Marlo. I think she might have suspected. She said something about Horace Bellow paying too much attention to characters' shoes. Men don't tend to notice shoes.

The meeting had been to ask me to write exclusively for them. And to give them first right of refusal on publishing my first book if I ever wrote one. They want to expand to publishing novels, you see?

Anyway, when they found out I wasn't just Horace Bellow but also half a dozen other writers, they were very excited. They had several magazines at the time, not just *Strange Crime,* and were hurting for quality content. They asked if I'd be willing to take a discounted word rate if they guaranteed to take a certain number of stories every month.

I said yes. Though I couldn't agree to write exclusively. They couldn't pay me that much. But I agreed that Horace Bellow would be exclusive to *Strange Crime,* and I created a couple other pseudonyms just for them.

So I said yes.

LP: *With whom do you share your work? Before you send it off?*

HQ: While it's in progress? No one. Whyever would I?

LP: *For advice? To work through a difficult narrative problem?*

HQ: Oh, no. No, no, no. I don't think I would like that. If I come to a point where I don't know what happens next, I'll sit on my fire escape and have a cigarette and eventually the solution comes to me. I don't think inviting anyone else into the process would be a good experience for me or them.

LP: *You said you write several stories a week. Where do you find your inspiration?*

HQ: The news, mostly. Snippets of conversation I overhear on the street, on the train. Other books and stories. Just inspiration, never plagiarism. I'm very careful.

I know why you're asking that. You're wondering if I got the idea for one of these stories from something I overheard or read somewhere. Did the killer and I intersect?

I've already thought of that. I've thought about that quite a bit. But I just don't find it likely. Some of these stories were written years before the murders occurred, after all. Besides, I can't come up with a single instance of seeing or hearing something, much less three. Because it would have to be three, wouldn't it? I would have to be stupid not to realize it. And I'm not stupid.

LP: *I don't think you are.*

HQ: Good.

LP: *Who do you talk with? On a regular basis?*

HQ: No one.

That's not true. But not many people. There's Mr. Cosmo. My neighbors, but only to say hello. My mother. I visit her every week. Tuesday mornings, usually.

LP: Do you talk about your stories with her?

    HQ: I talk to her, though rarely about my stories. And she doesn't talk back. Over the last few years, she's . . . Her mind has . . . She doesn't talk back.

LP: Who else?

    HQ: There's Brent and Marlo, obviously. We have dinner or drinks on occasion. And of course I see them when I drop off my manuscripts.

LP: You don't mail them, like you do the others?

    HQ: No. Sometimes they have notes and I like to attend to those right away. It saves time and postage. And I do occasionally like to talk to other people. I'm not a shut-in, Ms. Pentecost.

LP: Of course not. Is there anyone else in your life? Anyone you confide in?

    Miss Quick?

    HQ: There's my psychiatrist. Dr. Lydia Grayson. I see her once a month. I used to see her twice, but with the rising costs of my mother's home, I had to cut it back to one.

LP: Have you been seeing her long?

    HQ: Six years. You can ask, if you want. Why I see her. I don't mind.

LP: What brought you to Dr. Grayson?

    HQ: I wanted to . . . examine my problems with intimacy. No, it's not like that.

LP: I made no assumption.

    HQ: Miss Parker did. I can tell.

Will Parker: I really don't think—

    HQ: You think it's about sex. Of course this uncomfortable woman must be hung up about sex.

WP: I never thought that.

    HQ: I've had a number of sexual partners.

WP: All right.

    HQ: All right?

WP: You nailed me. I'm sorry for jumping to a conclusion I

*shouldn't have. Can we strike it from the record and maybe you
can tell me what conclusion I should have hopped to?*

   HQ: Fine.

   I have difficulty trusting people. Being emotionally open—
that's how Dr. Grayson puts it. It limits my ability to form lasting
relationships.

   Anyway, that is why I went to Dr. Grayson originally. We talk
about many things, though.

LP: Do you talk about your writing?

   HQ: Sometimes. She asks me how my week has been, and
mostly my week is writing, so sometimes I talk about it. Rarely
in detail, though.

*LP: Other than your editors, your mother, your psychiatrist, and
some small interactions with your neighbors, you have no other
regular interactions?*

   HQ: I do not. That's why I believe these questions are point-
less. Whoever is doing this is finding their . . . inspiration in my
stories. Not me. I live a very circumscribed life.

There were a couple dozen other questions. Ms. Pentecost's switchback style usually leads to an "Oh, I forgot about
this or that or so-and-so" moment on the part of the client.

   Not this time. Holly Quick stuck to her story.

   At the end, my boss turned to me.

   "Is there anything I've missed?" she asked.

   Holly looked at her watch, obviously fed up with the questioning. But there were a couple of bases I wanted to cover
before we called it quits.

   "Have you ever heard the name Jessup Quincannon?"

   "Of course," she said. "It was in several of the stories about
Mr. Checchetto."

   "Before that?"

   "Only in passing. About his club, of course."

"Ever thought about attending?" I asked.

"Why would I?" she asked back.

"He runs a club dedicated to killers. You write about killers. Could be good inspiration."

"No," she said. "I really don't think it would."

I didn't feel like yanking at that particular molar any more and moved on.

"Magazines get letters from readers, right?"

"Of course."

"Any addressed to Horace Bellow?"

My thought was that if our killer had an obsession with Bellow and his work, he might have typed out a letter or two.

Holly swiveled her chair and opened up one of the desk drawers. She pulled out a thick bundle of envelopes secured with a rubber band.

"Here—you can take them."

"You've read them all?" I asked.

"Of course. But I never respond. And all of them seem perfectly . . . benign."

Benign. A lot of killers seem that way. The nonfictional ones, I mean. Until they don't.

I saved the kicker for last.

"Do you have an alibi for the time of the murders? I only ask because we're keeping the cops out of this and that would be their first question out of the gate. Also, I personally want to make sure we're not collecting a fee from a killer."

As expected, Ms. Pentecost got flustered. Or as flustered as she gets.

"I apologize for Miss Parker's bluntness. She sometimes—"

"When Mr. Perkins was killed—this is the man who was hanged—I was having a late dinner and drinks with Marlo Chase," Holly said. "If the papers are correct about Mr. Checchetto, I was with both Brent and Marlo at their apartment.

We stayed up late talking about possible nonfiction pieces. I'm afraid I was home alone when Mr. Haggard was killed. He was the one who was stabbed."

I don't want to call that speech rehearsed, but it definitely wasn't improvised.

"You know all that off the cuff?" I asked.

"Of course not. I looked at my calendar," Holly said, as if addressing a small child. "I assumed you would ask. I'm surprised it took you this long to get around to it."

And on that ignominious note, we were done.

CHAPTER 8

It was after ten o'clock when we made our way back down the steps and out of the battered apartment. I found the Cadillac blessedly unmolested. It was the kind of street where that couldn't be taken for granted. We had one more appointment to keep, but that wasn't until midnight.

We had skipped our evening repast, so I drove the two of us to an all-night diner where I knew the food to be edible, the silverware clean, and the booths spread far enough apart that you could have a halfway-private conversation.

Ms. P had a hamburger, I went with fried pork chops, and we both ordered chocolate egg creams, which were on the fizzy side.

"It's like once you're over the Brooklyn Bridge nobody can manage it," I lamented. "It's three ingredients, for God's sake. Mrs. Campbell can do it and she boils chicken."

Once we were done digging into—and throwing digs at—the meal, we tucked into the interview.

"What did you note about Miss Quick?" my boss asked.

I could have rattled off a laundry list, but I kept it simple.

"I don't trust her," I declared. "I know what you're going to say, and you're right. She rubs me the wrong way. Some people do and there's no fixing it. But I don't think that's it."

Ms. P gave one of her slow, considered nods.

"Do you think she was lying?" she asked.

"I still can't find her tell," I admitted. "But I definitely know she was playing footsie with the truth."

"How do you mean?"

"The way she went on and on in some places and cut it short in others. And there were topics she was being very careful about."

"Can you provide an example?"

I could.

"How about when she mentioned sex?" I asked. "She says she's no virgin, but she didn't mention anyone special. Or even anyone not so special. Also, there was the way she phrased it. She's had 'partners.' "

"Ah, yes, the gentleness around pronouns."

"You caught that? You didn't press her on it."

"I assumed it was less about evasion and more about reasonable caution."

That was a new one. Two new ones, really. Usually Ms. Pentecost treats people like oysters—prying them open and scooping out everything, meat and pearls alike. In this case, not only was my boss holding pat with an assumption rather than confirming it, but she was apparently content to let our client keep her secrets to herself.

"Reasonable caution or not, if her partners are of the female variety, that adds a wrinkle," I said.

"How so?"

"You don't just sidle up to a woman you don't know and make an offer. Not unless you're particularly daring, and I don't read our client as that," I said. "So I'm guessing clubs, bars, salons. That would make her life a lot less circumscribed than she'd have us believe."

My boss stirred the chocolate that had settled at the bottom of her glass.

"Did you see anything that would corroborate this assumption?" she asked.

"Well, she didn't use the secret handshake, so I can't be sure."

She did that thing with her lips she does when I'm being especially funny.

"All I'm saying is I don't trust her," I said. "I don't think she's playing it straight, and I don't like the handcuffs she's snapped on us."

I settled back into the booth. Ms. Pentecost leaned back as well, tilting her chin up and resting her head on the cracked vinyl. She stayed like that long enough that I started to wonder if she was playing checkers on the tin ceiling tiles. Finally she spoke.

"I think . . ."

We should shake Holly Quick out of bed and demand she fill in any blanks.

We should inform the police.

We should drop this client like a hot potato.

". . . that it's time for our next appointment."

I waved for the check.

CHAPTER 9

A morgue at midnight has a certain ambience. Maybe it's the lighting, simultaneously too dim and too bright, where you can see more than you'd like but there's always one corner left dark.

Or the smell—bleach and rot in equal amounts.

Or maybe it's that just down the hall are the recently deceased, waiting patiently to be picked apart.

Hiram was one of the people that did the picking. He was a compact, delicate-boned man with deep-set eyes and a dark beard trimmed short. An always-reserved caretaker of the dead, he was the very picture of dignity.

Usually.

"They're bastards, Will. Bastards!"

Spittle flew down into his neat beard, but he didn't care.

"Trading the Hebrew Hammer away like that. Twelve seasons in Detroit. Forty-four home runs last year. They throw him away. And to where? Pittsburgh! What kind of city is Pittsburgh?"

"I've heard it has a very nice—"

"I have a cousin who just moved to Detroit. I was going to visit her this summer and take her boys to a game. Now . . . psssht!" He threw up his manicured hands in disgust.

"You can still see him when the Pirates play the Dodgers," I said.

I'm not sure he heard me. He just continued on a career retrospective of Hank Greenberg and how much he meant to the American Jewish community and how if he should have been traded anywhere, it should have been to a New York team.

I nodded in agreement while Ms. Pentecost leaned patiently against the wall. Hiram was just getting into Greenberg's wartime service when we heard whistling in the hall outside.

It was a tune I almost recognized. Its only accompaniment was the intermittent squeaking of the wheels of a gurney. I moved to hold open the double doors and let in our guests.

Both were clad in white—one draped in a sheet, the other in an orderly's uniform at least a size too small for his lanky frame. That is where the resemblance between the two ended. While the man on the gurney had been quieted forever, Sam Lee Butcher was, I am convinced, incapable of going half a minute without speaking.

"Miss Parker, Ms. Pentecost! So good to see you! Mr. Levy was real cagey. All he said was that I should expect company tonight and I should keep Mr. Checchetto's body handy. But I knew. Midnight visitors? Murder victim with claw marks all over him. Sam Lee, I told myself, that can only mean one thing. Pentecost and Parker are on the case!"

After situating the gurney under the room's brightest lights, he shook our hands with enough vigor to loosen my wristbones.

"Is it just me, or have you grown?" I asked.

"It's not just you," Sam Lee said. He held out his arms, demonstrating how his uniform jacket ended a good two inches too soon. "This thing fit when I first got it. I'm going through a spurt, I guess. Mrs. Henry—that's my landlady— she thinks I'll top six feet by the time I'm . . . by my next birthday."

Sam Lee was guarded about his exact age, but I was pretty sure he wasn't legally able to buy a drink in a bar. When we'd met him the summer before, he'd been working roustabout at the Hart & Halloway Traveling Circus and Sideshow, my former employer.

A month later, the circus gave its last performance. There weren't a lot of good jobs available for somebody with Sam Lee's circus-acquired skill set, especially a Negro somebody.

Having once been in Sam Lee's position, I didn't want to leave him high and dry. Ms. P talked to Hiram, and by the time Sam Lee got off the train at Penn Station, there was a midnight shift at the morgue waiting for him.

It was a dead-end job. Sam Lee knew that. But we'd impressed on Hiram how sharp his new attendant was, so he was providing anatomy lessons on the sly. Hiram could read a dead body as easy as most people read the Sunday funnies.

"Samuel, would you please uncover Mr. Checchetto?"

Sam Lee pocketed his smile and carefully pulled the sheet down, exposing the head of the man on the gurney. Mid to late fifties, dark hair, a tidy mustache, ears that could have doubled for jug handles.

Then he pulled the sheet lower and I saw why the cops' first thought was animal attack. A set of four ragged tears ran from the man's throat down to his groin.

In Holly's story "The Curse of the Red Claw," these tears were created with a specially made glove affixed with panther claws. Of course, we couldn't tell Hiram that.

That was another reason I didn't like the setup Holly was forcing us into. Dumb was a look I try my best to avoid, and having to play it was a chore. But I threw myself into the role with vigor.

"I guess cause of death is no mystery," I said. "Police still thinking animal attack?"

"The police do not confide their thoughts to me. However, there may be more of a mystery here than meets the eye," Hiram said. "Samuel, could you better expose the center wound? At the belly, please."

Sam Lee took a pair of forceps and used them to pry open the largest of the tears. It made a sound that I'll do you the favor of not describing. Hiram came forward, took a pencil out of the pocket of his white coat, and inserted it into the wound.

"As you can see, it's rather shallow," he said. "All four of the lacerations are. Ugly, yes, but even the worst did not cut very deep."

Ms. Pentecost leaned close enough that she could read DIXON TICONDEROGA on the pencil. After a moment's peering, she leaned back.

"What about the artery in the neck?" she asked, pointing at the upper end of the tears. "Did it strike the carotid?"

Hiram smiled. "An excellent question. It did hit the artery. But it was only a small cut and . . . Here, let me show you. Samuel, could you please bring the photos?"

Sam Lee put the forceps aside and went to a metal filing cabinet. He retrieved a folder while Hiram cleared off a counter. Sam Lee laid out a series of eight-by-tens of the crime scene. They showed Checchetto splayed out on top of his desk in the back room of his antiques shop. There was no official reason for Hiram to have crime scene photos, but he was the curious sort and had friends throughout the NYPD who traded favors.

My boss and I hovered over the snaps. I had to admit, the scene looked a lot like what Holly had dreamed up in her story.

There was something off, though.

"Do you see it, Will?"

I usually answer my boss's unnecessarily vague questions with a wisecrack, but out of respect for the dead, I played it straight.

"Not enough blood," I said. "There's a stack of papers right next to him. If he got gutted on that desk, they'd be soaked."

I sorted through the other shots. No blood pools anywhere. I looked at Hiram.

"Killed elsewhere and moved?"

"Perhaps," he said. "However, there was only a moderate amount of blood on the body and clothes when I received it. And there was no evidence that it had been cleaned. So I have another suggestion. Samuel?"

Sam Lee went and stood attentively by the body.

"Could you explain the function of the carotids?" Hiram asked.

"The carotids—that's the arteries on either side of the neck—they carry blood from the heart to the brain," Sam Lee explained. "Cut them off and your brain stops working. You're out cold. Cut them off too long and you're dead."

"And if they're severed or even nicked?"

"Then you bleed out. Even if it's just a nick, you'll probably bleed out pretty fast."

"Is there any time when you'd cut into the carotid and there wouldn't be an excessive amount of blood?"

Sam Lee paused, his eyes tracking up to the ceiling in thought. Apparently this wasn't a question he'd been prepped for, but he got to the answer quick.

"Sure," he said, bending over and peering closely at the victim's neck. "If the guy was already dead. Because his heart wouldn't be pumping anymore."

He looked at his boss to see if he'd nailed it. Hiram nodded. Sam Lee smothered a grin.

"Is that what happened in this case?" Ms. Pentecost asked. "Was Mr. Checchetto already dead when he was mutilated?"

Hiram shrugged.

"That's for the police to decide. Or you, perhaps," he said, with a little twinkle in his eye. "If he was dead, it happened very shortly before his mutilation. And there are no other marks of violence on the body."

"Poison?" Ms. P suggested.

Another shrug.

"There's no evidence of the obvious ones but . . ."

But there were a lot of poisons, and not all of them were obvious, is how that sentence would have ended.

"It's also possible he was administered some form of narcotic. Something that wouldn't kill, but would incapacitate. Something that would significantly slow the heart."

"You mean someone could have slipped him a Mickey?" I asked.

"If you mean chloral hydrate, that's certainly possible. Or some other sedative not easily detectable in the blood following death."

So whoever was doing this wasn't following Holly's blueprint. Not really. In her story the victim fell back on his desk and was brutally killed using the clawed glove. Here it was only made to look that way.

I spread my hand out over the body, lining my fingers up to the four parallel tears. It took some doing, and not just because I wear a ladies' size-small glove. For one thing, the rightmost tear was a little too far removed from the one next to it. I needed to stretch my pinky to make it reach.

Sam Lee watched what I was doing.

"I told them that wasn't any animal," he said.

"These were the detectives?" Ms. P asked.

"Yeah, Detective Staples. I told him these weren't claws— not real claws. I don't think they paid me any mind, though."

"Why do you not believe this was done by an animal?" my boss asked.

"Okay, so . . . feeding the tigers was my job at the circus. And we had a bear for about a month. Carlotta was trying to get it to do tricks but it never worked out. Anyway, I've seen what big claws can do to meat, and it doesn't look like this. Here, take a look."

The cork was out and Sam Lee was off. We all leaned over the body.

"The tearing is right, but you'd never see all the claw marks so even like this. One would be shallower or trail off before the others. And they're not going to be perfectly straight. They'll curve a little. Not to mention that the spacing between the claws is all wrong."

Sam Lee stepped back and let us see for ourselves what he was describing. Not that we'd ever suspected the mutilation was actually animal-related. But it was nice to see someone else coming to that conclusion without having Holly's story to tip them off.

"I believe Samuel is correct," Hiram said, apparently taking our silence for doubt. "While I do not have his experience with large carnivores, I have seen other animal attacks. A single swipe of a paw is an unlikely scenario. And the wound is unnaturally . . . neat."

Neat. Not a word I'd have picked for a corpse, but he'd nailed it. The whole thing, even the crime scene photos, was very neat. Arranged.

"Thank you," Ms. P said. "Both of you. I have no doubt Sam Lee is correct. It was a very astute observation."

Sam Lee let out the breath he'd been holding and smiled. I knew that feeling. A compliment about your deductive prowess from Lillian Pentecost. I've never tried cocaine, but I imagine the rush is similar.

"Thank you both for your help," Ms. P added. "Hiram, do you mind if I borrow these crime scene photos?"

"Of course not. They are yours."

I scooped up the photos and retrieved our coats from the rack in the corner.

While Ms. P bundled up and Sam Lee wheeled Mr. Checchetto back from whence he came, I slipped Hiram an envelope containing a handful of bills. It was more than on previous visits since we were buying Sam Lee's cooperation as well. It would go in the expense report under "Specialist Consultation," which was my preferred spelling of "bribe."

"You two seem to be getting along well," I said.

"We are. He's a curious young man, in both senses of the phrase."

"It must be nice to have someone to talk to," I said, slipping on my coat and squaring my fedora.

"I'm never short of people to talk to, Will," he said with a straight face. "It's just that they so rarely talk back."

CHAPTER **10**

It was nearly one o'clock by the time we slipped into
the Caddy, slamming its heavy doors against the icy teeth
of the wind. As I navigated the car through winter-vacant
streets, we talked about what we'd learned.

By "talked," I mean I rambled and Ms. P *hmmm*ed and
nodded in the right places.

"I don't think we really expected someone might be walking around with a panther on a leash, but I think we can cross
that off," I said. "Hiram was right. That crime scene looked a
little too neat to be real. Which is appropriate, since it started
as fiction."

A nod here.

"That's an interesting thing about him being dead before
getting gutted. We've got to get the medical examiner's report
on the other two victims. See if there's any weirdness there.
Beyond the obvious, I mean."

A *hmmm*.

"But it's telling, right? If Checchetto's murder was nuts-
to-bolts staged, then it's not about somebody reading Holly's
story and wanting the thrill of re-creating things. He wants to
re-create the look. I'm saying 'he' as shorthand. No reason a
woman couldn't be—Jesus Christ!"

I was directing the Caddy over the Brooklyn Bridge and a

gust of wind broadsided us, shaking the two-ton automobile like a child's toy. I crossed the rest of the span in silence, fighting the wheel the whole way.

Once we were back on solid ground, I picked up the thread.

"But painting a gruesome picture is the result, not the motive, right? We still don't know the why. Which leads us back around to the questions we'd be asking in any case. Who was Checchetto? What was his life like? Who were his friends, his family? How was his store doing? Did he owe anybody money? Rub anybody the wrong way? Specifically anyone in this club he belonged to? You lie down with dogs, you get fleas, right? In this case, you sip tea with murderers, you get murdered."

No agreement from the backseat, but no dissent, either.

"Anyway, I know we spent a lot of time getting me installed at Shirley and Wise," I said as I eased the sedan into a spot across the street from the brownstone. "But figuring out how a victim intersected with a killer can be a heavy ask in the best of times. Three simultaneously? There's no way I can go around asking all the questions that need asking if I'm behind a desk playacting Jean Palmer eight hours a day. It can't be done."

I opened the door and got out. The wind whipped my hair about and drove needles into my cheeks. I didn't even bother putting my hat on, for fear of losing it. As I helped Ms. P out of the car, she said something but the words were blown off course before they reached my ear.

"What was that?"

"I agree!" she shouted.

"Good. I'll call Shirley tomorrow and say I've got the flu. Which I just might catch for real if we don't get inside."

She was already hurrying across the street toward the

shelter of our front door. Cane or not, she could move fast when she wanted to. I could tell she was talking, but again I couldn't catch it.

"What?" I yelled, running after her.

"I said you should—please get the door open before I freeze to death—I said you should continue at Shirley and Wise as planned."

I managed to get my numb fingers to work the key and swing the door open.

"But I agree it's too big a job," Ms. P said as she shouldered past me into the wall of radiator-warmed air. "Before you leave tomorrow, call Darryl Klinghorn. Tell him we'd like to procure his services."

I was seven swear words in before I remembered to close the door.

CHAPTER **11**

If you've never heard of Darryl Klinghorn, then congratulations. You probably haven't suspected your spouse was stepping out on you and wanted someone to get the candids.

That was Klinghorn's specialty.

He also hunted embezzlers for small businesses; tracked down poison-pen writers and blackmailers; did in-depth background checks—all the usual independent PI gigs. But most of the time he stuck to sex.

I heard him brag once that he'd taken more pictures of couples in flagrante than most pornographers.

He made such a name for himself, he ended up scoring an article in *Life* magazine. It included a picture, likely staged, of him on a ladder outside a hotel room. His wife, Dolly, was holding the ladder steady while he aimed a camera through a window.

The *Life* writer let his distaste show in the article, but Klinghorn didn't care. He was peacocking for weeks after. He and his wife even uprooted and moved to Los Angeles, hoping to turn the minor fame into some kind of deal consulting on movies.

When that didn't manifest, he went back to doing what he did best—pointing camera lenses into bedroom windows. Whispers on the grapevine had it that during one job he'd caught a big studio leading man in the buff with his male co-star.

Klinghorn managed an under-the-table payday, but it was made clear that he had to choose between Tinseltown and his kneecaps.

The next week he was back in New York like he'd never left, reclaiming his slimy little niche in the private-investigator food chain.

Now he was getting that slime all over our office's best guest chair.

Not that it showed—not unless you knew him. By all accounts, he should resemble a slug crossed with Dracula. Instead, he looked like a second-rate accountant at a third-rate firm: pushing fifty, on the short side, on the bald side, with a pencil-thin mustache and an inoffensive, perpetually smiling face, a guy who bought his suits off the rack and thought fifty-cent aftershave was a replacement for five-dollar cologne.

Definitely not the kind of man who would scale a three-story trellis on the chance of catching a bank president's wife in bed with his best friend. Or the kind of guy who would drop a security guard with a right cross while running to his car.

But there you go. Books and covers.

"Would you care for a drink, Mr. Klinghorn?" Ms. P asked.

"I wouldn't mind some of that," Klinghorn replied, nodding at the glass of honey wine my boss was cradling.

It was ten-to-one he actually liked the stuff. But he knew Ms. Pentecost did, so it was his way of ingratiating himself. I walked over to our drinks cart to play stewardess, stifling a yawn on the way.

I wasn't bored. I came by that yawn honestly.

After we'd gotten home from the morgue I'd stayed up another two hours to get a start typing up our notes from the interview with Holly. That afforded me four hours of sleep before my alarm rang.

I downed three cups of coffee, swallowed at record speed in the kitchen, while Mrs. Campbell tried to brush off the lint that had appeared from nowhere to cover the rear of my third-dullest skirt. Then I spent five minutes calling Klinghorn to arrange the appointment, answering his barrage of questions with the thesaurus entry for "wait and see."

I walked into Shirley & Wise nearly fifteen minutes late, apologizing to everyone in sight. No one cared. Mr. Shirley didn't even stroll in for another half hour.

I spent most of the day trying to keep both eyes open, with at least one of them tracking the office for more clues about what Waterhouse had been looking for. By the end of the day, I had nothing new.

There was just the safe and the files therein.

Back in Brooklyn by six, I ate an early dinner at my desk while I finished typing up the notes and still managed to squeeze in ten minutes of arguing with my boss.

"Klinghorn's a weasel," I told her. "He's the PI equivalent of an ambulance chaser."

Ms. Pentecost sat behind her desk, pouring her first glass of wine for the night.

"There's no dirt he won't wade through," I continued. "He practically has it on his business cards: 'Darryl Klinghorn: Have Mud? Will Muck.'"

A sip, a nod.

"He is as you describe him," Ms. Pentecost said. "But the reason he is so well known is that he's very good at what he does. Even if many find the cases he takes distasteful."

I made a face, but she pressed on.

"Can you name another freelance operator in this city who could gather vast amounts of information on three separate victims, who can do it surreptitiously, and who we can trust to be thorough?"

She had me there.

That was the thing about Klinghorn. When he turned in a report to a client, it wasn't just the dirty snaps. It included a whole narrative, laying out when and where the couple had met, how many times they'd gotten together, even speculation as to what had sparked the relationship in the first place.

Sure, it might not help a husband sleep better to know his wife's lover spoke French and could double as an underwear model. But a divorce lawyer could certainly make hay of it.

"All right, I'll pack my distaste away," I said. "Though if we have to work with him, I'd prefer he take the secretary gig so I can work the murders. I'll even let him borrow my pumps."

I was only half joking. I'd floated the idea of siccing Klinghorn on Shirley & Wise while I worked the Quick case. Ms. Pentecost nixed that immediately. We were keeping Waterhouse to ourselves.

Not that we were being much freer with details of the Quick case. We were giving Klinghorn the names of the victims and a Christmas list of what we wanted, but not the real reason why.

I handed him his glass and returned to my desk. He pretended to enjoy the wine while looking through the three typed pages detailing the job. They didn't amount to much: names of victims, addresses, details of their murders, and instructions to procure a full background as well as any interesting sundries, the definition of which we were keeping purposefully broad.

There was no chance that Klinghorn would say no to the job. The man was a whore for the press, and he knew if Lillian Pentecost took an interest in a case, there was a good chance headlines would follow.

Of course he still had questions.

"Do you think these murders are connected?" he asked.

Ms. Pentecost shook her head and lied with a straight face.

"Not at all. They are three killings that either have baffled the police for months or, in the case of Mr. Checchetto, have some obscure elements that drew my attention."

"Obscure is right," Klinghorn said. "You don't see a lot of maulings in Manhattan."

I was usually the only one who was allowed to make quips in our office, but I let it slide.

"As you know, I sometimes take an interest in unsolved cases," Ms. P continued, "if I feel I can contribute something the authorities cannot. These seem likely candidates."

"It all seems straightforward enough. Any reason Parker isn't tackling it?" he asked.

"Miss Parker is currently assisting me in another matter, which is taking up the bulk of her time."

Klinghorn gave me an appraising look. My boss can tell fibs with the best of them, but Klinghorn had a nose for lies.

He also had an eye for my job. He wasn't aggressive about it, but I knew that he'd asked around. Questions about how I was faring, how Ms. P and I were getting along, had I spilt any milk lately.

Problem was, the people he asked liked me more than him, so word got back.

I couldn't blame him. Being the right hand of Lillian Pentecost was a plum gig. Big cases, big headlines, big paychecks. Any PI with ambition and a crumb of ego would want the job, and Klinghorn was seeing this as an opportunity to shoulder his way to the front of the line.

"Any excuse to work with the brilliant Lillian Pentecost," he said, grinning.

"One restriction in your assignment is in regards to Mr. Checchetto and his relationship with Jessup Quincannon," she told him. "You are under no circumstances to question Quincannon directly. In any approach to his associates, I would suggest a ruse. Perhaps say that you have a contract with Mr. Checchetto's life insurance company."

"That could fly," Klinghorn said. "Some kind of payout they're trying to wriggle out of. Why the dodge?"

"I am concerned about attracting the attention of the police," Ms. P explained. "They have almost certainly focused their attention on Mr. Checchetto's relationship with Quin-cannon and might have the latter under observation."

"You don't want them to know you're poaching on their territory," Klinghorn said.

"Not until I decide if I will officially take the case," she lied. "Discretion should be a watchword throughout your investigation."

Klinghorn nodded. He knew an exit line when he heard one.

"I'll get started tonight and send you the results when I have them. I'm grateful you thought of me, Lillian."

There wasn't much left to do except cut him a check for his advance and get him a stack of bills out of petty cash to use as bribe money. Once that was done, we all smiled and shook hands and I managed not to kick him in the ass on his way out the door.

I walked back into the office, where Klinghorn's cheap aftershave lingered in the air.

"That went as well as can be expected. I'm so happy you thought of him, Lillian. What a lovely man, Lillian. He is always such a pleasure to work with, Lillian."

My boss rolled her eyes. Well, really just one eye. The false one remained more or less glaring at me. She came out from behind her desk and picked up Klinghorn's wineglass, still mostly full.

She walked it to the kitchen. I followed, then hopped up on the counter and watched as she poured it down the sink.

"That was a good thought about Quincannon," I said. "But it seems to me we'll need to have a chat with him even-tually. I mean, if something else doesn't pop up. The guy runs a murder club. The cops wouldn't be wrong to keep him in their sights."

I watched the last of the criminally expensive beverage swirl down the drain.

"Why don't you call him yourself?" I suggested. "The guy sends you two invitations a year; he'll probably be willing to chat."

She made a face and shook her head.

"Absolutely not," she said. "Jessup Quincannon is cunning, curious, and purported to have numerous connections within the police department. If he were to learn I was investigating Mr. Checchetto's death, he might ask questions. Consequently the police would learn of my involvement and that might endanger Miss Quick's privacy."

Again with the deferring to our client.

"Well, if there's two things Klinghorn is good at, being sneaky is one of them," I said.

She rinsed out the glass and grabbed a dish towel. Don't ever say Lillian Pentecost isn't above the occasional housework.

"One last note," I said. "The first question out of Klinghorn's mouth was whether the three cases were a matching set. I think you sold the lie, but what if he finds a thread and starts pulling?"

"If he discovers a link between the murders, then that means we likely have our killer—or will be several steps closer. We should be grateful," she said.

"Sure. But after he forgives you for fibbing to his face, his next question will be how you knew in the first place. How are you planning to dodge that?"

"If Mr. Klinghorn asks why I suspected the three cases were connected . . . well, I'm the 'brilliant Lillian Pentecost.' What other answer does he need?"

CHAPTER 12

I did manage to convince Ms. Pentecost that there was at least one thing I could do that Klinghorn couldn't. Other than look good in a three-piece.

After he left, I started going through Horace Bellow's fan mail. All of the letters were on the positive side, some excessively so. One woman—I assume woman, but anybody can type "Janet"—even proposed marriage.

Not a weirdo in the bunch. Which I found remarkable.

I wasn't a celebrity in the conventional sense of the word, but I was a professional woman who'd been mentioned in the paper and whose address was easy to look up. I'd had a few letters. Some palatable, some poison, and a whole lot of strange.

Maybe it was because "Bellow" was a man. Maybe men didn't get strangers writing to ask what brand of stockings they preferred.

"It's possible our guy's not a letter writer," I suggested to Ms. Pentecost. "If he wanted to pass on a compliment, he might prefer the phone. Shoot—he might even have showed up at the *Strange Crime* offices in person."

She thought about that.

"It's possible," she said. "Though it would be rather imprudent."

"Three murders under his belt. I don't think our guy's the prudent type."

My boss, because she's a genius, saw the destination before I announced it.

"Because this is not an avenue we can ask Mr. Klinghorn to follow, you wish to do so."

"Obviously," I managed not to shout.

"We could ask Miss Quick to inquire herself."

It was a good three seconds before I realized my mouth was open. Discretion was one thing, but asking a client to play detective? To trust that she would not only do the job but do it correctly?

What the hell was my boss thinking?

My mouth didn't say that, but my face probably did, because my boss said, "Do you have a better suggestion? One that does not reveal our involvement in these murders, or at least our involvement as hired by Miss Quick?"

As it happens, I did.

Our client wasn't happy.

To be fair, I'd never seen her happy, so I wasn't sure the feeling was in her wheelhouse. But the idea of walking me into the *Strange Crime* office made her particularly disgruntled.

I assured her over the phone that it was necessary, and I laid out a program that would keep her and Horace Bellow's involvement in three homicides a secret.

That is, if our client could lie with a straight face.

On Thursday, I clocked out at Shirley & Wisc; took the subway uptown; hopped into a diner bathroom to change; stuffed my Jean Palmer gear into an oversize handbag I'd brought for the purpose; and met Holly on the sidewalk outside our destination.

If anyone were to challenge the offices of *Strange Crime* to a game of hide-and-seek, they'd have to settle for second place.

The entrance was located on the sixth floor of an unassuming building on West Thirty-eighth Street, tucked between two fabric stores and across the street from three others.

Even if you made it to the lobby of the building, you still had your work cut out for you. *Strange Crime* was not included in the list of the building's residents that was hanging on the wall. And you had to hunt for the stairs, since the elevator was out of order. Then, if you made it up six flights, you had to squeeze past the hopeful ingenues lined up along the wall outside the Steadman Casting Agency.

We got a few predatory glares before it became clear we weren't there to audition.

"Don't worry, girls," I said. "No competition from this quarter."

The hall took two more rights and ended at a nondescript door with a sign etched into the glass that read s an e cr me, the type having worn away. Or maybe the owners were dodging bill collectors and had scraped it off themselves.

It was just after six p.m., but Holly assured me the owners would be there. She didn't bother knocking and just walked in.

I hadn't had much in the way of expectations for the offices of a nationally distributed magazine of detective fiction, but what I had held were deflated. Most of it was contained in a single room with half a dozen desks spaced in a pattern Mrs. Campbell would refer to as higgledy-piggledy. In one corner was a door with a hand-lettered sign taped to it: CABINET OF MYSTERIES.

There were assorted tables lining the walls. Most were covered in paper of one sort or another—typed pages, photographs, stacks of printed magazines. A bulletin board took up most of the back wall. Pinned to it were sheets of paper with what I assumed to be pencil sketches of page layouts.

There were three people still there—two men and a woman. Not a one took notice of us when we walked in.

There was the man on his feet, peering through a set of horn-rimmed glasses at the layouts. He was young and slim, with navy pinstripe trousers and matching suspenders. He had a shock of blond hair that desperately needed a barber and was sticking up at odd angles.

He ran a hand through the shock and gave it a yank.

"Where's the jump for 'The Poisoned Pensioner'?"

The question was directed at the woman at the desk beside him. She had maybe a decade on him. Enough that there were strands of gray woven through her brunette bob. Her sleeves were rolled up and her hands and wrists were covered in smears of ink.

I couldn't see much of her face, since she was hunched over, taking a red pencil to a stack of typed pages.

"Bottom of fifty-two," she said, without bothering to look up.

At least that's what I think she said. She was drowned out by the last of the trio. He was sitting at a desk on the opposite side of the room, feet propped up, telephone receiver tucked between his ear and shoulder while he flipped through a stack of advertisements.

"I'm looking at your portfolio now and I'm telling you, you don't want to do this piecemeal," he was saying. "You do that, you're throwing money out the window. What you want to do is get a package—one full page, one half, one quarter— and lock it in for two years. Listen to me . . . Harry, Harry, Harry."

His patter reminded me of a hundred salesmen my father had run off our porch with a stick or a shotgun. Most of those had been college-age boys trying to make some extra scratch. This guy hadn't seen college in a while, except maybe a twentieth or even thirtieth reunion. His hairline was beating a hasty retreat and the years had worn worry lines across his forehead. He could have used a visit to a university dining hall, though. His sweater—a cardigan in a vicious shade of green—looked like it had been borrowed from someone fifty pounds heavier.

He was the first to glimpse us. He smiled and waggled his fingers at Holly and gave me a curious but not unfriendly look. Holly gave him the bare minimum of a wave and bee-lined for the other two. I followed on her heels.

To be honest, this was why I was really there. Asking about phone calls and visitors was all well and good. But I wanted to get a look at the couple that made up a good fifty percent of our client's address book.

I was convinced Holly hadn't been entirely straight with us during our interview. If I could ferret out a lie, maybe I could convince Ms. P that this case—or at least the guardrails we were being forced to stay between—wasn't worth it.

Our footsteps tipped them off and both looked our way.

"Holly!" the man exclaimed. "I didn't expect to see you today."

The woman jumped up and ran around the desk for a hug.

"Holly-Bear!" she said, squeezing our client, who had an unfamiliar look on her face. It took me a moment to identify it as a smile.

So happiness was in her wheelhouse.

When she was unpinned, Holly started into our prepared script.

"This is Will Parker. She works—"

"Will Parker? *The* Will Parker?" the man said with kid-at-Christmas excitement. "Marlo, do you know who this is?"

"I'm guessing it's Will Parker."

"Yes! She works for Lillian Pentecost. You work for Lillian Pentecost."

"That's what I put on my tax returns," I said.

He put out a hand and I shook it. He kept shaking while

he asked, "Did you really chase down and tackle that guy? The one leading the kidnapping ring."

It was hard to talk while being palpated, so I pried my hand back.

"The papers may have exaggerated that a bit." Or I may have exaggerated for them.

"I can't believe it!" Brent buried both hands in his hair and gave it a two-handed yank. "Holly, you brought me Will Parker and it's not even my birthday."

His wife held out a hand.

"Hi, Marlo Chase," she said, treating me to a more reasonable handshake. "That's my husband, Brent, who has utterly neglected to actually introduce himself. If you're wondering, yes, his enthusiasm is why I married him."

Now that I got her full face, I was reminded of a knife block. Everything had sharp edges—sharp nose, sharp chin, cheekbones that would slice you open if you slow-danced. But welding those elements together were a pair of bright, watery blue eyes. That and her cockeyed smile took a lot of the edge off.

Her husband flipped some internal switch and went from Stage Door Brent to Editor in Chief Brent.

"Miss Parker, I'm guessing this isn't a social visit. What brings your to our pulpy hovel?"

I dove into the fabrication that Holly had reluctantly agreed to. It helped only slightly that it was a Pentecost-approved pack of lies.

Holly, I explained, had been receiving harassing phone calls. Most were limited to heavy breathing, but some included full sentences delivered in a muffled voice. The sentences, I told Marlo and Brent, suggested that the caller knew Holly Quick was actually Horace Bellow.

While I was laying out our cover story, I re-evaluated

their respective ages, edging his up and hers down. Up close
I could see the webwork of cracks around Brent's eyes and
mouth, along with a set of laugh lines you could have buried a
body in. Marlo's complexion was relatively smooth, and I was
guessing her gray hair had arrived early.

So less May/September and more June/August.

There was a lot of fluttering from the two of them when
I finished.

"That's awful."

"That's terrible."

"How can we help?"

"Why didn't you tell us?"

The latter is something Holly and I had worked on.

"I didn't want to bother you," our client said with a
straight face and only a moderate amount of twitching. "And
you know I've always wanted to meet a real detective to see
how they operate."

She pitched the lie pretty well. I'd have believed it if I
hadn't known different.

"What do you need from us?" Marlo asked me.

"Have you or anyone at the office received any disturbing
phone calls? Anyone mentioning Horace Bellow? Or maybe
one of his stories?"

Marlo and Brent looked at each other then turned back
to me.

"I don't think so," Brent said.

"What about visitors?" I asked. "Anyone stopping by who
shouldn't have been?"

"We don't get much in the way of walk-ins," Brent said.
"You might have noticed that our office isn't visitor-friendly."

"I traversed the labyrinth, yes."

"It keeps the rent low and the foot traffic down. As for
phone calls, Marlo and I haven't gotten any. But you're wel-

come to ask around. There's only six of us. Me; Marlo; Mort over there; Kenny, our copy editor; Frances, our illustrator; and a Columbia student who works part-time helping with layout whose name I can never remember."

"It's Joy, honey," Marlo said.

"Right. Joy. Everyone should be in on Monday. We give them a three-day weekend since we pay them a pittance."

"And the two of us work Sundays to play catch-up," Marlo added.

Six people seemed like a small crew for a national magazine, and I said so.

"'National' doesn't mean much when you're a one-title shop," Brent explained. "It was different before the war. Along with *Strange Crime*, we had *Midnight Detective, High Class Crime, Dark Romance*. This place was really jumping then."

"What happened?" I asked.

"There was the paper rationing, of course," Brent explained. "And then I and quite a few of our regular contributors got to go on a tour of Europe. That really put a crimp in things. Danny—he was our layout guy—he never made it back."

"But we managed," Marlo said, reaching out to give her husband's arm a squeeze. "The real problem was the market changed. *Dark Romance* lost distribution. It edged too steamy and newsstands got pressure from the morals crowd, so they refused to carry it. As for the others, radio has been strangling the pulps to death for years. Who's going to pony up a quarter when you can get *The Shadow* and *Inner Sanctum* every week for free on the radio?"

I had the good grace not to pipe up that I was a regular audience for both programs.

"The plan is to get enough feed stored up so we can start publishing collections from our regulars. Then original paperbacks," Brent said. "Holly, a.k.a. Horace, will be on the top of the list. She's got a novel in the works that's gonna sell like gangbusters."

Holly's complexion didn't really lend itself to blushing, but she managed it.

"It's not all that," she said. "I don't like to . . . I'm still writing it, so I can't think about . . . Well, I mean sales are so—"

"One other question," I said, rescuing our client. "Who knows that Holly Quick and Horace Bellow share a wardrobe? I'm assuming everyone who works here is on that list."

This was purely a cover question. One suggested by Ms. Pentecost. Since our story was that someone had put Holly and Horace together, Brent and Marlo might find it odd if I didn't ask it.

"Actually, I think it's just me and Brent and Mort," Marlo said. "And Mort only knows because he's here with us Sundays and that's when Holly usually drops off her work."

"What about payroll?" I asked. "Somebody's got to cut a check to Holly Quick."

"I handle Holly's checks personally," Brent said. "She's very careful about her secret identity."

This line of questioning was derailed by the arrival of Mort, now off his phone call and coming to join us.

"What's the hubbub?" he asked. "Thought I heard my name."

"Holly's getting some threatening calls," Brett said. "She's hired Lillian Pentecost to investigate."

"Jeez, that sucks, kiddo. Hi—Mort Cohen." He extended his paw for a shake. "So you're Lillian Pentecost?"

Brent slapped a hand against his forehead. "Holy Christ, Mort. This is Will Parker, Lillian Pentecost's assistant. How could you not know who Lillian Pentecost is? She's only one of the most famous detectives in New York City."

I decided not to quibble with "one of."

"Look, Brent. It ain't my job to read crime stuff, just sell it," Mort said. "By the way, I've got Schulman and Sons on the hook for an annual package, but I had to cut him a deal."

"How deep a cut?" Brett asked.

"Fifteen percent off the annual rate. Before you start into a speech about cows and magic beans, he's putting me in touch with his brother-in-law, who's got a mail-order truss company he says could be good for at least a half page."

A shadow passed over Brent's face, and any illusion of youth vanished. I had a feeling *Strange Crime* might be headed the way of its fellows.

"Dang it, Mort. We can't afford to give away the store," Brent said, hands plunging into his hair and yanking. "Seems half our ads are getting a special just-for-you deal. Vita-Glow's getting half price, even. Half price for that full-page survey of theirs. They started off with the usual rate. How'd that happen?"

"They were gonna pull their business and—"

"Then get someone else in. Someone who can pay full." Brent's voice had risen and was within spitting distance of yelling. "I don't want to tell you how to do your job, but—"

Marlo nudged his shoulder with hers and gave him a look.

"Yeah, okay," Brent said. "I'm sorry, Mort. I don't mean to get hot. It's just frustrating, is all."

Mort was a little red in the face, but had taken the drubbing in stride, like it was a semi-regular occurrence. He shrugged and smiled. "I know, Brent. I know. I'll keep the discount to ten percent. And I'll talk to the Vita-Glow folks. Tell them we gotta raise the rates again." He turned to me. "I hope you can help Holly. She's a good kid. Now if you'll excuse me, I've got some more calls to make. Speaking of, where does Lillian Pentecost advertise?"

"The front page of *The New York Times*."

He flicked his fingers and a business card seemed to appear out of nowhere.

"Good press is a crapshoot. Paid advertising is an invest-ment. I can give you a great deal. Think about it."

I tucked the card in a pocket and told him I would.

I wouldn't have minded poking around further. Ask some indelicate questions, see if I could learn a little more about our client from her nearest and dearest. But I had reached the end of the script, and I had assured both Holly and Ms. Pentecost that I wouldn't deviate.

I thanked the pair and said I'd be back on Monday to ques-tion the rest of the staff. Marlo grabbed Holly to get her opin-ion on a piece by another writer. No goodbye from our client. Not even a wave.

Brent asked if I wanted copies of Horace Bellow's stories, and I said sure.

"Let me see if I can find all the issues with Horace in them," Brent said, before plunging into the piles of back issues. "I hope you can figure this out. Holly—she's kind of the unofficial third pillar around here."

"About that," I said. "Hiring someone to ghostwrite so much of the magazine. How outside the box is that?"

"Plenty of rags print multiple stories by the same author in the same issue," he said, pulling magazines out of the pile and making a separate stack. "They even have pseudonyms they lend out so readers don't get tired of seeing the same name all the time. But if you read enough you can pick out writers, no matter what name they use. Same voice, same writing style. None of them do it like Holly, though."

"How do you mean?"

He looked back at the two women now huddled together. Marlo was pointing at something on the pinned-up layouts and Holly was nodding vigorously.

"I mean she's so versatile she can give each pseudonym a different voice. Peter Wylde writes sort of dry-witted who-dunits. Like if Agatha Christie embraced irony. John Gallagher is all car chases and shoot-outs. Super macho. You'd never believe a woman wrote it. Grant LeClaire specializes in spicy damsel-in-distress pieces. Or damsel-in-no-dress, as Holly likes to put it. Can't print the really spicy ones these days. We're saving those for an anthology. Believe me, they are gonna fly off the racks."

"And Horace Bellow?" I asked. "He's exclusive to you, right?"

"Yep, Horace is all ours. He's the weird stuff. The twisty, blood-and-guts, psycho-thriller revenge tales," Brent said with more than a little relish. "Marlo and I like to say that Horace puts the 'strange' in *Strange Crime.*"

Exactly the sort of writer a real-life killer might glom on to.

"I think this is everything we've printed by Horace over the last five years," Brent said, pressing the not-insubstantial stack of back issues into my arms.

I thanked him for the complimentary copies and he walked me to the door. I was on my way out when he stopped me.

"I know your boss is pretty shy when it comes to personal interviews but what about you?"

"What about me?"

"An interview with Lillian Pentecost's leg-woman would be a great seller," he said. "Or you could write something yourself. Take the readers through a case and how you caught the guy. Or gal. Readers love femmes fatales."

I made some noise about client confidentiality.

"We can work around that," Brent said. "Names and details changed enough that nobody could figure out who was who."

I opened my mouth to decline again, but he held up a hand.

"Think about it," he said. "Because I promise you, there's a market. Our readers would kill for it."

CHAPTER 13

When I returned to the office I found Ms. Pentecost at her desk. She was just hanging up the phone.

"That was our client," she said. "She was not pleased."

"I don't know why," I said. "Everything went as planned. She stayed on script and her editors seemed to buy the cover story."

"She said she is uncomfortable lying to her friends."

"She certainly did it easy enough."

I gave my boss a quick summary of the visit, gifting her with the stack of back issues. I finished with "I'll head back on Monday, maybe during my lunch hour, and hit the rest of the staff. Ask them about calls and strange visitors."

Ms. Pentecost was shaking her head before I even finished the sentence.

"Miss Quick was adamant," she said. "You will refrain from any further involvement. At least until Mr. Klinghorn provides us with his report."

I could feel my collar starting to scorch, but I managed to keep it out of my voice.

"Look," I said, "these questions need asking. There's no secretary at that office. Any of the staff could have picked up the phone or answered a knock at the door. They might have actually laid eyes on our killer."

"Miss Quick said that she would have her editors put the question to the staff themselves," my boss said.

I was dumbstruck. Not only was Ms. P putting the handcuffs back on but she was having civilians do my job for me.

"What if they don't ask it right?" I finally managed to say. "What if one of the staff gets evasive? Are they going to notice? You want to do this right, you need me there doing the asking."

No dice. I was to keep away from the Quick case until Klinghorn came through. And knowing Klinghorn, he wouldn't feed us information piecemeal. He'd wait to send us the whole lot. Who knew how long that would take?

There was some more back and forth, but to be honest, I was too pissed to remember much of it.

Finally, I said, "What the hell am I supposed to do when I'm not warming a desk at Shirley and Wise? Just sit on my hands? All because our client got squirmy over some little white lies?"

Ms. P suggested that there was plenty of work in the office to catch up on. Correspondence and the like that we had let slide.

"Certainly enough to keep you occupied," she assured me.

I didn't have a blood pressure cuff handy, but I was pretty sure I knew what it would show. Through gritted teeth, I told her that was an excellent idea and I would get right on it.

"There's no need to hurry," Ms. P said. "I believe dinner is almost ready. Mrs. Campbell is making spaghetti Bolognese."

I told her I would take my noodles at my desk. We couldn't let that correspondence slide any further, could we?

My boss knew that when I got hot it was best to leave me alone to simmer. So when the dinner cry came, she retired to the dining room with some issues of *Strange Crime* and I stayed at my desk, typing away, and trying not to let ragù drip on the keys.

It didn't help my mood that she wasn't wrong about the correspondence. Our outstanding letters had crept up into the high teens, something I tried never to let happen. These included a number of requests from journalists about the Baby Wyatt Kidnapping (the *Times*'s capitals, not mine); half a dozen letters from assorted lawyers trying to schedule depositions; and various citizenry seeking to pique Ms. Pentecost's interest.

I'd already run these by my boss and had gotten noes across the board.

No to the Boston hotelier accused of murdering his partner. No to the French diplomat who was being blackmailed. And a firm but gentle no (this was the third) to the grieving husband who wanted Ms. P to prove his wife's suicide was foul play.

We'd had a similar case the year before and it had gotten some press. Now everyone thought we knew the secret alchemy to transforming suicides into homicides.

I stayed up past my bedtime finishing the lot. More out of spite than diligence.

I'd like to say I didn't go to bed angry. But, like our client, I avoid little white lies when I can.

CHAPTER **14**

By Friday afternoon, the anger had boiled itself off, leaving a thick sludge of discontent. I could stand playing a secretary by day as long as I got to be a detective at night. Now I didn't even have that.

I didn't even have any correspondence left to answer, having gone through the whole stack the night before.

This is probably why, when Peggy asked if I wanted to get a drink after work with some of the other girls, I said yes. I justified it to myself by saying it would be a great opportunity to uncover any dirt worth digging at Shirley & Wise.

But really I just didn't feel like going home and twiddling my thumbs, and this was as good a distraction as any.

So at 5:01, me, Peggy, and a dozen of the secretarial staff headed across the street to Milligan's, a tastefully bland watering hole catering to the grist of the Wall Street mill.

Not long after we arrived, we were joined by a pack of low-to-mid-level number crunchers in new suits and fresh haircuts. The bartenders at Milligan's poured with a heavy hand and the men were buying the girls drinks in the hopes of beating a path toward a weekend dalliance.

I was doing the same thing, except my goal was to loosen tongues, not inhibitions. I shelled out for a round of cocktails, very quickly becoming everyone's favorite temp, all the while nursing a straight seltzer. Asked about the deep, dark underbelly of their place of employment, they were more than happy to open up.

There was Alfred from billing, who kept a fifth of vodka in the bottom drawer of his desk in an accordion file labeled DEAD ACCOUNTS.

There was Dianne, who had stopped coming to happy hour over a year ago when she'd started an affair with Ron Hempel, one of the company's senior accountants. Ron said he was going to leave his wife, but all the smart money was on the thing ending in tears.

Then there was Charlie, who ran franchise accounting, and was, according to all the girls, a very nice guy but had been seen coming out of one of "those places" in the East Fifties and they were debating whether they should tell Mr. Wise, because they were sure the senior partner wouldn't want a queer being in charge of such big accounts.

The usual muck swirling around any office drain.

Not a whiff of anything at the level I was looking for. No secret clients. No money laundering. No mob activity.

A few of the women had even been around in the summer of 1940, when Olivia Waterhouse was playing dress-up as Emily Ginsburg, but not a one could remember a damn thing worth remembering.

My discontent only grew thicker.

One by one, the women allowed themselves to be culled away from our corner table, and went off with their wolf of choice to hear opening bids. Soon it was just Peggy and me left. We eavesdropped as a junior suit took his best shot with a pickup line involving pork futures—how he'd hopped on them first and now he had a brand-new Lincoln convertible and did she want to take a ride in it this weekend up to Westchester, where his folks had a lake house they weren't using.

His target smiled and nodded in all the right places, but if I were in her place it might have put me off men entirely.

"I can't stand people like that," Peggy said quietly enough so she wouldn't be overheard.

"Pork-pushers, you mean?"

She laughed and took a healthy sip of her G&T.

"I mean people who are so gangbusters about their job. Ten minutes and the man hasn't talked about anything else."

I thought that was a bit hypocritical coming from the rah-rah office social director, with her rotating selection of Chanel suits.

"What should he have led with?" I asked.

"Anything. His hobbies, his passions. Ask her a question, for crying out loud. Show me a man who's one-sided in his conversation and I'll show you one who's one-sided in the bedroom. Mark my words, if Stacey goes to Westchester, she better be resolved to taking matters into her own hands, if you know what I mean."

I barely managed not to snort seltzer up my nose.

"I'm sorry," she said quickly. "I get a couple of drinks in me and I get a little too frank."

I told her I didn't mind a little frankness, and soon we were picking apart every man in the room—from the aspiring Rockefeller who kept flashing his billfold under a girl's nose to the blank who thought a colorful necktie was a substitute for a personality.

It was silly and petty and apparently the cure for my mood. I might even have giggled.

I would have suspected Peggy of making a slow-burn pass at me, but I didn't get that feeling. She was just being friendly. She liked Jean Palmer, and it made me feel a little bad that Jean didn't really exist.

Eventually happy hour ended and the girls started to head out, most alone, some on the arms of a suit. Stacey, we were pleased to see, was flying solo.

Peggy looked at her watch and told me she needed to head

out soon, too. She had tickets to the revival of *Sweethearts*, which had just opened at the Shubert.

"My weekend is just packed," she said.

Saturday morning, she told me, would be spent at her swim club, followed by dinner with friends. Sunday would be spent taking her nieces ice-skating. She pulled some wallet-size snaps out of her purse and I made the appropriate compliments.

"I never wanted kids—one of the reasons Fred and I ended up getting divorced," she confided, "but I don't mind borrowing my sister's for an afternoon."

When she asked me what I had planned, I said something about chores and housework and washing my hair.

"Oh, honey, you need to get out and do something," Peggy said. "I'm not saying you need to get on the dating scene again. I know you're not ready for that. But go to a movie or a Broadway show. Find a friend to go dancing with. You need something else in your life. Otherwise you'll be like that jerk and his pork futures. Work, work, work all the time."

I promised I would spend my weekend more frivolously, then walked with her to the subway, where we hopped on separate trains.

On the way back to Brooklyn, I thought about her warning. How all work and no play makes for a dull girl.

But that was Jean she was throwing advice at. The widowed temp secretary whose greatest accomplishment was a seventy-two-word-per-minute typing speed.

Surely it didn't apply to Will Parker, who got to corner murderers and chase kidnappers through alleys and grind her heels to nubs tracking down clues.

Except, at the moment, she wasn't doing any of that. Darryl Klinghorn had been handed those responsibilities and the fun that came with them.

I examined the other straphangers in the car. Yeah, they

looked tired and aching, sweltering in their wool coats. But they all had family and friends and swim clubs and cute nieces. I had my job. And I wasn't being allowed to do it.

As I pushed my way out of the car and trudged up the stairs into the frigid January air, I thought maybe Peggy's advice wasn't so ill-aimed after all.

CHAPTER 15

The next day provided an opportunity to, if not shovel away my discontent, at least ignore it for a few hours.

On Saturdays we hosted a regular open house at the brownstone. Anyone with a mystery, a complication, or a thorny situation was free to take a spot in line. The unspoken rule being that these spots were reserved for women below a certain tax bracket.

Men showed up occasionally, some for legitimate reasons, and we didn't turn them away. As for the money thing, we found that clients who could afford Ms. P's services were willing to pay not to wait in line between a meat-packer and a midwife.

Also, we didn't advertise. The open house was word of mouth and women mostly talked to women in their own social strata. So the whole thing pretty much worked itself out.

Most of the reasons women walked in the door had to do with money (too little), men (too much and of the wrong sort), and the law (they'd gotten caught on the wrong side of it).

Among our visitors that Saturday was a prostitute who worked out of a no-name hotel on the edge of Chinatown. She and her co-workers were being squeezed by a sergeant at the nearby precinct, who was demanding free favors and a deep cut of their weekly profits.

There was also the war widow whose sister had gone missing. She had three boys under four at home and her sister had moved in last spring to help take care of them. The sister had vanished a week earlier with no note and no trace.

Then there were the pair of riveters who'd gotten the sack from a shipyard for what their supervisor called their "moral degeneracy" while on the job. After taking our temperature, the two admitted they were lesbians, but were not a couple and had never so much as brushed knuckles while at the factory.

The missing sister was the easiest. Ten minutes of chin-wagging got us a family tree. A couple of phone calls found the sister hiding out at a cousin's place in Savannah, having fled the winter wind and the screams of her three nephews.

The hooker's problem was a little tricky. We could pass the sergeant's name on to his superiors. But tattling would consequently shut down the women's business. Even if they stayed out of jail, they'd have to find a new hotel, with a manager who was amenable to renting rooms by the hour on the sly. They'd had the deal going for years and didn't want to uproot. Not only that, but the sergeant might have friends on the force who'd seek retribution.

I suggested that justice was nice, but having a precinct sergeant under your thumb was nicer. I made a call to another PI—someone who was in the same kind of business as Klinghorn but was less odious.

The next time Sergeant So-and-So came over, this guy would be stationed at a peephole with his camera to memorialize the occasion. I didn't feel great about the girl who'd draw the short straw, but if everything went as planned, the ladies would soon have a new protector who'd be more than happy to keep fellow flatfoots from hassling them. That or risk his job, marriage, etc.

As for the riveters, we put them in touch with a law firm

that did a lot of pro bono work in those sort of situations. We made sure to keep their hopes low, though. A lot of women were losing their jobs now that the war was over, and the line for grievances was long.

Around one I left Ms. P on her own and headed down to the basement, where a dozen women dressed in a motley assortment of sweat-clothes were waiting for that week's lesson.

The basement of our brownstone was a mostly open space, save for a few stacks of boxes against the wall and one corner dedicated to a special project of mine.

There was a square of wrestling mats that allowed me to lead the ladies through a series of self-defense drills without any of us accumulating too many bruises. Over the last couple months I'd hung additional mats on the walls, so that the whole basement was starting to look like a padded cell at Bellevue.

The wall mats were because I'd started using the basement as a makeshift shooting range and they kept the sound of gunshots from alarming the neighbors. Last summer I had occasion to fire my pistol at a would-be killer and missed him by a country mile. I didn't want that happening again.

That day I walked my students through a basic grab-and-toss I'd learned from a doorman in Baltimore. He was a runt, so he opted for moves that brought guys down quick and where size didn't matter. The doorman always followed this move with a knee-drop to the head, but I recommended the women run. No point sticking around to give the mutt a second chance.

By the end of the hour, everyone was flushed and breathless. Most of them had the move down pat, or were well on their way.

When the last guest walked out the door, I took an inventory of my desk. There were notes that needed filing and a bank account that needed balanced. I could probably burn five minutes changing out my typewriter ribbon.

Screw it, I thought. I'd take Peggy's advice.

"I'm heading out," I told my boss, as I slipped on my coat and hat. "Don't wait up."

Determined to prove I was more than the sum of my interrogation technique, I headed into Manhattan. My destination was a penthouse apartment on the Upper West Side, whose owner hosted regular soirees for the city's literati. That evening's focus was on poetry, which wasn't exactly my bag. But I'd been invited by a bookstore clerk who had been giving me the eye, and she broke out into a wide smile when I actually showed.

The poets were mainly of the tormented sort, and the poetry mostly pedantic. However, one woman—the host was insistent that she join in—read a poem that stuck with me. It was about living in New York City, and her words didn't paint a very pretty picture.

There was a refrain—"And I shall sell you sell you/sell you of course, my dear, and you'll sell me"—that made me think about the hookers in that hotel. Leaping at a honey-trap scheme so they could keep renting their bodies to whoever was willing to shell out the dough.

I thought about the suits in the bar, with their big wallets hiding small minds. The nine-to-fivers I swayed and sweated with on the train. Feet sore, backs aching, suffering death by a thousand paper cuts to buy themselves a weekend of freedom.

They were selling their bodies, too. Just at different rates.

The poem left a bad taste in my mouth, so I talked the clerk into following me to a club where they didn't care who danced with who as long as you spent money on the overpriced drinks.

The clerk struggled to keep up, and soon we were paired off with others who were more our speed. The kiss good night landed on my cheek. We both agreed that we enjoyed each other's company, but the chemistry wasn't there.

Well, Peggy, I tried.

If anything happened on Sunday, I don't remember it.

CHAPTER **16**

Even before I got to work Monday morning, I already knew that my second week as Jean Palmer wasn't going to be an easy one. My skirt felt too tight, my blouse clung to me in all the wrong places, and my stockings chafed.

I felt like a Broadway chorus girl looking down the barrel of a two-show day she didn't have the stomach for.

As soon as I sat down at my desk, Peggy came over to fill me in on her weekend, showing off the big bruise on her elbow she got from trying to pirouette on a pair of ice skates.

"I don't know what I was thinking. Probably that I was ten years younger than I actually am. How was your weekend? Did you end up doing anything?"

The best lies are ones that can't be corroborated, so I told her I'd stayed home, did housework, washed my hair.

"That's all right, dear," Peggy said, patting my shoulder. "But if you ever want to go out and you need a bookend, you let me know. Winter can get mighty glum when you're spending it alone."

Another pat and a smile and she went back to her desk. I was left with worms roiling around in my stomach.

I don't know why I felt so shitty. I'd passed off bigger lies to nicer people. When this gig was over, I'd never see Peggy or any of this lot again. And in a month's time, they wouldn't remember a damn thing about the three-week temp girl.

That's what I told myself as I went about my day, smiling and laughing, trading gossip and fashion tips, debating whether it was worth the trouble to adjust our hemlines now or wait until the spring.

Worms in my gut or not, it needed to be done.

Ms. P hadn't given me the go-ahead yet, but I knew eventually I'd be cracking that safe. By the time she pulled the trigger I wanted to be just another friendly part of the landscape.

I'd already gotten in touch with Jules, our safecracker friend. Starting that afternoon, I began spending an hour after work each day in his basement apartment, which doubled as his workshop. He'd procured the same make and model as the safe in Shirley's office and began putting me through my paces.

Tuesday was a carbon copy of Monday.

On Wednesday, there was finally some excitement, though it had to wait until I got back home. I had just slipped out of Jean Palmer and settled in at my desk when there was a knock at the door. I opened it to find a certain Detective Donald Staples, asking somewhat politely to speak with Ms. Pentecost.

"Somewhat" because a truly polite person would have called ahead.

I'd never laid eyes on Staples but I'd heard tales. Our pal Lieutenant Lazenby was considered the top homicide cop in the city, but Staples was the young Turk hot on his tail and racking up solves at an impressive rate.

He was in nearly every way Lazenby's mirror opposite. He was svelte, clean-shaven, and fair-haired, and he bought his suits, or at least the dark wool number he was sporting that evening, off the rack. That didn't count as a demerit since he had the physique of a department store mannequin. He had an easy smile, and an open-faced friendliness that I was convinced was carefully cultivated.

Cops, in general, ain't friendly.

But Staples was making an effort. If Lazenby had caught us poaching on his turf, he'd have blustered and raved for a while before settling in. Staples, sitting with perfect ease in one of the chairs facing Ms. P's desk, showed that he didn't do bluster.

"Thank you so much for seeing me, Ms. Pentecost. I know I don't have an appointment and I'm sure you're a busy woman."

Polite, and he got the "Ms." on the first go. He really was trying.

"I'm always happy to be of assistance to the NYPD, Detective Staples." She was trying, too. It never pays to piss off the men with badges.

"As I told Miss Parker, I wanted to speak with you about the murder of Flavio Checchetto. I believe you're familiar with it." A statement, not a question. But my boss responded anyway.

"I am."

"It's come to my attention that a certain Darryl Klinghorn has been making inquiries into Mr. Checchetto, as well as into some other cases. When I questioned him, he said he was doing it on your behalf."

I wondered how long Klinghorn had held out before spilling the beans. Ten seconds? Twenty?

"That's true," Ms. P said. "I hired Mr. Klinghorn to gather some general information about the crimes and their victims."

Staples nodded thoughtfully.

"I'm curious," he said. "I'm not as familiar with these other murders, but as far as I know, Mr. Checchetto doesn't have any close family. At least none that we've been able to find. I was wondering who your client is."

Ms. P and I hadn't rehearsed for this, but unsurprisingly she stuck to the story she'd given Klinghorn.

"When I'm between cases, I occasionally look into unsolved crimes, particularly murders," she said. "I hired

Mr. Klinghorn to gather information on a number of recent homicides. To see if I could be of assistance."

She actually did like to go fishing in the city's pool of unsolved murders, so technically all of what she told Staples was true. But a lot of obstruction cases are built out of technicalities.

"That's what Klinghorn told me. But I've found him to be less than reliable, so I wanted to confirm it with you," Staples said. "I have to be honest—I find it surprising that someone of your prestige would need to go hunting for work. Surely, you don't need it."

"That's true," she said, barely glancing at the compliment. "I do not need the work, in a financial sense. But I believe I have a certain civic duty. I live in this city. If I'm capable of assisting in bringing a murderer to justice, client or not, I think I have a moral obligation to do so."

Staples blinked, probably wondering whether he was being played. I marveled at my boss's ability to pivot from the sort-of truth to the genuine article with the grace of a ballet dancer.

"I find that commendable," the young detective said, deciding to buy the line. It wasn't that far-fetched, after all. She'd made big headlines not far back working a firebug case in Harlem. She didn't have a client then, either. The crime just pissed her off.

"I hope that, should you come upon any information on the Checchetto murder you think might be useful, that you'll share it with me," he continued. "Right now I've got a dozen men working on this case. I'd hate to waste their time."

"Of course, Detective," she said. "I have the greatest respect for this city's police force."

She pitched that with a straight face, too. She had respect for a handful of individual cops. The force itself she could take or leave. Mostly leave.

Staples nodded and stood up. After a round of handshakes,

I escorted him into the hall, where he grabbed his coat from the rack.

"Your boss is a very interesting woman," he said as he bundled up. "I didn't buy Klinghorn's line. About Lillian Pentecost fishing. But I guess it makes sense."

"How so?" I asked.

"Well, if she were really interested in these cases, she'd have sent you."

I wondered what he was buttering me up for. He settled his hat on and was half turned to the door when he stopped.

"It's curious, though," he said, his face still friendly and cheerful. "When Lillian Pentecost looks into murders on the side, the victims are usually women. Sometimes Negroes and the like, but mostly women. All the victims she asked Klinghorn to investigate are Caucasian men."

He stood there for maybe three seconds, face open, door open, the January cold creeping in, before I realized he was waiting for an answer.

"Well, we've got nothing against Caucasian men, Detective," I said. "My father was one."

If the answer ticked him off, he didn't show it. He just smiled and nodded and left.

Back in the office, I reclaimed my seat at my desk.

"That man is a lot smarter than he looks," I said. "I think it's a coin flip that he bought it."

"I agree," my boss said. "Notice how he never asked a single question, yet got as much information as we were willing to give."

"Yeah, I caught that. I'd love to watch him in an interrogation room. As long as I'm not on the receiving end."

We talked a little bit about the implications of Staples's visit, eventually deciding that he was only fishing and we shouldn't be terribly concerned. I expressed some anger at Klinghorn for tipping our collective hand.

Ms. P reminded me of my own appraisal of Staples, that he was sharper than the average cop.

Regardless, once she was out of the room I gave Klinghorn a call. I got his wife, who said he was out and that she would tell him to call back. When he finally did, he gave the same defense Ms. P used.

"Staples has his men locked down tight," he explained. "He's a real charmer. but he's not afraid to be vindictive if someone crosses him. Officers try to get on his good side and stay there."

"That's what bribes are for," I reminded him.

"Bribes are for getting you the information," he said. "The shelf life on buying someone's silence is real short. You know that."

I did know that, which didn't make me any less annoyed. There was some more back-and-forth, but eventually I conceded the point.

Then he said, "Could you be a dear and ask your boss if it's all right for me to approach Quincannon directly now about Checchetto's involvement in his club? Since the police know she's interested?"

I was about to ask him to be a dear and shove the phone receiver somewhere unpleasant. Then I had a thought. That thought rubbed up against a second thought, which gave birth to a plan.

"Actually, Darryl, she still wants you to stay off Quincannon," I said. "We'll take care of that interview ourselves."

"Is she sure?" he asked.

"Oh, she's sure," I answered. "Good night, Darryl."

"Good night. And tell Lillian I'll have the full report to her very—"

I hung up. I had a plan to nurse.

CHAPTER 17

Okay. It wasn't so much a plan as a bit of behind-the-back detective work. The back in question being Lillian Pentecost's.

Of all the possible routes to our killer, I figured Quincannon for the surest. Damned if I was going to let Klinghorn do the trailblazing.

I looked up Quincannon's number, and on Thursday morning, while the rest of my co-workers were still settling in, I gave him a call. I had to go through an answering service and an assistant, but after explaining I was working at the behest of Lillian Pentecost, I was eventually given his direct line.

The voice that answered was more Vincent Price than Peter Lorre, velvety smooth with an undercurrent of wry humor. He seemed genuinely pleased to schedule a meeting.

"Of course I've heard of you, Miss Parker. I've followed Lillian Pentecost's career for many years. I'm not at all surprised she's taken an interest in Flavio's death. So tragic. Please stop by whenever you'd like."

I told him what I'd like was twelve-thirty. He said he'd give word that I was to be admitted.

Thursday was Ken Shirley's day to have a long lunch, so I figured I wouldn't be missed. A little before noon, I told Peggy

I had a dentist appointment—only the whitest of lies, so the worms in my stomach stayed quiet—and was taking a long lunch.

Then I caught a cab and gave the hack an address in Washington Heights. Half an hour later the car pulled up to a sprawling Victorian manse, the kind that was being systematically wiped out in favor of less-haunted-looking homes.

"You sure this is the place, miss?" the cabbie asked, eyeing the looming monstrosity with its wraparound iron fence.

"Don't worry," I said, as I got out. "I get on well with ghouls."

He gave a grunt and pulled away before Lon Chaney lumbered out and grabbed him.

I was about to press the buzzer by the gate when the front door of the house opened and an hourglass walked out. At least that was my first impression as she glided down the walk toward me. She was dressed in a white jacket, soft at the shoulders and snug at the waist, and a voluminous skirt in black silk.

She practically glided, which is a neat trick when you're tackling cobblestones in three-inch heels.

The parts not covered by cloth were lily white, blood red, and inky black—skin, lips, and hair respectively. The latter was put up in a swirling braid that would have done Ms. P proud.

"Miss Parker," she said, unlocking the gate and letting me in. "I'm Alathea, Mr. Quincannon's assistant. I'll show you up."

I followed her up the cobblestones to the house, feeling like a foundling in my secretary togs and taking one and a half steps to every one of hers. Alathea's getup was definitely not meant for the late-January cold, but if there was a goose bump on her, I couldn't find it.

"Nice jacket," I said, as we took the porch steps.

"Thank you. Christian says it will be in his Paris show."

I didn't know who Christian was, but I made an appropriately impressed noise.

Inside, Alathea didn't slow her pace, and we rushed through an entryway and a sitting room, past a high-ceilinged conservatory, then up a flight of curving stairs, eventually ending in an office not entirely unlike the one in our Brooklyn brownstone.

There were bookshelves and Tiffany lamps and a Persian carpet in muted reds, and some tastefully upholstered chairs, as well as a large wooden desk in walnut instead of oak. There was even a painting on the wall behind it.

It was one of those curvy, reclining nudes you can still find hanging behind the bar in certain high-end establishments. Except this particular painter didn't quite have his brushstroke down. One thing smeared into another, and it was hard to tell whether the dark splotch across the woman's stomach was a shadow or evidence of evisceration.

I barely had time to critique the decor when a man came through the door behind us. He was about six feet tall and well built; given his denim shirt and stained dungarees, I took him for a workman. Then he spoke, and I recognized the velvety voice from the phone.

"I'm so sorry. I had to take a call," he said, then turned to Alathea. "Silas is on the line. He's securing the Mudgett lot and will need some assistance arranging for shipping. Give him the particulars, will you, love?"

She nodded, then left, shutting the door to the office behind her.

"Miss Parker, it's such a pleasure to meet you. I apologize for my attire. I'm doing some work on the exhibit room and have fallen behind, as usual. So much to do, so little time. Here, let me take your coat. Please, have a seat, have a seat."

My coat was deposited on a rack by the door, then we

deposited ourselves in our respective chairs—him behind the desk, me in front of it.

"So," he said, "how may I be of assistance to Lillian Pentecost?"

For a man who was obsessed with murder and who counted his personal wealth in the low eight figures, he didn't advertise it. According to the papers, he'd just celebrated his seventieth birthday, but he didn't look much older than sixty, with a ruddy complexion, a full head of wavy, white hair, and a long mustache to match, its ends sharply waxed.

The only thing villainous about his appearance was the way his skin pulled tight over the prominent bones of his face. But even that was more striking than sinister.

"As I said on the phone, Ms. Pentecost is looking into the murder of Flavio Checchetto. To be clear, she is not actively engaged. She's just seeing if she can be of assistance, or if the police have everything in hand."

Quincannon snorted, causing his mustache to quiver.

"I've spoken with the police at considerable length, and I would say that they have a firm grasp on very little."

"You weren't impressed?"

"Detective Staples is an excellent example of the city's police force. Incredibly persistent and exceptionally unimaginative. He seems determined that Flavio's death was committed by a member of our—well, our little group."

"The Black Museum Club."

"We don't call it that," he said. "We don't call it anything, actually. We don't advertise, so there's never been a reason to give it a name."

"But you do invite—well, you invite murderers to speak, don't you?"

"Also pathologists, police officers, scholars of all sorts."

"Still, it seems like a good place to start an investigation."

He leaned back in his chair and fiddled with one end of his mustache, resharpening its point.

"What do you know about our group?"

"About as much as anyone else who's read the papers," I admitted. "You're interested in murder and murderers. Some of your members have pretty fat checkbooks. That's about it."

"So, really, very little."

I shrugged, conceding his point.

"It's true that some of our members, although I think of them more as friends, have been fortunate with their fortunes. I myself inherited much of my wealth. My father was rather cunning when it came to investments. However, many of my friends would be considered average American citizens."

"I don't know if the average American has such an interest in homicide."

"Oh, I think you're being disingenuous, Miss Parker," he said. "If, as you say, you read the papers, you know exactly how much the average American is fascinated by murder."

I felt a little like I did when I waded into a philosophical argument with Ms. Pentecost. Like I was playing chess and my pawns were getting gobbled.

"Flavio might not have been average, but he wasn't a millionaire," I said, trying to get back on track. "How did a curio-shop owner rate an invite?"

Quincannon looked disappointed to be pulled from philosophy to facts.

"He purchased some blind lots at an estate sale," he explained. "When examining their contents, he recognized their historical and cultural value—value that he thought I in particular would appreciate."

"When was this?"

"Oh, nine or ten years ago now. Afterward Flavio kept an eye out for similar items of interest. I paid him handsomely, of course. More than he made hawking curios or selling the work of struggling artists."

"And he attended your meetings?"

"He did, though not regularly. Usually only when he had something to show me. Something I might buy."

"Was he at your last meeting?" I asked.

"He was."

"To sell something?"

"Not that time. He came to hear our special guest. Baxter Hill. He was convicted in 1925—"

"I know who he is."

"The police were very disappointed when Mr. Hill proved to have been in Philadelphia the night of the killing," Quincannon said.

He cocked his head up and back, gazing at the painting above his head. Like he was searching for something in its spilled-gut shadows.

"I have to admit my disappointment, as well, Miss Parker. I expected a detective trained by Lillian Pentecost to do more than simply parrot the questions already put forth by Detective Staples and his associates."

I knew I was being baited. But since my goal was to keep the man talking and hope he said something worthwhile, I decided to oblige him.

"Why murder?" I asked.

He brought his eyes back to me.

"What do you mean?"

"You've got the money to . . . well, to do most anything you want. Travel. Collect Rolls-Royces. Why murder?"

The little smile under his mustache told me he liked that question. I knew he would. Not because of any detective jujitsu. If you want to make a man happy, ask him about himself. They're really very simple to train when you know the tricks.

"I think we should dispense with a misconception first," he began, because men also like to tell you about your misconceptions. "I am not merely interested in murder, nor are the attendees of my salons. Not in murder or murderers, but in the alchemy of the one upon the other."

I didn't follow that last turn and told him so.

"Much of modern psychology says that a murderer is different from so-called normal people. That variations in his mind cause him to kill," Quincannon explained. "But I hold that the converse is also true. That murder changes a man. Or a woman. It changes them at an elemental level."

His voice had developed that husky quality usually reserved for the bedroom.

"Some are born killers. Some become killers. The rest of us would do well to learn from both. Don't you agree, Miss Parker?"

"I guess I'm just old-fashioned," I said. "Born or bred, I say lock 'em up."

He laughed—hearty, full-throated, and fake as a Cracker Jack diamond.

"I had much the same conversation with your employer once upon a time. Before she decided to . . . shun me."

Something about his face shifted. Maybe it was a change in the light coming through the second-floor office windows. His skull seemed to stretch against the edges of his too-tight skin. Like it wanted to tear free.

"You know, Miss Parker, while Lillian refuses to attend our salons, you are most welcome. I'm sure my guests would love to hear you speak."

"I think there are better people for that job," I said. "More experienced detectives."

He leaned across his desk, hands flat against the walnut.

"Oh, no, dear. Not because you're a detective. Because you're a killer. Throwing a knife into a man's back—it doesn't have the intimacy of a stabbing, but I don't think that matters. Especially considering it was the entryway into your profession. Which is proof that the experience changed you. That it made you a different person. Don't you think?"

My throat had gone dry. I felt light-headed. Like I was in danger of floating up or falling over.

"I . . . um . . . I don't think—"

"Then of course there is your sex," he continued. "We've had so few women speakers. I am sure our members would be terribly excited at the opportunity to hear you describe your . . . journey."

At that moment, a sound came from the window. A light tapping. I glanced over and saw a blue jay sharpening its beak on the windowsill.

That simple reminder, that there was a world outside that included blue jays, was enough to nail me firmly back into my body.

I decided I'd had enough.

"I knew a guy," I began. "This was back when I was working at the circus. Anyway, this guy, he liked to be spanked."

Quincannon recoiled.

"Excuse me?"

"Perfectly nice guy. All his ex-girlfriends said so. But the plumbing wouldn't work unless you went at him with a paddle like he'd gotten caught pilfering the cookie jar."

I got up and went for my coat.

"All I'm saying is that I've met plenty of men who need something extra to get their rocks off. It's really not all that special. I think I'll pass."

Quincannon smiled. But it was a different kind of smile.

" 'Get their rocks off.' How deliciously vulgar. And how disappointing."

"Sorry my vulgarity let you down," I said, slipping into my coat.

"Oh, no, Miss Parker. That's not why you disappoint me. I'm disappointed because you didn't ask the obvious question. Detective Staples didn't, either. Though I don't think I would have answered him even if he had."

I paused between one button and the next.

"What question?"

"Why am I so very certain Flavio's killer is not a member of our group?"

To give myself some credit, I didn't have to think about it long.

"You know something. Something that points somewhere else."

"Your employer received an invitation to our forthcoming meeting on Wednesday of next week. She declined. Convince her to reconsider. Oh, and tell her to bring tribute. She'll know what that means. Now, I have work to do. And you've ceased to be entertaining. Alathea will show you out."

I opened the office door and found the secretary already standing there, posed like a model in a Macy's window. Certainly not eavesdropping at all.

We followed the bread crumbs back downstairs, out of the house, and down the cobblestones to the gate, which she unlocked for me.

I was stepping through when she tapped the side of my purse with a manicured fingernail and said, "If you come on Wednesday, do please leave your firearm at home."

I was feeling pugnacious, so I responded, "Or you'll do what?"

She smiled, big and bright, showcasing a set of pearly whites.

"Or I'll cut you," she said. "Someplace it'll show."

She locked the gate.

"You walk safe, now."

CHAPTER 18

I wasn't much good at Shirley & Wise that afternoon. Not much good with Jules, either.

"Your fingers. They are made of mush. Go home. You waste both our time."

I went home.

"Honey, I'm back from the wars," I yelled as I walked in the door.

No answer.

I went into the kitchen, where I found a meatloaf roasting in the oven and a stewpot filled with water sitting out on the counter. At the bottom was something that would have been right at home on an autopsy table.

I opened the back door and poked my head out. If you were to do the same, you'd see a small courtyard with tall brick walls on either side, each containing a narrow gate that leads to the alleys that flank the brownstone. On the opposite end of the courtyard you'd see the renovated carriage house that Mrs. Campbell calls home.

Both gates were usually kept locked, except on Saturdays, when they were used to let in visitors who didn't want to announce to the world they were calling on a private detective. I bring it up, because one was standing open. The sun had long set, but there was light enough that I could make out our housekeeper on the other side of the gateway, kneeling in the alley and scrubbing vigorously at a wooden bench.

I walked over. Mrs. Campbell, who usually favored cotton skirts and wool jumpers, was clad in a many-stained boilersuit, her tight-packed curls bouncing with each go of her brush.

The stream of soapy water trailing away from the bench and down the drain looked more blackish than red. Blood does that in the moonlight.

"I don't want to be charged with aiding and abetting, otherwise I'd warn you you're leaving fingerprints everywhere," I said.

"You're a very funny lass, you are." The cold transformed her growl into a cloud of white. "You wouldn't like me doing this inside. The smell would settle for days."

"This" was the tending to of a lamb's stomach, heart, and lungs and various other disembowelings, all in the name of good Scottish cooking. Mrs. Campbell got the bug about once a year to make haggis. I thought it was an awful lot of construction for what could just as easily be served as hash. I mentioned that the first time I saw her make it. I have not made that error again.

"You need a hand?" I asked.

"I've got this sorted. Once I'm done, I'll get the meatloaf out of the oven and set the spinach on. I've also got rice pudding chilling in the fridge."

"If I didn't know better, I'd think you were a witch trying to fatten me up."

"You don't know better," she said, putting the brush to work on a stubborn spot.

"Point taken. The boss in her room?"

"I think she's up in the files. She said she wanted to reacquaint herself with some old cases."

"I'll go check on her. If a cop comes by, slip him a fin and tell him to give you a two-minute head start."

I hurried out of the cold before she could reply.

The third floor of the brownstone is a single open room almost entirely taken up by rows of tall shelves packed to bursting with boxes of files, clippings, case notes, and assorted evidence.

Most are arranged by date, but some are organized by criminal, by type of crime, and a dozen other exceptions to the rule. I could usually put my hands on the right file within a few minutes; Ms. Pentecost could do it instantly; anyone else would be out of luck.

The skylights peppering the high ceiling were dark, but the only electric light Ms. Pentecost had bothered turning on was the standing Tiffany lamp that illuminated an open island in the center of the room. Ms. P had opted against the perfectly comfortable armchair in favor of sitting, legs akimbo, on the massive Egyptian rug.

She had a stack of file folders next to her and a couple dozen photos spread out in a semicircle. The photos were all horror shows.

"Haggis prep or a murder scene?" I asked.

"Pardon?"

"Never mind. Dinner's soon. What awfulness are you wading through?"

"I thought I would reacquaint myself with a certain species of killer."

"What particular breed are you looking at?"

"Most killings are the result of the usual handful of motives," she said. "Money, revenge, lust, love. There are also those murders committed without forethought. Done in the heat of passion or intoxication."

She picked up a photo and turned it to better catch the light. It showed an open trunk. A woman's body had been folded to fit inside, her limbs bent at angles they were never meant to go.

"Then there are those murderers who kill for reasons that are decipherable only to them. Albert Fish, H. H. Holmes, Daniel Truelove, Earle Nelson."

The names all rang bells, some loud, some faint. Nelson raped and murdered landladies; Holmes slaughtered women in his so-called Murder Castle, just a few miles from the Chicago World's Fair; Truelove went after prostitutes, earning him the nickname the "New York Ripper."

Fish was the worst of the lot. It had been more than a decade since he'd ridden the lightning at Sing Sing, but his name was still used to scare Brooklyn children into obedience.

You better behave or I'll feed you to Al Fish.

"Are you familiar with these cases?" she asked.

"I've picked up this and that. Mostly from the pulps. I remember reading a piece on famous New York City slashers that included a few of the big names. Actually, it might have been in *Strange Crime.*"

"Really?" Ms. P said. "I'd very much like to read that."

"You think our killer is looking for a space in the next issue?"

"I think we should be prepared for it." There was something in her voice that gave me pause. Like she was at Coney staring up at the Parachute Jump and contemplating giving it a try.

"What does this preparation entail?"

She shook her head. "I'm not sure. An adaptation of our usual methods."

The usual methods she was referring to involved centering the victim and spiraling outward, looking for patterns and aberrations to patterns, finding where the victim's path intersected with their killer.

In short: learn about their life to understand their death.

It was generally successful. But it depended upon a more or less logical progression of human desire. Man wants woman; woman doesn't want man; man kills woman. It isn't pretty, but there's a terrible rhythm to it.

The men in the files spread out before her danced to a beat all their own.

"If our guy is anything like these, he's going to kill again, isn't he?" I said.

"Almost certainly. Likely sooner rather than later. August, November, January. Three points makes for a loose pattern, but the style of the murders suggests our killer is gaining confidence. From shooting to stabbing to the grotesque theatricality of Mr. Checchetto's murder."

"Yeah," I agreed. "Not to mention that 'The Curse of the Red Claw' came out in the December issue. That didn't hit newsstands until just before Christmas. Our guy only had a few weeks from inspiration to execution. No pun intended."

This was why I'd wanted to get Lazenby involved. We were racing against a clock and we didn't know where the hands stood.

"How much experience do you have with this kind of killer?" I asked. "Personally, I mean."

"Not enough," she said. Then after a moment, "And too much."

That was a side street I was tempted to drive down. But I figured I'd put things off long enough. I took a deep breath and squared my shoulders.

"Speaking of our usual methods and how sometimes they aren't up to snuff . . ."

She looked up, my tone tipping her off that I wasn't delivering good news.

"What?"

"I went to see Jessup Quincannon."

I don't know if a spike in blood pressure can cause a glass eye to pop out of its socket, but I think it came close.

"I expressly forbade you from directly working on the Quick case," she said with something nearing a snarl.

"You told Klinghorn not to approach Quincannon because it could alert the police to our interest. Well, the police are tipped."

"That is not the only reason. And I'm sure you suspected that—otherwise you would have informed me ahead of time. Quincannon is a dangerous man."

"I got that impression," I said. "But I know my way around dangerous men. Look—you've got me sitting on the bench. I just wanted in the game."

"This is not a game."

"That was a goddamn metaphor and you know it!" I took a breath and turned down the volume. "All I'm saying is you've got Klinghorn out there doing my job and I might not have hit a home run with Quincannon, but Klinghorn wouldn't have done any better. If you think he would have, maybe you should cut me loose and give my desk to him."

Her brow collapsed into a furrow.

"Don't be ridiculous," she said. "Whatever would make you suggest that?"

I didn't have the presence of mind to pin the blame on some photos of Peggy's nieces and a poem and the nagging worry that if you relieved me of the weight of my job I'd blow away like a scrap of yesterday's newspaper.

All I got out was "I don't know. Quincannon got me riled, I guess."

She began shoving photos back into their respective folders.

"I have you pursuing the Waterhouse lead because you are the most capable for the job. As for Quincannon, I did not want Mr. Klinghorn or you approaching him directly. He, of all people, could connect—"

She snapped her mouth shut so quick I heard her teeth click.

"Connect what?" I asked. "That Checchetto's murder was based on a short story? There's probably a ten-year-old kid in Hoboken who'd have a better chance. Quincannon's obsession seems rooted in the real world, not in fiction."

She wouldn't meet my eyes. I crouched down so we were on the same level. She kept her gaze fixed on the files in her lap.

"You know something, don't you?" I said. "Something about this case. There's a reason you're bending over backward for Holly Quick. Is it Quincannon? Do you have something on him?"

She opened her mouth to say something, stopped, opened it again, stopped. She set the files aside and pulled herself up off the floor and into the armchair.

Once settled, she looked me in the eyes and asked, "Do you trust me, Will?"

It wasn't quite as rhetorical as "Is the sun warm?" or "Is water wet?" But it was close.

Of course I trusted her. If Lillian Pentecost asked me to put on a blindfold and walk a wire, the only question I'd ask is if she wanted it done barefoot or in heels.

All I said was "Yes."

"Then trust me that we can serve this case better than the police."

"What is it?" I asked her. "What aren't you telling me?"

Someday I'm going to teach Lillian Pentecost to play poker and we're gonna make a goddamn fortune.

Eventually I answered for her.

"I'm guessing a whole lot. But that's your prerogative. So, good idea or bad idea, do you want my report on the meeting with Quincannon?"

She nodded.

I gave her the lot. I stayed standing, as she had the only chair in the room and I'd spent most of the day on my rear. By the time I got to Alathea's not-so-veiled threat, the smell of meatloaf had reached the third floor.

"She didn't show a knife, but I gotta say I believed her."

"You should," Ms. Pentecost said. "Alathea is not Quincannon's secretary. She's his bodyguard."

"Really?"

"You sound surprised."

"I guess I shouldn't be. The man invites killers into his home—of course he'd want protection. I'm not surprised he'd go with someone like her. He probably thinks it's . . . I don't know . . . playfully ironic."

"By all accounts she is exceptionally dangerous," Ms. P said. "I have a file on her, though it's very thin. Alathea—last name unknown."

"I'll look it up when I need some light bedtime reading. Now, what do you think of the rest? Do you think he's got something on the Checchetto murder?"

"I do," she said. "If for no other reason than that he requested tribute."

"What does that mean, by the way?"

"An exchange. Quincannon is, for all his talk of spiritual alchemy and human elevation, like most wealthy men. He believes in a transactional world. It would never occur to him to gift me information I find valuable. I must purchase it. With my presence. And a gift."

I was saved from asking just what kind of gift by Mrs. Campbell bellowing from the first floor.

"Dinner!"

Ms. Pentecost heaved herself out of the chair, grabbed her cane, and started for the steps.

"Do you want me to put the files away?" I asked.

"No," she said. "Leave them out. I may want to consult them further."

"Let's hope Klinghorn turns up a link and you don't need to."

I waited until she'd made the safety of the door before turning off the lamp, plunging her collection of madmen and murderers into darkness.

CHAPTER *19*

When I stub my toe on the corner of a case, I like to throw myself headlong in another direction to prove to my boss and to myself that I'm not habitually clumsy.

So I got up bright and early Friday morning, determined that, if I was going to be stuck as Jean Palmer, I was going to make the most of it. I was "capable," goddamn it. Surely I could dig up something more than a locked safe that I had yet to be given permission to break into.

But I couldn't get my head right. Ms. P had asked me if I trusted her, and I had answered in the affirmative. But I kept coming back to the fact that she was leaving me in the dark.

What did she know that she didn't trust me with?

And because being Ken Shirley's secretary took only the smallest fraction of my attention, I had plenty of mental real estate where I could run in circles.

At five o'clock, I booked it for the door, stopping only long enough to beg off happy hour. Jean Palmer had a migraine.

So did Will Parker.

I sweated through my hour with Jules, managing to get out of my own way long enough to crack the practice safe in a little under fifteen minutes.

"That is a terrible time," Jules said. "But it is as good as you will do, I think."

I had the fingers, he said, but not the ear. Still, we both

agreed that I was good enough to crack Shirley's little clinker. I handed him an envelope containing his fee and promised to let him know how things went.

On the train ride back to Brooklyn, I tried to screw my head on straight. I dreaded the thought of spending another week as Jean Palmer. Especially after my conversation with Ms. P the night before, and having taken a gander at those files filled with gore.

Was the killer going to strike again? How much time did we have? Certainly not enough to waste another week at Shirley & Wise. I needed to be out there. I needed to be doing something.

I was going to put my foot down. Ms. Pentecost was going to spill the beans or . . .

Or what?

I was still hammering out the second half of that ultimatum when the short hairs on the back of my neck rose to attention.

I'd long ago learned not to ignore that tingle. It usually meant that while the brunt of my brain was occupied elsewhere, some sharp-eyed sliver had noticed I was being watched.

I let my gaze brush across the other people in the car. I caught one guy staring, but his eyes were fixed firmly on my legs. Otherwise, nobody was paying me more attention than was warranted.

Still, my pulse wouldn't slow.

The doors opened at Chambers. I waited until they were about to close, then dove through. I glanced back as I headed for the steps. It was the tail end of rush hour, so half a dozen other commuters had squeezed off the train along with me. All of them were suits and secretary types. Not a one looked out of place.

That tingle was still there.

Once I made it topside, I doubled my pace, looking back over my shoulder every chance I got. The sidewalk was crowded with people plowing their way home. Was that a figure keeping pace a block behind? It was hard to tell.

Taking a page from Thomas Kelly's book, I made a sudden left into an alley and began running. My plain pumps didn't have the traction of my boots, and I almost lost it on a patch of ice. But I managed to keep my feet under me and got to the end of the alley without incident.

I looked back. No one was following. But there was someone at the other end, silhouetted by the light of a street lamp.

Then they were gone.

A tail? Alathea with a knife up her sleeve? Or just a civilian wondering why a woman had suddenly decided to sprint through an alley?

I walked to a nearby dive where I was friendly with the bartender. He let me use the office phone. A couple minutes later, a cab pulled up and I hopped in.

By then my pulse was steady and all my hairs were lying flat. By the time the cab crossed over into Brooklyn, I was half convinced I'd spooked myself.

"Too many pictures of corpses in steamer trunks," I muttered to myself.

The cabbie gave me a look, but it was New York City, so he'd heard stranger.

We pulled up in front of the brownstone right behind a paint-worn Ford sedan. As I paid the driver and he sped off, a familiar figure hopped out of the Ford, climbed our steps, and pushed the buzzer.

I muttered a bad word. Technically it was four words, but the other three wouldn't make sense without the fourth.

"Did you call ahead?" I asked. "She disconnects the buzzer after six on Fridays."

Startled, Klinghorn turned to see who was speaking. I

was greeted with a look of blank confusion. I had forgotten I was still wearing my Jean Palmer costume, complete with glasses.

I was about to ask what he wanted when I saw the thick accordion file tucked under his arm. His report.

"Hang on—I've got my keys," I said, pushing past him.

"Parker? You . . . um . . . Well, I didn't recognize you. You look very . . . Well, anyway, I have my report. And let me tell you—"

I didn't let him tell me. Instead, I pushed Klinghorn inside and got him installed in the usual guest chair in the office, then I found Ms. Pentecost on the third floor and informed her we had a visitor. On the way back down, I stopped at my bedroom long enough to ditch my coat and glasses, and scrub off the concealer so my freckles could breathe.

Once all three of us were settled, Klinghorn ceremoniously placed the accordion file—it looked to contain half a dictionary's worth of paper—on Ms. Pentecost's desk.

I hoped that he'd ask for his check and scoot. But no. He had to make a speech.

"This was the fastest I've ever gotten a report together," he said. "In there are general backgrounds on each victim, as well as interviews with friends, family, neighbors, and coworkers. Now, I'm sorry that Staples rousted you. But all that digging around, it was inevitable that the cops would twig to me. Especially when I was given such a broad brief."

"I assure you, Mr. Klinghorn, I do not blame you for Detective Staples's interest. He seems the perceptive sort."

"Yes, he is," Klinghorn said. "Smart, too. He knows the score. Two weeks and no suspect in the Checchetto murder? He's worried this is gonna sit on his desk like a dead fish."

Impatience is not one of my boss's casual vices. I have seen her sit, rapt and unmoving, through a three-hour lecture on fingerprint dust, all so she could ask the lecturer a single question.

However, even her supply of patience is limited, and we were both anxious to jump into the report and start hunting for a connection between our victims.

"Perhaps I can be of some assistance to Detective Staples in that regard," she said.

"There's two copies of everything. I've typed up a summary for each victim. We can go through those now, if you'd like," he said. "Or I don't mind walking you through the entire report. In case you have questions, or if anything's unclear."

Looking at the size of the thing, I imagined that would see Klinghorn still in our office come sunrise. Not my idea of fun. Not my boss's, either.

"I'm sure you've done exemplary work, Darryl. Miss Parker has your check."

The use of his Christian name made him blink. But this time he ignored the exit line.

"Um . . . well . . . if you're going to follow up on these cases, I have a few ideas. I think I can be a real asset."

I made a show of opening a drawer in my desk and pulling out the envelope containing the check for the other half of his fee.

"I'm sure you will be," Ms. P said. "We have your number in case we need anything further."

She forced the issue by standing and holding out a hand. Reluctantly, he shook it.

"It's been a . . . a pleasure working with you, Lillian."

At the door, I handed him the envelope. The check was healthy—his rate and a half for two weeks' work, even though he'd managed the job in nine days. He had the manners not to open it.

"Come on, Parker, tell me the truth," he said, putting on

his coat. "These are connected, aren't they? I'm telling you I can be a big help here."

It was the second time that week a man had tried to pry me open on his way out the door. Unlike with Staples, I didn't care about staying on Klinghorn's good side.

"We've got it from here," I said. "But if we need someone to peep in a window, we'll let you know."

He called me a word that is considered rude in polite society. Even if it is true. I responded in kind and shut the door in his face.

Then I went back into the office to dive into a trio of homicides, ultimatums and phantom tails conveniently forgotten.

CHAPTER 20

Victim: Michael Perkins (born 7/5/1900, Poughkeepsie, New York)

Relatives: Mary Anne Perkins, née Bard (wife, 37, divorced 2/13/1944); Emily Perkins (daughter, age 6); Theresa Perkins (daughter, age 12); Lorraine Perkins (mother, age 72); Thomas Perkins (father, age 75); Sandra "Sandy" DeAngelo (sister, age 52); Steve Perkins (brother, age 49)

Profession: Inspector, Division of Generalized Food Inspection, New York City Department of Health (1933–death)

Date of death: Wednesday, August 7, 1946, shortly before 12 a.m.

Circumstances: Found in his apartment, hanging by the neck from a rope (twisted cotton; sold at most hardware stores) attached to a ceiling fixture. He had also been shot in the head (.22-caliber) either immediately before or after death (see attached medical examiner's report).

State of investigation: Unsolved; death by suspicious circumstances

Summary: Michael Perkins was born in
Poughkeepsie and moved to New York City at
the age of seventeen (1917). He worked ten years
installing high-end plumbing fixtures before the
company went bankrupt (1927). What followed was
a series of dead-end jobs that ended when he found
stable work at the Department of Health (1933).

His remit was to inspect food services at education
and health facilities, where he regularly held the
annual Department of Health record for most
citations written. There were several outstanding
disputes against specific citations, but no complaints
against the subject personally (see p. 14 of main
report). However, other inspectors referred to him
as "no-nonsense" and a "hard-ass." (See attached
Perkins Co-worker Interviews.)

In 1935 he married Mary Anne Bard, whom he
met when she was working as a secretary in his
office. They moved into a two-bedroom apartment
in Jamaica, Queens, that same year and had two
children.

When interviewed, Mary Anne could not identify
when exactly her husband's drinking got out of
hand, only that he began spending more time in bars
and less time at home.

Possible reasons for excessive drinking: three missed
promotions, financial difficulties due to doctors' bills,
discipline issues with oldest daughter (see attached
Theresa Perkins School Record), general depression.

Mary Anne took the children and left her husband
(September 1943) to move in with her father. Mike

Perkins moved into an apartment in Stuyvesant Square following the divorce (uncontested and relatively amicable: February 1944).

From February 1944 until his death in August 1946, Mike Perkins's schedule was as follows:

9 a.m.: Report for work at Department of Health

9:30 a.m.–4:30 p.m.: Conduct activities related to his job as a food services inspector. This included regular site visits to hospitals, schools, etc.

5 p.m.: Return to apartment at Stuyvesant Square

7–10 p.m.: Have dinner at The Lucky Ticket, a bar and grill two blocks from his apartment. Following dinner he would drink until closing.

On Saturdays, he would spend much of the day at The Lucky Ticket.

On Sunday, The Lucky Ticket is closed and all evidence points to him drinking at home.

Shortly before midnight on August 7, neighbors heard a gunshot from the subject's apartment. Police were called and discovered the victim hanging from a light fixture by a length of rope. He also had a gunshot wound to the head (see attached photos).

The apartment door was unlocked when police arrived and there was no gun present. One theory held by police is this could be a suicide. That the victim rigged the hanging, then chose to shoot himself to ensure death. After he fell from the stool and dropped the gun, it was stolen by a third party, who heard the shot and entered the apartment after the suicide (see interview with Officers 1 and 3).

More experienced police believe this unlikely (see interview with Officer 2).

However, as Perkins had no known enemies, no notable troubles at work, no friends, and no legal entanglements remaining from his divorce, there are no other theories or suspects currently being pursued by the NYPD.

DK NOTE: It is my opinion that this is a homicide and warrants further investigation.

Victim: Connor "Conny" Haggard (born 11/4/1920, Staten Island, New York)

Relatives: Solomon Haggard (father, age 82); Sarah Haggard (mother, deceased 1936); Lydia Soule (sister, age 41); Darren Soule (brother-in-law, age 46)

Profession: Machinist, Collins Steelworks, 1937–1942; private, United States Army, 1942–1944

Date of death: Sunday, November 17, 1946, between 6 and 8 a.m.

Circumstances: Found stabbed to death (weapon: bone-handled hunting knife, 6″ in length; see attached medical examiner's report) on the rear-facing porch of his sister's home.

State of investigation: Unsolved homicide

Summary: Haggard grew up in the New Brighton neighborhood of Staten Island to a blue-collar family. Father, Solomon Haggard, had a steady job as a machinist at Collins Steelworks in Jersey City (1921–1935). Union-organizing activities resulted in his sudden dismissal, along with twenty other senior line-workers. Solomon Haggard did not hold regular employment after this.

Mother, Sarah Haggard, died (stomach cancer) in 1936 and both children left school to support the family. Connor took a job at Collins Steelworks on the same line his father had previously worked.

Solomon was unhappy with this decision (see attached Haggard Neighbor Interviews) and demanded Connor quit. Connor refused and moved out shortly after.

DK NOTE: I understand you have some familiarity with the former owners of Collins Steelworks, who might have more information about Connor's or Solomon's employment. I would gladly follow up should you supply an introduction.

Connor moved into a riverside tenement in Battery Park and continued working at Collins Steelworks. He was well liked and former co-workers remember him as a "swell guy" and a "real man's man." (See attached Collins Steelworks Interviews.)

No exceptionally close friends. Regular girlfriends, but none that lasted longer than a month.

Continued visits to his sister, Lydia. No contact with his father.

In July 1942, Haggard enlisted in the army. Following six months of training at Camp Shelby, Mississippi, he was shipped to England, where he remained until June 6, 1944 (see attached synopsis of D-Day, Operation Overlord).

While storming Omaha Beach (Normandy, France), Haggard received a fragment of mortar shell in his upper right thigh and another in his right knee. He did not lose the leg, but his walking was severely impaired (see attached Haggard Army Medical Report).

Returned to New York City in September. Received full army disability pension. As he could not remain standing for more than an hour without pain, he was unable to continue his position at Collins Steelworks.

He moved into a spare bedroom at the home of his sister and brother-in-law (Lydia and Darren Soule) in Sunnyside, Queens. Interviews with neighbors suggest that this was mostly Lydia's idea, as Darren had a long-standing dislike of his wife's family. Employed as a manager at the Dime Savings Bank of Queens, Darren was heard by several of his co-workers, following Connor's arrival, calling his wife's family "beer-swilling trash" (see attached Darren Soule Co-worker Interviews).

Soule agreed to house his wife's brother for a few months "while he got back on his one good foot." Connor Haggard stayed with the Soules for over two years. The few interactions he had with the Soules' neighbors were brief and unpleasant.

One example involves Haggard's fondness for cheap and, by all accounts, foul-smelling cigars. His sister did not allow him to smoke in the house, and so he would spend many hours on the back porch smoking one cigar after another. When a neighbor complained about the rancid smoke drifting into his own yard, Haggard threatened to "gut him like a [expletive] Jerry" (see NYPD Complaint, May 1946).

In July 1946, Lydia Soule discovered she was pregnant. She and her husband requested that Connor move out of the spare room so they could turn it into a nursery. As of November 17, Connor had yet to seek regular employment or other lodging.

There were regular shouting matches between Haggard and his brother-in-law throughout October and the first half of November (see attached Noise Complaints #2–7).

On Thursday, November 14, the Soules traveled to a resort in the Catskills for a long weekend. Connor was given an ultimatum: find new lodging by the time they returned on Sunday or be forcibly removed.

The Soules returned early Sunday afternoon and found Connor Haggard dead on the back porch of their home. He was discovered sitting upright in a chair, a knife lodged in his stomach. (See attached crime scene photos.)

Darren Soule remains the primary suspect. While he has a relatively solid alibi for the estimated time of Haggard's death, police are investigating the possibility of murder-for-hire.

DK NOTE: While the lack of fingerprints, minimizing of blood splatter, and the seeming ease with which the murder was committed seems to rule out an amateur, a professional would have been more likely to use a gun rather than a knife, especially one so distinctive. Also, Darren Soule does not travel in circles that include many professional hired killers.

Victim: Flavio Checchetto (born 1/17/1889, Milan, Italy)

Relatives: None found living in the United States

Profession: Sole owner, Checchetto Curios and Consignment (1928–death)

Date of death: Thursday, January 16, 1947, between 8 p.m. and midnight

Circumstances: Found in the office of his store; multiple slash wounds running down length of torso

State of investigation: Unsolved homicide

Summary: Due to the lack of official records, much of the subject's life prior to immigrating to the United States in 1926 cannot be confirmed. Most information has been gathered from interviews with regular customers, neighbors, and shop owners (see attached Checchetto Associate Interviews).

According to Checchetto, he ran an art gallery in Milan from approximately 1910 to 1926. He was a vocal supporter of the Italian Socialist Party, and his gallery was regularly vandalized during the Fascist rise to power in the early 1920s.

In late 1926, Checchetto closed his art gallery and took a passenger ship to New York City. The sale of the paintings that he brought with him helped fund the purchase of his store near the corner of First Avenue and 59th Street in 1928.

He originally named it Checchetto's Fine Art, hoping to attract high-profile art lovers. However, the location of the store made this difficult, as did Checchetto's Italian-immigrant status. The business was struggling in 1929 when the market crash dried up the demand for fine art.

Checchetto used the situation to his advantage.

According to Mrs. Caroline Daily, the owner of Daily's Dainties, a perfumery located down the block from Checchetto's store, Checchetto "might have been a Commie, but the son of a gun knew how to squeeze nickels out of other people's misery."

"The [expletive] went around to all these estate sales, buying up whole rooms of [expletive] for pennies on the dollar. He'd sell off all the cheap [expletive] to other stores, then he'd keep the good stuff and sell it in his shop for three times what he paid. These blue-collar [expletives] and [expletives] would come in and be like 'Holy [expletive], a Tiffany lamp for ten bucks.' Like they knew a Tiffany from their [expletive]. Checchetto was a vulture but the [expletive] knew how to make a buck." (From Checchetto Associate Interviews. Uncensored version available upon request.)

Checchetto changed the name of his shop to
Checchetto's Curios and Consignment in 1932. The
"consignment" referred to his side concern of selling
paintings by local artists. According to neighboring
shop owners, this did not account for a substantial
portion of his yearly profit.

Regarding his relationship with Jessup Quincannon:
This seems to have begun around 1937, when he
came into possession of a teapot reputedly owned by
English poisoner Mary Ann Cotton.

DK NOTE: This detail is "common knowledge"
among other antiques and rare-items dealers, but
I was not able to substantiate it to my personal
satisfaction.

Checchetto's body was discovered around noon,
January 17, 1947, by a driver delivering a truckload
of antique furniture. He found the shop dark and
the door locked, but discovered the alley door open.
He entered and found Checchetto lying on his desk.
Cause of death was assumed to be blood loss caused by
four parallel "claw marks" running the length of the
victim's torso. However, there is some disagreement
on this. (See attached medical examiner's report.)

While I was unable to get copies of Checchetto's
books, other store owners were unaware of any
outstanding debts and I could find no one with active
grudges against him.

DK NOTE: The restriction placed on my
investigation—that I was not to approach Jessup

Quincannon or his associates—has limited my
ability to flesh out the details of this case. I strongly
urge you to allow me to pursue this line of inquiry,
as it seems to be the most fruitful. It is doubtful that
Det. Staples and his fellows will have much luck
with Quincannon personally as, in the words of one
sergeant I spoke with, "Someone in Quincannon's
tax bracket can tell us to eat it, and all Donny Staples
can do is smile and swallow." I believe I would have
success following a more surreptitious route.

CHAPTER **21**

Say what you will about Klinghorn, the man could compile a report. If there was a nook or cranny he had failed to stick his nose into, I didn't see it. We went through the whole pile twice, which took us well past midnight.

"Thoughts?" Ms. P asked when she finished her second pass.

I was on my third pot of coffee, but it still wasn't enough to get my spark plugs firing properly.

"I've got nothing," I admitted.

"Nothing?"

"Maybe it's because I started the day at seven a.m. and the hour hand is approaching one. But if there's a link between our victims, I don't see it. Klinghorn obviously didn't see it, either. If he had, he'd have been shouting it from the rooftops. 'Lillian—you'll never guess what I found.' Instead what I see are three men who don't have anything in common. Other than a killer."

Ms. Pentecost shifted in her chair and grimaced. From stiffness or frustration, I didn't know.

"Let's look at this from the other side of the equation. What does this report tell us about our killer?"

"Okay, I'll bite," I said. "Looking at the crime scene photos, our guy is definitely copying what he's read in *Strange Crime*."

"Without question."

"Though not exactly," I added. "He's more into looks than actually acting the scene out. If Hiram is right, Checchetto was staged. Also, he used a bone-handled knife on Haggard. Maybe it's just too hard to stab someone with an antler. I've never tried."

Ms. P stood up, pushed her chair back to give herself room, and began a series of stretches. Her doctor had recommended them, but I rarely saw her actually comply.

"What else do you see?" she prompted.

"I don't know what you're looking for. If it's why this guy is doing what he's doing, I have no clue. And I don't see how we get there from what we have here." I tossed the pile of pages onto my desk. "Unless the motive is actually one of the usuals and these murders are only dressed up to look bent."

"Perhaps there are questions we can pose now that address both possibilities," she said, bending over to touch her toes. "Pretend you are the killer. What are the challenges you face?"

"Aside from being a complete wacko?"

"If you must conjecture about the killer's mental state, please be specific." At least that's what I think she said. Her head was between her knees. "For the moment, put aside motive. You have a task to complete. The murder of three men. Each will be brutal and elaborate. What are the challenges before you?"

I started to see what she was getting at.

"Okay, so first I've got to learn about these three guys," I said. "Even if I'm in their lives, it's unlikely I know everything I need to know. Where they live, what their schedule is. I've got to find all that out. Because if I'm going to go out carrying a rope or a gun or whatever, I don't want to be haphazard about it."

Ms. P uncoiled her spine.

"Which makes you a planner."

"Sure it does," I said. "Mind you, it wouldn't be that hard. These guys all had pretty set routines. Checchetto had business hours and was the only employee. If Perkins wasn't at work, he was home or at the bar. Haggard seems to have spent his entire life at his sister's place."

My boss began reaching for the ceiling, first one arm, then the other.

"Killing Perkins would be easy," I said, ignoring the floor show. "He's a drunk. It wouldn't be hard to shadow him, maybe even hold the door to his apartment building open for him. After that, I've got a gun, so I can move him around some. Maybe he cooperates. Sticks his head in the noose. Or I shoot him first. But then I've got to get him hoisted. And the neighbors have heard the shot."

I took a mental step back.

"So I've got to get him in the noose first," I said. "But what are the chances Perkins goes along with it? He'd rush me. Take his chances with the gun. That's what I'd do."

"Perhaps Mr. Perkins was made of weaker stuff," Ms. Pentecost suggested.

I wasn't so sure.

I thought of Checchetto. Taken at the end of business in his shop. Did he open the door after-hours to someone he knew? Maybe someone he'd met at Quincannon's?

I thought about the wounds and what Hiram said about blood flow and arteries and poison and drugs. There wasn't much blood with Haggard, either.

Knockout drops for all three? Easy enough for Perkins. Not so easy for Haggard and Checchetto. How would you get them to drink it? Good sense and fairy tales say you don't take sips from strangers.

So maybe the killer wasn't a stranger. But Klinghorn dug deep. If they shared someone close in their respective orbits, chances are it would be in that report.

I downed the last of my now-cold coffee. A few drops dribbled onto my blouse.

"Damn," I muttered. I walked to the drinks trolley, splashed some seltzer on a cloth napkin, and began rubbing. "I'm gonna have to spend a dollar on dry cleaning so Jean Palmer doesn't get a reputation as a slob."

Ms. P had her arms out at ninety-degree angles and was making some kind of twisting-rolling motion with her head and shoulders.

"You want to have a chance of winning the Harvest Moon Ball, you've got to work your hips more," I told her.

She reversed directions.

"It's late," she said. "You've had a long day and you're tired. When you're tired, you resort to sarcasm."

"I'll have you know that was pure wit. But I concede the point. And may I replace the wit with a thought?"

"You may."

"Thinking like the killer got me thinking like a detective," I began. "If the victims were all of a type—curvy blondes, let's say—I could see our killer walking down the street and going eeny meeny miny murder. But they're all different sorts, these men. And the killings are elaborate. He had to do all this work, all this planning. I can't believe they're random."

"What are you suggesting?" Ms. P asked.

"Klinghorn's report shows there's no close connection between them," I said. "But what if it's there, just not close. Maybe he barely knows them, but they tickled his fancy, right? Which means we need to look at the fringes of these men's lives."

She let off with the rolling and started working at the joints in her hands and fingers. The cracks they made—it was like the ice breaking up on the Gowanus.

"How do you suggest we proceed?" she asked.

"We need lists. A list of where Perkins was counting rat

droppings. A list of Haggard's army buddies. A list of Chec-chetto's customers, a list of his suppliers. While we're at it, maybe a list of *Strange Crime*'s subscribers. It's my fault for not asking for it when I was there. Hopefully in a dozen lists, with two hundred names each, we'll find someone in common and pray to God our victims didn't all ride the same train once in 1937 or something obscure like that."

My boss stopped her creaks and cracks and dropped wearily back into her chair.

"We'll make a list," she said.

"A list of lists?"

She nodded. "But not tonight. First thing tomorrow. Before visitors start arriving."

"Who is going to be collecting these lists?" I asked. "You go back to Klinghorn with this and he'll know you're doing more than fishing."

My boss could see the hook a mile away.

"You would like to leave your role at Shirley and Wise to pursue this."

"Sweet Jesus, yes. Two weeks and all I've got is that safe, which I'm ready to crack as soon as you give the nod."

She pursed her lips.

"I'll consider it," she said.

"Come on, Boss!" It wasn't a whine, but it was embarrassingly close.

"Nearly a year." Her voice was a third rail, vibrating with anger. "A year working on Olivia Waterhouse and we have had a single, solitary lead."

"Okay," I relented. "Once we get our list—our list of lists—we can work out how to track everything down."

"If no other solution presents itself, I can take on the task myself."

I couldn't do a look of withering skepticism as well as she could, but I tried.

"Much of the initial work can be accomplished over the phone," she explained. "I am not, as of yet, an invalid."

"I never suggested otherwise. I'll have a list of lists and the phone numbers to match when you come down tomorrow morning. Good night."

She nodded a good night to me and I trudged upstairs, already dreading Monday, when I'd have to slip back into Jean Palmer.

I thought about Ms. Pentecost's point, not giving up on a lead until you knew it was played out. And I thought about the anger in her voice.

Sure, Olivia Waterhouse was dangerous. But so was Holly Quick's plagiarist-cum-killer. And Waterhouse seemed so remote. Barely there. Blood in the water.

Now that we had Klinghorn's report in hand, Holly's killer felt much closer. Maybe he'd already found his next victim, I thought. It might already be too late.

CHAPTER *22*

Saturday morning I woke with the dawn. I break-fasted at my desk, went through Klinghorn's report cover to cover for a third time, and made a to-do list for my boss.
It included:

- Get a list of Perkins's inspection jobs.
- Get a list of Haggard's army buddies. Everyone in his company, if possible. Better too many names than too few.

The army wouldn't be quick to give something like that up. The best avenue might be to approach Haggard's sister and brother-in-law. Haggard might have letters and photos from his army days. I crossed my fingers they hadn't tossed them. I crossed another set, hoping they'd cooperate. The brother-in-law being in the police spotlight could cause them to clam up.

- Get a look at Checchetto's business records. These were probably in a police lockup somewhere. But Ms. P had as many connections with the cops as I did. She should be able to make some calls. Could she do it without Staples finding out? That was the question.

—   Ask *Strange Crime*'s editors for a subscription list. If
    I could get it without our client finding out, and
    thus throwing another tantrum, even better.

There was more, but I won't waste paper on them. Not
because they weren't good ideas. Some were excellent notions.
It's just that circumstances aligned to keep us from pursuing
them.

The first hint I had that the day wasn't going to go as
planned was a glance at the clock. Ms. Pentecost was half an
hour late getting up.

Not usually a big deal, as she frequently slept in. Except
this was Saturday and she knew we'd soon have visitors.

About fifteen minutes later, I heard the distinctive thump of
her getting out of bed and heading to the bathroom. Actually, it
was a triple-thump—two footsteps and a cane. Not a good sign
that she was reaching for her cane for such a short trip.

I waited until Mrs. Campbell had delivered her breakfast,
then went up and knocked on the door, typed to-do list in my
hand.

"Are you decent?" I called.

There was a two-second delay, then "Enter."

I found the lady of the house sitting in the armchair by the
window, still in her nightgown and working on a plate of eggs
that Mrs. Campbell had situated on a folding table beside her.
She had the Saturday *Times* open on her lap.

I walked in on her mid-bite. The hand holding the fork
was shaking and a clump of scrambled eggs fell onto the opinion page. She uttered a very unladylike word.

"Bad morning?" I asked.

She nodded.

"Scale of one to ten?"

She picked the eggs off her lap and dropped them back on
the plate.

"It's not . . . so bad, but . . ."

But it wasn't great.

Usually when her voice starts getting that hitch—the volume pitching up and down against her will—it's after a long day. The fact she'd woken up with it suggested it was going to be a rough one for my boss.

"Should we cancel the open house?" I asked. "It's not too late to get the word out."

She shook her head.

"I'll be . . . better once I . . . bathe and . . . get moving."

That was a lie. A good wash might do away with the grime, but it wasn't going to scour off the multiple sclerosis.

"How much sleep did you get?"

All I got was a shrug. She went for another bite of egg and managed to successfully dock the fork.

Ms. P's symptoms could come and go with frustrating irregularity. But one thing we knew made them worse was stress. I slipped the to-do list into my back pocket.

"So we don't cancel," I said. "But I'll stick to the office. No basement training."

She started to object but I talked over her.

"You'll need the extra hands. I'll tell my ladies to go practice their flips at home."

"Make sure . . . Mrs. Campbell . . ."

"Yeah, I'll make sure they get a hot meal before I send them off."

That was a bonus for anyone coming to Saturday open house. Mrs. Campbell made grub like she was the Bowery Mission, but with better food and shorter lines.

"Can you get yourself ready, or do you need me to scrub your back?" I asked.

Lillian Pentecost would never give anyone the one-finger salute. But the look she shot me was a decent substitute.

I left her to her eggs.

———

I won't run through that Saturday's clients. Let's just say that the day went about as badly as I expected.

With each successive visitor, Ms. P's symptoms got a little worse. By the time the clock struck four, the hitch in her voice was so bad she could barely sweat out a sentence.

We would usually keep the doors open until five, but I called it quits an hour early. My boss didn't even argue.

After I ushered out the latecomers—instructing them to write, or to come back the following weekend—I helped my boss up the stairs to her bedroom.

I got her back into her nightgown and propped up in bed, a stack of newspapers and a few copies of *Strange Crime* sitting nearby. Never once during the process did she chide me for mothering her. Which told me everything I needed to know about how bad she was feeling.

"I'm gonna have Mrs. Campbell bring up dinner," I said. "Something easy."

Translation: Something that doesn't require too much utensil work.

"Maybe try and get to sleep early tonight."

She shot me that single-digit look again.

"I know, I know," I said. "You're an adult woman who can manage her own life. But you're juggling three murders and the Waterhouse caper, and you know how a bad day can turn into a bad week at the drop of a hat."

She mouthed, "Thank you."

I left the room, went downstairs, and gave Mrs. Campbell her dinner instructions. Being a smart woman, she already had a collection of finger food at the ready.

"How bad is it?" she asked.

"She wouldn't give me a number, so I have to assume it's at least a six."

She grunted something in Scots.

"I'm going to mix up some cookies. She likes the oatmeal raisin."

"So do I," I said. "Better make a double batch."

She retired to the kitchen and I to the office, where I started planning for worst-case scenarios.

Or maybe not worst-case. But worse-than-average.

That would be Ms. P having a full-on bad week. Those were where she was consigned mostly to her bed for the duration. There was a phone line in her bedroom. I just needed to take the receiver from her desk and move it upstairs.

But if the dysarthria—that was the five-dollar word for the vocal troubles—stuck around, phone calls were out of the question. Which meant her pitching in with our to-do list was out as well.

I weighed the chances she'd let me drop Shirley & Wise for a couple of days and didn't like the odds. I started making a new list: other independent operators we could hire.

Sure, we could go back to Klinghorn, but he was already suspicious that the cases were connected. Also, I didn't like him.

Besides, taken separately, the to-do list didn't require all that much skill. There were plenty of private investigators in the city we could trust to do it. We could even farm it out piecemeal to lessen the chances of anyone connecting the cases.

I was mid-alphabet when the phone rang. I looked at the clock. Seven o'clock on the dot. I picked up the receiver.

"Hello, Miss Quick."

I have no psychic powers. Holly had been calling us nearly every evening since we'd taken the case, asking for updates. I haven't mentioned it previously because I'd given her the stock answer every time: "We're working a number of promising leads and should have information for you shortly."

Sure, we were treating her with kid gloves, but that didn't mean giving her more than we'd give any other client. When we needed her to know something, she'd know.

Consequently, the calls were brief, awkward, and unsatisfying for both parties.

This call was different.

"I wanted to let you know that I'll be out most of the day tomorrow," she said. "It will probably extend into the evening. Just in case you tried to get in touch with me."

"I'm sure if we have anything to report, it can wait until Monday morning," I told her. "Planning a Sunday outing?"

"Hardly," she said. "I've finished my latest round of stories for *Strange Crime* and I'll be delivering them to the office. Brent and Marlo and I sometimes go out to dinner after. Not always, but usually."

After that, she transitioned into her usual barrage of questions: Did we have any news? Any updates? Any more information about the victims?

I wasn't listening. I was thinking about the paper still tucked in my back pocket. Specifically the fourth item on the list.

I dove into her stream of questions.

"How would you like a ride?"

"I'm sorry—a . . . a ride to where?" she asked.

"To deliver your stories. Trains are sparse on Sundays. Cabs are expensive. Also, we need a list of *Strange Crime*'s subscribers."

"Well, I can get that for you myself," she said. "There's no reason for you to come. I really was not comfortable last time, and I don't want to put on that—that charade again."

If my boss was within earshot, I'd have employed some finesse. But it had been a long day and I didn't have the patience.

"No offense, Miss Quick, but I don't trust you to get the job done."

She started sputtering, but I kept going.

"It's not that you're inept," I clarified. "It's just that these are your friends and you've already admitted you aren't comfortable lying to them. When you ask to see the list, you'll have to stick to the cover story. Maybe you'll decide last minute that you don't want to do it. Or maybe they'll sidestep. Tell you they can't really hand out that kind of information. You'd have to give up. Whereas I could employ some elbow grease."

She waited a beat until she was sure I was finished.

"I'm afraid the answer is still no."

I covered the mouth of the receiver, said a few words, then got back on.

"Let me be honest with you, Miss Quick. I am going to ask them for the subscription list. In person, because I like looking into a person's face whenever possible. Now, I can do that with you by my side, where you can keep an eye on me and make sure I don't say or do anything compromising to you. Or I can go on my own."

Unspoken, but certainly implied, was that if I was to go alone, I would absolutely be asking as many questions as I could before they threw me out.

"I would like to speak to Ms. Pentecost, please."

"She is indisposed and not taking calls at this time."

"I . . . I would . . . I demand to speak—"

"Miss Quick!" It wasn't a shout. I promise. More like a firm, verbal slap. "You have hired us to do a job. And you've placed some pretty severe tethers on what we can and can't do in the course of that job. Against my better judgment, we have honored that deal. I even went to the trouble of concocting this whole harassing-phone-call story just so you don't have to tell your friends the truth. I would appreciate it if you would meet us halfway. You do that and, I swear on my mother's grave, I will do my damndest to keep our deal."

Silence from the other end of the line. Then, "Okay."

"Okay?"

"You can pick me up at noon. In front of my apartment. Good night."

A click and a dead line.

After a week of little white lies, it felt good to have success with simple, brutal honesty.

CHAPTER 23

Seventeen hours later, I pulled the Caddy up to Holly's tenement, its grit and grime all too evident in the bright sunlight.

If you're wondering whether Ms. Pentecost's bad day had stretched into two, so was I. She'd still been asleep when I left. I hadn't wanted to bother her the night before, so I wrote a note for Mrs. Campbell to deliver with lunch.

Accompanying client to magazine office to get subscription list. Will be on best behavior and home swiftly.
Will

I was a good fifteen minutes early, but apparently that wasn't enough for our client. Holly was already waiting on the stoop, working on the last half inch of a cigarette.

I didn't feel too badly. It was one of those unseasonably warm days that we occasionally get in New York City around the beginning of February. Each year I start to think that maybe I can pack away my wool frocks and each year I'm disappointed when, a day or two later, the bottom gets pulled out of the thermometer and winter clamps its hungry jaws back down on the city.

Even though I knew better, that day I decided to let myself be fooled. I'd broken out a cadet-gray two-piece suit over a short-sleeved blouse the store clerk had called plum. Daringly, I'd neglected a coat.

All of that's to say if Holly decided she needed to be early to her own front stoop, at least it was a balmy fifty degrees Fahrenheit. She'd decided to celebrate this faux spring with a bluebird ensemble: a robin's-egg-blue blouse paired with a navy plaid skirt and cardigan. She had her ten-gallon bag slung over her shoulder.

She'd also made some adjustments to her face: rouge, blue eye shadow peeking out above the frames of her clunky glasses, a touch of Victory Red lipstick. The blue didn't do her tawny complexion any favors, but overall she looked good.

She dropped the cigarette, the filter now smeared red, and toed it dead. I leaned across the seat and opened the Caddy's door.

"One personal taxi service for Holly Quick," I announced, hoping cheerfulness might erase the less-than-pleasant tone of our last conversation.

She slid into the car with the enthusiasm of a woman dipping into an acid bath.

"How are you today?" I asked, pulling out from the curb.

No answer from the passenger seat.

"Me? Well, as our housekeeper sometimes likes to proclaim, I'm not doing too shabby," I said. "Sure, I'm working on the Sabbath, but I've never been the religious sort. And it's a nice day for it. If a guy with a Lincoln convertible propositioned me in a bar, I might actually say yes."

She gave me the kind of look you'd expect.

"It *is* very nice out," she said finally.

"You make that sound like a demerit."

"No, of course not, it . . . May I smoke?" I gave her a reluctant nod and she rolled down the window. "It's just that usually I would visit my mother on Tuesday, not Sunday. But she likes to go for walks, or I think she does. I imagine she does.

It's hard to tell these days. So I think I should probably go today to take advantage of the weather."

"That sounds like a good idea," I said, making conversation as I navigated toward Manhattan.

"But if I did it after dropping off my stories, I would have to cancel dinner with Brent and Marlo," she said. "And who knows if this weather will even last into the afternoon."

She bent her neck to try to catch a view of the sun through the windshield, then looked down at her watch, then back at the sun. She sucked in a frustrated lungful of Chesterfield and chimneyed it out the window.

"Another thing we could do . . ." I began.

Which is how I came to be pulling the car into the tiny parking lot of the Golden Green Convalescent Home, which was situated on a tiny hill next to the historic Green-Wood Cemetery in Greenwood Heights, Brooklyn.

That's a lot of green, which was probably true in the summer months. That afternoon, the sun was shining down on dead grass, lingering piles of dirty slush, and the unrelenting gray of parking lot, building, and tombstones.

It was rather grim, I thought, as I followed Holly into the sprawling one-story building, to give its residents such a good view of the next stop on the line.

The lobby space had low ceilings, low lighting, and was about five degrees too cold for comfort. The receptionist at the front desk—a woman in her forties who bore a striking resemblance to a Romanian strongwoman I used to know— had a gray wool cardigan pulled as tight as her shoulders would allow.

She looked up from her copy of *Screen Romances,* this one with Gregory Peck looking out from the front cover. She gave a few quick blinks to shake off whatever warm fantasy she'd immersed herself in and attended to the reality in front of her.

"Oh, Miss Quick. I didn't expect to see you today."

She didn't sound disappointed, but she was a long way from thrilled.

"Good afternoon, Mrs. Simpson. I thought I'd take her outside, since it's so nice."

"That sounds just fine," the receptionist said. "Could you and your friend sign the guest book, please?"

As we scribbled our respective John Hancocks, Holly asked, "Is Mr. Dobbin in?"

"Oh, I don't think so," she said. "It's Sunday, after all. But if you leave a message, I'll be sure he gets it."

"That's strange," Holly said. "I remember him saying that he likes to be here on Sundays because that's when families like to visit. And I'm sure I saw his car in the parking lot. He drives a new Plymouth, doesn't he? I never notice cars, but this one is that bright shade of blue, so it's really very hard to miss. Maybe that color is popular, I don't know. I don't drive. But I don't think I've seen another like it."

It was educational seeing someone else be on the receiving end of Holly's verbal barrage. Before the receptionist could entirely crumple under the weight of it, a door behind her opened and a man stepped out dressed in his Sunday best.

"Holly, I thought I heard your voice. What a pleasant surprise."

He came around the desk and gave Holly the kind of lingering handshake that made me wonder if he was trying to read her palm. Unnoticed by anyone but me, the receptionist was giving them a poison-wallflower glare.

Dobbin wasn't Gregory Peck, but he could play his older brother. Tall, lanky, with a swoop of hair that was now more silver than brown, and a face that was all cheekbones and eyebrows. You could probably rig up a daydream or two involving him if no one else was available.

"Mr. Dobbin, hello. Yes, I thought I would take my mother for a walk," Holly said, gently repossessing her hand.

"The weather is unseasonably nice, isn't it? And, please, I keep having to remind you—call me Jerry."

Holly made a noise that was open to interpretation, but I had the feeling she would be doing no such thing.

He turned to the strongwoman at the desk.

"Go find Terry, please. Tell him to bring a chair to Mrs. Quick's room."

The receptionist went off to do as instructed, but she wasn't happy about it. Not that Dobbin noticed. He only had eyes for our client.

"I wanted to ask about a charge on the latest bill," Holly was saying. "Four dollars and seventy-five cents for specialized laundry service. If I'm not mistaken, all of my mother's clothes are simple cotton and wool and I don't see—"

I looked down to make sure I hadn't turned invisible before taking the initiative and holding out my hand.

"Hello, I'm Miss Parker. Holly's friend."

Both of them were startled. Not invisible, just forgotten.

Dobbin took my hand. It was the standard shake. No palmistry involved.

"A pleasure to meet you, Miss Parker." Then back to Holly. "Why don't I walk you to Naomi's room and we can talk about those charges?"

Dobbin and Holly took the lead, running into the weeds about dry-cleaning costs and Irish wool sweaters. We navigated a series of narrow corridors with patient rooms spaced on either side. Most of the doors were closed, but when we passed an open one, I took the chance to peer in.

Through the open doorways I saw men and women,

sleeping or sitting, mostly vacant-eyed, some listening to the radio, several looking out a window at the cemetery on the other side, not a one tucked into a book or thumbing through the Sunday *Times*. We paused to let an old man wielding a pair of canes squeeze by. He probably cracked six feet when you straightened him out. As it was, he barely reached my chin.

"Good morning, Solly," Dobbin said.

He gave us a toothless smile and muttered something Henry Miller would have cut as too obscene. I wasn't expecting it, and he had shuffled past before I arranged a comeback.

Dobbin turned back to me.

"Please pardon Solly. It's the dementia."

"Ah. Most men can only blame poor breeding."

It didn't get a laugh, but it probably didn't deserve one.

Eventually we reached a room located deep inside the maze. Dobbin stopped just short of the door.

"I'll leave you to your visit. And I'll write a note to our laundry service to see if they can't do all of Naomi's things together. Have a lovely walk, Holly. Miss Parker."

She got another lingering handshake. I got a nod.

I waited until he was around the corner and his footsteps had faded to say, "Call me a detective but I think he has a crush on you."

She made a face like I'd shoved a lemon wedge in her mouth.

"I'm very aware," she said. "Early on I made the mistake of flirting back. I thought it might get my mother some more attention or a better room, and it's only flirting, after all. But it certainly didn't help with the bill, and now I'm stuck with it."

With that bit of cheerfulness, she opened the door to her mother's room. If this was what flirting got you, I'd hate to see the alternative. It was two paces smaller than my bedroom, with painted cinder-block walls broken up by a single modest window. Its view was of a narrow courtyard. No green there. Just more concrete.

The woman in the bed didn't seem to mind, though. She was looking out the window when we walked in and didn't stop, even when Holly sat down beside her.

Naomi Quick was doing her own impression of a bird with pale, paper-thin skin stretched over a set of fragile bones and long wings of gray hair falling down either side of her face. I looked for a resemblance, but couldn't find it under the wrinkles.

"Hi Mom," Holly said. "It's Holly. How are you feeling?"

If the elderly woman heard, she didn't let on.

I noticed that someone had carefully applied makeup to the old woman—lipstick, rouge, a little powder. At least I assumed it had been a third party. I was pretty sure Naomi Quick wasn't up to the task.

"No, you haven't lost track of the week," Holly said. "It's not Tuesday, it's Sunday. But it's a nice day out, so I thought we might go for a stroll. Do you want to go for a stroll?"

Her mother's fingers twitched in her lap. The muscles in her face did something, but the expression was open to interpretation. Holly took it for joyous assent.

"I thought you would," she said, smiling.

Embarrassed to be peeping on such an intimate moment, I busied myself taking inventory of the room. A narrow bed piled high with handmade quilts, a nightstand with a vase of fresh flowers, a set of drawers with a Philco sitting on top of it. No bookshelves. I guess Naomi Quick was beyond reading.

A photo on the nightstand of a straw-haired fellow with a face that was all nose and teeth. Holly's father, I presumed, caught somewhere between marriage and Spanish flu.

The only other art was a small, sloppy oil painting hanging on the wall across from the bed. It showed a smeary sun setting over a rocky coastline, its rays turning the water into bloody foam. It was even less cheery than the concrete courtyard.

I was running out of places to put my eyes when there was a polite cough from the doorway. A compact young man in a white orderly's uniform waited there, smiling, gripping the handles of a wheelchair. He had blue eyes, a pomaded blond mane, and a Rhett Butler mustache. Just the type to clean up at an NYU mixer.

"Are we taking Mrs. Quick for a walk today?" he asked.

"Yes, we are, Terry," Holly said. "If you wouldn't mind."

I squeezed into a corner while Terry and Holly got the old woman into the wheelchair. Mama Quick might have looked like a bird, but she must have had some weight to her, and the operation required all four hands and careful coordination.

Once Naomi was settled, Terry took one of the quilts from the bed and draped and tucked it over his charge's legs. Then he navigated the wheelchair through the halls, expertly cutting corners and dodging wandering patients.

"Any changes?" Holly asked.

"Nothing since last week," the attendant said. "I heard her singing some along with the radio. And I've been putting birdseed outside her window so she'll have something to watch. Got a goldfinch on Thursday. Might have to stop doing that, though. Mr. Dobbin complained about the droppings."

"Has she said anything?" Holly asked.

"No. No talking. Not for a while. Just that little bit of singing. To be honest, it was mostly humming."

If Holly was disappointed at the news, she didn't show it. Once we were out the front door, he stepped aside and let Holly take over.

"Tell Doreen to fetch me when you're ready to take her back," he said before disappearing back inside.

Holly navigated the wheelchair onto a narrow, concrete path that meandered a little ways down the hill in the direction of Green-Wood. A short walk brought us to a wrought-iron bench that provided a good view of the massive cemetery. Holly situated the wheelchair next to it and sat down.

"How are you doing? Having a good week? I heard that you made a goldfinch friend."

No response from the old woman.

I stood an awkward distance away, hands in my pockets, wondering if I'd left a book in the car. This wasn't the sort of conversation I was interested in eavesdropping on.

Holly patted her coat pockets and scowled. She looked in my direction.

"Cigarettes?" I asked.

"In my bag."

"I'll fetch them," I said, probably a little too quickly, and hurried back inside.

After two wrong turns I found my way back to the room. I rummaged in Holly's cavernous purse until I dug out her Chesterfields and lighter. I was about to leave when I stopped.

Why hurry?

I checked the nightstand first. Five different kinds of pills, a fistful of lozenges, a scattering of pennies. While I was there, I knelt down and peered under the bed. Two pairs of slippers and a fluffle of dust bunnies.

I went to the set of drawers next, starting at the top and working my way down. The top drawer was unmention-ables, the middle drawer a collection of nightgowns in differ-ent shades and the aforementioned Irish wool sweaters. The bottom drawer contained carefully folded dresses that were a quarter century out of date.

The dresses on top had a thin layer of dust.

Naomi Quick hadn't had a reason to go out on the town in a while.

I knew from experience that it was drawers like these where you tend to hide things if you have things to hide. I lifted up each dress, careful not to disturb the dust. Not that I thought Holly's mother was going to notice.

Beneath the lot, shoved almost to the back of the drawer, I found a photograph.

It was cracked and creased and its corners were rounded smooth. It showed a woman and a child sitting on a stoop. The woman was Naomi with a couple decades shaved off. The girl, about eleven or twelve years old, was on the step below her. She sat stiff-backed, hands folded in her lap.

The stiffness might have been from the bandage taped to the top of her chest. You could see it peeking out above the neckline of her dress.

I peered closer. There was a look on her face I'd never seen on a girl that age.

That's not true. I'd seen it in the mirror once upon a time.

Utter despair. Like the camera was catching the last, flickering moments as her world collapsed.

I heard the footsteps just in time. I managed to shove the photo back and get the drawer closed, but when Terry turned the corner holding a stack of fresh sheets, he found me on my knees.

"Here it is!" I said, holding up Holly's lighter. "Thought I'd lost it."

As I left he gave me a look I imagine he usually reserved for residents like Solly.

I delivered the smokes and the lighter to Holly. Then I went and sat in the Caddy while Holly . . . what? Chatted? Communed?

Comforted?

I wondered how much of Naomi Quick was still left in there. The idea of my body and mind fading, failing, until I was a prisoner in my flesh?

Not a pleasant one.

I replaced that thought with another. The photograph.

The look on Holly's face. Something that went far beyond grief.

The fact that it was hidden. Who hid it? Holly or her mother?

Was it because it reminded one or the other of something they didn't want to remember? I thought about fists and feet and the fragile nature of adolescent girls' bodies. That bandage looked a little high for cracked ribs. A cracked sternum, maybe? Collarbone?

Maybe Holly's mother wasn't so loving. Or maybe her love was punctuated with rage.

Or maybe I was seeing what I wanted to see, and it was a poultice for a chest cold. Either way, it didn't matter to our case, so why bother speculating?

Still, I was thinking about the photograph half an hour later, when a bank of clouds obscured the sun and Holly wheeled her mother back inside.

A few minutes later, she was back in the shotgun seat, puffing smoke out the window as I aimed the Caddy toward Manhattan and *Strange Crime.*

CHAPTER 24

Again we walked the labyrinth, though there was no line of ingenues blocking our way this time. Again Holly walked in without knocking.

We found that the office census had dropped by one. Mort was working his phone, and Marlo was busy at her desk, but no Brent in sight. Both looked up when we walked in. Marlo smiled, Mort look distressed. The latter probably wasn't due to us.

"Look, Sarah, an ad in *Strange Crime* is a billboard in forty-eight states, the District of Columbia, and a bunch of Canadian provinces I can't pronounce. Every single place has people with hemorrhoids who are going to want to buy your pillows. You're not gonna find a better deal. . . . Well, no, I don't have this month's circulation numbers. But I've got December's in front of me. And let me tell you—"

And so on.

Marlo looked up as we approached.

"I love that dress," Marlo said. "But we need to get you a hat. Something in heather gray or a dark blue. To balance out the colors."

She pointed her sharpened chin in my direction.

"Miss Parker. Are you still looking into Holly's problem?"

"I am," I said. "And I was wondering—"

"Where's Brent?" Holly asked. "I thought we were sched-
uled for dinner tonight."

"Hoboken," Marlo said. "Dropping cover art off at the
printer. They need it first thing in the morning. Don't worry,
he'll be back in time."

Rather than volley the conversation back to me, our client
kept going, emptying her handbag and laying out typewritten
pages in paper-clipped chunks while she talked.

"I have the Horace Bellow piece at about twelve thousand
words and a Peter Wylde at seventy-five hundred. The one I
was telling you about with the murder on the ship I'm sending
to *Black Mask*. It's a little too locked-room mystery for *Strange
Crime*," Holly said. "But the rest that you asked for are here.
Oh, and the LeClaire ran a little long. Over eight thousand."

She picked up the Grant LeClaire story and began flipping.

"There's a section you might want to look at. It's—well,
it gets a little risqué. Not as bad as 'The Dame Burned Hot,'
but leaning in that direction. I'd rather make the corrections
myself than just have the section cut."

Marlo gave me a knowing look and a smile. She held
up a "just a minute" finger and joined Holly in peering at
the pages. Left to wait, I wandered over to Mort, who was
between phone calls.

"How go sales?" I asked.

He looked up, startled.

"What? Oh, uh . . . good. I mean, not good. *Good's* too
strong a word. But all right. Why do you ask?"

I looked over my shoulder, where Marlo and Holly were
hunched over the manuscript, each wielding a red pencil.

"Just killing time."

"Well, you know, crime still sells. Sells pretty well. Too
damn well, really. There's about a hundred magazines out
there you can choose from. *Strange Crime's* up in the top

twenty most months. Sometimes the top ten. But that's not exactly king of the world, money-wise. So, uh, if you don't mind . . ."

He nodded at his phone.

"Sure," I said. "Dial away. I'm surprised people pick up on Sundays."

"Folks I call on Sundays hold to a different Sabbath."

"Got it."

Marlo and Holly were still commiserating. I saw a copy of the Sunday *Times* sitting on an empty desk, so I helped myself, both to the paper and the seat.

The front page had a story on the rash of home break-ins that Lazenby was working. Although it seemed less like a crime wave and more like a slight elevation of the water level. But a few percentage points citywide was enough to get elected officials sweating.

Lazenby was quoted as saying, "We've got fingerprints. We've got witnesses. We're pressing on every outlet for stolen goods. We expect to be making arrests very soon."

"Outlet for stolen goods" translated as "fence." Finger-prints and witnesses and "making arrests very soon" trans-lated as they had bupkes. When the cops are closing in, they don't advertise.

It was interesting that the police suspected a single crew. The robberies were happening all over the five boroughs. Usually a burglary crew stuck to their home turf. I made a note to ask Ms. P what she thought about it.

I shuffled through the paper, looking for the sports sec-tion, and noticed Mort giving me a look that wasn't exactly friendly. I was about to apologize for the crinkling when there was a tap on my shoulder.

It was Marlo. Holly had installed herself behind a type-writer and was pecking away.

"She's rewriting the scene," Marlo said.

"Too spicy?"

"Ten years ago, even five, probably not. These days, some-one will make a stink. Holly said you wanted a list of our subscribers?"

"If you don't mind," I said. "I know you might be reluctant to hand that kind of thing out."

She waved away my concern.

"It's not a problem. Here, follow me."

We went through the door labeled CABINET OF MYSTERIES and I discovered it wasn't so much a mystery as a mess. Rows of boxes stacked one atop the other, the ones at the bottom crumpling under the weight. We were walking on a carpet of loose magazines.

"I know," Marlo said. "Once we trimmed a secretary out of our budget, this place went to hell."

"You can find the subscription list in all this?" I asked.

"That's easy," Marlo said, immediately putting her hand on a thick sheaf of papers held together with an industrial-strength staple. "We've got a couple of copies floating around, so feel free to keep it."

I looked at the pages—a few thousand names and addresses. One item to check off of my list of lists.

"Do you really think this guy bothering Holly—that he could be a real problem?" Marlo asked, arms crossed tight across her chest.

"I'm afraid he could be," I said.

"And Holly could actually be in danger?"

"Mokes like this, they don't usually stop unless you smack their nose. And sometimes they up their game, so . . ."

I let her imagination do the lying for me.

I saw her make a decision. She turned and pulled a shoe-box off a stack of boxes. It was bursting at the seams, its lid held on tight by a thick rubber band. She handed it to me. I read the handwritten label taped to the top.

"The 'Creep File'?"

"We don't give Holly all the letters that Horace gets," Marlo explained. "I read through everything first and set aside the . . . well, the odd ones."

"Odd?"

"Ones that might be upsetting. Ones that are mean or . . . just disturbing."

"You do this for all your authors?"

She shook her head.

"Why Holly?" I asked. "You don't think she can handle the weirdos?"

"Oh, I'm sure she could handle it," Marlo said. "But I don't want to fill her head up with gunk if I don't have to."

I hefted the shoebox, wondering how many dozens of letters it held.

"You should have handed this over sooner."

"I know," she said. "But Holly doesn't know we screen her mail, and I didn't want to upset her. Besides, I've read all of these letters. None of them connect Horace Bellow to Holly. So I didn't see how they could help."

I couldn't tell her that we weren't actually looking for someone who'd connected Holly and Horace but were hunting anyone with an unhealthy fascination with Bellow and his stories.

"Well, you never know," I said.

"Do you have to . . . I mean, do you have to tell Holly?" she asked.

"Probably not," I said. "Not if you're right and they don't link Holly and Horace."

"Good. I'd like to . . . I mean, we like to protect her when we can, you understand?"

I told her I did. Though I suspected Holly had tougher skin than Marlo gave her credit for.

I thanked her for the letters and the subscription list and made for the door. Holly didn't look up from her typewriter, but she did deign to toss a wave in my direction.

Progress.

CHAPTER 25

Ms. Pentecost stayed in bed until dinnertime.

Haggis leftovers again, this time accompanied by something Mrs. Campbell refers to as neeps and tatties. Neeps are swedes, which I've discovered are turnips. Tatties you can figure out for yourself.

I told Ms. P I'd bring her up a plate, but she insisted on making the perilous journey to the dining room.

"I am . . . not spending my life . . . in bed."

Because Sunday is traditionally our day off, my boss usually likes to dress down. To her, that means forgoing the jacket and loosening the knot in her tie. But a bad day called for a whole different level of casual: a blue-and-white-striped polo, gray sweatpants, and a navy blue cardigan that could have wrapped around her twice over. All were things that could be slipped on and off with ease.

Her hair had never made it up into its customary braids and hung in barely brushed waves down her back.

I kept an eye on her hands as she forked ground lamb innards into her mouth. There was only minimal fumbling, which made me think she was on the mend.

Though it was always possible she could wake up the next day feeling worse than ever. It had happened. But every once in a while I like to impersonate an optimist.

During dinner I gave her my verbal report—from my

journey to Golden Green to my conversation with Marlo Chase. If she had objections to my taking the initiative, she kept them to herself.

Regarding the photograph I'd found of Holly in her mother's drawer, Ms. P gave no opinion. Or at least none that she shared.

When told about the Creep File, she exhibited the same excitement and annoyance that I had. Excitement that we might find a lead inside; annoyance that we hadn't known of its existence sooner.

Following dinner, we propped ourselves at our respective desks to digest our neeps and start in on our assignments. Mine was typing up the notes from the day. Hers was plowing through the letters and back issues of *Strange Crime*.

She was trying to shuffle them so she could read them in some semblance of order—first the magazine, then any letters connected to it, rinse, repeat.

By the time I typed, "Exited *Strange Crime* offices at 2:45 p.m.," she was maybe a third of the way through the lot.

"Let me play catch-up," I said, grabbing the stack of letters Ms. P had already gone through.

"Do you . . . want the magazines that . . . accompany them?"

"Only if I need to cross-reference. I'd like to see my bed before I see the sun."

Four or five letters in, I could feel my love for my fellow man start to wilt. When I'd read the bundle of letters Holly had given us, I'd noted the lack of nastiness, chalking it up to Horace being a man.

No dice. Horace got the nasty, too. It just came at him a little sideways. An example:

```
Dear Mr. Bellow,
   I very much enjoyed your story "Girl with
the Cast-Iron Heart." However, as a fellow
```

writer, I find it curious that you made
Susanne, the titular character, a waitress.
In my experience a woman, especially one as
poorly educated as a diner waitress, would
not have the wherewithal to initiate such a
plot.

It is intimated (paragraph 2 on p. 49)
that she initiates relations with the thief
as a way of extracting information from
him. Perhaps, I thought as I read, she is
secretly a prostitute. I was surprised when
I reached the end and found she was not!

A whore might have the necessary cunning
and desperation, and would freely use her
body as barter in a way a waitress would
not.

I urge you in future printings to consider
this revision. It would require only a
few sentences, I think, and would more
accurately reflect humanity.

For further accuracy, I suggest perhaps
she could die at the end. Perhaps the thief
could carry through with this threat. As I
have observed, women who live this kind of
life do not survive long.

I trust your judgment to make the correct
choice.

Sincerely,

William Ormston III

I folded the letter and put it back into its envelope.

"Wonder what waitress turned you down, Billy."

Ms. P looked up.

"I think I'm going to have to pay Billy Ormston a visit,"

I said. "He's got a bloodthirsty side. And the envelope has a Staten Island postmark, so he's local."

She nodded. "I concur that . . . Mr. Ormston . . . is disturbed," she said. "Though if he were . . . our killer . . . I believe our victims . . . would be women."

"Fair point," I said. "I'm going to need a shower when I'm through with these. Maybe a delousing."

"They are . . . decidedly unpleasant," Ms. P responded.

"It's the dirty-raincoat ones that get me."

She looked up from her own pile of letters.

"They're like a flasher in a raincoat," I went on. "You think they're normal, then you're three paragraphs in, and—"

The phone kept me from finishing the simile. I picked up the receiver. It was our client, or I thought it was. I could barely hear her over the hyperventilating.

"Holly? You're going to have to speak up."

"I'm home and I . . . I think someone's been in my apartment."

"All right. Stay calm. Can you ring Mr. Cosmo?"

"It's Sunday night. Sunday nights he has dinner at his sister's house on Long Island and spends the night. I think I have her number somewhere, but I don't know where and— I don't—I don't—"

"Deep breath, Holly. Deep breath."

She took a long, shuddering one.

"Whoever was here . . . I don't know if they're gone," she whispered.

CHAPTER 26

I spent twenty seconds failing to talk Holly into calling the police, five seconds convincing her to lock herself in the bathroom, ten seconds getting into my coat while relating the situation to Ms. Pentecost, another ten retrieving the Colt and making sure it was properly loaded, ten rummaging through my desk to find my massive ring of skeleton keys, and fifteen seconds getting out the door and down the block to the Cadillac.

I made it from our corner of Brooklyn to her corner of the Bronx in what must have been record time even for a Sunday night. The street door of the tenement building was locked. The third key on the skeleton ring did the trick.

I took the steps two at a time, pausing at the first landing to take out my gun. I stopped outside Holly's door and yelled, "It's Will Parker!"

No answer.

"Holly!"

Silence. I tried the door. If she'd set her four locks when she got home, she'd had the presence of mind to unlock them for me.

"Holly, it's Will Parker. Are you all right?"

This time I got a muffled response.

"I'm in the bathroom."

"Okay," I said. "Stay there for a minute. I'm just going to check the place out."

I did a quick sweep of the apartment. Living room, kitchen, bedroom, closets. At last, I went to the door of the bathroom and knocked.

"It's clear," I said.

After a few seconds, I heard the lock turn on the doorknob.

Inside the bathroom I found our client. She was shivering, from either fear or the cold. All she had on were her glasses and a pink silk robe that was more for show than function.

Her eyes went wide when she saw the gun in my hand, and she retreated to the far side of the tiny bathroom.

"It's okay," I said, slipping the gun into my coat pocket. "There's no one else here."

She spent a few moments finding her voice.

"Okay, okay, okay. Thank you. Okay. Thank you."

"You can come out."

"Okay, I think . . . I think maybe . . . I think . . ."

I recognized panic when I saw it and adjusted accordingly.

"Hang on."

I went back to the front door and set all the locks. Then I returned to the bathroom, closed the door, and locked us both in.

"There," I said. "All the locks are set and you've got an armed guard. Take all the time you need."

She slid down the far wall and propped herself against the toilet. She tried for a few more words, but they turned into choking sobs. I transferred my gun to my trouser pocket, then took my coat and slipped it over her shoulders.

Then I put as much space between us as I could in the small room, sitting on the floor with my back against the door. After a few minutes the sobs stopped and her breathing returned to normal. When I thought she might be able to speak again, I asked the obvious.

"What made you think someone had been in the apartment?"

"Things were . . . out of place," she said. "Or I thought they were out of place. Maybe I was wrong. Maybe . . ."

"What things?"

"Papers on my desk. The . . . drawers. I thought I'd left one open but when I got home it was closed. And there was something else. A feeling. The feeling that someone had been in here. Someone had been breathing the air. But it wasn't until I came in here to take a bath that I got scared. The bottles in the medicine cabinet. I always keep the labels facing out. So I don't make a mistake. Two of the labels were turned sideways. But . . . maybe I was wrong. I was in a hurry earlier. I wanted to be outside to meet you and I . . ."

I let the monologue run its course. I could have interrupted it to tell her that when I was locking her front door I'd checked the lock on the hall side. There were scratches—faint but fresh. Somebody had gone at it with a pick.

I kept that to myself for the moment. I didn't want to spark another bout of anxiety.

Sitting there, pretending patience, I noticed that when I'd slipped my coat over her shoulders, it had caused her robe to fall open a little, revealing a round divot right over her breastbone.

She noticed me noticing and pulled the coat tight.

A lot of people would mistake a divot like that for a pockmark. But I'd seen that photo of Holly with the bandage around her chest. And I'd seen old bullet wounds before.

I stowed the question for when she wasn't in quite as much distress.

She tucked her chin down, like she could burrow her way to freedom through my coat collar. The shivering was starting to get worse.

There was cold water available, but I didn't think she'd appreciate that treatment. I settled on a different tactic.

"So," I said, "you got home right before you called. About eleven o'clock? Is that right?"

Her shiver turned into a nod.

"Okay," I said. "Now I'm going to ask you a question. It's very personal, but I think it's relevant. So brace yourself. Are you sleeping with Brent, Marlo, or both?"

Her head snapped up, eyes shooting daggers.

"Excuse me! I don't—"

"Before you start into the denials, please let me remind you that I've seen the three of you up close. And I have experience with people showing affection without showing affection, if you catch my meaning."

She was like a deer in headlights. A very angry deer, body frozen stiff except for her chest, which was rising and falling so rapidly I worried she was going to start hyperventilating again.

Eventually she came out with: "You said it's relevant. How is it relevant?"

"An hour ago, maybe it wasn't," I said. "But somebody cracking your apartment—and, yeah, I think somebody did— puts the possibility out there that whoever's doing these murders knows that Horace and Holly share an address."

I waited for her to process that before I continued.

"If that's the case, that throwaway question I asked Marlo and Brent—about who else knows about you—that becomes a real concern," I explained. "That means we have to get a handle on the relationships of everyone who knows and who they might have let it slip to. If Ms. Pentecost were here, she'd give this whole speech about nothing being irrelevant. But all I'm going to say is that to date we've kept your connection to three murders under wraps. We can keep your love life to ourselves as well. But we still need to know."

During my little speech, she'd gotten very agitated. Head darting this way and that; fingers tapping madly on the tile floor, as if typing out her distress on invisible keys. As I watched, she forced herself to become still, shoving her hands into my coat pockets.

Her eyes met mine for a solid ten count. I felt like I was under a jeweler's loupe. What would the vote be? Diamond or glass?

"Both," she said.

"Both?"

"Marlo and Brent and I. We have an arrangement."

Diamond it was.

"Are we talking about mix-and-match pairs, or is everyone invited?"

"Sometimes all three. Sometimes just Marlo and me," Holly said. "It began when Brent was in the war and after he returned, it . . . evolved."

I thought about her alibi for Checchetto and put two and two together.

"The night Checchetto was killed. Was that really a talk about magazine articles?"

"We talked about the magazine."

"And then . . ."

"Then we stopped talking," she said. "I stayed until morning."

"Does anyone else ever appear on the dance card?" I asked. She shot me a dirty look.

"I don't appreciate your levity," she said.

"I'm not making light," I assured her. "I've found most people would rather come at this kind of conversation obliquely."

"I prefer to be direct," Holly declared. "For the last several years, Brent and Marlo and I have been in a relationship. Yes, that relationship is sexual, but not limited to sex. We go to movies. We have dinner. Sometimes we stay up late and just talk. And, no, it is not a perfectly equal relationship. But it is one that . . . that makes us happy. That makes me happy."

Her hands came out of my pockets. She'd found a pencil and began worrying it between her fingers, twisting and bending.

"I do not . . . I do not make relationships easily," she said. "I know what I'm like, Miss Parker. I know that I don't say the right things. Or I say too many things. I am not comfortable in unfamiliar situations or with unfamiliar people. I do not trust easily. But I think that I still deserve love and in whatever way I am comfortable finding it. Because I am still—"

The pencil snapped.

"I'm sorry," she said, placing the two halves carefully down on the bathroom tile.

"That's okay," I told her. "I buy them by the gross."

My rear was starting to find the floor cold, so I stood up.

"Of course you deserve love. For what it's worth, this isn't the first arrangement like yours I've come across. I've got a story about a dwarf, a clown, and an ex-showgirl that makes your setup look like a Rockwell painting. But you never really answered the question. Is this an exclusive club? Or are others allowed in?"

She got to her feet as well.

"I'm not jostling for an invite," I assured her. "I'm just wondering who might have been part of some loose pillow talk."

The daggers came back to her eyes.

"While we are free to see other people outside of the arrangement, no one else is invited. It is not an orgy, Miss Parker!"

"A nice orgy never hurt anyone. But thank you for your honesty. I know those aren't easy questions to answer."

She looked like she was trying to choose between a slap or a kick.

"Are you angry?" I asked.

"Obviously!"

"That means you're probably feeling better. I'm going to do a more thorough once-over. Feel free to join me."

I was out of the room before she could launch.

I did a second pass of the apartment, this time with an eye for anything out of place. I'd never been in the bedroom before that night, so I couldn't say whether things were disarranged. The bed itself was a twin size, barely big enough for one, much less three.

The floor was scattered with clothes, empty cigarette packs, assorted lipsticks, and at least two dozen books. In contrast, the closet was impeccably clean and meticulously sorted. All of Holly's clothes were indeed arranged by color.

I went into the living room and took a look at her desk. There was a stack of manuscript pages—carbon copies from her recently submitted stories. I peered close, hoping to see an errant inky fingerprint.

"Those were moved, as well."

Holly had grabbed some clothes from her closet, mixing a blue jay blouse and wren slacks.

"When I'm done with a story, I straighten the carbons so their edges are even, and I use that nail sticking out of the desk there to help. Then I leave them sitting right there against the nail. It smells funny, doesn't it? The room, not the manuscript."

I gave a sniff. All I got were layers of cigarettes and the floral perfume Holly favored.

No, I thought. There was something else. Something out of place. I couldn't quite put my nose on it.

I went into the kitchen. Holly followed.

There I found clear evidence of tampering. I'd done enough bag jobs to know the signs.

A tea towel hanging from a drawer was caught in the

cabinet below it, like someone had quickly opened and shut each in turn. There was a scattering of sugar and flour where someone had unscrewed the canisters.

People like to hide valuables in flour or sugar containers, and any self-respecting burglar knows that. Although a burglar wouldn't have tried to be neat. I was explaining this to Holly when the phone rang in the living room.

I made a noise, but Holly made a louder one.

I didn't think she was in any state for conversation, so I went and answered.

"Good evening. Holly Quick's residence."

"Will?" said a voice identical to my boss's. "What . . . did you discover?"

"A frightened but unharmed client and an apartment that does look like it's seen an unwanted visitor. Nothing missing, on first glance. If Holly's up for it, I might have her go through things more thoroughly and then—"

"No."

Ms. Pentecost is a big proponent of phone etiquette, so the fact that she interrupted me let me know it was serious.

"Leave . . . immediately. Bring Miss Quick. Have her pack . . . a bag. Do not . . . tarry. She is . . . in grave danger."

I had all the same questions you have, but I knew better than to waste time asking them. I turned to Holly.

"It's Ms. Pentecost. You need to pack a bag. It's not safe to stay here."

"What do you mean? This is my home."

"And the boss thinks it's safer if you abandon it for the moment."

"I'm not going to be driven out of . . . This is my *home*."

I wasn't unsympathetic. No one likes to be bounced from the pad they pay rent on. I put my mouth back to the receiver.

"Our client is balking," I said. "She's had a fright and

wants to dig her heels in. The apartment's clear. I'm armed. I could camp out here tonight and—"

"Please put . . . Miss Quick on."

Two interruptions in one phone call. I wondered what was on fire.

I handed the receiver to our client.

"It's for you," I said.

Holly put the phone tight enough against her ear that I couldn't hear what my boss said. Whatever it was, it had an effect.

In the kind of stories Holly wrote, someone was always having a shock and the blood drains from their face. I'd never seen it happen in real life. Not until that moment. In a blink, our client's face went the sickly pale of cabbage and corpses.

"Okay," she said in a not-quite-whisper.

It took her three tries to get the receiver back onto its cradle.

"Can you please get down my suitcase?" she said. "It's on the top shelf in my closet. I believe . . . I believe I'm going to vomit."

She almost made it to the bathroom in time.

CHAPTER **27**

An hour later, we were all sitting in the office of Pentecost Investigations nursing drinks—Ms. P her honey wine, Holly a stiff bourbon, and I a coffee. It was shaping up to be another long night.

Holly had been installed in the second-floor guest room across the hall from Ms. Pentecost's bedroom and next door to mine. It shared a bathroom with mine, but was smaller and had a window that was permanently fastened shut and had been since I'd come to work there. Something about a reluctant witness doing a runner.

Whether Holly was pleased with the accommodations, I didn't know. She was so out of it when we arrived, I could have told her she was sleeping in the hall closet and she'd have gone along with it.

Now she was looking at Ms. Pentecost like she expected my boss to leap across her desk and bite her. Which was funny, since Ms. P hadn't changed clothes and looked more like she was ready for a cozy cup of tea and a crossword.

I might have even smiled, except I was a little too perturbed to be amused.

Of the three people in the room, I was the one out of the loop. I wasn't used to that, and it chafed. But I was trying to learn patience, so I sipped my coffee and waited for someone to speak first.

My boss kicked it off.

"I'm handing . . . Miss Parker . . . a letter. Addressed to . . . Horace Bellow. . . . It is dated November second . . . of last year. . . . Will?"

I took the letter and did the honors.

```
My Dearest Mister Bellow,
   I have been an avid reader of your work
for many years and recently had cause to
revisit your story "Five-Minute Head Start."
When your heroine was being chased through
the woods—the desperation and fear. You made
them so real. How he toyed with her, took
away her power and control. You understand
it. The righteous anger of those who have
been wronged.
   The plight and rage of the powerless!
   Then the exaltation as she exacted her
revenge on the man who humiliated her. I
could practically feel it in my blood. Her
triumph!
   The blade. The bullet. The noose. You bring
them to life with your words.
   It is truth. And in truth, beauty.
   I am sorry that no one else appreciates you
or your work properly. I hope to show you
that appreciation soon. To show my truelove.
   An Ardent Admirer
```

Ms. Pentecost nodded at me to hand it to our client, which I did. Holly snatched the document out of my hand and began scanning it. While she did that, I talked.

"Okay, I can see why you think this is our killer. He's writing to praise a three-year-old story. The same one that gets used as a kill-by-numbers on Conny Haggard not long after the letter is sent. There's also the mention of the noose. No noose in this story, but there is one in the Perkins murder. A bullet, too. But I don't see how this—"

I stopped.

Our client's eyes had locked on something near the bottom of the letter. I thought she was about to upchuck again, though I doubted she had much left in her.

With a shaking hand, she put the page on my boss's desk.

Now, maybe you're sharper than me. Also, you have the luxury of flipping back to Chapter 18 while I had to react in the moment.

"Okay, I give up," I said. "There are times I don't mind being in the dark, given the right circumstances. This isn't one of them."

Ms. Pentecost looked at our client.

"Would you . . . like to explain . . . or . . . should I?"

There was about thirty seconds of head-jerking and hand twitching. Finally, she turned in her chair and almost met my eyes.

"My name isn't Holly Quick," she said. "I mean, it is Holly Quick. I changed it. Legally. Officially . . . that's my name. But my name used to . . . The name I was born with was Henrietta Truelove."

The first name was merely unfortunate. The second . . .

"As in Daniel Truelove? The New York Ripper?"

A jerk. Like she'd been shocked. Then a single sharp nod.

"He was my father," she said.

Over the following days I would become a world-class expert on Daniel Truelove, so I'll save you the time by laying out the basics.

Between December 1923 and September 1924 Daniel Truelove murdered between twelve and twenty-two people on New York City's Lower East Side. The tally is usually aver-

aged out at around eighteen, but the actual figure will probably never be known.

The early deaths looked like muggings gone bad. The
victims were mostly drunks and prostitutes who were blud-
geoned to death, then robbed of what money they had on
them.

As the year carried on, the killer began focusing solely on
prostitutes, mostly foreign ones. He also picked up another
weapon—a straight razor. The crime scenes got bloodier. But
it wasn't until June of 1924 that enough dead streetwalkers
had piled up that the press decided to nickname him the New
York Ripper.

The name wasn't all that special. There had been
half a dozen so-called Rippers since the original stalked
Whitechapel.

It wasn't all that accurate, either. The London Ripper had
mutilated his victims. This New York version was content
with a single, deep slash across the throat.

Despite the fancy moniker and the high body count, the
killer's exploits rarely made the front page. I'd eventually talk
that detail over with my friend and former newshound Hollis
Graham.

He figured that part of it was because Truelove stuck to
prostitutes. These were the days of the Committee of Four-
teen and social-decency laws and weekend vice raids. A lot
of people probably thought Truelove was doing the city a
service.

But Hollis—who I call "Holly" but won't in this document so as not to confuse you or me—thought the bigger reason this New York Ripper never made it above the fold was
that he "only killed them."

" 'Only'?" I asked.

"Sure, sure," Hollis said. "If he wanted to get the nose of
the press, he should have carved them up a little. Posed them.

Something reporters could translate to 'he interfered with the bodies.' Let the readers' imaginations do the rest."

"Have I ever told you the press are blood-hungry monsters?"

"No, honey. *People* are blood-hungry monsters. The press are the monsters in charge of keeping the trough full."

It wasn't until the evening edition of September 23, 1924, that the New York Ripper hit the front page and stayed there. Early that morning, just before dawn, Maria Hernandez was cutting through an alley, hurrying to catch the train so she wouldn't be late for her job as a maid at the St. Regis.

Maybe she saw him and tried to run. Maybe he fumbled the cut. Whatever happened, people heard Maria scream.

The neighborhood was adjacent to the Ripper's usual territory, but it might as well have been a world away, surrounded as it was by mostly respectable apartments and houses full of families, many of whom were up and stirring even that early.

People didn't come running. This was still New York, after all. But they peered out of windows to see what was the commotion.

They saw a man stumble out of an alley and toss something into the gutter. It turned out to be the straight razor used to open Maria Hernandez's carotid.

Someone—several someones, actually—turned to their spouses and said something along the lines of, "What's Dan Truelove doing running through alleys at this hour?"

Everyone knew Truelove. The jovial handyman had been in their homes to fix leaks and adjust radiators and clean out flues. Half the supers on the block used him for jobs they didn't have the time or talent to tackle.

Everyone liked Truelove. More or less. Him and that young Mexican wife of his—Josefina, her name was—and their quiet little daughter. They liked him more when he was fixing their electrics. Less when he casually made comments about his wife. How she was lazy, but that wasn't her fault. It was her people. How he'd met her when he was serving in the army on the Mexican border. How he wasn't even sure his daughter was his because Josefina had been friendly with a lot of soldiers.

So when a pair of beat cops showed a few minutes after Maria Hernandez stopped breathing, a dozen witnesses were able to tell them right where they could find their suspect.

"It had been one of my bad nights," Holly told us twenty-three years after the fact, fingers thrumming madly against her bourbon glass. "I used to have these nights where I couldn't sleep. I couldn't keep still. I'd pace and pace and try to read myself to sleep, or my mother would read to me, but it wasn't working that evening, and he got so angry. Not at me. He never got angry at me. Just at Mama. It was her job, he said. Her job to get me to sleep and she couldn't do her job because she was . . . Didn't she know he had to get up early to go to work? That he needed his sleep? Didn't she understand how tight money was? And didn't she . . . ?"

Holly lost control of her hands and her expression for a minute, and I took the glass away from her. Ms. P and I waited, silent, until she could continue.

"He went out. I guess I finally fell asleep. I'm not sure how long. When I woke up, he was back and he was yelling and there was blood. I remember thinking he'd had an accident."

Holly's mother must have known different. Because when her husband turned and went into the bedroom, she grabbed her eleven-year-old daughter and ran out the apartment door. She made it all the way to the end of the hall.

"She was carrying me and we were almost at the stairs and . . . there was a sound," Holly said. "Mama fell but she didn't let go. I was trying to yell for my father. I didn't know it was him we were running from. But I couldn't get the words out, she was holding me so tight. Then there was another sound. It was so loud. I felt something punch me in the chest. It hurt so much. I couldn't breathe."

It was a good thing she couldn't get the words out. If she'd been able to make a sound, things might have turned out differently. As it was, Daniel Truelove put two bullets from an army issue revolver into his wife's back, one of them traveling through and hitting his daughter, its speed diminished so much that it only embedded halfway into the bone of her sternum.

Figuring them both for dead, he spent a third bullet on himself.

"There were people everywhere. One of our neighbors pulled my mother off and I heard her say, 'Oh, he's killed them. He's killed them both.'"

Holly fumbled out her pack of Chesterfields, and my boss and I silently decided to throw out our no-smoking rule. The flame did a jitterbug under the cigarette, but eventually she got it lit.

I went to the kitchen to fetch a bowl to serve as an ashtray and used the seventeen steps it took to order my thoughts. There were questions that needed asking, and I wanted to shift the more important ones to the front.

When I got back in my chair, Holly pre-empted me.

"How did you know?" she asked Ms. Pentecost. "Because you did know, didn't you? Before this letter."

That was at the top of my list.

My boss opened a drawer and pulled out a yellowed newspaper clipping. She slid it across the desk. Holly picked it up. I set the bowl on the table next to her and looked over her shoulder.

The clipping was a photo of a tenement stoop, a mass of policemen milling about, a sense of excitement. One policeman was caught walking down the steps carrying a young girl. Her arms were wrapped around his neck like he was the last life preserver on a sinking ship.

The news ink turned the blood on eleven-year-old Henrietta's nightdress pitch-black, but you got the idea. The girl was looking almost directly into the camera, eyes wide and filled with something that went a good way past shock.

"I had . . . not spent much . . . time with the details of . . . Daniel Truelove's crimes. But this photo . . . stayed in my mind. The . . . resemblance remains."

She wasn't wrong. It was a memorable snap.

Holly put the picture back on the desk.

"I guess the next question is how you got from Henrietta to Holly," I said, going back to my chair.

Holly downed the rest of her bourbon.

"I really did spend my life in the library. Anytime I could be there instead of at home," she said. "Naomi was a librarian there. Naomi Quick. She's the one who found me books she thought I'd like. She's the one who gave me paper and pencil and let me write in a corner by a window. I think . . . I think she knew things weren't going well at home. I doubt she knew just how unwell. The stories I wrote—the little childish fantasies? Many were about how Naomi and I lived in a secret room above the library and never left and were so happy."

She sucked in as much nicotine as her lungs would allow and let it loose in a billowing cloud.

"She was the only one who came to visit me in the hospital. The only one who wasn't a police officer, that is. She was a widow. Her husband died of Spanish flu, just like I said. They never had children and . . . And she loved me. Or at least liked me immensely. Eventually, they let me go home with her. Except everyone in the neighborhood knew who I was, who my father had been. I don't remember them saying anything, not to my face, but I know they said things to Naomi.

So we moved to the building I live in now, where no one knew either of us. She started working at a new library. Everything after . . . is much the same as I told you."

Not a bad lie, I thought. So close to the truth it was easy to tell with a straight face.

Holly used one cigarette to light another, then snuffed the first out in the bowl.

"Were you . . . legally adopted?" Ms. Pentecost asked.

"I was," she said. "That was when I had my name changed. 'Holly' was a nickname that Naomi called me. Because of a sweater I had with holly berries stitched on it. I wanted to sever everything, you see?"

But she couldn't sever everything. The point of Ms. P's question was that there was a paper trail. Somewhere in some dusty filing cabinet in some city building was a piece of paper saying that Henrietta Truelove and Holly Quick were one and the same.

And that was just one of a hundred ways someone might have made the connection.

There were plenty of corners that needed dusting, but the Swiss clock on the wall was approaching three a.m. and our client was starting to list sideways. Whatever adrenaline rush she'd been riding was on the wane.

I squeezed in the question at the top of my list.

"Who else knows?" I asked. "About your past?"

"No one," she said, which wasn't true, and I gave her a moment to realize that and do an actual tally. "Let me see. There's the man who filed the paperwork for the adoption. But he was very old—or I remember him as old—and I doubt he's alive. There's Naomi. But you've seen her. I don't know if she actually remembers much of anything anymore. And my therapist, Dr. Grayson. She knows."

"Have you told Marlo and Brent?" I asked.

She shook her head.

"I haven't," she said. "It was easier not to. They just know I don't like to talk about my childhood."

Ms. Pentecost leaned back in her seat and closed her eyes. She was probably pondering the same thing I was.

That wasn't the full list. There was my boss and me and probably a killer. How did he find out? What would he do next?

Ms. P opened her eyes.

"It is . . . very late, Miss Quick, and you . . . have had a traumatic . . . evening. Sleep . . . if you can. Miss Parker and . . . I have much to . . . discuss."

Damn right, I thought.

CHAPTER 28

I got Holly settled, explaining to her that breakfast could be obtained as early as seven, and that if she heard someone singing "Five Minutes More" in a Scottish brogue, not to be alarmed.

I had barely crossed the threshold of the office before Ms. Pentecost started in on it.

"Will. I know . . . that you must be—"

I held up a hand.

"Save your energy. You don't have the stamina to spend on a labored, heartfelt apology for keeping me in the dark, which is, I'm sure, what you were about to launch into. Even if you did have the stamina to spare, I would stop you. Because I understand."

She blinked. Three quick ones, real eye and false together. I always get a kick when I take her by surprise.

"You do?" she asked.

"I do," I answered. "I've been ordering my thoughts— some classified as questions, some as conclusions—and I understand why you did what you did. Specifically, keeping me in the dark that Holly Quick was really Henrietta True-love, daughter of the New York Ripper. Would you like to hear these thoughts?"

She gave me the nod. I grabbed my coffee cup, plopped

down in the armchair Holly had recently vacated, and pulled it up as close to Ms. P's desk as I could.

"The first question that popped into my head, not the most important, was how long have you known, but I was able to answer that for myself. It was the first time Holly was here. We were sitting here and your mind wandered for seven seconds. I know it was seven because I counted. At the time I was worried I'd have to have a conversation with your doctor, but really your brain was shuffling through the third-floor files trying to remember where you knew her face from. Correct?"

Another nod.

"So you basically knew from the jump. It's why you insisted on taking the case. And agreeing to Holly's stipulations. It didn't make sense to me at the time, but now . . . You *had* to take the case."

A line appeared between and a little above her eyes.

"Because you weren't taking on Holly Quick as a client," I said, leaning forward and tapping the newspaper clipping with a finger. "You were taking on *her*. You were taking on the girl whose father murdered eighteen people, then killed her mother and tried to kill her. No matter how it shook out, you figured you could handle it better than the police. They'd tear her life apart, and there's no way it wouldn't leak. Jesus Christ—I can't even imagine the headlines. Anyway, that's why you took it. Because it checked one of your boxes. But of course you couldn't tell me that. It wasn't your secret. It was Holly's. Talking about it here, to us, it almost did her in. So of course you couldn't tell her you knew, and you couldn't tell me anything."

I stopped for a sip of coffee, which had long gone cold.

"How am I doing so far?"

Her mouth twitched into something that was almost a smile.

"Very well," she said. "Thank you for . . . your forgiveness."

"No, no, no," I said. "Hold your horses. I didn't say anything about forgiveness. I said I understood, not that I agree. Even with all that, you still should have told me."

"I . . . understand . . . you're angry," Ms. P said.

"I'm not," I told her. "Check my pulse if you don't believe me. You see, I know you probably played it how you did because you didn't want to burden me. To have to go into Shirley and Wise every day and answer phones and pretend to be Jean goddamn Palmer when we've got this case—*this* case, with *this* client—in our lap, with Darryl goddamn Klinghorn doing the . . ."

I stopped and felt my pulse.

"Shit. I am angry," I said. "Here I've been going around wearing out brain cells, worrying about why you weren't letting me do my job, and why you didn't trust me anymore, and generally feeling like a ten-pound sack of crap in a five-pound pencil skirt. All for nothing. So, yeah, I'm angry. If the roles were reversed and I held something back about a case—and there is precedent for this—you would be rightfully pissed, too. After everything we've been through, I deserve to have all the facts. I understand why you didn't, but . . . Aw, nuts."

A tear was rolling down Ms. Pentecost's cheek. It was quickly followed by another. Then a third. I grabbed a handkerchief off my desk.

"I didn't mean to go that hard."

"Don't be . . . foolish," she said, taking the handkerchief and dabbing at her face. "You . . . know this . . . happens."

Meaning that during her symptom-heavy days, she was prone to crying jags.

She popped out her prosthetic eye, gave it a quick polish, and set it on the desk. Its not-quite-right shade of blue peered up at me from the nestled fold of my handkerchief.

"But I *am* sorry," she said. "Of course . . . I trust you.

I'm sorry if . . . I gave you reason to . . . believe otherwise.
I should . . . not have . . . prioritized . . . a client's secret over
our . . . relationship."

"I accept," I said.

She nodded and gave me that half smile mixed with what
I'd call chagrin if it were on another face.

"Many people . . . will need to . . . be questioned."

"Yeah," I said. "Holly's neighbors, to start with. See if anyone saw a stranger lurking. Someone watching the building.
Then there's our list of lists. We've got *Strange Crime*'s subscribers, but the rest still need fetching. I am assuming with
this latest development we don't want to farm this work out."

She shook her head.

"Certainly not," Ms. P declared. "Tomorrow morning . . .
you will call . . . Shirley and Wise and . . . give notice."

"Absolutely not," I told her. "I have not spent the last two
weeks being prim and proper and wearing those god-awful
pumps for nothing. Tomorrow I'm taking a crack at that safe.
Pun absolutely intended. Then I'll quit."

Shortly after, we retired for the night.

There was one last incident worth relating before I can
finally put a period on that very long day.

I was lying in bed, listening to the tick of my clock and
wondering if my brain would allow me to sleep before the sun
came up. I heard the other door to the bathroom open, then
running water, then a quick *shhtk-shhtk* of a lighter, then, a
minute later, the sound of quiet sobbing.

I got up, turned on my bedside lamp, slipped into my
robe, and knocked on the bathroom door.

"Yes?" Holly croaked.

I cracked open the door. Our client was sitting on the rim
of the tub in the dark, dressed in a set of wool pajamas, using
her cuff to smear salt water across the lenses of her glasses.

"I wanted a cigarette, but I couldn't get the window

open," she explained. "It's been nailed shut. Did you know that? I didn't want to make the bedding smell of cigarettes, so I came in here, and then my lighter wouldn't work, or more accurately my fingers wouldn't. This is so . . . *Embarrassing* isn't the right word. It isn't big enough. *Mortifying,* maybe. But the word is so overused its meaning has been lost."

I think she would have gone on like that if I didn't offer to escort her to the courtyard, where she could have a cigarette and some fresh air. I loaned her my second-best robe and slippers and we padded downstairs, through the kitchen, and out the back door.

We sat on the back step and she smoked and I looked at her sideways, trying to decide if I could have matched her face with that twenty-three-year-old newspaper photo if I didn't know to look for it.

I decided it was a fifty-to-one shot and that's why the business fell under "Pe" in the phone book and not "Pa."

I don't mention this incident to prove my boss was a genius. There are plenty better examples. And I don't bring it up to show how good I am at calming crying women—two in one night!

I don't even bring it up because of something she said or I said, because if either of us said anything during those few minutes, I don't remember it.

I include it here because trying to decide if I could see Henrietta in Holly, I had to think about that girl. The one who took a bullet in the chest and had to get up and keep going. About the secrets and the shame she'd had to lug along with her.

Somewhere in there, as we sat in silence and I watched Holly blow out smoke and frozen breath in equal measure, she went from nuisance to actual client.

I've had a lot of time with this. Time to think about my own childhood. My father had never murdered anybody—at least none that I knew of—but he'd caused plenty of pain. He'd helped usher my mother to an early grave and sent me on the run.

Did I see those parallels between Holly and myself, then? I'm not sure.

All I know is that Holly had rubbed me wrong. I hadn't understood why we were letting her dictate terms, so I was seeing her more as an obstacle than a client. An irrational annoyance. Consequently, the case had been about the puzzle.

Now it was about the person.

A woman who was doing the absolute best she could to hold herself and her world together. Probably better than I would have done, given the same circumstances. We're going to get this guy, I thought. We're going to find him and keep Holly and her secrets safe.

Eventually I walked her back upstairs. She thanked me and we exchanged good nights. Back in my bed, the smell of Chesterfields still clinging to me, I wondered if she would be able to sleep.

I wouldn't have been able to, if I were her, I thought.

But I wasn't her. So I did.

CHAPTER 29

I have performed many difficult feats in my life. Managing to be at my desk at Shirley & Wise at nine a.m. Monday morning, properly bathed and dressed, having forgotten only lipstick, ranks as one of the most impressive.

Mrs. Jean Palmer was not the picture of health or efficiency that Monday, but people forgave her. It was her sister, you see? The spinster sister who lived in Oakland, California? She was very ill and Jean was concerned that she didn't have anyone to look after her.

Peggy was especially effusive, asking if there was anything I needed. I told her no, I would be fine.

Again, I felt bad about lying to her. But I wouldn't have to do it for much longer.

Jean's sister was going to take a turn for the worse that evening, and Jean would call in the next day and say she had to make an emergency trip to the West Coast. After which Jean Palmer would cease to exist, having hopefully served her purpose.

The day went by like any other, except instead of spending lunch in the Automat, I ate a cold ham sandwich at my desk and made a couple of personal calls, first making sure no one was in earshot.

One was to the office to see how things were in my absence. I was told by Mrs. Campbell that Ms. Pentecost was on the upswing and that her flare-up seemed—fingers crossed—to be of the forty-eight-hour variety.

I was also informed that Holly was settling in fine. She'd slept until nearly noon, then devoured three fried eggs, four slices of toast, and enough coffee to raise the dead.

"She's a queer one, that girl," Mrs. Campbell said. "I think I make her nervous."

"Don't take it personally. She's naturally nervous."

"How long will she be staying, do ya think? I've got shopping to do tomorrow."

I told her I couldn't even hazard a guess and to shop on the side of caution.

The second call was to Holly's super. I told him about the possible break-in, that Holly didn't want to involve the police, and that she'd be staying with us for the time being. Mr. Cosmo was properly abashed.

"This is so terrible, that someone would do this," he said. "Why, if I had been there, I would have—"

He finished the sentence in a language I didn't know. But a threat's a threat in any tongue.

"If you don't mind, I'd like to stop by the building tomorrow and talk to your tenants," I said. "There's the possibility they saw someone hanging around who didn't belong. Would you mind making introductions?"

He said he would be happy to, and would be installing a new lock on the front door and on Holly's door, even if he had to pay for it out of his own pocket.

I spent the rest of the day trying not to obsess over that evening's assignment.

Which was this:

Stay at my desk an extra half an hour to finish up on some typing. Long enough so the office was mostly vacant.

Pack up my things like normal and head down the hall to the women's restroom.

Choose the least popular stall. There's always one, and I'd been there long enough to identify it as the one farthest from the door, with the wobbly seat.

Hang my coat and bag—a satchel so big it put Holly's to shame—from the hook on the back of the stall door, sit, and wait. Only one person came in during that time. I tucked my feet up and held my breath until she left.

When my watch said seven p.m., I slipped out of the booth, out of the bathroom, and down the hall to Shirley & Wise. I didn't stop and press my ear to the door. A temp secretary who forgot her apartment keys in her desk drawer wouldn't do that, and that's what I was if anybody asked. I just strolled in like I was supposed to be there.

Not a typewriter was stirring, and only the minimum number of lights were left on. For the mice, I assumed.

I walked straight to Ken Shirley's office, went inside, closed the door behind me, and flipped on the lights. I put my bag on the desk and took out a notebook, a pencil, and the stethoscope Jules had lent me. Remaining in the bag were my brand-new Leica and a dozen rolls of film, which I'd use to photograph the contents of the safe, should I be successful.

According to Jules, the stethoscope was unnecessary and "God must love thieves, because the naked human ear is the perfect instrument for the detection of a lock's manipulations."

I liked my naked ear fine, but I was an amateur and never turned down an edge.

With the stethoscope plugged into my ears, I used one hand to dial and the other to hold the diaphragm of the stethoscope over where the safe's innards would be.

Then I turned the dial and listened, turned the dial and listened. Occasionally I would make a mark in my notebook. Then back to listening.

A good safecracker can get a simple three-turn job open in under ten minutes. Five, if you're of Jules's caliber. I was approaching the twenty-minute mark when I got the second digit. What I'd taken for a click had apparently been something else, and I'd had to start over.

I was so intent on the job at hand I didn't hear the footsteps until they were right outside Shirley's door.

If I've ever moved faster, I don't know it. I swung the painting shut, grabbed my bag, and practically leapt over the desk. I crouched down just as the door opened. I caught the briefest glimpse of Ken Shirley as he stepped in.

Luckily the front of the desk was a solid wood panel. I squirmed past the wheels of his chair and squeezed into the hollow under the desk.

Shit, I thought. The lights!

Would he notice? Or would he assume he'd left them on himself?

There was the sound of the painting swinging open, then three spins of the dial and the squeak of the safe door. Papers flipping. A muttered, "Here it is."

Footsteps, followed quickly by the sight of the feet themselves. I was positive that Shirley was going to pull his chair out, have a seat, wheel forward, and run his shins right into his secretary's head.

I was working through what choke holds I could throw on him when, still standing, he picked up the phone and gave the operator a number.

"Simon? It's Ken Shirley. The opening date on the Hawkins account was June seventh, 1943. . . . That's right. I'm sorry for the confusion. . . . Thanks. . . . You have a good night, too."

The tapping of the switch hook. Another request to the operator.

"Vivianne. . . . Yes, I'm heading there now. . . . I know. . . . No, I didn't do this on purpose. . . . I like your sister immensely. It's that layabout husband of hers I can't stand. Just tell them I'll be there in half an hour."

The sound of the phone hanging up. Then a string of words that reinforced Shirley's opinion of both sister- and brother-in-law.

The sound of the file being put back into the safe, the safe door closing, the painting closing, and then footsteps to the door, open, out, close.

I let out the longest, shakiest breath ever exhaled. I counted to three hundred, then got out from under the desk. My legs almost collapsed beneath me. All I could hear was the panicked beating of my heart. Naked or not, my ears were shot.

Jules had told me that the best thieves were in and out of a place in fifteen minutes. Any longer and the chance of getting caught skyrocketed.

I thought about calling it quits.

Then I thought about what I'd heard when Shirley was leaving. Or more specifically, what I didn't hear.

I didn't hear him spin the dial on the safe.

I unlatched the sailboat, grabbed the handle of the safe, whispered a prayer, and pulled.

It swung open.

Jules was right. God must love thieves.

CHAPTER 30

I made it home in time to catch the tail end of dinner. Photographing all of the documents in the safe had taken another twenty minutes and burned through my entire stock of film.

I dropped my bag off at my desk before walking into the dining room, where I found Holly and Ms. Pentecost working through the last of their plum pudding and keeping up a breakneck pace between swallows. The latter was back in real clothes, her hair in its usual braids, which was another good sign.

"That must be part of the job," Holly was saying. "At least a small part."

"Of course. Though I do not know if when you say the word 'clue,' we are both thinking of the same thing."

"Oh, of course not. Words are so vague sometimes. So imprecise."

"Absolutely."

"But, anyway, what was I saying? Oh, yes! Clues are the hardest part of my job. Figuring out how to slip them in. A scrap of paper on the windowsill, a bird's feather stuck to the bottom of a dead man's boot. Of course I know these things don't really happen, or if they do they're mostly meaningless."

"Patterns and coincidences," Ms. P said.

"What do you mean?"

A pause for mastication.

"Other words for clues. Patterns and coincidences. A feather on the bottom of a shoe might break a case, but only if you know that it's an anomaly. And to know that, you must know, well, everything you possibly can about a victim. When understanding a person, every detail becomes relevant."

I'd been part of this conversation with Ms. Pentecost many times, but never from the outside. Occasionally, when I was feeling bored or snippy, I would wade into the argument with "Many things, taken singularly, don't have anything to do with anything. If it wasn't for the person they happened to having gotten murdered, nobody would care, including us."

To which she would respond with something like "Once you start picking and choosing what is relevant in a life, you edge closer to picking and choosing what lives are relevant."

Which would usually shut me up.

Holly finished scraping her bowl clean and turned to see me in the doorway. She actually smiled. I'd seen her smile before. I'd just never been the recipient.

"Hello," she said. "We were just talking about—"

"Clues and patterns and relevance. I heard."

I addressed my boss. "The errand has been run."

"And?"

"Satisfactory. I'm going to pop into the basement. I should have everything done by bedtime."

Holly studied the back-and-forth, trying to figure out if any of it pertained to her. Deciding it didn't, she swerved back to talking patterns and clues and so forth.

Seeing I wasn't needed, I slipped out and descended into the basement. If you'll recall, I mentioned a corner had been given over to a project of mine. That project was a darkroom.

I'd nailed up some plywood and hung black velvet drapes, creating a lightproof box the size of a largish closet. I sourced the equipment from a handful of pawnshops and a photography studio in Harlem.

I'd like to say I did all this because—as Peggy suggested—I needed something in my life besides work. Really, I was just tired of waiting for prints to come back from the developer. Also, occasionally we might not want a third eye to see what we'd been taking snaps of.

Photographs taken during the commission of a felony, to use one example.

Developing took me past midnight, and by the time I was finished I reeked of chemicals and was in possession of several dozen photographs and a sore back.

I left the photos lying out on the mats to dry and went up to the office. Finding it dark, I headed upstairs. At the second-floor landing I caught the sound of typing coming from the guest room. I recognized the cadence as being from my portable Underwood. I had told Holly she was free to borrow it.

I thought about knocking and warning her about the dodgy return but I figured she'd discovered it by now.

On the third floor I found Ms. Pentecost seated in the armchair, Klinghorn's report on one knee, the Truelove file on the other.

"Any new insights?" I asked.

"Merely checking to see if there are any intersections," she explained. "A name or place."

"Like maybe the son of Truelove's fifth victim was Perkins's next-door neighbor? Something like that?"

"I admit it feels like grasping at straws. But better to be thorough now than feel foolish later."

"Well, I have a straw, but I don't know how useful it'll be to pluck at. I would have brought it up last night, but I didn't want to do it with Holly present. She was overwhelmed as it was. Then I got distracted by revelations and apologies. Anyway, here's the deal."

I told her about Holly's relationship with Marlo and Brent.

"You think this could be relevant?" she asked.

"I don't know," I said. "She says they don't know about her history, but maybe she talks in her sleep. All I know is the question needs to be asked. I'll have to come up with a clever way of asking it that doesn't out our client. Bring up Truelove somehow and see what their reaction is."

She nodded. "Perhaps Miss Quick will have a suggestion."

"Perhaps," I said. "I'll run it by her in the morning. Right before I leave to interview her neighbors and right after I package the photographs off to Sid."

Sid was a former mob moneyman who now served as our expert on all things financial.

"Nothing leapt out at me when I was taking the snaps," I said. "At least nothing that would interest Olivia Waterhouse. But if there's a nugget in there, Sid will dig it out."

With the program for tomorrow set, I bade her good night and went downstairs to my bedroom. A quick shower did away with the chemical smell and some of my backache.

Again, I thought about knocking on Holly's door, this time to say good night. But the typewriter was still going, and I didn't want to interrupt.

I tucked myself in, and let the clatter of the Underwood lull me to sleep.

It was the scream that woke me. I sat up in bed, heart pounding. Had it been real, or a dream? It was still dark. I peered at my clock to see that I'd only been in bed an hour.

Hurried footsteps sounded from the third floor.

I jumped out of bed, threw on a robe, and went into the hall. The guest room door was open. I looked in and found the lamp on and the room vacant. I ran to the stairs and caught Ms. Pentecost on her way down from the archives.

"The courtyard," she said, letting me get ahead of her.

I took the stairs two at a time, flying through the kitchen and out the back door, nearly barreling straight into Holly. She was wide-eyed, cigarette still clutched in her trembling fingers. She used it to point to the left-side gate. It was open, which it shouldn't have been. I walked toward it, wishing I'd had the presence of mind to grab a gun.

A lamp came on in the carriage house, Mrs. Campbell's silhouette at the window. The light was just enough to illuminate something lying in the open gateway.

The closer I got, the more details I could pick out.

A pair of feet, one shoe missing. A dark overcoat spread open to reveal a bloody shirt. One arm tucked under, the other pointing back into the alley.

A familiar face, white and bloodless, mouth open.

I crouched down to examine what was shoved between his teeth. Business cards. A whole stack of them. One had fallen out and was sitting on his collar. I picked it up.

"What is it?"

I turned to see Ms. Pentecost standing in the kitchen door, one arm wrapped around our client.

There was a spot of blood on the card, but it was still plenty legible.

DARRYL KLINGHORN
Private Investigation Services

CHAPTER 31

Nine hours. That's how long the brownstone was given over to the police.

Mrs. Campbell brewed so much coffee and baked so many scones I was starting to suspect some officers were lingering just to fill up on baked goods. The police photographer, who took snaps of just about every corner of the house, inside and out, ate three of the scones all by himself, which I can testify weigh about half a pound each.

Mrs. Campbell's efforts may also be why we were allowed to be questioned in the office rather than taken to a station house. No scones there, and vastly inferior coffee.

So I sat at my desk chair and told the same story first to a beat cop, then a sergeant, and then finally to Detective Donald Staples, who showed up about an hour into the process, looking criminally fresh for three in the morning.

He'd ditched his no-questions questioning method, and was the one who came closest to tripping me up.

Detective Staples: Are you in the habit of going outside for a cigarette so late in the evening?
Will Parker: Not in the habit, no.
DS: So why tonight?
WP: I'd been up late and couldn't get to sleep. A cigarette relaxes me.

DS: Why go outside? You have a window in your room, don't you?

    WP: That lets the heat out, and it takes forever to get that room warm again.

Then later on.

DS: And you said you saw him from the doorway of the kitchen?

    WP: No, I said I was almost on top of him when I saw him.

DS: You didn't notice the gate was open?

    WP: It was dark. And it wasn't open very far.

DS: The neighbors said they heard a scream.

    WP: I'll have to apologize for waking them up.

DS: I didn't take you for a screamer.

    WP: You trip over a corpse in the middle of the night and see what sound you make.

And so forth.

You might be asking why a private investigator would risk her personal liberty and professional license by lying to the police.

The answer? Orders.

As soon as I told her that Klinghorn's corpse had been dropped on our back door, Ms. Pentecost realized what we had on our hands and that the police would have to be called. Lights had come on in some neighboring houses. Just our luck that we caught the one time that New Yorkers weren't going to roll over and go back to sleep.

She ushered me, Holly, and Mrs. Campbell into the kitchen and started throwing orders.

To Mrs. Campbell: "Eleanor, will you please go up to the guest room and move all of Miss Quick's possessions into Will's room? The closet should do. If they bother to look there, the searchers will be men and unlikely to notice any difference in sizes."

To me: "Take Miss Quick up to the birdhouse. Make sure she is well provisioned. She could be up there for many hours and it is quite cold. Feel free to go through my own clothes."

To all three of us: "The police will soon be here. It's likely they will search the brownstone and the carriage house as well. I would like them to find no evidence of Miss Quick's presence as a guest in this house. Will—you will tell them you were the one to discover the body. I'll leave it to you to devise a plausible scenario."

Holly tried to interrupt here but Ms. P talked through her.

"The police are aware that Mr. Klinghorn was employed by me to gather information about three murders. It is inevitable that they will conclude that the culprit of one of these crimes is responsible for his death. If you are found to be a guest here, they will ask who you are and why you are here. A cursory investigation will reveal your pen names and, eventually, their link to the murders. Armed with that information, and with the fact that you were the one to discover the body, they will thoroughly question you, perhaps going so far as to arrest you as a material witness. Sooner or later—likely sooner—your past will be revealed."

Back to Mrs. Campbell and me: "This will require extensive lying to the authorities. It will place us all in legal jeopardy. I cannot order you to—"

I don't remember who stopped her first. But we assured her that if she was willing to lead, we were ready to follow.

"Good," Ms. P said. "Then let's get to it. I will phone the police. I shall feign vocal weakness to buy us some time."

That's how you know she was serious. Playing up her disease wasn't something she did for kicks.

While Mrs. Campbell cleaned out the guest room, I grabbed my second-best overcoat and then went rummaging through my boss's things, coming out with a heavy wool sweater, a pair of long johns, socks, gloves, and a five-foot-long scarf that had been sent by a women's group in Topeka in thanks for Ms. Pentecost corresponding with them.

Then I took Holly up to the third-floor archives.

"Get into all that. Like Ms. Pentecost said, I don't know how long you'll be up there."

If she had questions, she held them, and started stripping down so she could build from the long johns up. Meanwhile, I started an operation that involved a tall ladder and the unlatching of one of the skylights.

I went up the ladder first, then she followed, nearly unrecognizable under all the layers. At least the wind wasn't blowing, I thought. And the temperature was double digits, though that first digit was a two.

I've never had cause to describe the roof of our brownstone before and I'm not going to spend many words on it now. All you need to know is that someone who lived there used to keep pigeons and the frame of the coop was still intact.

Also on the roof was a beach chair that I'd brought up three summers back when I decided to try tanning. That bright idea cost me two bottles of calamine lotion and a layer of skin, but the chair fit inside the old coop, so Holly wouldn't be sitting on cold tar paper.

I unfolded the chair and handed Holly a bag of goods I'd grabbed from the kitchen. There were apples, bread, cheese, a dozen homemade oatmeal raisin cookies, and a quart of milk.

"I'll try and sneak up something hot, but I can't make any promises," I said. "Stay in the coop. There are buildings within eyeshot once the sun's up."

I was about to leave when she grabbed my wrist.

"Will? That man . . . ?"

"I know. It wasn't pretty."

"No, I . . . I've seen that before. I've *written* that before. It's from 'Death Gets a Dial Tone.'"

"I don't think I know that one. Is it Horace Bellow?"

"Yes," she said. "You don't know it because it's not published. It's one of the stories I just turned in."

"Are you sure?" I asked.

"Yes! The protagonist—he's a private detective—crosses a gang of thieves, so they murder his old partner as a warning. Except it wasn't business cards. It was pages from a phone book."

That sparked three dozen questions but I forced myself to shelve all of them.

"Okay," I said. "We'll work that out later. Right now, just keep quiet and try and stay warm."

I was almost to the skylight when I ran back to her.

"Give me your cigarettes and lighter."

"What?"

"First, you can't smoke up here. What if a cop looks up at the wrong moment and sees a trail of smoke? Second, I need a story for being out in the courtyard at two in the morning and that's as good a one as any."

Very reluctantly she handed over the Chesterfields and her lighter.

By the time I got back downstairs, the guest room was clear, Ms. Pentecost was off the phone, and the police were on the way. At the last moment, I remembered the photos drying in the basement. I ran down, scooped them into a stack, and tucked the lot of them underneath one of the wrestling mats.

If a flatfoot managed to find them, he deserved a promotion.

Ms. Pentecost and I had about three minutes to ourselves, sitting in the office, waiting for the first wave to arrive. I told her about Holly's revelation—that Klinghorn's murder was another plagiarism job.

"I'm assuming the killer found the carbon copy when he broke into her apartment," I said.

My boss paused to think it over, but we didn't have time for pauses.

"This is going to be tricky," I told her.

"I know."

I gave her a look. We'd been around each other long enough for her to decipher it.

"Yes," she said. "I'm sure I want to commit to this stratagem. I'm not sure it's the correct one. But I'm ready to commit."

I gave a sigh and leaned back in my chair. Again—I trusted Lillian Pentecost. Even when she led me unto perjury.

She must have read the sigh as frustration because she felt the need to expound.

"I told Miss Quick that we were doing this to prevent her life from becoming public, but that's only half the reason. There is a good chance the police will arrest her for these murders."

"She's in the open for Haggard. But she's got an alibi for Perkins and Checchetto."

I found the flaw before I even finished the sentence. Her alibis were her married lovers. Not only would the cops toss them as fabricated, but Holly's arrangement with Brent and Marlo would become public knowledge.

"Okay, you're right," I said. "Her alibi might be worse than not having one at all. Of course they'll arrest her. The stories are hers. She's a Truelove. Like father, like daughter. That's the frame they'll build. Everything else will be window dressing."

"Indeed," Ms. P said.

"In case you were curious, Klinghorn had a good bit of gore on his shirt. I kept half an eye on Holly while she was changing. If she had any blood on her, I didn't see it."

Ms. P raised an eyebrow.

"Hey, I'm just covering our bases," I said. "She's starting to grow on me and I don't want to get bitten."

Ms. P grunted. Then said, "The kitchen sink?"

"Spotless and dry. Same for the bathroom."

She nodded. I nodded back.

After a moment I said, "You ever think we might be a little too suspicious?"

Another easily decipherable look.

"Yeah, I got it. No such thing. Now get your lying face on—I think I hear the cops coming up the steps."

The nine hours had begun.

CHAPTER *32*

While the flow of information was mostly from us to them, I was able to learn a few things by delivering coffee and scones and keeping my ears open.

Klinghorn had been killed sometime between midnight and two a.m., stabbed twice in the chest. One of the two looked like it had slipped through his ribs and hit his heart. That would have been an instant kill, and either it was a lucky shot or the killer had practice.

There was a blood pool in the alley. Not a big one, but enough to suggest Klinghorn was killed there. Some of it was smeared, which made the cops think the body had been moved after. They surmised it was to get at his pockets. I had money on the killer wanting to arrange the body to better fit Holly's story.

Regarding the more faded bloodstains around the drain, I told them to talk to Mrs. Campbell.

"Ask her about the haggis," I said. "Just don't expect her to give you the secret recipe."

In addition, the padlock on the gate had been snapped with bolt cutters. None were found in the vicinity. There were plenty of fingerprints, most of them on the business cards stuffed in Klinghorn's mouth. To the naked eye, they all belonged to the victim.

That was the lot.

Ms. Pentecost had her own hour-long session with Staples. I wasn't in the room for it, but I knew all the best places to eavesdrop.

Detective Staples: You've had Mr. Klinghorn's report on these murders for three days, and you say you've done nothing with it.

    Lillian Pentecost: I've read through it, but I have not pursued any avenue of investigation.

DS: You've had no contact with him since then?

    LP: I have not.

DS: What instructions did you give him after he turned this report in?

    LP: None. I thanked him and paid him for his time.

DS: When you spoke with him, did he give any indication that he knew the identity of who killed any of these men?

    LP: He did not.

DS: Is there anything in this report that indicates that Mr. Klinghorn stumbled on something, or someone? That he'd uncovered a murderer?

    LP: There is not.

DS: So, if I go through that file, I won't find any possible suspects mentioned.

    LP: You will find many names. But no one whom Mr. Klinghorn suggested as a suspect for any of the murders.

DS: Uh-huh.

We're talking with his wife right now. She keeps the books. She also keeps copies of all his paperwork. We'll be taking a look at her copy of this report as well. Will we find anything in there that isn't in your copy?

    LP: If you are suggesting that I removed anything from my copy of the report before giving it to you, I did not. If there's something in Mr. Klinghorn's personal copy that was not in mine, it was his doing.

DS: *Uh-huh.*

And you didn't hire him again? A follow-up job, maybe?

LP: I did not. I took his report and paid him his fee for services rendered. Miss Parker can show you the check stub. I have not seen or spoken to Mr. Klinghorn since, and I had not employed him for any additional jobs.

DS: *That should be easy enough to confirm with his wife. What moves have you made in regards to the Checchetto case since we last talked?*

LP: What moves?

DS: *You're actively investigating it, aren't you?*

LP: I am not.

Though if you're referring to Miss Parker's visit to Jessup Quincannon, that was part of my original inquiry. I had asked Mr. Klinghorn not to approach Quincannon, believing he would not be admitted.

DS: *But Miss Parker was. What did he tell her?*

LP: That none of his members were responsible for Mr. Checchetto's death.

DS: *Anything else?*

LP: Nothing of use. It was a short conversation—one that ended by Mr. Quincannon making a somewhat rude suggestion to Miss Parker.

DS: *Uh-huh.*

Now, going back . . .

And so on.

Staples left with one of our two copies of Klinghorn's report and little satisfaction from me or my boss. My naked ear wasn't around for his chat with Mrs. Campbell, but I had faith in her ability to stick to a script.

I managed to sneak out of the brownstone exactly once. To a pay phone at the deli two blocks away. Jean Palmer's sister in Oakland had taken a turn for the worse and she passed on her regrets to Ken Shirley.

I bought a pack of Chesterfields at the deli in case anyone wondered where I'd gone. No one noticed or asked.

When the door closed on the last flatfoot, Mrs. Campbell immediately got to cleaning. There were muddy footprints from our front door all the way through to the back.

I moved to the stairs, intending to rescue Holly, then thought better of it. Staples was exactly the sort to find an excuse to circle back for one last question. I decided that if Holly hadn't frozen yet, she could stand another ten minutes.

I placed a call to a courier service relied upon for its discretion and arranged for them to pick up the photos and deliver them to Sid. I told them to come through the right-side alley. The front door might be watched and the left-side alley had a chalk outline.

Then I went up to the second floor and knocked on Ms. Pentecost's bedroom door. She'd retired there after her interview, pleading exhaustion. I found her sitting in her chair by the window, an issue of *Strange Crime* open in front of her.

Looking over her shoulder, I expected to find one of Holly's stories. Instead, it was a full-page ad for Vita-Glow— a medication for nervous exhaustion. It was one of those deals where you fill out a survey about your health and habits and they send you a free sample and a catalog of not-so-free samples.

"If you're placing an order, make it a double," I said.

She squinted up at me, her good eye scattershot with red.

"Nearly two-thirds of the ads in this magazine are for health products," she said. "And the questions this survey asks are surprisingly personal."

"The price of putting more pep in your step," I said. "All the crime pulps lean heavy on the snake-oil salesmen. Must be reading about all that death. Makes a person keen to keep spirit and body attached."

"Have you retrieved Miss Quick?"

"Not yet. I'm counting to five hundred in case one of the cops forgot a notebook or something."

She looked out the window. The sun was just clearing high noon.

"At least the wind has not been severe," she said. "And the sun has been bright."

"Yeah, it's practically swimsuit weather. What's the program once I fetch her?"

She flipped the magazine closed, stood from the chair, and immediately stumbled. I caught her arm and propped her up.

"The program is to sleep for a few hours," she said. "Then we will discuss a path forward."

Ms. P usually resents it when I play lady-in-waiting, but she let me help her swap her blouse and trousers for a nightdress. Her fingers were giving her issues, so I plucked the pins out of her braids, breaking the levee on that streak of iron gray. It looked to be about an eighth of an inch thicker than the last time I'd checked.

I left her to tuck herself in, then headed up to the roof. I expected to find a wreck—physical, emotional, or both. At the very least, Holly should have been chewing at the tar paper for want of a smoke.

I heard her before I saw her. Curled up on my sunning chair, snug inside her borrowed clothes, snoring away.

I almost felt sorry to wake her up.

CHAPTER 33

We are committed now. Not just to solving these murders, but to doing so swiftly, covertly, and without revealing Miss Quick's background. Preferably, without revealing her involvement whatsoever. She will remain sequestered here, at least for the time being, and not venture anywhere unchaperoned. Not until the killer is caught.

"To be clear, this is not a simple task. The police outmatch us in manpower, and while they do not know of the real relationship among the three original murders, they will consider them linked by Mr. Klinghorn's death, at least temporarily.

"I will entertain all suggestions. Where will the police not go? Where might we find success where they will not?"

It was quite a speech. Ms. Pentecost usually saved them for the office, but the three of us—she, Holly, and I—had just done away with a ten p.m. breakfast of scrambled eggs and sausage, so we got the speech in the dining room. Even Mrs. Campbell, who was standing in the doorway, thumbs hooked around the strings of her apron, was included.

I kicked things off by sharing my theory about the killer seeing the copy of "Death Gets a Dial Tone" when they broke into Holly's place.

There was the counterargument that there were others who'd seen the story—namely Brent and Marlo—and they weren't in the clear. Holly had been with Marlo for the Perkins killing, but not Brent. And while she had been with both during Checchetto's murder, I assumed that at some point in the evening, sleep had been involved. Which means either Marlo or Brent could have slipped out.

I did not voice this counterargument, because it was too late in the day to start a fight with the client. She had recovered from her rooftop ordeal but hadn't quite shaken off the cold. She was bundled in a sweater and skirt, both heavy wool in variations of yellow, more buttercup than canary.

"Essentially, knowledge of this unpublished story does not narrow our suspect list," Ms. P summarized.

Holly raised her hand.

"This isn't Miss Reeder's third-grade English class," I told her. "Just let it fly."

"So if I understand properly, this man, Mr. Klinghorn— you hired him to gather facts about the three victims, yes?"

"We did," I said. "The reasons are convoluted and somewhat confidential. We wanted a lot of facts as quickly as possible, and Klinghorn could manage that."

Holly cocked and twiddled, and just when I thought she was going to drop it, she said, "Then Mr. Klinghorn's murder does narrow things down, doesn't it? I mean, he must have met the killer. Or come in contact with him—assuming it's a him. I've been picturing a him. How else would the killer know Mr. Klinghorn was on the case, or that he was working for you?"

I looked at my boss. "One of us should have thought of that," I said. "I vote you, since you're the genius."

"Did Mr. Klinghorn document who he spoke with?" Holly asked.

"Boy, did he."

I went into the office, opened the safe, and pulled out our last remaining copy of Klinghorn's report. Then I went back into the dining room and dropped the file on the table.

We all looked at it. Somewhere inside a killer was lurking.

"May I?" Holly asked.

I raised an eyebrow at my boss. She nodded.

"Go to town," I said. "Raise your hand if anything rings a bell."

Holly opened the file and dove in.

"You should talk to his missus."

That came from Mrs. Campbell, still standing in the kitchen doorway.

"The cops have been all over her," I said. "The way Staples was playing it, I get the feeling she couldn't tell them much."

Mrs. Campbell shook her head. "They were all men that asked her, weren't they? She might have something to say to you she wouldn't let slip to them."

We didn't just keep her around for her neeps and tatties.

"First thing in the morning," Mrs. Campbell said. "Nice and early."

"You don't think she'll be a wreck?"

"Grief's a funny thing. It can take some time before it comes on. Besides, women are usually more resilient than you think."

Ain't that the truth.

CHAPTER 34

The time I'd spent worrying whether Dolores Kling-horn had any interest in seeing me were wasted minutes.

As soon as she saw who it was knocking at the door of their basement apartment in the East Village at ten a.m., she yanked me inside, telling me how good it was to see me and how nice I was to come and would I have a slice of cake, everyone had been dropping off food and she was running out of counter space, and how about a cup of coffee to go with that?

Which is how I ended up sitting at the kitchen table with Dolores "call me Dolly" and nibbling at an apple-cinnamon number.

"Neighbors I say hello to maybe twice a year have been dropping off this and that. I appreciate it. I'm from the Mid-west. Cleveland, originally. I understand the impulse. Some-body dies, get out the bundt pan. But I wish they'd let up."

I'd met Dolly Klinghorn in passing, and there had been a picture of her in the *Life* article with her husband, but I'd never noticed before how much of an odd pair she and her husband made.

He was nailed to my memory as a sly weasel of a man, always on the come, always searching for the spotlight. Dolly was the picture of a happy housewife: pushing fifty, blond rolls turning gently to gray, wearing the years well in a pink button-front she'd probably stitched herself from a McCall's pattern.

The softness to her husband's slickness.

"Of course I know half of them are just nosy. The police were in and out all yesterday. Then there's this."

"This" was the Wednesday edition of the *Times* sitting on the kitchen table between our plates. DETECTIVE FOUND SLAIN OUTSIDE LILLIAN PENTECOST'S BROOKLYN HOME. Front page and above the fold.

At least they'd specified "outside."

It didn't have much. After the fifth call from a reporter, I'd turned off the ringer on the phones. A couple journos had come knocking the night before. We kept Holly away from the windows and I shouted, "We are not taking questions!" through the mail slot.

"Mrs. Strazynski from down the hall?" Dolly was saying. "Eighty if she's a day and even she was all 'Do they know more about happened yet, dear? Was it someone's husband, do you think?' Bloodthirsty old bat."

Maybe not so soft.

"Do they know more?" I asked.

"The cops are clueless," Dolly said, grabbing another tissue from a quickly depleting box. "All they had were questions. What was he working on? Did he have any fights? Any arguments? Owe anybody money? One of the detectives had a bunch of questions about you and your boss. I didn't tell them much. Darryl never trusted the cops. Not after California. He used them when he could, but he always watched his back around them."

"So do you mind if I ask some questions?" I said. "I know it's not a good time."

"Honey, there's never gonna be a good time for this. So fire away. Don't mind the tears. I can't get them to stop."

I led her through the last couple of weeks, tracing where

her husband had been and when. No surprises. It was the schedule of a man frantically doing background on three murders simultaneously, and it lined up with what he'd included in his report.

"What about after he turned in the report on Friday?" I asked. "What was he up to?"

"He was out of the office most of the weekend. We had two cases on the books. One looking into a woman pulling an insurance scam. One basic peepshow. That's where we try to catch a cheating spouse in the act. Both were cut-and-dried. The cops are following up on both, but I don't think they'll find anything. He hadn't gotten far enough in either to piss anyone off. I think like you think—his death came from looking into those murders."

I did away with the last bite of cake and leaned back in my chair. I don't know what I expected to find out. If Klinghorn had tripped over the killer, it's not like he'd know it. He wouldn't come home and say, "Hey, honey, guess who I ran into today?" I'd never found a four-leaf clover and saw no reason for my luck to change now.

Then Dolly proved me wrong.

"You gonna ask about off the books?"

I leaned forward and complied.

"What about off the books?"

"He had something else going. He wouldn't tell me what, but I think he kept working your murders. I think he was working it all weekend," she said.

She got up, took my fork and plate, and walked to the sink.

"He had this idea, you know? That he could make people respect him. That was what the whole movie thing was about. Respect. Hollywood went sour, but he still had that itch. He figured working for you and your boss might be his last chance."

As she talked, she rinsed and scrubbed and rinsed again.

"I always told him, 'Who cares what anyone else thinks? I respect you. I think you're a good man. I know you're a good man.' But it wasn't enough for him. It was this thing he'd always had. Wanting people to take him seriously. After he turned in his report to your boss, he came back and he couldn't stop talking. How he knew all along he'd get edged out. But he was going to show Lillian Pentecost he was good for more than background work. He was going to deliver."

I pried the dish out of her hand, grabbed a tea towel, and began drying.

"You know what line he was following?"

She shook her head.

"I don't know. Sometimes he did that. Worked on stuff on the side. He never talked about it because he was afraid it wouldn't pan out. All I know is that he was out until late Saturday and Sunday. And he left early Monday morning. I never . . . I never saw him again."

She folded her arms in front of her, squeezing so hard she threatened to leave bruises.

"And they never found his notebook," she added.

"What notebook?" I asked.

"He always had a notebook on him," she said. "You know how it is."

I told her I did.

"But the police didn't find one on him. They didn't find it here, either. Or in his car."

"They found his car?"

"That's what they told me," she said. "A couple blocks away from your office."

That was news to me.

"They tell you what they found in the car?"

She shook her head.

"No. But I got the feeling it wasn't . . . I mean that it

wasn't . . . it wasn't a mess inside, or anything. They said I could get it back right after they were done."

The question was, did Klinghorn drive it to our neighborhood? Or did the killer? Either way, the killer likely took Klinghorn's notebook, which held with Holly's theory. Klinghorn and the killer had crossed paths. Maybe even spoken.

"The only record I have is his expense report."

"He kept expenses? On a job he wasn't getting paid for."

"Honey, I do the books. I made him keep expenses on everything."

She walked into the living room and returned a few seconds later with her purse. Eventually she pulled out a paper-clipped collection of handwritten slips. She handed me the lot. We sat back at the kitchen table to sort through them.

"You didn't show these to the police?" I asked.

"They didn't ask."

I gave her a look.

"You know how many times the cops roughed him up because some asshole with money didn't like getting caught with his dick out?" she asked. "Screw the police."

Except she didn't say "screw."

Scribbled on each slip of paper was a date, an amount, and what it was used for. Most also had names written in the bottom right corner. I asked Dolly about them.

"Those are our clients," she explained. "So the ones from this weekend, the ones without names at the bottom, that's from whatever he was working on that he didn't want to talk about."

There were two.

Sunday, Feb 2. D.S. $20. Research.

Sunday, Feb 2. Amos Hardware $5.25. Assorted supplies.

" 'Research' was our code for when he bribed somebody," Dolly explained.

So Klinghorn was working an informant. I knew only one "D.S." in the mix.

But I couldn't picture Donald Staples snitching for Klinghorn. Certainly not for a measly twenty bucks.

But I'd been wrong before.

Maybe it wasn't initials. Maybe it was some kind of personal shorthand.

I asked Dolly about it.

"Sure, Darryl did things like that all the time. I was always having to ask him what this or that means. But if 'D.S.' is one of his codes, I don't know it."

Whoever D.S. was, did they lead him to the killer? Or was the informant the killer?

"Do you think your husband—do you think Darryl—would leave something out of his report on purpose?" I asked Dolly. "So that he could fly solo? Try and prove something to my boss?"

To give her credit, she didn't answer on automatic. She thought about it. Finally she shook her head.

"I don't think so," she said. "He wanted to prove he was good at his job. That means he wouldn't fudge a report."

I didn't know about that. Sure, she knew her husband better than anybody. But I didn't know how many pairs of rose-colored glasses she owned.

"Thanks for this, Dolly. You know how it is. Every bit helps with a case. And I'll ask my boss about cutting a check. Some kind of bonus."

The smile she gave me was a sad, fragile thing.

"You think I blame you?" she asked. "I know who I married. I knew it was going to be something. Angry husband. Jealous boyfriend. Wrong place, wrong time. I'd hoped it'd be a little longer coming, but . . . what can you do?"

She stood up and smoothed the wrinkles out of her dress.

"But I won't turn down the check," she said.

Before I left I asked if I could take a look at Klinghorn's office.

"You can, but it won't do you any good," Dolly said. "The cops took it down to the carpet nails."

She led me to a small room tucked away in the back corner of the apartment. There was a writing desk, two filing cabinets, and a bookshelf. That was about all the tiny room could manage. The only decoration in the space was the wallpaper—dancing blue elephants.

Dolly saw me notice it.

"We were gonna use this as a nursery. Then . . . Well, things didn't work out. Darryl never took down the wallpaper."

I didn't ask a follow-up. Besides, I knew the answer would just make me sad or angry or both.

Dolly wasn't kidding when she said the cops had been through the place. Every drawer was open, every book was off the shelf, and the floor was awash in loose paper.

"They find anything?" I asked.

She shrugged. "If they did, they didn't tell me. You're free to take a crack. I'm gonna go put that cake away."

She left me alone in her dead husband's office. I sat in the chair and spun around and thought about the last time I saw Klinghorn. He'd seen it coming. How we were going to cut him loose.

When we tossed him, he went hunting on his own. To prove he was good for more than grunt work.

Cross that out. When *I* tossed him. Pretty hard, too. If I'd soft-pedaled it, maybe he would have let it be. But I didn't and he didn't and now he was dead and I was surrounded by his goddamn blue elephants.

The guilt settled in my gut like a stone. I didn't like it.

Dolly had asked if I thought she blamed me. Of course I thought that. I blamed me. To make matters worse, it should have been me working the case. It should have been me following the leads. It should have been me who stumbled on the killer.

It should have been me dead in an alley.

I kicked a pile of papers and caught a flash of color beneath them. I reached down and uncovered more.

When I realized what I was looking at, I had to bite my tongue from cursing.

Then I leaned over and looked closer.

"Klinghorn, you son of a *bitch*."

CHAPTER 35

It was well past noon by the time I pulled the Caddy up to the curb in front of the brownstone. A familiar figure was lumbering down the steps. Lieutenant Lazenby aimed a frown in my direction before sliding his bulk behind the wheel of an unmarked and driving away.

In the past I've described Lazenby as a thundercloud of a man. Not just because of his storm-gray beard and the kind of eyes that hide lightning strikes. It's also because when you see him on the horizon, it usually means it's time to batten down the hatches.

Inside, I found Ms. Pentecost in her usual spot. The widest of the guest chairs was centered in front of her desk, a mostly full glass of beer on the side table.

"Is that the German stuff?" I asked.

"The Porter. Yes."

"He didn't finish it. That doesn't bode well. Did he meet our houseguest?"

She shook her head. "When he knocked, she retreated to her room."

I sat down in the seat he'd just vacated while she gave me the synopsis. It wasn't until later when I was typing up notes on the case that I asked for the conversation in full, as best she remembered.

Lieutenant Nathan Lazenby: *Not bad.*

Lillian Pentecost: It was a gift from a German neighbor. For helping her brother's family navigate United States immigration laws.

NL: *You're not smuggling escaped Nazis, are you, Pentecost?*

LP: My neighbor and her family are Jewish, so that's unlikely. How can I help you, Lieutenant?

NL: *I'm going to make a speech. You don't have to respond, but I need to make it. Okay?*

LP: Proceed.

NL: *This thing with Klinghorn. I talked with some of the officers on the case and I know you're working an angle. I don't know what it is, but I know it's there. You've taken a flier on cases before. But three murders at once? All with some bizarre element attached?*

You have a connection between them. I know it. I can't prove it, but I know it. Staples would know it, too, if he had one piece of information I have that he doesn't: Parker doesn't smoke.

Which means she lied about the circumstances of finding the body. Which means that's probably just the tip of the iceberg.

Now, I have my feelings about Staples, and they aren't always charitable. Don't mistake me. He's a good cop. As straight a shooter as you're going to find in the department. But he's also a political beast who's as interested in making a name as he is in making cases.

Under normal circumstances, if you wanted to tweak his nose I might applaud.

These aren't normal circumstances. These are four murders. I worked Haggard personally. I'd have worked Checchetto, too, if I wasn't trying to get a handle on this goddamn burglary thing.

I've spoken with Connor Haggard's family. His sister. His father—eighty-two years old and can barely remember his name, but he knows enough to understand his son is dead.

So don't tweak my nose.

LP: Lieutenant, tweaking your nose is the furthest—

NL: I rescind the comment. How about I call it what it is: lying to the police so you can chase down a murderer yourself.

So?

LP: You said, at the beginning of your speech, that I would not be required to reply.

NL: Right. I see how it is.

I'll end with this. Staples isn't dumb. He'll clue in eventually. His next stop won't be here for a chat—it'll be to the DA's office for a pair of material-witness warrants. Probably even one for your Highlands housekeeper.

You've got some juice with the DA right now on account of the Baby Wyatt thing. So if worse comes to worst and they pin an obstruction charge on you, he might wave it off.

But if there's another murder. If anyone else dies while you're— and pardon the crudity—dicking us around . . . ?

There's not enough juice in the world for that.

"He then apologized for not being in a better mood to enjoy his beer, and left," Ms. Pentecost finished.

"I'm going to tape a note to my desk," I said. "Just to the left of the typewriter so I'll see it every day: 'Nathan Lazenby is nobody's fool.' "

"Indeed."

"Does it change our program any?" I asked.

"No," my boss answered. "Our goal goes hand in hand with the lieutenant's threat. Stop this before anyone else dies."

"Well, I don't know if this furthers that goal or not, but it certainly rearranges some things."

I pulled a magazine out from under my sweater, where I'd tucked it so as to smuggle it out of the Klinghorn apartment. I tossed it on Ms. P's desk.

She glanced at it.

"*Strange Crime*, December 1946. The issue containing 'The

Curse of the Red Claw.' I believe we have at least two copies of this already."

"Yeah, but look closer. This one is a collector's item."

She leaned over and peered at the address label: Holly Quick, etc., etc.

As usual, my boss connected the dots a full two seconds quicker than I had.

"Was this taken from Miss Quick's residence?" she asked.

"We'll have to ask her, but that's my guess. The way her place was searched—going so far as to check the flour canisters and all—that's somebody who's sifted a joint before. And here's another thing . . ."

I moved over to my desk, took a seat, and found my most recently filled notebook.

"When I was over at Holly's place right after the break-in, I noticed something, but I couldn't put my finger on it." I flipped pages until I found the shorthand I was looking for. "Here we are. 'Something in the air. Intruder-question mark.'"

I flipped it shut.

"It was Klinghorn's goddamn aftershave. I was reminded, because his office still reeks of the stuff. I couldn't get a good enough whiff the night of the break-in, because Holly steeps her apartment in Chesterfields."

"Did you find any indication to his purpose?" she asked.

I told Ms. Pentecost about my conversation with Dolly Klinghorn, including her notion that he was working an angle, the list of expenses, and the thing about him wanting to prove himself.

I kept out the part about the stone in my gut. No need to clutter things.

When I was finished, I pulled out my current notebook, tore out the page where I'd copied Klinghorn's expenses, and added it to the collection on Ms. P's desk.

"Now that I have that magazine, I think they tell a story in three acts. Want to hear the synopsis?"

"Please."

"Klinghorn bribes somebody. This 'D.S.' Could be Donald Staples, but I didn't think that was likely before I found the magazine. Now I'd lay ten to one against. Why? you ask. Because I think whoever this D.S. is gave him a name and an address—Holly's. And if Staples had Holly's name, she'd be in an interrogation room right now."

"Why do you think that's the information this D.S. provided?" my boss asked.

"Because after he shells out that twenty dollars, he pays a visit to Amos Hardware. I could give Amos a call and ask what Klinghorn bought that cost him five dollars and twenty-five cents. But I won't do that."

I waited until my boss took the cue.

"And why won't you?"

"Because I wouldn't get a straight answer. After I found that magazine, I asked Dolly a couple follow-ups. Turns out Amos has a few side gigs. One of those is that if you come to him with a brand of lock, he'll sell you the best skeleton key at five bucks a pop. The twenty-five cents was probably for rubber gloves."

Those were enough bread crumbs for Ms. P to follow.

D.S. gives Klinghorn Holly's name and address. Klinghorn swings by her apartment building, finds an absent super and a tenant out for the day, and scopes out the lock on the front door. Then he pays a visit to Amos, makes his purchases, and heads back to Holly's for a quick breaking and entering. The skeleton key took care of the front door. His picks took care of her apartment.

But what was he looking for? Proof that Holly was Horace Bellow? Proof that Holly was Henrietta Truelove? What was his goal? Even more importantly, who pointed him to Holly in the first place?

My boss's thoughts were running on the same track.

"If Mrs. Klinghorn is correct—that her husband would leave out nothing relevant from his report—then whatever theory he was following is contained within."

I told her my concerns about wives and rose-tinted glasses. Also, there are a lot of ways to bury a relevant fact in a pile of nothing.

"Either way, we're at least half as smart as Klinghorn," I said. "If it's there, we'll find it."

We talked about other ways this new revelation reshuffled the deck. Including one angle in particular that was helpful in terms of winnowing suspects.

By the time we were done, the clock was chiming five o'clock. We had a date with Jessup Quincannon and his merry band of murder-lovers at seven.

"Are we sharing this lot with our client?" I asked.

Ms. Pentecost nodded. "For all intents and purposes, Miss Quick has entered into what could be considered a criminal conspiracy to obstruct justice."

"Right," I said. "In for a penny."

I went upstairs and knocked on the guest room door.

"Come in."

I found Holly sitting on the floor under the window. Scattered around her were pages from the report. Someone, either Holly or Mrs. Campbell, had pried the nails out of the window and it was now cracked open. An ashtray was sitting on the sill and Holly had a lit Chesterfield hanging from her lip.

"Don't catch any of that on fire," I warned. "It's our last copy."

"Mr. Klinghorn's narrative style is fascinating," she said without bothering to look up. "It's very concise in places and incredibly bloated in others. Like here. He describes a friend of Michael Perkins as poverty-stricken, filthy, having poor hygiene, slurred in his speech. He could have called him a drunk and been done with it. Although I suppose if you don't know how important someone is to the story, you err on the side of too much rather than too little."

She reached up to the ashtray and snuffed out the cigarette.

"Here's something that might further color your opinion of Klinghorn."

I gave her the lot. I didn't give her our conclusions, but she reached them on her own.

"If Mr. Klinghorn really was the person who broke into my apartment, then something in this report led him to me. Which means there should be something in here I recognize."

"Anything ring a bell?"

"It's very difficult," she said, lighting another cigarette. "I've read extensively about these three murders. All of it rings a bell. Take Conny Haggard, for example. I have this very clear memory—déjà vu, almost—of thinking, 'Oh, *Haggard*—what an evocative name. I'll have to use that somewhere.' But was it before or after I read about this case? I don't know."

"Your homework is to keep looking," I said.

"Also . . ."

"Yes?"

"If it was Mr. Klinghorn who broke into my apartment, and he obviously isn't the murderer, then . . . then how did the killer know about 'Death Gets a Dial Tone'?"

That was the winnowing of suspects Ms. P and I had discussed. The killer must have had contact with either Holly or the folks at *Strange Crime*. Otherwise, how else would he have seen the yet-to-be-published story?

"We'll need to talk with Brent and Marlo, won't we?" Holly said. "To find out who else could have seen the story."

I nodded. I did not bother to mention that Brent and Marlo were still very much in play as possibilities.

"They'll have heard about Mr. Klinghorn's murder. They'll know I haven't been home. They'll have called. I'll have to tell them I'm staying here. I'll have to . . ."

She mulled that over until the ash on her cigarette threatened to topple onto the pages in front of her. I took it out of her mouth, tapped it on the ashtray, and returned it to her lips.

"Thank you."

"We can come up with another cover story," I said. "We'll say Klinghorn was working on your stalker. He found out something and we don't know what. It has the benefit of being mostly true."

She shook her head.

"I should tell them the truth. About who I am. About my father."

"You don't have to."

She shook her head again.

"I should have done it ages ago. I . . . It's dishonest not to. Not when . . ."

I took a seat on the edge of the bed.

"I get it," I said. "You're sharing one kind of secret, why not all the others? You think you owe it to them."

"Dr. Grayson says that it's okay to protect myself, but that . . . that in the long term, not being honest, especially with people I love, will do more harm than good."

I didn't know what to say to that. Telling all, even to someone I was in the sack with, felt like letting someone paw through my lingerie drawer. It wasn't that I was embarrassed; I just preferred to show off one item at a time.

I ended up just smiling and nodding and let Holly make of that what she would.

Then I went and tried to figure out what you wear when you're rubbing shoulders with monsters.

CHAPTER 36

A retired superior-court judge, an award-winning playwright, a shipping magnate, three professors, two deans, a man who'd stabbed his employer in the throat with a pencil, a suspected serial rapist, a scattering of wealthy unidentifieds, the world's premier female gumshoe, and her erstwhile assistant.

Those were the people gathered that evening at Quincannon's haunted mansion.

"This feels so weird," I whispered to Ms. P. "Even more than I expected. I think because it's so . . . normal."

When we'd arrived we'd been shown into a room with high ceilings, big windows, comfortable furniture scattered about, and tables covered with a healthy selection of hors d'oeuvres. We were among the last to arrive and guests had already clustered and started in on conversations.

I'd been to a few university functions—post-lecture shindigs where a bunch of highbrow so-and-sos stood around talking philosophy or archaeology or evolution. Except here they were chatting about murder.

One of the professors had pinned the pencil-stabber down and was grilling him about whether such a thing as insanity can really be temporary; the rapist and the steel magnate looked to be talking about the stock market; a large cluster was gathered around Quincannon as he held court on the psychology of crime and his whole idea of murder being transformative.

There were also a number of by-the-hour caterers keeping drinks topped and the plates of tiny sandwiches full. The whole affair had a relatively cheery air.

To be honest, Ms. Pentecost and I were the grimmest things there, both of us having gone for basic black—she in a three-piece with matching tie, I sticking with two and going tieless. We didn't look exactly like undertakers. We had better tailors than that. But we were definitely dressed for death.

"It is certainly unexpected," Ms. Pentecost responded. "Which I think is the point. The normalization of the abnormal."

"Do you think all these people actually buy into his whole obsession, or do they just want to rub elbows with his money?"

"Part of it is certainly Quincannon's wealth. He has been known to make or break political candidates. But I'm sure part of it is that they simply enjoy the topic of murder."

Which didn't exactly put me at ease.

I mean, yeah, it was one of our frequent topics, as well. But when we discussed murder, it was more like a pair of exterminators talking cockroaches. This crew were writing the vermin fan mail.

Speaking of unease, Alathea was stationed in a doorway, keeping watch over the whole scene. She'd dropped the couture for a basic gray tweed suit and had lopped two inches off her heels.

On second glance, I noticed the subtle slits cut up the skirt. Ditto for the jacket. The tailoring would allow her a lot more freedom of movement. I wondered if the jacket was also tailored to conceal a holster.

I wandered over. She gave me a smile. A little like an alligator grinning at a passing swimmer.

"Miss Parker."

I opened my jacket.

"No firearms, as promised."

"There are other places to conceal a gun," she said.

She made it sound like a flip comment, but the way her eyes flicked over my body, I didn't think she was kidding.

"Don't be silly," I said. "An ankle holster kills the line of these trousers."

Another smile, equally reptilian.

Her eyes went back to surveying the crowd. I turned to join her.

"So what's the deal? You're on hand in case Mr. Employee of the Year over there sees a pencil and goes for a repeat performance?"

"I'm here to ensure that Mr. Quincannon and his guests have a pleasant evening."

The suspected serial rapist, who I'll just call "Ted" because typing his full name makes me nauseous, headed in our direction, his eye on a serving tray of little cream puffs. Then he looked up, caught something from either Alathea or me, and decided he was watching his waistline.

"Piece of shit," I muttered.

"Agreed," Alathea muttered back.

I looked at her in surprise. Maybe she wasn't Quincannon's pet. I decided to push it.

"What I don't get is, Ted there's a rapist. Not convicted, even, thanks to his daddy's money. Why does he score an invite? I thought Quincannon's obsession was limited to killers."

She didn't answer, but gave me a look that I managed to decipher even without her personal codebook.

"Teddy's not just a rapist, is he? And Quincannon knows it. What happened? Did one of the girls fight back and he got violent? More than one?"

There were no more forthcoming looks. I made a mental

note to take a real close look at Teddy in my spare time. When I had such a thing again.

Across the room, I saw Quincannon approach my boss, followed by his coterie of hangers-on. I hurried back in that direction. I didn't catch his opener, but I caught her reply.

"I'm afraid I know little that was not in the papers," she said. "Their coverage has been quite extensive."

"Well, can you blame them? A murder on the doorstep of Lillian Pentecost. My God, I can't imagine."

He chuckled, and his sycophants followed suit.

"But at least it was someone like Darryl Klinghorn, and not Miss Parker here," he added. "I don't think his death will be a great loss to the community."

I felt an unexpected surge of anger. Maybe it was from that stone in my gut. Or maybe it was simply that Klinghorn had been one of ours. I hadn't cared for him, but I'll be damned if I was going to let somebody like Quincannon spit on his grave. I had my mouth open to retort when Ms. Pentecost beat me to it.

"On the contrary," she said, "Mr. Klinghorn was an excellent investigator. He had a keen eye and a keen mind, and was dogged in his search for the truth. Those skills as a detective were likely what led to his death. He located a killer and paid the price for his ingenuity."

If Quincannon was impressed by her impassioned defense, he didn't show it.

"What about you, Lillian? Are you also on the trail of a killer?"

"Always, Jessup," she said. "Now, if you don't mind, I am a busy woman and we have business to attend to."

"Of course," he said. "Let's go up and see the exhibits."

CHAPTER 37

Much like our own archives, the third floor of the old Victorian was a single, open space. No skylights, though. No windows at all. Quincannon didn't want the sunlight to spoil his treasures.

Instead, illumination was provided by rows of hanging bulbs, each hooded in green glass. They hovered over waist-high cases filled with artifacts: bones, blades, hacksaws, and a hundred other curiosities. The walls were covered in framed pictures, pages from diaries, maps of cities, their streets scattered with tiny red X's. A woman's skirt—green chintz with golden lilies—was pinned to the wall like a dead butterfly.

Each item represented a murderer. There were weapons and diary entries, bits and baubles collected from the pockets of victims, scraps of lives cut short.

Quincannon's very own Black Museum.

Unlike at a real museum, there were no placards explaining what each item represented. Another power play. If you wanted to know what an item was, you had to ask.

Also, if Quincannon ever missed a bribe and the police decided to raid his house, all they'd find would be a room full of junk, with no way of concretely linking any of it to a particular crime.

While it might be legal to pay a convicted murderer for a memento or two, it was a gray area when the killer hadn't been caught yet. And downright criminal to bribe police or courthouse employees to accidentally "lose" evidence after a trial.

Though if the cops really got interested, they wouldn't be able to touch Quincannon. He had a pet lawyer who did the dirty work. Hanging around jails and courthouses, briefcase filled with cash, ready to make a deal for some piece of evidence or other.

Alathea joined us, stationing herself at the top of the stairs. Ensuring our privacy while keeping a close eye on her employer who was busy playing docent.

"These coins here were found in the pockets of John Wilkes Booth. This wedding band belonged to Lizzie Halliday. It was given to her by her sixth and final husband. These needles were a few of the twenty-nine that were found lodged in the pelvis of Albert Fish. Inserted there himself. He was quite the masochist."

"Well, it's nice to have a hobby," I said. "When you're not going around murdering and eating children, I mean."

Quincannon scowled. He didn't appreciate being thrown off his rhythm. My boss didn't let him get back on track.

"You intimated to Miss Parker that you had information regarding the murder of Flavio Checchetto," she said. "Was that true? Or was that just a ploy to ensure my attendance?"

He made a sound that you'd call a laugh if you'd never heard a laugh before.

"You think too highly of yourself," Quincannon told her. "I do have information. And, no, I haven't shared it with the police. I'm perfectly willing to give it to you. But . . . I believe I told Miss Parker there would be a price."

From an inner pocket, Ms. P pulled out a silver lighter. She held it out, displaying the initials inscribed on one side: G.S.

"Sendak?" Quincannon asked.

My boss nodded.

Barry Sendak had torched three Harlem tenement buildings. It was Ms. Pentecost's work that got him caught, and her testimony that put the nail in his coffin. We made use of a stand-in for the lighter during the trial, but this was the real deal. How Ms. P got her hands on it, I had no idea.

"Hardly the most prolific arsonist."

"As an arsonist he was mediocre. But as a murderer . . ."

"True. . . . Fifteen, wasn't it?"

"Seventeen."

Quincannon reached for the lighter, but Ms. P pulled it out of his reach.

"How do I know what you're selling is worth the price?"

Quincannon grinned and said one word.

"Truelove."

Ms. P and I are pretty good at keeping a straight face when under stress. But I guess between the two of us there was enough of a reaction for Quincannon to know he'd hit a mark.

His smile stretched wide and all I could see was skull.

"Here," he said, extending his arm toward a particular case with the flair of a circus showman. His hand hovered over an open straight razor lying on a square of black velvet, its blade pockmarked with rust.

"It's believed Daniel Truelove used several over the course of his brief but prolific career. As you can see from the cheap plastic handle, it was no precious heirloom. This was the one recovered just prior to his arrest. We know there were others because on at least two occasions, he cut deep enough to hit bone. Pieces of blade snapped off."

Ms. Pentecost asked the question we were both thinking.

"What is the connection between Daniel Truelove and the murder of Flavio Checchetto?"

"I don't know, dear. You tell me. You're the detective."

Apparently even the rich and disgusting can stoop to sarcasm when the mood strikes.

But Ms. P took his request at face value.

"You told Miss Parker that no one in your group was the killer. You would consider such a blatant lie to be gauche, so I'll take it as truth. While I know you're perfectly capable of withholding information from the police, I don't believe you'd protect a killer when asked directly. It would put you in too much personal jeopardy. This suggests that the murderer has been in contact with you, but not in such a way that has revealed his identity. For reasons of my own, I believe the killer enjoys correspondence. So that contact has likely been through a letter or letters in which he mentions Daniel Truelove. . . . So, *dear*, how did I do?"

With each word, Quincannon's smile withered a little more. By the end, I could see the thing living inside his paperthin skin. A bloated spider dressed as a man.

"Oh, Lillian, you take all the fun out of things."

"I do not find murder fun."

He wagged his finger at her. "Oh, you little liar. *Everyone* finds murder fun."

He walked over to the skirt on the wall and gently brushed his fingers across its bloodied hem.

"How many newspapers were sold on the back of Jack the Ripper? Not just in England, but around the world? So many that we're still christening killers in his honor. What about those kidnappers you yourself captured just a few weeks ago? Do you think it would have been front-page news if they hadn't left a dead little girl in their wake? It is the ultimate taboo and so it is the ultimate fascination."

Satisfied that he made his point, he gave a nod to Alathea. She walked over. In her hand, she held an unmarked envelope.

"A letter. I believe you will find it to be from Mr. Checchetto's murderer."

Ms. Pentecost looked from the envelope to Quincannon. "Is this all of it?" she asked.

"It's all I'm giving you," the spider hissed. "For a detective of your caliber, it should be enough."

She spent three seconds sizing him up, then gave him the lighter. He took it in both hands, cradling it like it was made by Fabergé. He opened it and flicked the wheel. There were only a few sparks, and no flame.

"Pity," he said, then nodded to Alathea. She passed Ms. Pentecost the letter.

"I believe our business is finished," my boss said.

We were turning toward the stairs when Quincannon said, "We despise in others that which we are ashamed to admit of ourselves. You and I, Lillian, we are identical in our obsessions."

Ms. Pentecost ignored him and kept moving.

"Oh, and Miss Parker. In case you're wondering, *this* is me getting my rocks off."

I was prepared to ignore him as well, but my boss stopped and turned. She pointed at the skirt hanging on the wall and demanded, "What was her name?"

"Hmmm?"

"The woman to whom that article of clothing belonged? What was her name?"

Quincannon blinked, stymied.

"It was . . . Well, one of the five, of course. Kelly, I think."

"Her name was Catherine Eddowes. She was orphaned young and was a mother of three herself. A cheerful woman, by all accounts. Always singing. Her friends called her Kate," Ms. Pentecost said. "We can show ourselves out."

And we did.

CHAPTER *38*

Dear Mr. Quincannon,
   You do not know me but I am, first
and foremost, a great admirer of your
philanthropy and your ongoing scholarship.
I was fortunate enough to procure a copy of
an article you wrote for a certain journal.
Your theories about the true nature of
mankind and the transformative power of our
basest instincts are revolutionary. I was
gripped, truly gripped in my soul, by your
declaration that "the violent instincts of
mankind are as ingrained in our species
as the urge to make love or to sing or to
create great art."
   That the editors of that journal chose not
to publish this article, instead leaving it
to be passed hand to hand among those who
know and understand, is a travesty.
   I am one of those who understand.
Intimately.
   But I believe that your associate Flavio
Checchetto is not. I have had dealings with
him and have found him to be the basest sort
of man. He cannot appreciate the more subtle

talents. He is, at best, a hawker of gewgaws.
He cannot create. Only sell.

I approached him recently to request an
introduction to you and your organization.
I felt, I still feel, that I have much to
contribute to your ongoing conversations. He
turned me down. Laughed at me, even, in the
most disrespectful way. He referred to it as a
"gentlemen's club." A club! Like the Elks. One
that was very lucrative to him personally. He
dared not chance his relationship with it or
with you by bringing with him a guest whose
"bona fides are so paltry."

I dared not share with him my true "bona
fides." But I would with you. I would like
to visit you and talk with you and see your
collection. I am especially interested in
anything you have commemorating Daniel
Truelove. I feel I could add to your
understanding, especially regarding your
belief that "These men whom we callously
deem monsters linger long in our collective
memory. Their work is resonant longer even
than that of the great poets and painters.
They imprint themselves on the very soul of
mankind."

I believe I will make for you a gift—
a tribute—by way of introduction.

Sincerely yours,

An Ardent Admirer

Ms. Pentecost read the typewritten letter out loud while I
drove back to our own brownstone, which was blessedly free
of bloodstained knickknacks.

Okay, so we had a few, but we didn't show them off to guests.

"That's our guy," I said. "Even if he didn't sign it 'Ardent Admirer,' there's something about the feel of it."

"You're not mistaken," Ms. P said. "The tone and the cadence are the same. Also, if I'm not mistaken, the *t* is slightly raised, as in the letter addressed to Horace Bellow."

No date on the letter. And Quincannon had given it to us in a plain envelope. So no postmark to work with. Was there something on the envelope that might have pointed to the killer? Or was it just Quincannon being difficult?

"If we take him at his word, he definitely knew Checchetto," I said. "It wasn't random. We really need Checchetto's address book, receipts, everything from his store."

"Specifically, I would like to see the list of artists who have sold pieces on consignment."

"You think our guy's an artist?" I asked, pulling the car up to the curb outside the brownstone.

"Or he considers himself one," Ms. P said. "Remember what you said about the crime scenes? How they painted a gruesome picture?"

"He also said that thing about beauty and truth in his letter to Holly. That sounds like the kind of bullshit an artist would say."

I paused the conversation to get us out of the car and up the steps. A nor'easter had shot the bottom out of the thermometer and threatened to rip away words and hats alike. I kept my mouth shut and both hands on my fedora until we were indoors.

"Okay, so what else does this thing tell us?" I asked, once the elements were safely locked outside.

"What thing?"

The question came from our office. I walked in to find

Holly sitting behind Ms. Pentecost's desk, papers strewn out in front of her. She quickly started clearing up.

"I'm sorry," she said. "Eleanor wanted to clean in the dining room. She said there were still footprints all over the floor from the police. Though I didn't really see much in the way of footprints, but I'm not as fastidious as she is. Anyway, I wanted to get out of her way and there's not much room in my bedroom and I really wanted to spread Mr. Klinghorn's report out. It really is very comprehensive. I would have liked to have met him. Alive, I mean. Even if he did break into my apartment."

By the time she got to the end of that little monologue, she had transferred herself and the report to the davenport under the window.

"So how did it go? The meeting? Salon? Party? I'm still unclear exactly what Mr. Quincannon's group is."

"Words cannot do it justice," I said.

Ms. Pentecost handed our client the letter. While she read it, I went into the kitchen for a sandwich. I found Mrs. Campbell on the floor, scrubbing some stubborn dirt that had accumulated in the corners.

"Pardon me while I scrounge up dinner," I said, inching around her.

"I thought they were serving food at that thing."

"It wasn't an atmosphere conducive to a healthy appetite," I said, stacking slices of ham, cheese, and bread in the traditional arrangement. "Really, it wasn't an atmosphere conducive to a healthy anything."

"Any luck?"

"That's a matter of opinion," I said, trying to choose between mayonnaise and mustard and settling on both. "You might as well step into the office. Your advice on Dolly Klinghorn was spot-on. Maybe you'll see something we don't."

She shook her head. "Oh, I don't think so. I don't like to get mucked up in your business."

"First, we both draw a paycheck from the same account," I reminded her. "Also, I believe the phrase Ms. Pentecost used was 'criminal conspiracy to obstruct justice.' You're already hip-deep in the muck, so you might as well dunk your head in."

I brought the sandwich and the Scotswoman into the office.

"I figured four heads are better than three are better than two."

I took a seat at my desk while Mrs. Campbell hovered in the doorway.

"I think this *is* the same person," Holly said, flipping from one letter to the other. "Do you think he's an artist? Does he think these murders are . . . art?"

I looked at my boss. "I wasn't keeping time. Did she get there faster or did you?"

"What person are we talking about?" Mrs. Campbell asked.

"Our killer wrote to Quincannon," I explained. "At least that's the working theory. Holly—do you want to do the honors?"

Holly read the letter out loud.

When she finished, we all gave it a minute's thought. Mrs. Campbell was the first to break the silence.

"The voice you did . . ."

"I did a voice?" Holly asked. "I didn't mean to do a voice."

"It was like a put-on voice," Mrs. Campbell explained. "Putting on airs, I mean."

"This voice made you think of something?" Ms. P prompted.

"It's nothing, really. This boy I knew back when I was a lass."

It was refreshing to see Ms. P aim her impatient look at someone else for a change.

"He was just a bloke," Mrs. Campbell said. "Nothing special about him. Martin, his name was. One day he was out in the country—he must have been twelve or thirteen—and he found this drawing on the underside of this little stone outcrop. Like a cave painting. People from university came to take a look. It was a big deal around there. I remember Martin leading them and what seemed like half the village out so they could study and take pictures. In the end, it wasn't all that old. Not in the grand scheme of things. But it really got in his head, that little bit of fame. Couple weeks later, Martin comes back, says he's found another painting. Oh—lightning strikes twice, people said. Called the university. But he'd made it himself, didn't he? They knew it right away. His father tanned his hide all the way home."

"I don't suppose he grew up to kill a bunch of people," I said.

Mrs. Campbell snorted. "Became a grocer, he did. Meek as a lamb. But those letters just reminded me of him. The way he's . . . I don't know . . . preening and . . . something—"

"Fawning?" Holly suggested.

"Yes! That's it. Preening and fawning. If he was a cat he'd be rubbing up your leg, desperate for attention."

I didn't have to think about it long to see how close she'd hit the mark.

"She's not wrong," I said. "Three showy murders. Letters to Quincannon and to Holly by way of Horace. Dumping Klinghorn's body in our alley like a mash note. I'm surprised he hasn't sent flowers to Staples yet. Or the *Times*. If he wants attention, I mean. The Ripper did that, didn't he?"

I glanced at Holly and stuttered, "I mean the original one. The London one. Jack, I mean."

For some reason my flustering made her smile.

"He's a connoisseur. Or wants to be," Ms. P muttered.

"What was that?" I asked.

"'He cannot appreciate the more subtle talents. He is, at best, a hawker of gewgaws. He cannot create. Only sell.'"

She looked at the three of us in turn, waiting.

"You're doing that thing where you're three steps ahead," I told her. "Just take a fourth and narrate it."

"That's what he said about Mr. Checchetto," she explained. "Not only does that suggest he thinks of himself as someone who creates, but that he seeks approval and attention from those who would properly appreciate his creations. Look who he has reached out to. A writer whom he admires, though perhaps as much for her proximity to tragedy as for her skill. To Jessup Quincannon, a wealthy aesthete who elevates murder to a philosophical event."

"And he reached out to you by way of Klinghorn," I added. "The greatest detective in the five boroughs and beyond."

She made a face, but she didn't disagree.

"So he's a snob. How does that help us?" I asked.

"It helps us in that he is less likely to contact the police or the press. I believe he would consider them—and the general public—beneath him."

"Let me rephrase," I said. "How does that help us catch him?"

Silence. I gave it another try.

"Okay, I'll get a little more specific. The big hurdle is discovering how this guy knew his victims. We assume he maybe tried to sell a drawing or two to Checchetto and got snubbed, but remember what they say about assumptions and asses. Anyway, that's one victim. What about Haggard and Perkins? You've got a white-collar civil servant and a machinist-turned-soldier-turned-layabout. Nothing to do with a sort-of-high-end antiques dealer. At least nothing Klinghorn dug out. I joked about eeny meeny miny murder, but what if that's the case? What if this guy is throwing darts at the phone book? Or what if—"

Holly had her hand raised again.

"The student in the front row has a question?"

"Well, not so much a question as an . . . an observation, I suppose." She picked up Klinghorn's report and began flipping through it. "While there's no link between these three men—four men, I suppose, since Mr. Klinghorn shouldn't be forgotten. While there's no physical link, there is a . . . a link of character, I suppose."

Ms. P asked the question for all of us.

"What do you mean, a link of character?"

"I mean . . . Here, if you look at the words people used to describe Michael Perkins: fussy, stickler, rule-lover. And then Conny Haggard: pugnacious, abrasive. And Flavio Checchetto: snide, standoffish, weasel."

I saw the picture before she'd finished the paint-by-numbers, but I let her continue.

"Then there's Mr. Klinghorn. I know he was likely killed because he discovered something about the killer, or was about to, but the way Will talks about him, it seems like he was . . . well . . ."

I saved her the trouble.

"Assholes. They're all assholes."

Holly nodded. "Or at least they're of a type. The kind that would . . . well, piss people off. Especially the type of man who would write this letter."

"What do you mean?" I asked.

"He thinks he's better than other people. Smarter. More talented," she explained. "I've found that men like that can be particularly fragile, especially when confronted with someone who refuses to recognize their superiority."

I was aware of Ms. P and Mrs. Campbell following this

exchange like a tennis match. I was also aware that, as sharp an observation as Holly's was, it didn't actually help us find the link between killer and victims.

Ms. P must have been aware of it, too.

"Excellent theory, Miss Quick," she said. "In order to help prove it, I believe we need Mr. Checchetto's list of the artists he sold on consignment. That is one of a number of items—lists of people connected to our victims—we had discussed procuring. With this letter sent to Mr. Quincannon, I believe it should become our first priority. It is, unfortunately, in the possession of the police."

We tossed around the names of some cops we might be able to ask—read this as bribe—to get us a copy of Checchetto's consignment list. He apparently didn't sell much, so it couldn't be too long.

But there was a problem.

Considering how quickly Staples got tipped when Klinghorn came around asking questions, it made a bribe a chancy proposition. Like Klinghorn told me, a bribe buys compliance, not eternal silence.

The payoff wasn't even guaranteed. Checchetto might have refused to sell the killer's work. That would account for the anger. The killer might also not have used his real name. The list—assuming there was one—could be useless.

I relayed these thoughts to the group.

"It's still a tangible lead," Ms. P said. "We cannot afford to ignore it."

As we worked out how to beg, bribe, or steal the list, I noticed Holly getting more and more twitchy. Her fingers traced the seams of her skirt, back and forth and up and down.

"You have another brainstorm?" I asked.

"I wonder . . ." she started.

"Yes, Miss Quick?" my boss said.

"I wonder if I shouldn't just go to the police. Maybe to

the man who came and saw you. Not the rude one, the other one."

"Lieutenant Lazenby."

"Yes, to him," she said. "Maybe I should go to him. Tell him everything."

"I'm not sure that would be possible now," Ms. P said. "At least not how I had originally suggested. Mr. Klinghorn's death and our subsequent deceit of Detective Staples would hamstring the lieutenant. I do not believe he would be able to protect you, either from public exposure or from becoming a suspect yourself."

The idea that she'd move to the front of the suspect line didn't seem to faze her. She'd apparently figured out that likelihood on her own. Holly Quick wasn't dumb.

"Perhaps I should come forward anyway. I could . . . I could tell them I made you lie. That I convinced you. It's just . . . Having this letter. It makes him real. No, *real* isn't the right word. It sounds stupid, but—"

"I understand, Miss Quick. It's a perfectly adequate word. Because, yes, this letter does make him real in a way his letter to the magazine does not. He lets his mask slip here."

She got up from her desk and walked to the drinks trolley. She picked up the bottle of honey wine, then put it back down and went for the bourbon instead, pouring a healthy three fingers, then considered and added two rocks from the ice bucket.

"I've brought many criminals to justice, Miss Quick. Few of this particular ilk, but still . . . I have a sense of when things are on the verge. I feel we are on the verge now."

That was news to me. The only thing I felt on the verge of was exhaustion.

She took the drink back to her desk and sat there, ice clinking against the glass.

"If I did not feel that way, I would consider your suggestion. But I would like, to whatever extent possible, to protect you."

"Why?" Holly asked. "Why do you care?"

A swirl, a clink, a sip. A grimace. When Ms. P drinks bourbon, it's not for the taste.

"The world often defines women by the worst thing that's ever happened to us," she said. "It won't let us be otherwise."

Another sip, a smaller grimace.

"You've managed to create a new life," she continued. "Despite your past, despite your tragedy, you've carved out a place for yourself in the world. If you go to the police now, I believe that will be lost and irrecoverable. I would fight to protect it."

Turned out that I would, too.

CHAPTER 39

We talked things over, namely how what we knew about the killer could help Holly's and my discussion with the *Strange Crime* employees the following day. Out of deference to Holly, I didn't call it an interrogation. But that's what it would be.

Somehow the killer had seen Holly's story, and unless her apartment had been broken into twice in short order, that limited the pool. The plan was for me and Holly to go over the next morning. If one of them was our killer, I wanted to be armed with questions that would root them out.

If they had somehow shared the story with someone else, that could make things more complicated, but still doable. There was also the possibility the killer got access to the *Strange Crime* offices some other way. I made a note to ask about cleaning staff and to check the locks for tampering.

After that was settled, Holly asked if we thought it would be safe for her to go back to her apartment.

"If Mr. Klinghorn was the person who broke in, then it shouldn't be a problem, should it? Mr. Cosmo changed the locks."

The rest of the room was unanimous that Holly going home was a bad idea.

"If the killer knows who you are, he can find out where

you live," I told her. "Until now he's been happy fawning from afar. But maybe he has some literary criticism he wants to share in person."

It was an excellent argument, but Holly dug in her heels.

"I understand your fear. I do," she said. "But I want to be back in my own home and to sleep in my own bed. I can't sleep here. I mean, I can, but not well. . . . I have dreams."

Eventually Ms. P and I relented, but on the condition that I spend the night propped in one of Holly's armchairs. She made some grumblings about how that wasn't necessary, but they weren't very loud, and eventually we both went upstairs to pack our respective bags.

Mine, as usual, included some specialty items.

"How many guns do you own?" Holly said when she caught me trying to choose between the Colt and the Browning Hi-Power.

"Three more than the police know about," I said before tucking both in with my pajamas. "Before you ask, no, I do not think they'll be necessary. But I didn't think the Cardinals were going to take the Dodgers in the playoffs, and look what happened."

She looked at me blankly. "What happened?"

"I'm just saying, better safe than sorry."

Properly supplied, I drove myself and Holly to her apartment. She called Mr. Cosmo before we left, and he was waiting on the curb when we arrived.

"Miss Holly, it is so good to see you. So awful what happened," he said as he took Holly's suitcase and tucked my overnight bag under his arm. "I am so sorry I was not here. I tell my sister—no more Sunday dinners. Not for a long time."

I told him that wasn't necessary.

"You got cracked by a pro," I explained.

"I talk to owners. Locks are old, I tell them. They do not want to replace. I tell them it will cost less than if building gets a reputation as unsafe. Eventually, they agree. Miss Holly's door and the front door first. Next week I do the rest."

He dropped the bags outside Holly's door and handed her the new keys.

"It is very good to have you back," the super said. "If you need anything, you call."

She assured him she would, then let us into her place.

I took a big whiff. Stale air, baked-in cigarettes. Nothing to raise my hackles.

We spent an hour sorting and cleaning. Sure, it hadn't been a killer in her apartment. But it was still an invasion.

Her apartment wasn't exactly spotless when we were finished, but Klinghorn's presence had been erased.

Holly brewed some tea—an herbal concoction that didn't quite taste like grass—and we spent another hour chatting, she sitting at her desk, I in one of the armchairs.

After a while, she started talking about her father.

"I remember the police asking me why he'd killed all those people, but I didn't know. He just seemed normal to me. Although I guess all parents seem normal to their children, no matter how off they are."

Her hands were surprisingly still. Not a twitch or tic in sight.

"I've thought about it a lot since," she said. "I remember him and my mother fighting. Mostly about money. So I think it might have started out about that. Because he was robbing them at first. And sometimes it was men. Drunks. Then . . . then it became something else. He must have enjoyed it, mustn't he?"

I didn't know how to answer that, and it didn't look like she expected me to.

"I think he was thinking of her. My mother," she said. "I think he was killing her over and over again. Until he finally did."

She stared down into her empty teacup, like she was looking to read an answer in the dregs.

" 'Parker' isn't my real name."

Her head snapped up.

"What?"

"I changed it when I ran away from home. I took 'Parker' from a detective story I read. Not one of yours. Part of the reason was so I could kick dirt over my tracks. But mostly I didn't want to drag my father's name behind me for the rest of my life."

"What about 'Willowjean'?" she asked. "Is that fake, too?"

I shook my head.

"No," I said. "My mom named me Willowjean. So I kept it."

I told her a little about my childhood. My time at the circus. How I ended up stumbling knife-first into the detective business. That sent us back into her case, the letters from the killer, Quincannon and his club—trying to transform a bunch of ugly, little men into something more.

"That's what it always seems to come down to," I said at one point. "Men who think the world's shortchanged them, and that they can murder their way to even."

Not long after, Holly announced she was going to bed.

"Usually I'm awake until much later," she said. "But I'm just so tired."

"I'll be right here if you need me."

"Are you sure you'll be comfortable?"

"Trust me," I said. "I could sleep standing up if I needed."

"Good night," she said.

"Good night."

I might have overstated my ability to sleep anywhere. I tried half a dozen positions before finally settling on one where I squeezed my rear to one side and threw both legs over the opposite arm of the chair.

I'd brought my holster, but sleeping with a gun in your

armpit is a dangerous prospect. I put the Colt on the end table within easy drawing distance.

I was midway through a dream where I was trying to brush knots out of my hair and it was coming out in clumps when a voice snapped me awake.

My hand was halfway to the gun when Holly said, "It's just me."

"What's up? What's wrong?"

"Nothing's wrong," she said. "I just . . . I wanted to tell you that you don't have to sleep here if you don't want to."

"That's all right," I told her. "Your first night back, I'm not going to leave you alone."

"I don't want to be alone," she said. "I just mean you don't have to sleep *here*. If you don't want to."

Then I noticed she was wearing that pink silk robe I'd seen her in before. My eyes were at the level of her navel, a dark eye winking at me through the sheer fabric.

I stood up a little too quick and she took a step toward me, close enough I could feel her breath on my face. She was only the slightest bit taller than me, but she seemed to loom. She'd ditched the glasses and was looking at me with those big brown eyes.

No, not brown. There were flecks of amber and green in them. How'd I not notice they were hazel? I thought. I was a detective, for Christ's sake.

She ran a hand through her thick wave of ink-black hair and I caught a whiff of shampoo. Something sugary. The wave fell back over one of her eyes. My hand was halfway up, ready to brush it aside, when I caught myself.

I took half a step back. Just far enough that I couldn't smell her.

"Look," I said, my voice cracking only a little, "I have a personal and professional rule. When it comes to mixing the two, I mean."

"Really? You've never . . . mixed the two?"

The way she said "mixed" would have gotten her banned in ten countries.

"I find that hard to believe," she said.

My mind flashed back to recent instances where I'd let my libido take the lead during a case. The first was with a client, the second with a cop. Neither had proven the wisest decision.

"Oh, no, I've done plenty of mixing," I admitted. "The bartenders at the Copacabana have nothing on me. That's why I made the rule."

She took her own step back.

"Right. Sorry."

"No, it's . . . it's not you."

"I understand," she said, crossing her arms over her chest.

"In other circumstances—"

"It's fine, Will. Really. We're both adults. I'm not . . . I just thought we were—I thought it would be nice. Good night."

She turned and walked back into her bedroom. She didn't slam the door, but she definitely closed it with emphasis.

I sat back in the chair, heart still pounding. I thought about going and knocking on her door, but I eventually nixed the idea.

I wasn't entirely sure what I would do if she let me in.

CHAPTER 40

We arrived at the *Strange Crime* office at 10:15 Thursday morning. Holly had called ahead and was informed by Marlo that the entire staff was present and available for questioning.

We'd had a perfectly pleasant breakfast, followed by a perfectly pleasant drive over. No mention was made of Holly's pass the night before, or of my turning her down.

So it wasn't a big deal, she was pretending it wasn't a big deal, or it was a very big deal but she was preoccupied with the impending conversation.

When we came through the door, a total of five faces looked up to see who had arrived. There were Brent and Marlo, along with Kenny, the copy editor, Frances, the illustrator, and Joy, the part-timer from Columbia University. All of them were relatively easy to identify from age and sex. Only Mort was missing.

Brent and Marlo came to greet us as a pair, peppering Holly with a flurry of questions.

"What's going on?"

"Your house was broken into?"

"Are you all right?"

"What's going on?"

I suggested we adjourn to the Cabinet of Mysteries, where we could have a modicum of privacy. The eyes of the other employees tracked us, and I tried to track them in return, wondering if one of them seemed a little more interested than the others. I paid special attention to Kenny, since we were pretty sure our killer was a man.

He was a twig of a guy who looked like he'd get winded lifting a coffee mug. Not the sort who could manhandle dead bodies. His face told me nothing other than that he was curious.

Maybe one of the women had a boyfriend, I thought. I would have to ask about that.

Then we were in the storage room, and I focused my attention on the co-editors.

There were no chairs, so the four of us stood awkwardly. I positioned myself to the right of the door. Also, I kept my coat on. The better to hide my holster.

Holly might have trusted them, but I sure didn't. They were the two people I knew for a fact had read Holly's story, and I could easily imagine their fascination for crime getting kinked up somewhere down the line.

"What's going on?" Marlo asked. "Why the secrecy?"

"We read about the murder of that detective," Brent said. "Was that something to do with your stalker?"

That was a good line, I thought. Making it clear he still bought the stalker story. Was it calculated or on the level?

Holly gave me a look, and I nodded for her to take the lead.

"I haven't been honest with you," she said. "About my background. So I need to tell you now, and this is very hard, so please don't interrupt me until I'm finished, okay?"

The pair nodded. I'd watched them during Holly's prelude, paying close attention to their eyes, to the little muscles around their mouths, ones you can't control even when you try.

I saw something I didn't like.

I crossed my arms, bringing my hand to within inches of my gun.

Holly gave them the lot, up to and including the fact that there was a killer out there using her work as inspiration. The only thing she left out was that Klinghorn's killer had used her most recent story as inspiration, and she'd done that at my request. The thing about the business cards being stuffed in Klinghorn's mouth hadn't made the papers, so reading Holly's story wouldn't automatically tip someone off about the connection.

Unless you were the killer.

"Oh, my God," Marlo gasped when Holly was finally done. "I'm so sorry. For what happened and . . . I'm sorry you felt you couldn't tell us."

"I couldn't tell anyone," Holly said. "I mean, I didn't tell anyone. For a long time."

"So you didn't know?" I asked the pair. "About Holly's father?"

"Of course not," Marlo said. "I mean . . . how could we?"

I shrugged. The movement let my hand slip inside my coat.

"I don't know," I said. "How could you, Brent?"

Marlo and Holly gave me identical confused looks. Brent's face was blank, but you could see the panic if you knew where to look. Just like I saw that he knew what Holly's big reveal was before she dealt the final card.

"I don't . . . well, I don't know how . . ." he said.

Something in his voice tipped the other women off.

"Brent?" Marlo said. "What is she saying?"

"Did you know?" Holly asked.

The man backed up two steps and then he hit a stack of magazines and was stuck. He plunged both hands in his hair and yanked. His glasses had slid as far down as they would go while remaining on his face.

"Look, it's not . . . It was an accident!" he said. "We were putting together that piece on New York City's most famous killers and Daniel Truelove was in the mix. I knew we probably wouldn't have room for art, but I went looking for it just in case."

"You found the photograph," I said. "Of Holly being carried away after her mother's murder."

He nodded and had to catch his glasses before they hit the floor.

"It's not a huge resemblance, but it's there," he said. "I saw it right away."

Marlo took a step toward her husband.

"That was before you even got drafted, the August—no, the June—1943 issue," she said. "Four years? You've known for four years and you haven't said anything?"

"Actually, it's only three years and—"

"Don't you throw numbers at me!"

"It was Holly's secret. I figured she'd tell us when she was ready."

There were about five seconds here where all three women in the room looked at him with identical faces of disgust.

Marlo reacted first.

"You idiot," she said, punching him in the arm.

"Ow," he whined. "That hurt."

"You bet it did."

She hit him again. Harder.

"Hold off, hold off," I said.

Marlo stepped back and Brent looked at me in relief.

"Oh, I'm not rescuing you," I told him. "I just need to ask you a couple of questions before she resumes the beating. The most important one being: Who did you tell?"

"Nobody," he said. "I swear."

"Four years—I'm sorry, three years and change—and you

didn't spill that you had Daniel Truelove's daughter on the payroll."

"I didn't even tell my wife."

He was playing full defense now and it was hard to judge if he was lying. I asked the experts.

"Okay, ladies. You know him better than I do. Is he telling the truth?"

Marlo and Holly looked at each other, at Brent, back to each other.

Marlo nodded, then Holly mirrored her.

"He can't lie to save his life," Marlo said. "Which I'm seriously considering taking."

"You should have talked to me," Holly said. "You should have told me you knew."

Marlo's hand slid into Holly's and gave it a squeeze.

"Verdict is you're on the level," I told Brent. "So here's question two: Who did you show Holly's new story to?"

"Which new story?" Brent asked.

"The Horace Bellow piece. 'Death Gets a Dial Tone.'"

Marlo and Brent shared a look.

"No one," Marlo said. "We haven't even read it yet."

"Neither of you?"

"We've been working like crazy on the next issue," Brent explained. "That new stuff is for the one after."

"Where is it now? Holly's story?"

Marlo nodded at the closed door. "On my desk. It hasn't moved since she brought it over on Sunday. Why does that matter?"

So much for easy answers.

"Just curious," I said. "I'm going to go on out and nose around, ask some questions. See if anyone might have wandered into the office and taken a peek. Is everyone around?"

Marlo nodded. "Everyone except Mort."

"When Holly called, you told her there was a full house."

"There was, but Mort had a client emergency come up. Some error in one of the ads. He should be back later."

"All right," I said. "Commence the vivisection."

I left the three to work out what they needed to work out. I did not envy Brent, but I was starting to suspect he wasn't a killer. Just an idiot.

Back in the main room, I was intensely aware of the three pairs of eyes on me. I smiled and sauntered over to Marlo's desk. Holly's bundle of pages was exactly where she'd left it on Sunday, half-buried under a stack of proofs.

I stalled while I thought about how to approach things. The problem with an open office plan is that there's no privacy. Everyone would get a preview of the questions.

I could ask one person after another to step into the hall, but not only would that put them all on edge, there was another line outside the casting agency. I didn't want to air my business in front of the ingenues.

I considered getting them in a huddle and asking them questions as a group. See if anyone contradicted anyone else.

My gaze passed over the empty desk in the far corner.

Mort.

Who'd had an emergency right after Holly called to say we were coming over.

I aimed my saunter in that direction. Unlike Marlo's desk, there were no piles of papers cluttering Mort's. Everything was neat and tidy, a leather-bound calendar taking center-right position, a two-inch-thick address book taking up center left. I casually slid open one drawer, then another.

"Did Brent or Marlo announce we'd be coming over?" I asked the room.

"She didn't say, but we knew," Kenny said.

"What do you mean?"

"We all heard Marlo tell Brent how we were going to have visitors and one of them was his second-favorite detective."

Huh.

"Did Mort say what client was having the problem?"

"I don't think so." That was from Joy. "He just said there was a problem with an ad and he had to go see to it."

"That happen a lot?"

She shook her head. "Not since I've been here."

Frances seconded Joy. "Mort hardly ever leaves his desk," she told me. "He's practically glued to that phone."

I picked up the calendar, thinking to look up the days of the most recent murders. When I opened it to the current week, a card tumbled to the floor.

I recognized it at a distance. But I picked it up anyway.

DARRYL KLINGHORN
Private Investigation Services

"Mort lives in Jersey, doesn't he?" I asked with as even a voice as I could manage.

"No, he's down in Rockaway." This was Kenny again.

"You don't happen to have his address, do you?"

CHAPTER 41

An hour later I was on my way to Rockaway.

Why the delay? you ask.

I decided to play it safe and used Mort's phone to call the office before I went running after a possible killer. The woman who signs my paychecks might have a suggestion or two.

The call was answered by Mrs. Campbell, who, when I asked her to put our boss on the line, told me that wouldn't be possible.

"She went out."

"What do you mean she went out?" I asked. "Went out where?"

"She said she—why are you whispering?"

"Because bullpens make for great eavesdropping. Now, the boss said what?"

"She said she had a doctor's appointment. Left about an hour ago."

I knew my boss's schedule, and there wasn't a doctor's appointment on the books for months. Unless she'd made one on the fly.

"How did she seem?" I asked. "Is she having another flare-up?"

"Not that I could tell, but you know how she is."

Meaning if it was possible to hide her symptoms, she'd attempt to.

"Okay, well, when she gets back, give her this message."

Lowering my voice even further, I gave Mrs. Campbell the rundown of things at the *Strange Crime* office and my plan to go to Mort's house in the hopes of locating either the man in question or a pickable lock.

"If she were here, she'd tell you not to go alone," the housekeeper said.

"Well, she's not there, is she?" I countered.

"No, but I am. And I'm saying you best not go alone. I find out you did, I'll tan your hide. I don't care how old you are."

She was probably bluffing about the hide-tanning. But it's not good to piss off the woman who makes your meals.

"Fine. I'll recruit backup."

After hanging up, I briefly thought about grabbing Holly. But she was still in the storage room with Marlo and Brent, and from the sound of things coming from under the door, their issues weren't going to be resolved for a while.

Then I had a better idea.

It took three calls to the boardinghouse before its owner agreed to wake up her tenant, who, once conscious, couldn't say yes fast enough.

A quick trip to East Harlem, and Sam Lee Butcher was hopping into the passenger seat, a big smile on his face.

"Hey, Miss Parker. Thanks for giving me the call. I'm real happy you thought of me."

"Don't thank me yet," I said. "We don't know what we're going to run into."

As I pulled away, I waved at the scowling woman standing on the boardinghouse stoop.

"Sorry if I got you in trouble with your landlady."

"Oh, it's no trouble for me," Sam Lee said, settling back into the Caddy's leather seat. "But you might want to steer clear of Mrs. Henry. She's of the mind that white women are nothing but trouble. I told her you and me weren't involved like that but . . . she has her opinions."

"I just rousted you out of bed to go off chasing a man who might be responsible for brutally murdering four people."

"So?"

"So your landlady's right," I said. "I am definitely trouble."

After three traffic jams and more wrong turns than I could count, we reached Mort's street, in a quiet, residential neighborhood not too far from the beach.

Rather than make the turn, I parked on the corner and looked down the street to what I deduced was Mort's address. That deduction was based on the fact that I saw the man himself—easily identifiable by another loud sweater, this one in fire-engine red.

He was walking out of his garage carrying a box half as high as he was tall. I watched as he heaved the box into the back of a delivery van, then turned around and went back into the garage.

"That's our mark."

"Looks like he's getting ready to skedaddle."

"Yes, it does."

I let the Caddy glide past the intersection, then turned down the next street over. There were narrow alleys between the houses—thin strips of concrete and weeds, with tall wooden fences on either side.

I pulled up in front of a house halfway down the block and looked down the alley. I could see the side and rear of Mort's garage just on the other side of the fence.

"Here's the plan."

I told it to him. Sam Lee didn't like it. His principal objection was that he thought we should switch roles. But my role involved the part that would be frowned on by the cops if I were caught, and my first goal of the afternoon was to not get Sam Lee arrested.

Once I had him reluctantly on board, I hopped out and casually strolled across the sidewalk and down the alley. No furtive scurrying or looking this way and that. Remember the first rule of breaking and entering? Act like you belong there.

Once I got to the halfway point, I waited. After a moment, I saw the Caddy pass slowly by the alley on Mort's side of the line and heard it slow to a stop. Immediately after, I heard Sam Lee's voice.

"Excuse me! Excuse me, sir!"

A mumbled response from Mort.

"Yes, I'm trying to find 429 Jasper Street."

Another mumble.

"Any help you can give, sir. This car—it belongs to Miss Myrna Loy. The film star? She's in town visiting her sister on Jasper Street and—"

There was more, but I was moving. I leapt straight up, grabbed the top of the wooden fence, and pulled myself up and over. Then I lowered myself as gently as I could to the ground.

There wasn't much clearance between fence and garage, and I had to do a sideways shuffle around the back corner and into a postage-stamp backyard. No door on that side of the garage, but there was a back door into the house.

Its lock was rusty from disuse, but simple enough to force. I was inside in under twenty seconds. I'd been keeping a stopwatch running in my head, and that put me at about a minute since the Caddy pulled up. I knew how Sam Lee could talk when given free rein, so I figured I had another minute before Mort came back inside.

Fingers crossed he'd go into the garage, which was where it looked like he'd been taking that box from.

The back door opened onto a short hall. Before I'd left the *Strange Crime* office, I'd asked if Mort was married and was told he wasn't. So hopefully I wouldn't stumble on anyone.

The first door I came to was an unused bedroom. At least I thought that's what it was. There was a bed, but I'd have had to dig to find it. There were piles of fur coats and gowns, stacks of paintings, and a column of radios stacked floor to ceiling in the far corner.

I backed out and opened the next door in line.

It was a linen closet, equally stuffed. I glanced down and nearly shrieked when I saw a rotund troll squatting on the second shelf.

I peered closer. A carved wooden Buddha the size of a small child smiled blankly back at me.

My heart was still racing when I heard the Caddy's horn. Two honks.

"Shit," I whispered.

One honk was garage. Two was the house.

I didn't have time to think, so I hurried to the back bedroom and closed the door just as I heard Mort come in the front. I crab-walked around the piles on the floor until I was on the other side of the bed, then I crouched down.

I pulled out my gun and waited.

I heard Mort shuffling around somewhere in the house. He wasn't being quiet about it. There was a lot of stomping and muttering and the sound of things being moved about.

While I waited I thought about the paintings and the furs and the assorted bric-a-brac shoved into every corner and tried to piece things together.

Was Mort one of Checchetto's antiques and curio suppliers? Did he also specialize in murder memorabilia?

One of my calves was flirting with a charley horse, so I shifted my weight. My backside nudged something behind me. I had just enough time to mutter my favorite four-letter word before the column of radios came crashing down.

Luckily none of them hit me on the head. Unluckily they made the loudest sound I'd ever heard.

Mort was muttering his own favorite words as he stomped down the hall, flung open the door to the bedroom, and flicked on the ceiling light.

I'm assuming from the way his jaw dropped that he expected to find an accident of gravity, not a snooper. I rose to my feet, gun pointed generally in his direction.

"All right, Mort. I want you to—"

He never got to hear what I wanted him to do because he was already running. Fast. By the time I stumbled over the fallen radios he was out the front door.

I ran after him.

Outside I saw Mort half a block away and moving like he knew what he was doing. I gained some ground, but he had a serious head of steam. He was making a squealing noise as he ran—like a teakettle.

"Eeeeeeeeeeeeeee!"

We'd gone three blocks and he wasn't slowing and I wasn't gaining. How was I going to explain to Ms. Pentecost that I let a killer escape because I couldn't find second gear?

Mort was about to cross a fourth intersection when I heard the squeal of brakes and a wall of Detroit steel appeared in front of Mort. Unlike Thomas Kelly, he managed to dodge around the vehicle, but Sam Lee was already out of the Cadillac and moving.

He hit Mort with a running tackle that should have made the New York Giants consider desegregation.

By the time I caught up with them, Sam Lee had Mort in an armlock that I'm guessing he learned from one of the roustabouts at the circus.

"I got him!" Sam Lee said, grinning. "But he's pretty squirmy."

He wasn't kidding. Mort was twisting and turning, trying to break free.

"Mort. Mort!" He focused on me. I flashed open my coat and showed him the gun again. Something clicked in his eyes and he grew real still real quick.

I glanced around and was pleased to see that everyone on the block seemed to be at work or otherwise occupied. Regardless, I got us off the street as quickly as possible. We loaded Mort into the back of the Cadillac and I kept the gun on him while Sam Lee drove us back to Mort's house.

I got out and opened the trunk. It was mostly empty except for the spare tire and assorted emergency provisions. I fiddled with the lining on one side and popped open a secret compartment. Among the contents, some of which were not strictly legal, was a pair of police-issue handcuffs.

Mort was silent as the cuffs clicked shut. If that's not a sign of a man secure in his guilt, I don't know what is.

I left him in the backseat and told Sam Lee to keep an eye on him.

"You gonna leave me the gun?" he asked.

"I'd like to keep the list of possible charges against you to a minimum. He gets frisky, just chase him down again."

I went back inside, this time detouring through the garage on my way. It, like the house, was packed with things. A lot of paintings, bric-a-brac, and small pieces of furniture that looked old and uncomfortable.

If I didn't know better, I would have thought Mort was a fence. Except most of the goods—the tower of radios and the furs being the exception—was unfenceable. It was all one-of-a-kind stuff. Hard to shift on the sly.

It wasn't a mystery I was going to solve on my own, so I

hunted around the house until I found Mort's phone. I dialed the number I knew best. This time it was answered by the woman herself.

"Pentecost Investigations."

"Hello, Pentecost, it's Parker."

"What have you discovered?"

You might think this rude. Her not leading with an inquiry about my health or her concern for my well-being.

I didn't. It meant she expected me to handle myself and get results.

I gave her the batch in as few sentences as possible.

"When you say the items are 'unfenceable,' I take it you mean they are easily identifiable by the authorities."

"Exactly."

There was some rustling on the other end of the line. While she rustled, I thought out loud.

"Okay, so maybe Mort's connection to Checchetto is that he's a housebreaker and that was where he was unloading the stuff he couldn't move through a proper fence. The real hard-to-sell items. Mort doesn't look like a housebreaker, but he doesn't look like an Olympic runner, either. Somewhere along the way he asks Checchetto to help him get into Quincannon's little club. All the years of working for *Strange Crime,* he's picked up a twist or three, and he wants to be among his own. Checchetto says no and that sets Mort off. I'm not sure where he intersects with Perkins and Haggard, but I might find something if I dig around here long enough. What do you think?"

There was no answer.

"Boss?"

The sound of the receiver being picked up off the desk.

"I'm sorry. I had to put the receiver down. Did you say something?"

"Oh, nothing useful. Just being a detective."

"Good," she said. "Now tell me. Among the contents is there a Buddha?"

"Excuse me?"

"A hand-carved Buddha. A rotund figure about three feet high."

"Okay," I said. "I've always suspected it, but now I know. You're a witch."

"I take it that means there is."

"Yes, there is. Crouched in the closet like a goddamn goblin. You want to tell me how you knew that?"

"Yes, I do." I could actually hear the smile in her voice. "But I'd like to do it in person. Bring Mr. Cohen here. Now."

CHAPTER 42

Sam Lee drove. I played guard in the backseat. Mort sat quietly. Any energy he'd possessed had been spent on his attempted escape. His face was sunk in on itself, and he looked like a prisoner on his way to the chair. If death-row inmates were issued red woolly sweaters.

When we arrived at the brownstone, I draped my coat over Mort's shoulders to hide the handcuffs. Our neighbors were used to strangeness, but I didn't want to be seen in the process of what was technically kidnapping.

In the office, I removed the cuffs and planted Mort in the chair of honor while Ms. P got up to greet Sam Lee.

"Thank you so much for your assistance," she said, shaking his hand.

"Anytime, Ms. Pentecost. Whenever you need me."

"I'm afraid now I have to ask you to leave. The conversation we're about to have might involve information that's confidential in nature."

Sam Lee looked disappointed, but he took it in stride.

"That's all right, ma'am. I understand."

She took an envelope out of an inner pocket and handed it to him. He peeked at the sheaf of bills inside.

"Oh, no, ma'am. I couldn't. I was happy to help."

She smiled. "I also enjoy my work, Samuel. But I expect to get paid for it."

There was another round of handshakes and Sam Lee left.

That left me, my boss, and Mort Cohen, who hadn't budged. My boss and I took our respective chairs. I kept the Colt sitting on my desk, within easy reach of my left hand. I had a pencil in my right and a notebook open on my lap, ready to sketch out a shorthand confession.

Mort, I noticed, wasn't looking at my boss so much as what she had on her desk, which were half a dozen issues of *Strange Crime,* along with a thick file folder from our third-floor archives, open to display the stack of newspaper clippings they contained.

It wasn't the file I was expecting, but I recognized it. Things started falling into place.

"Mr. Cohen, thank you for joining us today."

"Look, I don't know what's going on here. This woman broke into my house. She had a gun! Then she and that Negro boy chased me down the street. This is . . . I'm going to call the police. I'm going to call the police and tell them everything."

Ms. P gave him a look of desert-dry amusement.

"You may use the phone on Miss Parker's desk."

"Wh-what?"

"To phone the police. You may do so now, if you wish."

Mort glanced at the phone then back at her. He didn't get up.

"I think we can dispense with the preliminaries," Ms. P told him. "While you might be able to explain your flight from Miss Parker as panic at finding a woman with a gun in your home, you cannot explain the items stored there. I, however, can."

She opened the file folder and patted the stack of newspaper clippings and police reports.

"Several years ago, the NYPD was faced with a string of burglaries on the Upper West Side. The burglars were very professional. They left no evidence and the police were never

able to recover any of the stolen property. Then late last winter the burglaries stopped. At least . . . they stopped there."

She moved her hand to one of the issues of *Strange Crime*
and flipped it open to a page she had marked. The Vita-Glow
survey.

"Was this your idea, Mr. Cohen?" she asked.

"No! Absolutely not," Mort said. "I mean, sort of. It's complicated. I never wanted to be a part of this, I swear to God. I
just got roped in and now I can't get loose."

Ms. P leaned back.

"Explain."

Mort looked at me. "Can I . . . um . . . can I get a glass of
water, please? Do you mind?"

I hid my smile. When suspects start asking for things—
cigarettes, drinks, and so forth—that means they're getting
comfortable. Settling in for a long chat.

I fetched him a glass of water from the kitchen. Taking
the Colt with me while I did so, because getting comfortable
didn't mean a suspect wasn't still capable of trying something.

"Thank you," he said, before downing half of it in a single
gulp.

"That was a pretty good chase you gave."

He gave me a smile that was half pride, half embarrass-
ment. "All-American track and field. Still got it, I guess."

"Mr. Cohen," my boss said, not a little impatiently.

"Right," Mort said. "So I have a regular poker game.
Mostly magazine people. One night—this was late in 1945,
around the holidays—there's this new guy at the game. Friend
of a friend. Raymond. Said he was in sales. But I'm in sales and
I know sales and he wasn't in sales. Anyway, during breaks I
was working on this ad for some kind of exercise gizmo. They
wanted a reader survey. Fill it in and get a free something or
other and a catalog. My friends were rubbernecking and, I
don't know how it started, but we got to talking about how

you can ask people anything in these surveys. If they think it's about making them healthy, about giving them a better life, they'll answer. We were making a joke out of it. What's your favorite sex position? How long's your . . . You get the picture."

He downed the rest of his water and wiped a hand across his mouth.

"Anyway, Raymond asked me out for a drink after. Really grilled me about the whole thing. Asked me how I liked my job, how it paid, and all that. I told him I did okay. Not great. Guys my age in advertising—we're a dime a thousand, you know? Anyway, that was that. A month later, he gives me a call. Says he has a full-page ad for me. He sends it over. Right away I notice it's all wrong."

"It asked the wrong questions." A statement from Ms. P, not a question.

"You bet it did," Mort said. "It had all these questions about work hours and habits and finances and—you know, it was just odd. I called Raymond and told him I could help him do it right. He says no. Run it as it is. So I did."

Ms. P leaned forward in her chair.

"So you weren't aware at the time of its actual purpose."

Mort shook his head. "Not until I started getting complaints. People who had filled out the survey weren't getting their free sample. I called up Raymond. He asked to meet. Same bar, same booth. This time he's got two other guys with him. None of them look like they're in the health business, unless it's on the subtraction side. That's when they let me in on the scheme."

It turned out, Mort explained, that Raymond and his friends were the crew who had been hitting those Central Park–adjacent homes. The heat was getting a little too much for them when Raymond sat in on that poker game, saw the advertising man working on his survey, and had a brainstorm.

The two big questions a good burglar wants answered

before a break-in are what's the family's routine and is there anything worth stealing. By crafting the right kind of survey, they could have victims mailing in the answers themselves.

The crew would sort through the few hundred survey responses they got every month, pick out the ones in New York City, then narrow those down to the most promising targets.

A side effect of this technique is that it spread the robberies out over the five boroughs, making it hard for the police to pin it on one crew. Instead, it showed up as—

"A citywide rise in burglaries," I said. "Exactly what Lazenby's trying to get a grip on right now."

Ms. Pentecost nodded.

"What happened when you found out what Raymond and his companions were using the survey for?" she asked.

"I said I was going to yank the ad. They said it was too late. I was part of it now. I was incriminated. I said who'd believe that, and they said who wouldn't. There were dozens of witnesses who'd seen us meeting at that bar. If I tried to pull the survey, they'd drag me down with them."

I looked at my boss to see if she'd caught a lie. She gave me the same look. I shook my head. I hadn't caught one, either.

"Okay, that was the stick," I said. "But then they gave you the carrot, right?"

Mort snorted.

"If you want to call it that. They said they'd take care of me. Give me a cut. I'm not gonna lie. Things were tight. I was excited about the money."

"But it wasn't money, was it?"

"Hell, no! It was stuff. Stuff they boosted out of houses," he said. "At first it was things like radios and furs. As good as cash, they told me. Just take it to a fence, but what do I know from fences? Then they started dumping other crap on me. Furniture and paintings and crap. Every week they come by with another load. I told them to stop, but they wouldn't listen."

To my knowledge, I'd never met Raymond or his crew, but I had to admire them. Not only had they found a way to get burglary victims to basically volunteer by mail, but they'd found a way to dump all the stuff their fence refused to take.

"You know what really bites the boot?" he added. "They stopped paying for the ad. I've had to pay for it out of my own damn pocket."

I made a sound. It wasn't a laugh, but it was close.

"Why did you flee your office this morning?" Ms. P asked.

"I heard Marlo on the phone. Telling somebody that the whole staff was in. Then I hear it's Parker coming back. I knew it had to be about me. I mean, that whole stalker thing didn't fly. I know what Holly makes. She's not calling in Lillian Pentecost for some heavy breather. It had to be a cover. The second time Parker was there, she was reading the damn *Times* story right in front of me. Taunting me. When I heard she was coming again, I knew that was it. I made an excuse and went to this truck rental place and started loading."

"Your intentions?"

"Jersey," Mort said. "I was going to heap every last stick of that crap in the swamp."

That time I did laugh.

By then I'd discarded the notion that Mort was our murderer. But there was still the fact of Klinghorn's business card on his desk, so I was holding out hope he knew something useful.

Ms. Pentecost was, too.

"Now that we have the essentials, I wish to suggest a solution to your problem."

"Ma'am, I'm open to ideas, because I'm fresh out. I can't eat. I barely sleep. I just want free of this."

"Do you have a personal lawyer? One experienced in criminal law?"

He shook his head. "Never needed one."

"I have frequently needed one, and I have him on retainer. After you leave here, you're going to call him. I'll tell him to expect to hear from you. You're going to tell him what you told me, and first thing tomorrow the two of you are going to make an appointment with Lieutenant Nathan Lazenby of the New York City Police Department. While you are certainly guilty of conspiracy and possessing stolen goods, I think that if your tale proves true and verifiable, the district attorney will drop those charges in exchange for your testimony against Raymond and his colleagues."

Considering how long that crew had been plaguing the cops it would probably be the quickest deal the DA ever made.

"First I need something from you, Mr. Cohen."

"Anything! I'll do anything."

"What do you know about the murders of Michael Perkins, Connor Haggard, Flavio Checchetto, and Darryl Klinghorn?"

A pause and then, "Nothing. Not a thing."

"Nothing?"

"I hadn't even heard those names until that Klinghorn guy showed up at the office asking."

"When was this?"

"Monday morning, bright and early. I was the first person there. Barely got off my coat when he strolled in. 'Hey—can I ask you a few questions?' That really put me over the edge, you know. Two detectives in as many days. Then he goes and turns up dead? I thought maybe Raymond and his boys had something to do with it, but I was too chicken to ask them."

My boss leaned as far across her desk as anatomy and propriety would allow.

"What did Mr. Klinghorn say to you? His exact words."

"I don't know about exact. He said he was working for Lillian Pentecost—for you, I mean—and that he had some questions. That's when he asks about the murders. He asks if we've ever done any articles on them. True crime pieces. I said, not to my knowledge but he was free to flip through the last couple issues. He asked how long Holly had been writing for us and I told him. He asked how many pseudonyms she wrote under and how much true crime stuff she wrote. I told him I was the sales guy and that he'd have to ask Brent and Marlo when they got in. Then he asked about her family—Holly's family—if I knew anything about them. I ask him what that's got to do with a stalking case and can't he just ask her, and he says thanks for the time and beats it. That was that."

I hoped that really wasn't that. Because if it was, we weren't any better off than when the day started.

CHAPTER **43**

We took him through it again, then a third time, for good luck. The details didn't change and the story didn't get crisper. Mort didn't have a verbatim kind of memory.

It was dark by the time I deposited Mort in a taxi and gave the cabbie his address. He had his instructions to call Ms. P's lawyer first thing. If he didn't, we'd get on the phone to the police and any hope for a deal would be gone.

Back inside, I plopped down in the chair Mort had just vacated. I didn't want to sit at my desk. If I did I'd be forced to look at my notebook filled with shorthand. The notes put a bow on a three-year-long string of robberies, but did nothing for our murders.

"What are the chances he does a runner?" I asked. "He's still got that truck parked outside his house. He could be in Canada by morning."

Ms. P shrugged. "You've had more exposure to Mr. Cohen than I have. What is your opinion?"

"My opinion is he's smart enough to know you're giving him a way out of a jam and scared enough not to want to go it on his own. I think he'll call."

"So do I."

"The Buddha?" I asked. "Just to cover all the bases."

"It was mentioned in one of the articles," Ms. P explained. "A gift from a favorite uncle."

"Hang on," I said. "I know your memory is good, but it's not that good. You had the file down here already, didn't you? Did you see this coming?"

"I thought the Vita-Glow ad odd compared to similar surveys. As an exercise I filled it out and was struck by how much personal information I was relaying to an absolute stranger. How useful it could be to a certain sort of criminal."

"Damn," I said. "You really are a witch. Or a wizard. Wizardess. Is that a word? I'm saying you're magic, is what I'm saying."

I kicked off my shoes and sank back in the armchair. The long day—the long week, month, and what there was of the year—had started to catch up with me.

"Are we saying that this whole robbery scheme has nothing to do with our murders?" I asked.

"So it seems."

"If you will recall, not too long ago we ran into another kind of crime ring in the same small town in which there was a murder. The consensus was that having two big crimes in such close proximity and not having them connected was too big a coincidence to swallow. What makes this one more palatable?"

"This is not a small town," she reminded me. "Though if you see a possible connection, I'm open to suggestions."

I shuffled some pieces around in my head.

"Maybe Raymond or one of the guys on his crew is our killer. Some of these second-story men—they're real freaks. Get off on breaking in when people are home. You should hear the stories Jules has. Anyway, one of them's a freak and at some point Mort lets slip about Holly being Horace and . . ."

My train of thought ground to a halt. I could actually hear the engine seize. Steam might as well have been coming out of my ears.

"Okay, I give up," I told her. "I don't like it being a separate thing, but I don't have a worthwhile alternative. I'm still going to pick at it, though."

"Of course you are."

I leaned my head back and counted cracks in the ceiling.

"I guess I should get back to Holly's place," I said, more to myself than my boss. "I ran out of the magazine office without telling her where I was going. I didn't want to chance anyone warning Mort."

"Miss Quick called just before your arrival with Mr. Cohen. She said that she would prefer to be alone tonight."

Ah.

"I explained to her again how that would not be wise, but this time she was adamant. Were there any difficulties last night?"

"None worth reporting."

My boss knew me well enough to recognize I was being evasive. She also knew well enough to leave it alone.

As for Holly—she wanted to take her chances with a killer over spending a night with me in the next room. Which let me know just how badly I had bungled things.

But she'd been the one who'd made the pass, damn it. Not me. Why's she the one with her feathers ruffled? It's not like I'd turned her down hard, right? I'd gently explained that she was a client and—

"Will?"

I blinked. Ms. P was looking at me expectantly. How long had I wandered? Probably not as much as seven seconds, but still.

"Swerving back to our murders," I began, "I'm open to what I do next. I know I'll have to go back to the magazine and interview the rest of the staff. Though I'm tentatively ruling Brent out, at least for the time being."

I gave her a précis of the storage room conversation.

"Brent's a moron. Or at least he did a good impression of one," I said. "But he doesn't strike me as the murderous type. Tentatively."

"I concur. Tentatively."

"So where are we?" I asked. "Speaking of where are we, where were you when I called? Mrs. Campbell said you were at the doctor's. Are you feeling all right? If you're hiding another flare-up, we're going to have a conversation and I can't promise there won't be yelling."

She waved me down.

"Eleanor misunderstood," she said. "I was not seeing my physician, but Miss Quick's. Her psychiatrist, Lydia Grayson."

Grayson was so far down my to-do list she'd practically fallen off it.

"You think there might be a connection through the psychiatrist? Holly spilled about her new story in therapy and Grayson squealed to someone? Or someone got at her notes?" I asked. "I swear, if we find out our killer shares office space with Holly's psychiatrist and has been eavesdropping, I'm just gonna—"

Again with the hand-flapping.

"No, no, no," Ms. Pentecost said. "Of course those questions needed asking. But it was more in the way of a consultation than an interrogation. I wanted to get her opinion on the psychology of our killer."

"How did it go?" I asked. "Any earth-shattering insights?"

Instead of answering, she picked at a loose braid, trying to get it back into the weave and warp. Eventually she gave up and began undoing the whole mechanism, taking out one pin at a time and laying them side by side on her desk.

"Should I fetch a brush, or were you going to answer?"

"No," she said. "No to a brush and no to any particularly

stunning insights. At least into our killer. Although she did help me to pinpoint the problem I've been facing with this case."

"Problem, singular?"

"On the surface it seems to defy our usual methods. That by understanding the victim, we can identify the killer."

I shrugged. "Well, yeah. What else are we supposed to do with this thing? The usual motives aren't in play."

"True," she said, staring down at the growing ranks of hairpins. "But that does not mean we should ignore our strengths."

"Okay," I said. "Whatever you think works. I'll line up some glasses of wine, put some jazz on the record player, and you can get that big brain of yours working."

"Not my brain," Ms. P said, looking up. "Yours."

I blinked, startled.

"My brain? My brain went on strike about half an hour ago. Around the time I realized that Mort was a dead end."

She shook her head, a smile playing at the corners of her mouth.

"Actually, I think he might have been quite useful."

"All right, I'll bite. How?"

"In helping us determine what Darryl Klinghorn knew and when he knew it," she said. "Let me explain."

"Please do."

She'd gotten to the last pin and shook out her mane.

"Let us assume that, on Friday, the day he delivered his report, Mr. Klinghorn did not know about Miss Quick or the connection between the murders and her stories. If he had, I believe he would have disclosed it. He would have wanted to show off his prowess."

I nodded. "I'm with you so far."

"By Sunday, he knew about Miss Quick. Enough that he located her address. This was the same day he paid twenty dollars to a 'D.S.' The notation suggests a bribe. Did this person provide him Holly's identity? Again—possible, even probable. I agree with you that it's unlikely this D.S. is Donald Staples, but we should not discard the possibility entirely. Or that D.S. is not a person's initials but a personal shorthand of Mr. Klinghorn's. Regardless, on Sunday Mr. Klinghorn broke into Holly's apartment. Searching for what, we do not know, but coming away, at least, with one of Miss Quick's complimentary copies of the magazine."

By then I could see the game she was playing. I took the ball.

"The next day he shows up at *Strange Crime*," I said. "He knows enough about Holly to ask questions. Knows she's our client. Knows about Holly's father, too, because he asks Mort about her family. The only thing that trips him up is the stalker angle. He didn't know we'd fed them that line. That gets him out of there quick. What he does next, we don't know. Whatever it is, it leads to him being dead in our backyard by two a.m. that night."

This time it was my boss who did the nodding.

"I miss anything?"

"Probably," she said, smiling to soften the blow. "But if you did, so did I."

"Now what?"

She got up and began slowly pacing the room, reaching out a hand occasionally to gently steady herself on whatever was within reach.

"We know what Mr. Klinghorn discovered and we know approximately when he discovered it. We know that somewhere along the way he crossed paths with our killer, that our killer became aware of him. Aware that his presence, his investigation, put the killer in danger. Yes, putting his body in our alleyway was a message, a boast, even, but his choice of victim was also self-preservation. We know all of that. Most important, we know Mr. Klinghorn's techniques, his desires, and his character."

She stopped mid-stride, right by my chair. She reached out and steadied herself on my shoulder.

"Will, I asked you to think like a killer," she said, looking down at me, her face framed by long, loose shanks of hair. "That was foolish. You know nothing about the killer other than the results of his work. But you know quite a lot about being a working detective. One who depends as much on action as on deduction. I'm not sure there is anyone more equipped to deduce from the facts at hand what Mr. Klinghorn's movements were and how he came into contact with our murderer."

I hoped there was more, but she just kept staring down at me, her face flushed in that way she gets when she's racing toward a solution.

"If you're waiting for me to come up with some kind of sudden revelation, you're out of luck," I said. "I wasn't kidding about my brain giving up the ghost."

She nodded and gave my shoulder a pat.

"I understand," she said. "Get some sleep and we'll reconvene in the morning."

Sleep.

Easier suggested than accomplished.

Ms. P was right. We had enough pieces to figure this out. We had Klinghorn's report: two hundred pages of everywhere he went and everyone he talked to while doing background on Perkins, Haggard, and Checchetto. We had all the little bread crumbs by way of the expense notes and the break-in and Klinghorn's questions to Mort.

Four years and change as a working detective. I should be able to figure this out.

I sat in my bed, lights on, staring at the ceiling, and thought. All I discovered was that there were fewer cracks than in the office. And that I could still smell the faint odor of cigarettes drifting in from the guest room.

I drew a hot bath and filled it with this lavender concoction that Mrs. Campbell had given me for my birthday. I lowered myself into the bubbles and soaked and tried to imagine that I was Klinghorn.

"So basically me, but sleazier," I muttered.

It was no good. I closed my eyes and tried to picture Klinghorn's second-rate-accountant face, but Holly's was the one that swam up out of the darkness.

How was she doing? I wondered. Alone again in her apartment. Alone like she's been so much of her life, wrapped in her books and the symphony of her typewriter and her secrets.

While somewhere out there was a killer. Someone who enjoyed taking Holly's imagination and twisting it for his own sick satisfaction.

He was going to kill again.

According to my boss, it was up to me to nail him.

An hour later I had pruned skin and no additional clues. At least the lavender overwhelmed the smell of cigarettes.

I pulled the plug and watched the purple, bubbly water swirl down the drain. Along with my hope of figuring this thing out.

"We're gonna have another body on our hands before we get this guy," I informed the emptying tub.

I changed into my warmest pajamas and tucked myself into bed. Looking at the time, I leaned over and turned off my light, then turned on the radio.

"Who knows what evil lurks in the hearts of men? The Shadow knows!"

In that night's episode, evil lurked in the heart of a mad surgeon who had kidnapped precious Margo Lane and was threatening to cut her open. The Shadow was hot on his trail.

I fell asleep before she was saved.

CHAPTER 44

I could tell you about the dreams I had that night. Some of them were pretty interesting. None are pertinent to this case.

Instead, I'm including some of Ms. Pentecost's conversation with Dr. Lydia Grayson.

My boss never actually told me the details of what she and Dr. Grayson talked about, and I never asked. Though I was certainly curious. That night—the one where she charged me with taking on the role of Darryl Klinghorn—she'd seemed as self-aware and focused as I'd ever known her. I wondered at the time what Grayson had said to inspire that.

It was only much later that I discovered she'd taken notes on that first meeting—a meticulous record of their conversation. She'd typed them up and put them away in her personal files.

I thought I'd share a portion of them here. I think it's . . . illuminating.

FROM THE FILES OF LILLIAN PENTECOST:

Dr. Lydia Grayson keeps her office at her home on the fifth floor of a building in Greenwich Village. Entering her home, you pass through a short hallway and into a room that is neither spacious nor cramped. It holds several comfortable chairs, the requisite couch, a table, and a watercooler, and is lit by a bank of high windows that let in a generous amount of sunlight.

Grayson herself is a large woman—large in voice, in body, and in personality. She reminds me of Eleanor in some ways, though she is younger, only in her forties, and speaks with the long-set dialect of a native New Yorker.

Replace her flower-print skirt and turtleneck sweater with a boilersuit and she would go unnoticed on the Brooklyn waterfront.

I asked Miss Quick to write out a letter of introduction that gave Dr. Grayson permission to speak with me about her patient's history. After she had a chance to read the letter, I gave Dr. Grayson a short summary of our case, first getting assurance that what would be said between us would remain confidential.

I notate our conversation for my own remembrance.

> *Dr. Grayson:* Well, isn't this just a big ol' bucket of awful? I'm going to have to give Holly a ring. This can't be easy for her. Though she's a lot tougher than she gives herself credit for.
>
> *Lillian Pentecost: I have found that as well. I assume the events of her childhood have provided certain defenses against further trauma.*
>
> *Dr. G:* It's not quite as simple as that, I'm afraid. Some of those defenses cause more harm than good. But that's neither here nor there. How can I help you? I'm not sure what use I can be. Unless you think I'm your killer, in which case I'll have to disappoint you. The only deaths I'm responsible for are three ficuses and a potted palm. I can't keep plants alive to save my life.
>
> *LP: You take notes on your sessions?*
>
> *Dr. G:* I'd be a poor therapist if I didn't. Ah, I see what you're getting at. I suppose someone could break in and go rummaging. But my notes are more like outlines. Just some key words and my own thoughts—you understand?
>
> *LP: But there is a record that Holly was once Henrietta Truelove.*
>
> *Dr. G:* That is definitely a key word.
>
> *LP: Let's talk about her stories. The ones she's currently writing. Does she tell you about those? And do you make note of them?*

Dr. G: Sometimes to the first question, almost never to the second. Unless I think it's somehow tied to other things she's working through. They frequently are. Holly employs words like a shield and a scalpel.

LP: *How so?*

Dr. G: A shield to defend her from the world. A scalpel to understand it. To slice open its guts and peer inside. I've had a number of writers as clients. It's not uncommon.

Anyhow, we usually talk about those connections between her life and her stories in the moment. So my notes on the plot and all that are sparse.

But Holly could have told you all this. You could have confirmed it with a phone call. So I guess we're back to that earlier question: How can I help you?

LP: *You've spent several years with Miss Quick talking about her past, her father.*

Dr. G: I have.

LP: *You've discussed what kind of man he was? His motivations? The kind of environment that leads to that kind of killer?*

Dr. G: We've stepped onto that dance floor once or twice. You want to know if our discussions of Daniel Truelove might shine some light into how this new killer thinks.

LP: *Any insights would be greatly appreciated.*

Dr. G: I don't know if I can give you any. My specialty isn't abnormal psychology. I've got some colleagues at Bellevue I can recommend. Though I don't think a single one has more experience with murderers than you have.

LP: *This particular species of killer is relatively foreign to me. Or I should say that my usual methods are of little use.*

Dr. G: What methods are those?

WILL HERE: No reason to go over Ms. P's methods of putting the victim first. It's nothing you haven't heard before.

Dr. G: I can see how that makes it difficult. But the way you describe things, it sounds like you didn't give your own methods much of a chance. You said this kind of killer is "relatively foreign." Emphasis on *relatively.* So you've had some experience.

LP: I have.

Dr. G: How did that go?

LP: Not well.

Dr. G: So you're second-guessing yourself.

LP: I'm exploring other methods.

Dr. G: While half-assing the old ones? See—that look you're giving me. That tells me I'm right and you know it.

LP: Time is of the essence.

Dr. G: Uh-huh.

LP: He will almost certainly kill again.

Dr. G: Probably. There's that look again.

LP: I don't appreciate your flippancy.

Dr. G: I'm not being flippant. I'm speeding things along. Usually I'm a lot more subtle, but usually I don't have someone like you in the chair.

LP: Someone like me?

Dr. G: Someone as intelligent as you. No. Holly would tell me *intelligent* isn't the right word. Someone who can swiftly sort through the bullshit. Who would almost certainly have done her research before showing up here. You'd have found out that my work and background couldn't help you a lick, not when it comes to someone like your killer.

So I'm going to ask you again. Third time's the charm.

What can I do for you, Ms. Pentecost?

LP NOTE: I considered walking out. There was much to be done. Will was, at that moment, at the offices of *Strange Crime.* It was possible that she might have discovered something. Perhaps even the killer. I did not have time to waste.

It was that thought that stopped me.

Time. And the lack of it.

LP: *You know that I suffer from multiple sclerosis?*

 Dr. G: I read the papers.

 That must have been something. When you first got the news. I'm sure you knew something was wrong. I mean, that kind of thing doesn't land on you all of a sudden. I had a patient with palsy. Not the same, but in the ballpark. Degenerative. Following a general path, but not one you can predict.

 That must be very hard. Having to live with the uncertainty.

WILL HERE: Ms. P started talking after that. For a long while. Things she'd never shared with me.

 I hope you won't mind if I don't share them with you.

 Instead, we'll jump forward a little.

 Dr. G: So when you said that time is of the essence, you don't just mean the case. You mean your own time. You don't know how much you get, so you're rushing to get as much done as you can.

LP: *Do you blame me?*

 Dr. G: Not in the least. Time's in short supply all around. But I imagine detective work is like any other profession. The more you hurry, the more you miss. I have a niece. Bought me this cross-stitching set. Thought it would help me relax. I didn't have the patience for it. I was rushing along, dropping stitches left and right. But I can sit here and tease out stories from patients for hours. Maybe because I don't know what the picture will end up looking like. The cross-stitch? I already know it's a kitten in a bed of daisies. I just wanted to get the damn thing stitched and over with.

Probably not the best metaphor. Should have stuck with "haste makes waste." Oldies are oldies for a reason.

LP: How does one balance that? Murderers are rarely so accommodating that they will wait for me.

Dr. G: Figuring out how to arrange your life? That's more than a single-session problem. In the end, it always comes down to the same questions. About desires and values and obligations.

LP: What I want to leave behind?

Dr. G: More like how do you want to live while you're here. In my experience, legacies are a fool's game. Worry about living and what happens after will sort itself out.

WILL HERE: There was more, but not much. Ms. P left soon after. She had a case to solve, after all. Or a case to task me with solving.

CHAPTER 45

I woke to the sound of a girl singing about toothpaste.
"Gets your teeth so white and pretty
Gets your teeth so cleeeeeean!"
I was humming along by the end. I felt practically electric.

I turned off the radio and looked at my clock. Minute and hour were about to shake hands on the twelve. No wonder I felt so energized. I'd slept double-digit hours for the first time in weeks.

Also, I had the answer. At least I thought I did.

I curbed my urge to race across to Ms. Pentecost's bedroom. I very deliberately went about my morning ablutions: brushing my hair, my teeth (*Gets your teeth so cleeeeeean!*), washing my face, choosing my outfit for the day. I settled on blue denim dungarees and matching jacket over a thin white pullover. It was an ensemble for early spring, but seeing the sunlight pouring through my window, I was feeling hopeful.

I even took a minute for lipstick, all the while thinking it through. Does it hold together? Is that how it really went?

I used a bit of tissue to blot my lips.

"Yep. That's how he did it," I said to the smug-looking redhead in the mirror.

I went out into the hall and found Ms. Pentecost's bedroom door open and the room empty. Going downstairs, I discovered the office equally vacant.

Hearing voices from the rear of the house, I went through the kitchen and out the back door. In the courtyard, I found my boss going to town on the weeds that had crept up through the bricks. Mrs. Campbell was in the alley, attacking the bloodstains and chalk outline with a mop.

I had, of course, seen my boss take part in manual labor before. Just never when we were in the throes of a case. She'd broken out her one pair of blue cotton overalls and her party hat. I call it that because its straw brim is wide enough to act as a serving tray. It was tied around her chin with a big yellow ribbon.

"Howdy, Huck," I said with a smile. "We whitewashing the fence later?"

She looked up. There were streaks of dirt across her forehead and sweat was pouring down her face.

"Both you and my doctor regularly berate me about my need for physical exercise."

She peered up at the sliver of sun peeking over the adjacent buildings. It was another unseasonably warm winter day.

"Regretting it yet?" I asked.

"My knees are. Here, help me onto the step."

She raised a hand and I pulled her into a sitting position on the back step. Then I sat down next to her.

"Turns out all I needed was a good night's sleep. I'm going to lay things out, then you tell me what's off about it. I'm sure something is."

She tilted herself to face me, looking at me expectantly.

"First of all, he's not a secret genius," I said.

"This is Mr. Klinghorn?"

"Right. That's been eating at me. Assuming the report is square, how did he get on Holly? Holly and *Strange Crime* and the connection between the murders and all of it. Because Klinghorn was, rest his soul, not a deductive genius. He was a straight-line thinker. He knew what he needed and kept going until he got it. If a brick wall appeared in his path, he'd blast through it or climb over it or whatever he needed to do. But—"

"It was still a straight line," Ms. P finished. "So how did he make these investigative leaps?"

"He didn't," I declared. "I mean, not really. He cheated."

I stood up and started pacing in a tight square. I had too much electricity in my limbs for sitting.

"Okay, so I'm Klinghorn. I've spent two weeks working on a trio of murders for the great Lillian Pentecost and that bitch of an assistant kicked me to the curb. That's not self-loathing. He actually called me that to my face. So here I am—I'm being Klinghorn again—on the outside and looking in. I know those cases are connected and I'm hell-bent on proving I can do more than sling muck on philanderers. But first I've got to know what Lillian Pentecost knows. So starting Saturday I park within eyesight of her front door and I watch and I wait. There's a slew of visitors, but I know about the Saturday schedule, so I don't get too excited. Pentecost and Parker—neither of them goes anywhere. I take a break to go home and catch a few. Then I do it again on Sunday. That's when I get lucky."

I stop pacing mid-square.

"He found Holly because I led her to him. I led him right to her goddamn door."

Ms. P made a little satisfied "hah."

"You wouldn't have noticed him following you?" she asked.

"Your average cop, maybe. But not Klinghorn. He would have done it right. That day, he'd have gotten everything. He would have followed me to Holly's apartment, to Golden Green, then to the *Strange Crime* office," I said. "That's where he really started scaling some walls. He sees me leave. Holly doesn't. Maybe he scopes her leaving with Marlo, follows them far enough that he knows they're not heading to Holly's place. He goes back there, checks out the locks, then heads to

Amos's to shell out five dollars and twenty-five cents for some skeleton keys, goes back to the apartment, and gets to work."

"How does he know which apartment is hers?"

I froze. Of course Ms. P would find the flaw.

"How would he know?" I pondered. "Her name isn't on the buzzer, so how could he . . ."

It clicked.

I dodged around the detective sitting on the stoop and went inside, through the kitchen, to the office, where I picked up the phone and asked the operator for a connection.

By the time I got an answer, Ms. P had caught up and was standing next to me.

"Golden Green Convalescent Home," the woman on the other end said. "How can I help you?"

"To whom am I speaking?"

"This is Mrs. Simpson."

"Doreen, isn't it?"

"Yes."

"Son of a bitch."

"Excuse me?!"

I hung up.

"Revise that timeline. After he figures Holly's not going home, he goes back to Golden Green. There he pays the receptionist, one Doreen Simpson, twenty dollars for information on Holly, up to and including her apartment number. Then on to Amos's. Then back to Holly's to go rummaging. The next day, he hits *Strange Crime*. He's seen her manuscripts. He knows she's Horace Bellow. He knows about the resemblance between her work and the murders, but he doesn't know about her being Daniel Truelove's daughter. When he asked Mort about her family, he meant Naomi. Who he knew was at Golden Green."

It wasn't all that many words, but I found myself breathless. Was this how Ms. Pentecost always feels? I wondered.

"How does that sound? Any gaping holes?"

"None that I can see," she said.

I was a few years too old to leap and whoop, so my heart did it for me.

"However . . ." she added.

My heart sat back down.

"Mr. Cohen was able to tell him little. It would have been another wall. What would he have done next?"

"That's the million-dollar question," I said. "After Mort, there are no markers."

"What would you do?" she asked.

I thought about it.

"When I hit a wall, I go back to my lead and see if I can get more meat off the bone," I said. "He got lucky staking us out before. Maybe he tried it again. His car was found a few blocks from here. I've been thinking the killer drove it there, but maybe he didn't. Maybe Klinghorn was nearby with eyes on our door. Though that means I missed him twice and I was pretty wired after coming back from safecracking. I'd hate to think . . ."

I trailed off because Ms. Pentecost had stopped paying attention. She was staring at the painting above her desk. Or not so much at it as through it. She had that look she gets when she's pondering a problem.

No, not a problem. A solution.

I held my breath and waited.

Suddenly she snapped out of it and looked at me. She had that gleam in her eyes—I use the plural because somehow even the glass one manages to glint.

"Does Golden Green have a cafeteria?"

That was not the question I was expecting.

"I don't think a cafeteria, but there's got to be a kitchen, since they serve meals. Why?"

"During our interview at her home, Miss Quick mentioned she was being charged a nutrition fee. Which they might implement if they needed to upgrade their ingredients or their equipment."

"Sure."

"A convalescent home might very well fall under Michael Perkins's purview as a health inspector. His remit was schools and medical facilities, remember?"

"Okay, I can see that," I said. "That might be one connection. But—"

"When you took Miss Quick to visit her mother, did she leave her new manuscript in the car or did she have it with her?"

"She had it in that big bag of hers," I said. Then the penny dropped. "Which she left in her mother's room while she went strolling."

"How long was it unattended?"

"Plenty long."

I had a sudden cascade of thoughts. They were still pouring while I dialed Holly's number.

No answer. I looked out the window.

"It's a real nice day, isn't it?" I said.

I called Golden Green again.

"Golden Green—"

"Is Holly Quick there?"

"Excuse me?"

"Holly Quick. Is she visiting her mother today?"

"Yes, she just—I'm sorry, who is this? Is this the same woman who called—"

I hung up.

"She's there now."

We shared a look and started moving.

CHAPTER **46**

"Do you think her danger is great?" Ms. P asked. "He has not harmed her so far."

"Here's the thing," I said, taking off my jacket so I could slip on my holster and the Colt. "Even discounting the saying that you hurt the ones you love, Holly's smart. Not as smart as you, but I think smarter than me."

I slipped my jacket back on and we hurried out the door of the brownstone and toward the car, Ms. P still clutching her party hat.

"She's got her routine. She's going to leave her bag in her room again. She'll probably remember the cigarettes this time, though. Maybe think to herself, 'Oh, I'd better remember my cigarettes. I left them in my bag last time.' Then she'll think of what else she left in the bag and the implications. If he's in the vicinity, do you think she can keep it from showing on her face?"

By then we were in the Cadillac and I was shoving the gearshift into drive with one hand and closing the door with the other. Ms. P had chosen to ride shotgun.

I was turning the car onto Bedford Avenue when I said, "Son of a gun."

"What is it?"

"Naomi," I said. "I had it in my head she was basically a mannequin. She doesn't talk; she barely knows where she is. But just five years ago, she was giving Holly advice on talking with Brent and Marlo. Which means she probably did a lot of her getting worse while at Golden Green."

I swerved around a slow-moving truck and floored it. Ms. P clutched the grab handle above the door.

"She could have told anybody anything. She wouldn't know better. That's how he found out about Holly's father. He sat and listened."

We should have caught that, I thought. We should have thought of that long before now.

After what seemed like an eternity of driving, Green-Wood Cemetery appeared on the horizon. I glanced at my watch. It had been eighteen minutes since I called. Eighteen minutes during which anything could have happened.

I screeched the sedan to a halt at the front entrance of the convalescent home and ran inside, Ms. Pentecost as close on my heels as she could manage.

Doreen was at the desk poring over the same copy of *Screen Romances*.

"Is Holly Quick with her mother?"

It took her a goddamn eternity to get her nose out of the magazine. She blinked once, twice.

"Holly Quick!" I repeated. "Is she still here?"

"You were the one on the phone, weren't you? I do not appreciate—"

But I was already moving, running as fast as I could through the labyrinth of narrow halls to Naomi's room. The door was standing open.

I'd learned long ago not to rush through a doorway without checking. I peeked my head around the corner.

Empty. No Holly. No Naomi, either.

Behind me came the sound of panting. Doreen hurrying to catch up. My boss not far behind.

"You cannot just barge in here! Only family members have—"

"Did Holly take her mother outside?"

Doreen looked like she was courting an embolism. She was opening her mouth to yell at me again when my boss put a hand on her arm.

"Mrs. Simpson," she said, "this is an emergency and we really need to locate Miss Quick."

I don't know if it was Ms. P's tone of voice or the fact that she wasn't me, but Doreen straightened her cardigan and said, "She took her mother outside about ten minutes ago. If you'd simply asked that before—"

I was moving again. I'd made it to the first corner when I stopped and turned back.

"Where's Dobbin?"

A blank look from Doreen. If I was in striking distance I'd have smacked her.

"Your boss, Doreen. Where's your boss?"

"I—I don't know. He was talking with Miss Quick about something."

"He went out with her?"

"Yes. She was really very—"

Very what? I don't know. I was already gone. By the time I hit the front door I had the Colt out.

My eyes went to the parking lot first. Squatting in a space marked RESERVED was a bright-blue Plymouth. I hurried to it, gun at the ready.

I glanced in the windows. No one in the driver's seat. No one in the back. I was about to move on when something caught my attention. Two somethings.

The trunk lid was open half an inch.

And there was a spot of bright red marring the fresh chrome of the bumper.

CHAPTER 47

I have a complicated relationship with God. I've seen enough that, if an almighty does exist, I think he probably resembles one of Quincannon's crew. A man with a sick sense of humor who delights in cruelty.

But in that moment I said a silent prayer. Please be empty. Please let Holly be okay. I reached out with my free hand and opened the trunk.

It wasn't empty.

Dobbin's lifeless eyes were staring up at me. It took a long moment before I managed to pry my heart out of my throat. See what I mean about a sick sense of humor?

There was a gash over his eyebrow and blood was trickling down his cheek. On the floor of the trunk by his head was a syringe. I didn't need a chemist to know it would be a high-octane Mickey. I was reaching for it when Dobbin blinked.

"Shit!"

I checked for a pulse. Slow and thready. But still there.

I heard a noise behind me. I turned, Colt raised.

"Did you find something?" Ms. P asked from the doorway.

"It's the manager," I said. "He's been drugged. He's alive, but barely."

Doreen appeared behind her.

"Excuse me! That's Mr. Dobbin's car. You can't just—"

She saw the gun and her eyes became saucers.

"I'm calling the police!" she shrieked and ran back inside. I looked to Ms. P.

"Pry the phone out of her hand and ring for an ambulance. See if you can stall on the cops. I don't want them to spook our killer."

No argument. No "Be careful." Just a single nod, and away she went.

I kept scanning—the parking lot, the street, the cemetery—hoping to catch a sign. My eyes landed on Holly's preferred bench.

It was empty. The wheelchair next to it wasn't.

I sprinted to it. I found Naomi, eyes wide, face frozen in a look of distress.

"Naomi? Are you okay?"

She moaned and her hands fluttered in her lap.

"Did he take her? Did he take Holly?"

She made a sound, a low groan, and with the last bit of control she had left over her body, she jutted her chin out toward the graves.

I turned and looked down the little slope. Five hundred acres of tombstones and dead grass. There were maybe a dozen people scattered about, most stationed at graves paying their respects.

I drew a line out from Naomi's eyes. It landed on a pair walking close together, not in a straight line toward a particular marker, but sort of weaving in and out.

One of the figures slowed and the other, clad all in white, yanked them along. Neither were looking in my direction.

"Thank you, Naomi," I said. "Don't you worry. I'm gonna go get our girl."

I slid the Colt back into its holster and began what I hoped was a natural pace down the slope toward them. If he had another syringe, I wanted to get as close as possible before he tried to use it. I didn't want any of the other visitors to spot a woman holding a gun and shout an alarm.

A hundred yards.

Seventy.

Fifty.

I got to within thirty before Terry turned and saw me.

I started running. He tried to run as well, dragging Holly with him. But it's not easy to pull an unwilling participant over uneven ground while dodging tombstones.

Eventually the pair stopped, blocked by an open grave. Chairs were stationed around it in preparation for a service. Terry whirled to face me. He had one hand gripped tight on Holly's arm. The other was jammed into her ribs.

It wasn't holding a syringe. He had a gun.

I skidded to a stop ten yards away. The pistol looked like a .22—probably the one he shot Michael Perkins with.

I shifted my arm slightly, making sure my jacket covered my holster. I glanced around for approaching mourners. None close by. Good. Fewer people who could get hurt.

Terry wasn't looking too put together. His hair had come unpomaded and was peeling away in ragged blond curls. He'd shaved the mustache. Probably to attend to the split lip, which looked to have been self-stitched.

Sweat was pouring down his face, soaking down into his orderly's uniform. His baby blues rolled in their sockets like a cornered animal.

"Stay back!" he shouted.

"He did it," Holly gasped. "He's the killer, Will. He's the—ow! You're hurting me."

"Don't worry," I said. "We figured it out. A little late. Sorry for the inconvenience. Are you okay?"

"Yes. I'm fine. But he did something to Mr. Dobbin," she said. "We were on our way out with my mother and I had realized who he was but I didn't know what to do and I saw Mr. Dobbin and I asked him to walk with us and he didn't want to but I insisted because—because—and then—"

"Terry clocked him and doped him and shoved him in a trunk."

The orderly smiled.

"It's just a little medicine," he said. "It's kind of ironic, when you think about it. Dobbin—he asked me to order a whole case of it to use on our difficult residents."

His voice was steady, even if his eyes weren't.

"Oh, yes," he purred. "It works wonders on difficult people."

He was practically begging for one of us to ask him the follow-up. Whoever do you mean? The men you killed? Please tell me all about it, Terry.

Don't remember Terry?

That's okay—neither did I. I didn't remember him interrupting me when I was searching Naomi's room. How afterward he would have had all the time in the world to rummage through Holly's bag and get a preview of the newest Bellow.

I didn't remember how the orderly was one of the only other people who had regular access to Holly's mother back when she could talk. Maybe talking too much about the wrong things.

Terry got tired of waiting for us to take our cue. He shifted Holly so she was in front of him, the gun pressed into her back. That way he could put his mouth right up next to her ear.

"I was saving him for later, you know. I really wanted to choose the perfect story," he said. "I was thinking 'The Beat of the Bloodstained Heart.' What happens to the father in that one. I see what you were doing with that story. Nobody else did because nobody else understands. But I do. I really wanted to make it perfect, but I've been having trouble finding a hearse—at least one I can set on fire. I think his Plymouth will have to do. All cars look the same when they're burning, don't they?"

Tears were pouring down Holly's cheeks. I didn't know what she was more afraid of, the gun pressed into her back or the fact that his voice was so . . . casual.

Terry felt her sob.

"Oh, no, no, no. It's okay. He's really not a very nice man. All he cares about is money. You should hear how he talks about the patients. Your mother. He's such an ugly, ugly man. You'd want him to burn, too. But this way—stop crying! This way, at least, he'll be made into something beautiful."

His head snapped up, like he suddenly remembered we were a threesome.

"That's what I do. I take ugly things and I make them beautiful. No, not beautiful. I know how words matter so much to Holly. Or maybe beautiful *is* the right word. Because truth is beauty, isn't it? Artists understand that. Holly understands that. She and I show the world as it truly is."

I was only half listening. I was too busy running the angles. Terry wasn't a big man. That would be a plus if this was hand to hand. But he had Holly in front of him. And the ground we were standing on was sloping down toward the open grave. Only half of his head was in the clear, and it was pressed right up against his hostage.

It would be a hard shot. Maybe impossible. Not without hitting Holly.

"Mr. Quincannon understands," Terry was saying. "He understands about the world. About rules and morality. How they're designed to turn us into blind sheep trudging toward the slaughterhouse. Our whole lives spent trudging. But a few—a very few—will see. And understand. And then . . ."

He kept going. Going and going, because he finally had an audience. He was an artist at a gallery opening and he wanted to preen.

I'd stopped listening entirely. I was remembering Mrs. Campbell's story. And what Ms. Pentecost had said. This man wants attention. Validation. He's desperate to be understood, desperate to be seen.

I took my eyes away from him and locked them on Holly. "How'd you figure it out?" I asked over Terry's monologue.

"Wh-what?" she stammered.

"You said you figured out he was the killer. How'd you do it?" I asked. "I told Ms. P it was going to be the bag. You'd remember leaving it in the room with the manuscript."

Terry looked confused. Didn't we know he had the stage?

"I did remember that eventually," Holly said. "But what tipped me off first was Solly. We passed him in the hall on the way out."

"Solly?"

"Solomon Haggard. The old man who made the pass at you? That's where I'd heard the name Haggard before. I would have recognized it, but everyone here calls him Solly. So stupid of me, really."

"Do you know what that son of his said to me?" Terry asked, wrenching the spotlight back on himself. "He asked how I could let his father just roam around embarrassing himself. Like it was my fault. One visit! He pays one visit in five years and—"

"My boss got it from the food angle."

Terry made a choking sound, gagging on the indignation of being ignored.

I'd pulled a trick like this in Virginia. Except that time I had Ms. P standing behind the crook with three feet of sharp steel. This time the only backup I had was an open grave.

By then Holly had figured out the play and went along with it.

"What food angle?" she asked, doing her best to ignore the killer and the gun.

"You mentioned having to pay more for Naomi's board. Ms. P figured it was because of a bad review from Perkins. Some hygiene problem caused by what's-his-name here."

"That son of a bitch!" Terry snapped. "He said the meals I served the patients were a disgrace. That the kitchen wasn't clean. Like those walking corpses even noticed. Like . . ."

I tuned him out.

"I got it from following Klinghorn's bread crumbs," I told Holly. "He followed us on Sunday, the tricky son of a bitch. That's how he got your name and address. I think he came back to Golden Green on Monday for more, and that's what did him in."

Terry smiled. Or not so much smiled as bared his teeth, like a dog at the end of a chain.

"That pathetic little man," he growled. "I told him I had information for him. He was so excited. I lured him out to the parking lot and introduced him to my needle. Then later I showed him my knife. Did you like it? Did your boss? Did Lillian Pentecost like my exhibit? I call it *Death of a Detective*. He thought he was so smart."

For the first time since the conversation started, I looked Terry right in the eyes.

"He got you, though, didn't he? Got close enough to touch. Maybe even close enough to hit. He clocked you one before you got the needle in?"

His tongue flicked out and ran across the raw stitches on his lip. "He was a sheep. A nothing. A nobody."

"Klinghorn might not have been everything he wanted to be," I said. "But he was a somebody. You want to see a nobody, look in the mirror, you talentless little shit."

He snarled, took the gun out of Holly's back and began pointing it in my direction. The move brought him about six inches out of Holly's shadow. As soon as I saw daylight, I drew.

The Colt cleared its holster like it was greased. Like the

hundred times I'd practiced down in the basement. No prayer this time. I barely bothered to aim before I pulled the trigger.

Terry and Holly both tumbled back into the open grave.

I ran up, gun ready. The sound of the shot was still echoing across the cemetery.

Terry was lying on his back, Holly facedown on top of him. There was blood on both of them. I couldn't tell where it was coming from.

"Holly? Holly!"

She rolled over. Terry tried to take a breath through the ragged red hole in his throat.

I eased myself down into the pit and took the gun out of his twitching fingers. Once that was safe in my pocket, I pulled Holly to her feet.

"Are you all right?"

She nodded, staring down at the man, who was gasping for air and getting only blood. He looked at me, then at her, mouth opening and closing, trying to speak.

Finally he stopped trying. His chest stopped moving and his eyes turned up to fix forever on the bright blue February sky.

I gave Holly a boost. Then I pulled myself out of the grave.

CHAPTER 48

Let me count the ways we got lucky.

There was, of course, Ms. P and me figuring things out in the nick of time. Then there was that shot. An inch either way and Holly would have gotten hit or Terry could have fired off a bullet of his own.

There were the witnesses. An elderly couple visiting their son's grave, as well as a brother and sister bringing flowers to their dear departed mother.

They'd seen enough of the events to be able to testify that I fired in self-defense. That made the exchange with the first officers on the scene a lot smoother than it could have been.

And by the time the ambulance was carting Dobbin off to the hospital, he'd started to come around.

After that I thought maybe our luck had run out. Staples was the first detective to arrive, and we were shipped off to the nearest station house.

Before his arrival, Ms. P and Holly and I had about two minutes of privacy to iron out our story. The problem was there were too many wrinkles. Too many people knew Holly had been our client. The connection to Holly's stories was going to be on the record one way or the other.

That meant admitting that we had lied to the cops after Klinghorn's murder.

So we decided to give them the lot. The only thing we left

out was Holly's real identity. If they wanted that, they'd have to work for it.

At the station we were split up so they could work us over separately in an attempt to trip us up. I spent six hours in an interrogation room. The entire time I was thinking about Holly.

Ms. Pentecost would be fine. She'd spent enough hours in the box that I wasn't concerned. But police could get rough when they started prying. I didn't know how our client would hold up.

As for myself, I held up fine. Though it wasn't pleasant.

After I went through the story the third time, Staples started in on the threats.

"You're admitting that you and your boss lied—you lied when I visited you the first time and you lied when I questioned you about Darryl Klinghorn's murder."

He was back to asking questions without asking questions. I gave him an answer without giving him an answer.

"I'd like to call my lawyer, please. I know his number by heart."

It didn't get easier from there.

Three hours in, Howie Clark showed up from the district attorney's office. I knew him from our work on the Sendak case. He'd been promoted on the back of that conviction. If he felt he owed us, he wasn't showing it.

He made me go through the whole thing again. I did, repeating my request for a lawyer. He ignored my request and left. I assumed he was off to get Ms. Pentecost's and Holly's versions.

They left me alone for more than an hour. I spent the time thinking about which would be worse, losing my detective's license or losing my liberty. The former was almost a certainty. When they handed you that card, there was a whole list of commandments that went with it. The first five were: Don't mess with the real cops.

As for whether I or my boss did any time, that would be up to the DA, and maybe a judge and twelve civilians in a jury box.

But losing my PI's license would be punishment enough. I'd gotten a taste of what it was like working a nine-to-five, and I didn't like it.

Ms. P and I could always move to New Jersey and get a license there. But then we'd have to live in Jersey. Maybe Philadelphia was hard up for private sleuths.

I was working my way down the East Coast when the door opened and Lazenby stepped in.

"Do you have my lawyer in tow?" I asked. "Or a sandwich? I haven't eaten today."

He eased his bulk into the chair across from me. His suit was wrinkled, his beard tangled, his eyes red and blurry.

"You look beat," I said. "You getting enough iron in your diet?"

He didn't smile.

"You're going to have to wait for your lawyer," he informed me. "He's otherwise occupied. I spent all day with him and a Mr. Mort Cohen. I'm going to be meeting them in Rockaway in an hour to identify some stolen property."

"I'll take my thanks in corned beef."

For a man who was on the verge of clearing three years of robbery cases and becoming the mayor's golden boy, he didn't look it.

"You're a real piece of work, Parker," he sighed. "You and your boss, both. By all rights, you and she should be under arrest right now. Obstruction of justice, at the very least."

I stayed silent, having picked up on the word *should*.

"Clark gave his boss a call, who gave a judge a call. I don't

know which of them called Jessup Quincannon, but somebody did. While Pentecost was telling her side of things, she
really hammered home Quincannon's involvement in all this.
That he'd received correspondence from the killer. That he'd
lied about it when questioned. That if this ever gets to court,
that fact will be front and center."

"What did Quincannon say to the DA or the judge or
whoever?" I asked.

Lazenby heaved his shoulders up and then let them drop.

"They don't trust lowly police lieutenants with that kind
of information. Whatever he said, it made everyone involved
decide it would be in the best interests of justice if we just forget this happened."

I don't know what I was expecting, but it wasn't that.

"How much are we forgetting?"

"Turns out you stumbled on a workplace dispute that
turned nasty. Your heroic actions resulted in the rescue of
Mr. Dobbin and the prevention of Miss Quick from being
assaulted by a lunatic. Everyone's going to keep it nice and
vague and let the press draw their own conclusions."

"And the four murders he committed?" I asked. "You
think the press aren't going to jump on that like it's a free
steak?"

Now came the scowl.

"We'll get around to closing those," Lazenby said. "One
by one, and we'll take our time doing it."

That might work, I thought. Tell the world a man was a
four-times murderer and it made headlines. But taken one at
a time, four deaths could get buried. A lot of things happened
in New York City. A lot of murders. You could lose a few in
the shuffle.

"Staples is going along with this?" I asked.

"He's not happy," Lazenby said. "But he's got his eye on

eventually becoming chief. He'll follow orders. Until he's the one giving them. Then you better watch out."

He stood up and tried to smooth the wrinkles out of his jacket.

"That's it?" I asked. "I'm free to go?"

He nodded. "There's some press out front. We're going to let you and Miss Quick have a few minutes to get your story straight. You think she can do that?"

I stood up and stretched.

"She tells stories for a living," I said. "She can pass a lie when she needs to."

Lazenby put a hand on the knob, then stopped and looked back.

"Before this all gets swept under the rug, I want to ask you something. If you'd come to us—come to me—about the connection between these murders right when you found out about it, do you think Darryl Klinghorn would be dead?"

I didn't have an answer and he didn't wait for one. He left the door standing open in his wake.

In the hall, I found Holly and Ms. Pentecost and Clark. As promised, Clark ran the story by us.

"Keep it simple," he told Holly. "You don't know why he did it. You don't know what he wanted. He just had a gun and he assaulted his boss and then grabbed you. Thanks to whatever he got dosed with, the manager doesn't remember anything past breakfast, so we're safe there. The Simpson woman is trickier. She'll know things won't line up. But we have her taking a bribe to hand out information on you and your family, and apparently she likes her job. We told her if she keeps her mouth shut, so will we."

He turned to me.

"Parker—you were in the right place at the right time. No mention of the murders. They ask for details, you tell them to talk to the police. Don't linger. Miss Quick has had a traumatic experience and you're going to take her home. There's a taxi waiting for you. Got it?"

We told him we did.

It went as planned. There were only three reporters, and none of them pushed too hard. Holly and I were mid-script when out of the corner of my eye I saw Ms. Pentecost walk down the steps of the station house and toward the waiting cab.

She passed within arm's length of the journalists, none of whom recognized the greatest detective in New York City. Turns out her hat isn't so silly after all.

CHAPTER **49**

Over the following weeks, our luck held.

The shooting at the cemetery made headlines for a day, then dropped off, replaced by the news that the NYPD had broken up one of the most prolific burglary crews the city had ever seen. Mort was referred to as a "confidential witness" so no one made the connection to *Strange Crime*. At least not right away.

Perkins's murder was closed in mid-March. Terry's gun was indeed the one he'd used to shoot Perkins after hanging him.

Between the continuing war-crimes trials, Truman pushing a loyalty order on federal employees, Congress proposing a Twenty-second Amendment, which would set term limits for the U.S. president, and the usual slate of fresh corpses, the solving of Perkins's murder got bumped to page six, and only in one paper.

Haggard's death would be officially closed shortly after, Checchetto's in early April. By then the front pages of the city's papers were filled with news of a smallpox outbreak and the heroic effort to vaccinate millions of New Yorkers.

Which is not to say the police didn't do their job. They took a shovel to Terry's life. I was kept appraised of their progress through Lazenby.

There's a lot I could tell you about our killer. I could

explain how he was an art school dropout who got expelled for making threats against an instructor. I could run through how he'd gotten a job at Golden Green using a résumé that was mostly fiction.

If I wanted, I could recite the list of complaints made against him by patients. How he stole from them. How he hurt them when no one else was looking. Then I could talk about how Dobbin listened to the complaints and promptly filed them away in a back drawer. These were old, unwell people, after all. A lot of them weren't in their right mind.

I could tell you about some suspicions Ms. Pentecost had. About how Perkins was too clean to be his first. A lot of people died in that convalescent home and nobody bothered with an autopsy. Again—they were old and unwell and swiftly forgotten.

I could tell you about the search of Terry's apartment. The stacks of crime magazines. The journals he kept, their pages choked with thick, tight scrawl. Fantasies he'd concocted about his life. Lists of slights and indignities—victims he hadn't gotten around to yet.

There were whole journals dedicated to Holly. There was some of the expected depravity, but most of the books were filled with elaborate screeds comparing his childhood to hers and how pain can be transferred down through the blood, and you either harness that pain, transform it into something beautiful, or are consumed by it.

I could almost agree with him. Except for his idea of beauty. Eye of the beholder, and all.

I could describe all the finished and half-finished paintings they found stacked like cordwood. How he'd started with landscapes. Even hung some in Golden Green, like the seascape in Naomi's room.

I could describe how his subject matter changed, grew darker, grimmer, bloodier.

They never found Terry's name in Checchetto's commission records. But there was a painting in his shop that could easily have been done by his killer. It was unsigned and had been marked down several times.

I could even tell you about a suspicion of my own. Remember that painting hanging in Quincannon's office? The one of the lounging, maybe eviscerated, nude?

I saw snaps of Terry's later work, and I'm no expert, but the similarities were striking. I told Ms. Pentecost about it, and reminded her of the promise Terry had made in his letter to Quincannon about sending a tribute.

"We had assumed the tribute was Checchetto's death," Ms. P said. "You think it might have been this painting?"

"Not only that. I think Quincannon hung it up right before I came over. As a little private joke."

I could also relate our discussion about whether or not there was more than one letter. I hadn't been taking notes during our graveyard standoff, but the way Terry talked about Quincannon made me think there might have been an ongoing correspondence. Which meant the philanthropist knew a lot more about the killer than he'd let on.

Ms. P had something to say about that. I won't print it here. Besides, you wouldn't believe she'd stoop to that kind of vocabulary.

Anyway, I could get into all that. But I won't.

You'll also notice I haven't dropped Terry's full name.

I won't do that, either. If you want it bad enough, you can go hunting in the newspaper archives.

He wanted fame. He wanted people of quality to know he existed.

I don't want anyone to know he existed. I don't want anyone to give him a clever little nickname. I want him forgotten.

Like his victims will almost certainly be.

CHAPTER 50

Our biggest stroke of luck had nothing to do with Holly's case.

On a Thursday morning in mid-March, Ms. Pentecost decided it was time to pick up the Waterhouse Project again. Sid had gotten back to us. There was nothing in the photos of Ken Shirley's documents that raised his hackles. No hidden crimes. No creative math. Just the usual paperwork you'd find in a mid-level tax firm.

Not a damn thing that would interest Olivia Waterhouse.

Subterfuge had gotten us nowhere. It was time for the direct approach.

"Bring Ken Shirley here," Ms. Pentecost instructed. "If he balks, concoct an appropriate story. I'd prefer he not know what I'm going to ask ahead of time."

You'll notice she didn't ask if I thought it was possible to get Shirley there. She just expected I had it in me.

I decided to get to Shirley & Wise a little before noon and catch him on his way to lunch. It was a Thursday, which was his long-lunch day. Whoever was warming Jean Palmer's chair wouldn't be alarmed if her boss went missing for a couple of hours.

Standing on the corner opposite the entrance, I decided I'd trail him to the restaurant and grab him right before he went inside. It meant leaving the Caddy and relying on a cab to get us to the brownstone, but it would catch him the most off guard. It would also prevent him from running back up to Shirley & Wise, where he had an office with a lock on the door.

I didn't have to wait long. At 12:03 on the dot, I saw Ken Shirley step out the double glass doors, smooth his overcoat, adjust his toupee, and start north.

I gave him a half-block head start and slipped into his wake.

He passed several promising eateries and then surprised me by heading down into the subway. It isn't an easy job, tailing someone on the train, especially if that person knows your features.

Luckily, Ken Shirley was in a world of his own and never bothered looking at the other end of the car, where he might have recognized a less demure version of Jean Palmer trying not to give him her full face.

He got off near Chinatown and went two blocks east and one block south before stopping in front of a building in the middle of the block and slipping through a set of nondescript double doors that definitely did not belong to a restaurant. I looked at the number on the building and almost tripped over my half-inch heels.

I picked up my pace until I found a pay phone. I dialed Ms. Pentecost.

"There's been a development with Ken Shirley," I said.

"A problem?"

"Actually, I think it's an opportunity."

I told her where I was and reminded her why we were familiar with the address.

"Interesting."

"I thought so. You want me to grab him on the way out?" I asked. "No chance he'll refuse now."

"No. I'll come to you. We'll question him there. When his

defenses are down," she said. "Though it would be best if our way were paved."

I directed Ms. P to the notebook in my desk where she could find the appropriate phone number. Once we got in touch with the right parties, things went smoothly. Favors were owed.

Forty minutes later, Ms. P and I were waiting quietly in a narrow hall, trying unsuccessfully to ignore the sounds coming from the other side of Room 340. There was a crescendo, followed by brief silence. Then a muffled woman's voice, followed swiftly by a muffled man's voice. A moment later, the door swung open and a woman stepped out, a bottle blonde with all the proportions of a Vargas girl, but even less wardrobe. She was carrying an armful of suit and trousers.

She gave us a wary look.

"Go easy on him, okay?" she said. "As far as johns go, he's pretty sweet."

"We'll pull our punches," I told her, then stepped into the room. My boss followed.

If you've been on the road and had to choose the cheapest hotel to stay in, you've seen that room. I won't waste ink describing it. Though your fleabag probably didn't have a naked tax lawyer sitting on the bed.

At first I thought we were in the wrong room. This guy was a cueball. Then I saw his toupee sitting upside down on the nightstand like a dead possum.

It took Shirley a second to realize the two women coming into his room weren't a buy-one-get-one-free deal. He squealed and yanked a sheet over himself.

"What's going on? Who are you? Who . . . Mrs. Palmer?"

"Parker, actually. Will Parker. Don't worry if you've never heard of me. The woman with the cane and the Italian-cut suit is Lillian Pentecost. Her you've probably heard of."

Shirley shuffled until his back was against the headboard.

That left the foot of the bed free for my boss to perch on. I stayed by the door, arms crossed, hand near my holster.

Shirley didn't look like a runner or a fighter, but recent experience had taught me to be prepared.

"Mr. Shirley, I wish to have a discussion about a woman—"

"Please get out!" Shirley cried. "You are not—you are not allowed to be here."

"This will go swifter if you let me finish," Ms. Pentecost said. "Hear my inquiry, then you may choose to lodge a protest. Though I would remind you of our relative positions."

In other words: One of us is married and has just spent an hour with a prostitute. The other is not.

Shirley quieted.

"As I was saying, I have questions about a woman who was in your employ in July and August 1940. She called herself Emily Ginsburg, though that was not her real name."

As soon as Shirley heard the name Ginsburg, he practically shriveled. My boss saw it, but she finished the pitch anyway.

"Shortly after her tenure, files were stolen from your office. I believe she was responsible for that theft. I wish to know what she was after, Mr. Shirley. I wish to know very badly."

"I don't know what you're talking about. I barely remember . . . whatever her name was."

I chimed in from the door.

"Ken, you're a shitty liar. Now, my boss there is being polite and skirting around the fact that we've caught you with your pants down and I have your home phone number."

Ken Shirley started crying.

I actually felt bad. I felt sorry for Shirley, who had been an okay boss if you're into that kind of thing. I felt sorry for the prostitutes whose business we were tracking mud into. We'd helped them with the sergeant who was shaking them down, and here we were, doing the same to one of their regulars.

I tucked all that away and waited patiently for the sniveling to stop.

"So, Mr. Shirley. Tell me what happened. What did Emily Ginsburg want in your files?"

"Nothing."

"Now, Mr. Shirley . . ."

"I mean she didn't want anything from the files," he said. "She didn't care about the files."

"Explain."

He wiped his nose, then spied his toupee on the nightstand. He reached over and wriggled it into place. He handled the maneuver with a surprising amount of dignity.

"It was here," he said. "She found me here. She was waiting outside one day after . . . after I'd seen Darla. She said the same thing you did. Do what she says or she'll tell Vivianne."

He looked over to me. "I love Viv. I really do. It's just . . . Darla's nice to me and Viv . . ."

I tried to look sympathetic. Ms. P didn't bother.

"Continue."

Shirley did.

The woman calling herself Emily Ginsburg told Shirley that he was to go to his office and take out the ten most important files from his personal filing cabinet. She had a list—all the big-money clients. The files represented thousands of man-hours and included documents that were irreplaceable. He was to bring them to the Bethesda Fountain in Central Park that evening.

"She met you there?" Ms. P asked.

He nodded. "Yes."

"You gave her the files."

He shook his head.

"She didn't want them. There was a metal bucket sitting on a bench. She told me to put all the files in it. She handed me a little tin of lighter fluid and said to douse the papers, so I did. Then she handed me a book of matches. She said to light them on fire and to watch and to not leave until the files were nothing but ash."

The way he talked, it was like he still couldn't believe it.

"I had to stand there and watch all this work go up in flames. She said not to look away. I had to keep watching until the fire was out. Or she would call my wife. So I stood and watched. I lost clients after that."

His eyes were leaking again. I don't think he was crying over burnt documents, but over how Olivia Waterhouse—or Ginsburg, or whoever—made him feel.

Helpless.

Probably like we were making him feel right then.

Ms. Pentecost led him through it one more time, but it was pretty clear he didn't have anything further to add.

"You never told anyone about the incident?" she asked.

"She warned me not to," he explained. "I told everyone at the office that I'd called the police and they were investigating, but that was a lie. I never told anyone."

"Have you had contact with her since?"

He shook his head.

"Never. For months—years, even—I was afraid she'd do it anyway. Call my wife. I waited for it to happen, but she never did. I'd . . . I'd almost managed to forget about her."

We left Shirley with a promise that we wouldn't be back. That his secret was safe. Again.

We passed Darla on the way out. She'd changed into something less gauzy. She had Ken Shirley's clothes in her arms, all carefully folded.

I thanked her and passed her a few bills. It didn't make me feel like less of a heel.

Ms. Pentecost and I walked a few blocks before hailing a cab to take us to where I'd parked the sedan. As we strolled, we talked about what Shirley's story meant.

"I never pegged Waterhouse as the sadistic sort," I said.

"Nor I," Ms. P replied. "What I know of her says that she does everything for a reason, everything to serve a larger purpose."

"What purpose did it serve to make Ken Shirley torch his own files?"

"I think I have an idea," she said.

She told it to me.

"That is kind of brilliant," I admitted. "Of her, I mean. Of you, it's just par for the course."

"If true, there might be a way to confirm it."

We went home and started making calls.

CHAPTER 51

Throughout all of this—from February through March and into April—I kept seeing Holly. Part of it was because I was worried about her. She'd been through a lot and I didn't know how she'd hold up. Twice now she'd almost been killed by a multiple murderer. Not something most people can shake off.

But Holly wasn't losing sleep. Or at least she said she wasn't.

The other reason I was checking in on her at least once a week was that I enjoyed her company. She'd grown on me. Or maybe I'd grown to better fit her.

I took her to the Copacabana. She said she couldn't dance, but that turned out to be a lie. We caught *All My Sons* on Broadway. I thought it could have used a chorus girl or two, but was happy to stay up late, sipping tea at Holly's apartment and listening as she took apart Miller's script to examine how it worked.

On the second-to-last weekend in March, I had dinner with Holly, Marlo, and Brent at a hole-in-the-wall Greek place in the Village.

Brent stayed mostly silent throughout the meal. The trio's arrangement had been patched up, but Brent would be in the doghouse for a while.

The new rule was "no secrets."

I told them I thought that was a great idea. I kept mum on what I thought of its viability. Holly seemed happy. It was a good look on her, and I didn't want to dent it.

Over Turkish coffee, Marlo told me the May issue of *Strange Crime* would be the last. Now that the robbers were making their way through the courts, their victims were learning about the magazine's role in the caper. How filling out the Vita-Glow ad had put a target on their back.

There were murmurings of lawsuits.

"Brent and I are insulated legally," Marlo explained. "But the magazine's assets will probably be wiped out."

"I'm so sorry," I said, meaning it. "What are you going to do?"

The three exchanged a conspiratorial look.

"We're going to start publishing books," Marlo declared. "We have some savings. We have the industry contacts. And it's what we always wanted to do. Our first title will be an anthology. Just to get our feet wet. The second will be a debut novel by one Holly Quick."

I turned to Holly. She had a twinkle in her eye. I think she liked being able to surprise me.

"You're ditching the pseudonyms? Are you sure?"

She nodded.

"I'm done hiding. My work is my life, and I want my name on it."

"What if someone makes the Truelove connection?" I asked. "What if they track down who you really are?"

Under the table, she took my hand in hers and gave it a squeeze.

"That's not who I really am."

One day in mid-April Ms. Pentecost and I arrived home, both of us freshly vaccinated for smallpox, to find a message from Lazenby. Darryl Klinghorn's murder was being officially closed.

There would be no announcement to the press. A body found on Lillian Pentecost's doorstep had been big news, but that was two months ago. The public has a short memory and newspapers like to accommodate.

The only mention of the name "Klinghorn" appeared in the classified section under a brief notice announcing that Klinghorn Investigations was again open for business. Dolly was taking up where her husband had left off.

I'd known about the move ahead of time and had delivered a decently sized check to be used as seed money.

"Somebody's got to keep the cheating bastards in line," she told me.

The evening we learned that the last of the murders was being officially closed, I steered the Caddy to Holly's apartment to give her the news in person.

"So, it's over? Really, really over?" she asked.

"As over as these things get."

She smiled. She was doing more of that now.

She was wearing a white sleeveless dress with hand-stitched flowers around the collar. She'd been to a hair stylist and her top lock was tight and trimmed and she'd swapped out her thick black frames for thinner ones. They showed off the green flecks swimming in the brown.

"That's really fantastic," she said. "I've been walking around on eggshells. I thought they would never wrap it up. I mean, in stories, the case is closed when the murderer is caught. If I had to add in all this rigmarole at the end, I'd never finish."

"Tell me about it," I said. I was standing just inside her doorway, fiddling with the brim of my fedora.

"Why don't you come in?" she said. "I just finished my writing for the day. I was going to have a drink. Mr. Cosmo dropped off a bottle of sambuca. I've never had sambuca before and I'm rather anxious. No, not anxious. Hesitant, I guess. What if it's awful? Why don't you stay and have a seltzer or tea or coffee—I just got some instant—and then if the sambuca is awful you can help me think of a way to say I didn't like it without hurting his feelings."

"Sure, sure," I said. "A drink of whatever sounds great."

She pointed a scowl at me.

"What's the matter?" she asked. "You have the face you get when something's the matter."

"Nothing's the matter," I told her. "It's just . . . Remember that night I stayed over. And you . . . Well, you made an offer. I said that I had a rule about mixing business and pleasure and—well, you thought I was making an excuse. Remember?"

Her eyes narrowed behind her specs. "Oh, I remember."

"It wasn't an excuse. It was on the level. And today you're officially not a client anymore. I know we've spent some time together socially. But I was wondering if you might like to make that more . . . official. Well, as official as we can get. Or not. I mean, if that pass was a spur-of-the-moment thing, I understand. You were under a lot of stress. Either way, I'd still like to see you. Even if it is how we've been going. I think the word is platonically. A movie, maybe? The Rivoli's got *Notorious* back in. You like Cary Grant, right? Also, I've got tickets to opening day at Ebbets Field. The Dodgers just signed Jackie Robinson, so that'll be a game to see. But I know you're not big on crowds, so if—"

Holly grabbed me by my lapels, pulled me in, and kissed me. You wouldn't expect Chesterfields to taste so good.

Eventually, she released me and we caught our respective breaths.

"You know," she said, "you're really very awkward."

I didn't disagree.

She took me by the hand and led me in the direction of the bedroom.

I didn't disagree with that, either.

CHAPTER 52

I wouldn't mind ending things there, Holly and I tangled in her too-narrow bed, guarding against the last of the April chill.

But like the woman said, real life just doesn't get wrapped up so easy.

It was the first day in May and I was making my rounds of the city's specialty bookstores. Ms. Pentecost had picked up the reading habit again and I had a laundry list of tomes, as well as a wish list of my own.

It was early evening and I had hit my last stop—the place near Union Square where I can find all the foreign periodicals Ms. P enjoys. I was loaded down with bags and heading for the subway entrance when a woman's voice called out behind me.

"Excuse me. I think you dropped this."

I didn't notice the speaker, just the copy of Elizabeth Bishop's *North & South* she was shoving in front of my nose. I didn't know how Holly felt about poetry, but I was interested in finding out. I was sure the book had been tucked at the bottom of one of my bags. How'd it fall out?

Something dropped over my head and the world went dark. There was a sweet chemical odor. I took a desperate lungful of air before I realized what was happening.

I heard tires screeching and I felt like I was floating.

Then nothing.

———

The first thing that returned was sound. A voice. Muffled like it was coming to me from underwater. Eventually I was able to make out words.

"—ing is wiped down and the files are in the incinerator. Should I bring the car around?" This was the voice of the woman on the street—very adenoidal, like she was talking through her nose.

"Go ahead. I shouldn't be too long." This was another voice entirely. I hadn't heard it in a while, but it was familiar.

Footsteps. A door opening, then closing.

Feeling was starting to come back into my extremities. I flexed my fingers, trying to move my hands, but came up short. By the time I had the idea to play possum I'd already given the game away.

"The effects will wear off quickly, Miss Parker. None will be lasting."

I opened my eyes. I was sitting in a heavy, wooden chair. My wrists were bound to its arms, my ankles to its front legs.

About six feet in front of me was an identical chair. Its occupant was a petite woman with short black hair. She'd had it colored and straightened since last I saw her, and had styled it in an asymmetrical bob. It went well with her midnight-blue wrap dress and black silk stockings.

A pair of blue heels were sitting on the floor by her chair.

She looked nothing like the mousy academic I'd met two years earlier.

Except for the eyes. Nothing you can do about those eyes, no longer hidden behind a pair of cheaters. Irises so dark they were almost black.

"You could have . . . called," I said. "Made an appointment."

My tongue was a little numb, so the words came out mushy, but she got the idea.

"I don't think I could have, Miss Parker," Waterhouse said. "Besides, I wanted to talk to you here."

I gave my neck muscles a go and found they had woken up enough to look around. I was in a large, empty room. There were a few desks pushed into the corners. The ceiling lights were off. The only illumination came through the frosted glass of the room's only door and from a bank of windows that ran along one side of the space. Through them I saw a row of office buildings, most of their windows dark, their occupants gone home for the night. The sound of traffic echoed from somewhere at the bottom of a Manhattan canyon.

The layout of the space was familiar. A lot like Shirley & Wise, but with the windows on the opposite side.

"Thinking of setting up shop?" I asked.

She smiled. It almost, but didn't quite, reach her eyes.

"Closing shop, actually."

"Son of a bitch," I said. "We were right."

She crossed her stockinged legs, clasped her hands together over her knees, and leaned forward in her chair.

"Please, Miss Parker. Tell me. I want to hear you explain it."

She was so close. If I could just get a hand free. But whoever had tied the knots knew what she was doing. I didn't want to be obvious. So while I talked, I very slowly rotated my wrists, one way, then the other, trying to create some space where I could slip a finger through.

"What do I call you?" I asked. "Olivia Waterhouse doesn't officially exist."

"That name will do," she said. "I've lived with it for as long as any other. Please. Run through it for me."

"It was a real stumper at first," I began. "All that time spent playing secretary to Ken Shirley, and for what? So you could destroy a bunch of files that didn't mean anything? It didn't make sense. What did you get out of it? Nothing. . . . Except proof that you could."

This time the smile did meet her eyes. I had maybe a quarter inch of clearance between wrist and rope. I needed to make more.

"You proved that you could spend a month as someone's personal assistant, learn all their deepest darkest, and then—at the drop of a hat—get them to do something they would never normally do in order to keep their secrets safe. It was an experiment, wasn't it? A proof of concept. To show that you could do it again."

She uncrossed her legs and stood, walking with liquid grace toward the bank of windows, silent on her stocking feet.

Shit, I thought. Out of reach. One hand wouldn't do anymore.

"Please continue, Miss Parker."

Keeping an eye on her back, I started working my wrists more quickly.

"Now that you knew you could do it once, you figured you could do it again. But a one-woman operation wouldn't work. Sure, Shirley had a skeleton in the sack, but you wouldn't be able to find that kind of leverage on everybody."

"You'd be surprised," she said, eyes fixed out the windows.

"I probably wouldn't," I replied. "Either way, it wasn't practical to do it all yourself. You had other irons in the fire. For this job, you needed help. And there you were, teaching classes filled with young, idealistic women. I bet some of them really leaned forward when you started going on about power structures and control and all that jazz. A little time, a little finesse, and you'd figure out your marks."

She turned. I stopped wriggling my wrists.

"Marks?"

"How about recruits?"

"How about co-conspirators?" she countered.

"Fine. Whatever you want to call them. I'm guessing the woman who's down in the car is one. Figure maybe one girl in every class. Multiply that by however many classes over the years. That's enough to keep a secretarial agency running, don't you think? A couple of branches, even, if you spread the girls out. This time you'd play with higher stakes. More important people. Ones whose secrets were deeper and darker. Ones you weren't going to let go with a slap on the wrist."

No smile this time. At least I didn't think. With her back to the windows her face was in shadow. I could feel her eyes picking me apart.

"Very astute," she said. "Rather a brilliant deductive leap, really."

"I have a very astute employer."

She shook her head. "I think you're being modest. I imagine Ms. Pentecost was the first to suggest my time at Shirley and Wise was a test. The phrase *proof of concept* sounds very much like her. But going from that to starting a temp agency. Recruiting like-minded women from my classes. That's you all over, Will."

So this is what being dissected feels like, I thought.

"I guess I had a hand in it," I admitted. Very slowly I began pulling my arms straight back, testing the loops. Almost there. I just needed a quarter inch more.

"You were smart," I continued. "The real estate guy who hanged himself? The D.C. lawyer? The zoning inspector? We found out they'd had temps working for them within a year of their death. But the records were missing. Nobody knew what agency they'd gone through. I warned the boss that we were going to tip you off. Going through the phone book and calling every secretarial agency of a certain size. Even if we kept the questions off topic, you'd have your girls on guard. Is that what happened?"

"Oh, no, Miss Parker. I've known you and Ms. Pentecost

were on this particular trail since your first day as—what was the name? Jean Palmer?"

Son of a bitch. How did she know? Did she have a plant at Shirley & Wise?

I remembered that evening my second week there, when I thought I was being followed. I'd crossed it off as nerves. But maybe it wasn't. Maybe it was Waterhouse or one of her girls keeping tabs.

I was going to ask, but then she swerved the conversation.

"How are you feeling?" she asked. "After having killed a man. Your second. At least the second that the authorities know about."

The fine hairs on my arms stood at attention.

"I'm feeling all right," I said.

"Some people might have trouble sleeping after taking a life."

"I sleep just fine. Besides . . ."

"He had it coming?"

"I was going to say it was self-defense."

She turned away again and pressed a hand against one of the windows. Like she could feel something through the glass. The rumble of the city speaking to her.

"There are far worse men out there, Miss Parker. Men who are responsible for far greater atrocities. They don't even have the excuse of madness to hide behind."

I could see what she was getting at. Trying to close the ethical distance. I wasn't going to take the bait.

"I'd tell you I'm sorry we queered your deal," I said. "But I'd be lying."

Abruptly she pivoted and walked back to the chair. She picked up her heels and slipped them on, one, then the other.

"That's quite all right," she said. "This phase of things was nearly at an end."

"Don't suppose you want to tell me what's next?"

She laughed. It was actually a pleasant sound. Musical, even.

"I don't think so," she said. "I think I'm done underestimating you and your employer."

She reached down and pulled up the hem of her dress, exposing a leather holster strapped to her thigh. From it she retrieved a long, thin blade.

Cold sweat started to trickle down my back.

She closed the distance.

"The last time we spoke, I told Ms. Pentecost that she and I were not so very different," she said, holding the knifepoint level with my throat. "I still believe that. But after spending more time observing you both, I think it's you, Miss Parker, who I have more in common with."

"I don't think so," I said, trying to keep the panic out of my voice, and failing.

She crouched down, perched on her heels like a dark peregrine. She looked at the knife in her hand.

"Believe me, Will. We do. Someday you might realize it, too. When you do, I'll be waiting."

With a sharp flick of her wrist she reversed her grip on the knife and drove it into the chair, leaving it upright and quivering between my bound legs.

She stood.

"Now I'm afraid I have to leave. So much work to do, you understand." She turned away and headed to the door. "Another minute and you should be able to get a wrist free. Your bags are here. The new piece by Simone de Beauvoir in *Les Temps Modernes* is excellent. I highly recommend it."

For the first time I noticed my bookstore parcels sitting unmolested by the entrance to the vacant office.

"Please give Ms. Pentecost my regards."

With that, she opened the door, was bathed briefly in the light of the hall, and walked out.

I wasted no time. I proved she'd underestimated me again by getting my wrist free at least twenty seconds short of a minute. Once that was done, I yanked the knife out of the chair and went to work on the rest.

Then I started moving. I ran to the door and cautiously looked out, knife at the ready. Nobody. Closed office doors and a dimly lit hall.

I glanced at the name painted on the hallway side of the door.

SUNSHINE SERVICES
SUITE 502

It rang a bell but I didn't have time to place it. I ran down the hall. I didn't feel like waiting for the elevator, so I found the stairs. I practically flew down the five flights.

I burst out into the lobby and stopped, confused. I knew this lobby. I knew this building. Jean Palmer had walked into it every morning for two weeks.

"Son of a bitch."

Waterhouse had been one floor above me the entire time. That's how she knew we were onto her. She or one of her girls had seen me.

I shook it off and ran out the front door into the emptiness of the Financial District after hours. I looked up and down the avenue. A couple cabs and a dark sedan taking the far corner at speed.

Waterhouse was gone.

But not for good, I thought. Not even close.

My boss was right. This woman wasn't going to get caught.

Not unless we were the ones doing the catching.

I went to find the nearest pay phone. I needed to call Ms. Pentecost. I trusted her to know what to do next.

WILLOWJEAN PARKER

LEAD INVESTIGATOR

PENTECOST AND PARKER INVESTIGATIONS

NEW YORK CITY

ACKNOWLEDGMENTS

The question I get asked most frequently is why I decided to set this series when I did. My answer has always been: Because I want to show how the Golden Age of America wasn't really so golden, and how it came at the expense of whole communities of people who were violently paved under in the name of prosperity.

Because history is viciously cyclical.

We know what history has in store for Will and Lillian: McCarthyism, the Lavender Scare, the Cold War, and all the other boots that are waiting to press down on the necks of people who stick out. There's nothing we can do to change that. History is written.

And so my first thanks go to everyone, everywhere, fighting for a future that's a damn sight brighter than the world our heroes have waiting for them.

As always, it takes a team to get this book from me to you. Special thanks to:

My agent, Darley Anderson, who saw the potential of Pentecost and Parker well before I did. And to the rest of his team, including: Mary Darby, Georgia Fuller, Kristina Egan, Rosanna Bellingham, and Rebeka Finch. Thanks for helping me turn a passion into a career.

My editors Bill Thomas and Margo Shickmanter for championing this series and Carolyn Williams for picking up the baton and running with it.

The rest of the lovely and talented Doubleday crew responsible for shepherding Pentecost and Parker through the production process. Those include, but are far from limited to: Elena Hershey, Jillian Briglia, Peggy Samedi, Milena Brown, Maria Massey, Maria Carella, Michael J. Windsor, and Ana Espinoza.

Jessica, whom I made wait three books before having one dedicated to her. This book is, at its secret center, a love story involving a writer. So I thought it was appropriate.

And, finally, all of the readers who have hopped on for the ride—thank you all so very much. You help make the journey worthwhile.

About the Author

Stephen Spotswood is an award-winning playwright, journalist, and educator. As a journalist, he has spent much of the last two decades writing about the aftermath of the wars in Iraq and Afghanistan and the struggles of wounded veterans. His dramatic work has been widely produced across the United States. He makes his home in Washington, D.C., with his wife, young-adult author Jessica Spotswood.